"WHAT THE HELL HAPPENED!"

The first shot cracked, reverberated, then piled onto two more. Shouts, obscene, desperate, angry, spilled over them outside.

The screams followed. Brock ran out and found the women and children being held back by a yelling FBI agent.

"What the hell happened?" Brock demanded, trying to be heard over the women praying and shouting at him, shoving to get past the armed men restraining them.

"She started running and she had a gun," one female agent said. "The bitch was going for someone."

Brock walked fifty feet away to the crumpled form in the dirt being frantically worked on by the paramedics. The woman's gray and blue blouse was torn open and bloody. As he leaned down toward her, her small boy was screeching and tearing to get to her.

"Killers! Killers!" the other women screamed.

He said sharply to one of the FBI agents, "Where's the gun she had?"

The stony-faced agent extended his hand, holding something dark.

Without another word, Brock took hold of a palm-sized black wooden cross.

QUICKSAND

William P. Wood

Pinnacle Books
Kensington Publishing Corp.
http://www.pinnaclebooks.com

PINNACLE BOOKS are published by

Kensington Publishing Corp.
850 Third Avenue
New York, NY 10022

First Kensington Hardcover Printing: September, 1998
First Pinnacle Printing: February, 1999
10 9 8 7 6 5 4 3 2 1

Printed in the United States of America

Whoso diggeth a pit shall fall therein:
and he that rolleth a stone, it will return upon him.

—Proverbs 26:27

CHAPTER ONE

Assistant United States Attorney Brock Andrews shifted his lanky frame and stared through binoculars at the large cargo ship berthed a half a mile away at Pier 20. The ship rode low in the turgid green-black waters of Los Angeles Harbor. Brock felt tickling sweat, drawn by the constant dry, hot wind, inch down his neck.

He said to the angry man behind him, "Ed Nelson and his bad guys are going to come rolling up in ten seconds. There's enough explosive on that ship to blow this harbor off the coast. Your problem can wait."

The undersheriff of Los Angeles County was crew-cut, craggy, and solid in a square suit, hands on his hips. "Listen, mister, I know your song and dance. This is still my jurisdiction and I still represent local law enforcement."

Brock turned from the second-floor open window. The crowded room was filled with telephone equipment, tape recorders, television monitors, and other electronics. The air buzzed with radio chatter.

"Lila, anything hot coming through?"

A young black woman from the Bureau of Alcohol, Tobacco, and Firearms, headset clamped on her head, looked up. "They're still full-speed ahead, chief. Nelson's parade is southbound. Coming right for us. ETA is just five minutes."

"Okay. This is to all positions," Brock spoke into a headset he picked up. "We will move when Nelson is on the pier. He is not, no matter what, to board the ship."

Brock swept his glance over the other men and women, four from the FBI's Technical Services, and two from ATF. He had surveillance teams outside the Beverly Hills Hotel bungalow of Edward Nelson, wiretaps on his phones, and the same coverage of a rented home in Marina del Rey that the Syrians were using. The Syrians had already given the signal; some arrived first and boisterously boarded the *Ramon Esquivel* while its cargo was being unloaded.

The deal was about to happen, Brock cursed inwardly, and the Sheriff's Department picked this moment to mark its territory.

"My immediate beef"—the undersheriff came to the window beside Brock—"is that your bozo Yee, your half-assed bullshitter ATF guy, just ordered my men back outside the pier gates. Now, why is he doing that, Mr. Andrews?" It was not courtesy but sarcasm behind his use of Brock's last name.

"My guess's he has a tactical reason. I'm not going to override Jimmy Yee, bullshitter or not, because he's the one with his neck sticking out."

Brock knew Lila was smirking. Together, five years ago, they all had gone through training at Quantico, joining so enthusiastically in the after-hours drinking parties held in an open field that DEA, ATF, and FBI agents present had dubbed them "The Three Muscatels."

"Bullshit, Mr. Andrews," the undersheriff shot back, so close to Brock's ear it was a shout. "Tell him to get my men back inside the perimeter, because I guarantee you, Mr. Andrews, the Sheriff's Department is not going to be sidelined by your federal grandstanders."

Brock stared at the rusting cargo ship, across the buildings of San Pedro, over the low harbor warehouses, willing nothing to go wrong. Six months of intense work and worry hung poised. The wait in the command center inside the Cafe Tanjore had gone on for five hours, well past one in the afternoon. He was sick of the Santa Ana wind, the exotic stink of red chile, coconut chutney, and fried oil in the South Indian restaurant, the gulls keening everywhere. He was sick of anxiously staring at the *Ramon Esquivel*, stacked high with steel and wood containers, knowing that if anything went wrong now, the ship's crew would finish unloading part of its cargo of auto parts, lightbulbs, and paper pulping cylinders, and it would leave the harbor serenely and continue onward down to Tampico, Mexico.

And I'll have wasted a lot of money and put my head on the block because Nelson's just moving oil drilling mud to Kuwait or maybe even to Syria, scamming everybody along the way, Brock thought. Or else he's really got sixty thousand pounds of C-4 explosive hidden in those drums of phony drilling mud.

Either way, Brock swore, he's not getting on that ship, and that ship isn't leaving the harbor.

He swung away from the undersheriff just as Lila, head canted listening to her headset, said briskly, "Chief, Syrians just made a wire transfer of half the buy money to Nelson's Cayman bank."

Brock stared at the scrolling numbers, words on the screens. Nelson would show up, cautious but elated he was making one of the biggest sales of his wretched career. Inspect the shit. Then demand the Syrians make the final payment. Squeeze them while he still had control of the contraband cargo. Brock smiled. That was how former CIA spook Ed Nelson played things.

Then we bag the whole damn shipload of them.

The undersheriff started in again. Brock had no time for it.

"Agent Martin," he said to Lila, "will you please escort this man outside. Right now."

"What the hell do you think you're doing, Andrews?" the undersheriff spluttered.

"You're giving me a royal headache," Brock said.

Lila rose, whipped off her headset, passing it to another

agent. She was taut, athletic, black hair clipped short, her
jeans evenly pressed. She had the undersheriff by the arm,
pushing him toward the door. "Do you work out, sir?"
she asked with exaggerated politeness.

"Get your goddamn hands off of me," he shouted as
they hurried down the stairs. "I'll have you arrested."

Brock heard Lila say calmly, "I think we'd arrest you
first, sir."

He grabbed his hand-held radio, got Jimmy Yee on it.
There were four teams arrayed undercover around the
pier, but Jimmy's people were closest to the ship and most
vulnerable.

"Jimmy," he said, picking up the binoculars, staring,
"are you all set? Nelson's onto the Vincent Thomas."

"Over the bridge and right past Terminal Island,"
Jimmy crackled gleefully. "Too bad we can't just jam his
ass into the lockup there." Terminal Island was a federal
prison.

Brock heard constant reports now of the three-car
motorcade as it drew inexorably closer. The Santa Ana
flapped the cafe's orange awning below his window. He
swiftly checked in with the other FBI, DEA, and harbor
police teams, and four coast guard ships riding just beyond
the breakfront on the sun-spangled water.

"Jimmy, we'll have visual in a second," he said, straining
to see along the street leading onto Pier 20.

It was just like one of those hunting afternoons with
Master Sergeant Terry Andrews and the other senior
NCOs. A bunch of the same jolly, profane men his father
collected at any of the ten postings Brock had shuttled to
as a kid. Always deer hunting. Maybe today is like that
particular time in the Rockies, when we lived at Fort
Carson.

Brock had had a beautiful five-point buck in his sights.
And suddenly, he'd realized he could not shoot such an
animal again. He still vividly recalled his father's startled
expression at the announcement.

But Master Sergeant Andrews would undoubtedly be

proud his son had a rogue like Ed Nelson sighted and would not flinch from pulling the trigger.

"Vests on everybody," Brock said to the command center personnel. He slipped into his ballistic vest as Lila helped him close it. She said quietly, "Don't worry about Jimmy, chief. He won't jump the gun."

"I wouldn't have put him there if I was worried."

Brock braced himself, reckoning the directions and speeds being called out by the FBI, his binoculars raised, spotting the cherry red cars splitting off the highway, turning onto the pier's access road. Jesus, don't go cowboy on me, Jimmy.

But into his radio, Brock said coolly, "Heads up, everyone. The bad guys are coming for the cheese."

Jimmy Yee held up silent hand signals for his team of three crouched inside the warehouse foreman's shack on the pier. His people nodded. Two minutes to go, or sooner if Brock gave the order.

The cherry red cars screeched to a stop; out piled the pukes, laughing, slapping each other, led by a taller, stocky, gray-haired man in white linen pants, rumpled tweed sportcoat, and wide aviator dark glasses. Nelson, with his two clowns Bower and Denny Lara, plus a couple of Syrians in tight jeans, gold trinkets around their necks and wrists glittering in the sun, along to show this was one big sweet good time. Jimmy wiped sweat from his forehead as he peered through the splotched window. Crane operators and longshoremen yelled back and forth bringing pallets of newsprint and barrels of fish meal off the rusting ship only a hundred feet away.

Ed Nelson snapped off the glasses, a great warm smile on his windburned face, an arm around the shoulder of the nearest Syrian, caught in mid-laugh with young Lara, the court jester in Nelson's enterprise.

Jimmy grinned wolfishly to his team, got returning grins. They had worked hard and long for this arrest, and it was at hand now.

Wish I could hear the assholes congratulating each other, pimping each other about what studs they are, he thought. Then Nelson's going to tell the other bad guys they can't have enough C-4 to keep every terrorist drooling unless he gets his full payment. Right now. Even as Jimmy thought it, the smile faded on the Syrian's broad face, and he angrily shook Nelson's arm from his shoulder.

Jimmy had an assault rifle and Sig Sauer pistol. He was in his mid-thirties, hair shaved very close, compact build. He wore a gray sweatshirt with a vest over it and black chinos and, like every task force member, an olive green windbreaker stenciled with the word POLICE in white.

Two drivers had stayed at the parked cars. Jimmy gestured, detailing two agents to take them. He gripped his gun. Even before his first days with ATF, when he did training at Quantico or Georgia, all the way to the crazy days and nights in paratrooper jumping, he had often felt this same galvanic sensation, like sparks ran along his fingers and arms. He was the wild man, the smallest guy, who always went out the jump plane first, tried the longest fall before reluctantly yanking the parachute cord.

Brock never quite understood. He was an armchair warrior at heart.

What Jimmy delighted in, to the terror and futile anger of his young wife Trisha and two little daughters, was the free fall, arms spread over the whole earth, the uprush of force and wind, and the knowledge that for an instant, just before the packed earth of the landing zone reclaimed you, you flew and were invincible. The world's longest orgasm, some jumpers called it.

He half rose from his crouch, the rifle ready. He gestured, bringing the team into position, coiled to rush out on Brock's signal. He checked his watch. Time was almost up.

Jimmy's hand raised, about to slice down and send them out.

Brock's voice buzzed harshly in his ear. "Hold, damn it, Jimmy. We've got major trouble."

* * *

Brock had just waved a ten-dollar bill, and said with a grin, "Okay, who wants in on the pool? The pukes are lying and buying right now. You win if you guess how much more to the nearest quarter mil Nelson screws over the Syrians."

It was a way to leaven the tension. Bids were called out. Then an agent swore. Lila shot from her chair.

"We've got media coming. Fast. Goddamn." She stared at Brock. "They're here."

He strode to the window as three TV news trucks roared down the access roadway, through the pier's gates, and screeched to a halt just to one side of the startled, edgy car drivers.

Nelson reacted instantly, lumberingly sprinting up the ship's walkway followed by Bower and Lara. The Syrians shouted and stumbled toward the cars, their arms flapping.

Brock swore and spoke brusquely into his radio. "Get him, Jimmy! Keep him out of the cargo hold!" The room behind him chittered with electronic sounds, his command center working frantically.

Brock saw Jimmy Yee running onto the pier even before he finished speaking, rifle pointed at a driver reaching into his blue coat. The other agents quickly surrounded the TV crews.

Brock shook his head. Thank God Jimmy was a cowboy. He spoke to the whole task force. "Move in immediately. Everybody move in. The door's wide open."

The pier filled instantly with armed men and women shouting curt orders. The waters around the ship clogged with Coast Guard and Customs boats. Longshoremen paused, cranes in mid-swing, and gaped.

Jimmy bolted from the pier, joining groups overrunning the cargo ship, ATF, DEA, and FBI agents pouring up passageways, down to the holds. In the brainstorming sessions preceding the raid, Brock had reckoned that the ship's crew wouldn't fight. "They're mules and union guys, so brush them aside if they try to help Nelson."

The bad boys were nowhere in sight, so gun out, Jimmy raced with his team down to the rearmost hold, where they had let Nelson load his lethal cargo. Let him think it was safe.

Passageways went by in a blur, his adrenaline high as he charged up heavily repainted steel stairs, yelling at the stunned crew to stay back. Heads peered from cramped, steamy cabins. Quick images: a photo collage of tanned, naked women taped to a bulkhead, a large cage of squawking parakeets in one cabin, a man punched, cuffed, held down, when he made a sudden reach for his grease-stained khaki pants pocket. Up came a cheap cigar.

Jimmy barely paused, moving on instinct, the ship's lay-out gleaming in his mind. Thirty other agents swarmed busily around him and his people. He jumped down stairs, through narrow steel doorways.

He sprinted into the last hold, loud, cracking gunshots bursting ahead of him.

CHAPTER TWO

"I'm going down there," Brock announced right after the first excited, confused reports of shots fired burst from the radios. He tugged on his POLICE windbreaker. "Lila, take charge. I want some fast answers why the media showed up."

The unspoken questions rattled Brock, and he knew they did Lila, too. How badly was the raid compromised? Were Nelson, Bower, and Lara waiting on the ship, picking off the feds as they boarded? Was Nelson going to threaten to blow the C-4 to bargain his way out?

Maybe he's desperate enough to set it off, Brock thought grimly. From the incomplete, shouted impressions spewing out of the two-way radios, filling the command center like frenzied insects, Brock had no answers.

He grabbed a radio, conscious of being armored in the ballistic vest. His worst fears were for Jimmy. And the other agents. I've got too many people's lives in my hands, he thought.

Lila said sharply, "You shouldn't go anywhere near the area until Nelson's nailed down."

"I've got to see what's going on." Sourly, Brock remembered the heated discussion he'd had in Alison's office three months ago. She had insisted he stay well back in any operation. "I don't want you hurt or shot or doing something you can't justify."

He had nearly leapt from the chair. "It's always public relations for you, Ally. You're scared of bad coverage."

It was a crass, vicious accusation and he knew it, but her attitude angered him. Their marriage was growing shaky enough that he was prepared to believe she cared more about not jeopardizing her upward career trajectory than his safety. He'd stalked to the door, where Alison already stood. "You think I'd make it if something happened to you?" she'd said softly.

"You'd pick yourself up."

"What for? There'd be nothing left."

Brock shook his head at the memory. He touched the simple silver ring she'd given him two years ago on their fourth anniversary. It had one tiny, elegant Latin word engraved inside: *aeternus*. For eternity, Ally, he thought. God, I hope so.

He pointed at Lila. "Okay, come on and keep an eye on me. I'll drive."

As they briskly headed for the door, the relief he felt jumping into the middle of the raid nearly overwhelmed him.

Jimmy Yee, assault rifle at the ready, cautiously peered around the tower of dull metal drums just inside the low steel hatchway. Two more shots went spang into the hull above his head in the twilighted, high-ceilinged rear hold. He cursed, waving back his tensed team and the agents filling in behind them in the corridor. He took in the babbling from his radio, and the smell of the ship's machine oil, stale grease, fresh green paint. Spanish signs were everywhere, exclamatory and incomprehensible.

It was easier doing that than thinking about the ferocious explosive stacked around them, wondering if Nelson or

Bower was manipulating some trigger to send them all up in a vast hot vapor.

He motioned to the four men with him, his radio burring that others were coming. No one was to return fire.

In the next ten seconds, Jimmy was startled when Brock, Lila right behind, gently pushed forward and crouched beside him.

"You screwup," Brock kidded quietly. "Where are they?"

"Back there, boss. Deep. Somebody's shooting, too," Jimmy replied in a whisper.

"Anybody said anything?"

Jimmy shook his head.

Brock nodded. "Well, let's not sit around." He half rose. "Nelson? This is Assistant U.S. Attorney Brock Andrews. I'm in charge. I want to talk to you."

A metallic clang over Brock's head followed the deafening thunder of a large caliber gun in the confined hold. Jimmy tried to yank Brock down, but Brock didn't budge. "Nelson. This is idiotic and that's not like you. I'll guarantee you and Bower and Lara will walk out of here with me, but you've got to say something right now. I've got armed agents and they are pissed."

Brock grinned down at Jimmy, then wiped sweat off his face, puzzled to realize he was sweating. Jimmy saw him twist the ring on his hand, a habit when he was very nervous.

Instead of the answering gunshot, they all heard a series of low, violent obscenities, then mixed yells. "Goddamn, that's the way I say it is, Bower," a raspy, liquor-thickened voice shouted. Then, "This is Ed Nelson, whoever the hell you are. Coming out. Hands up. So don't shoot, you bastards."

Brock turned to Jimmy and Lila, eyebrows raised. "Slowly," he shouted.

They watched three figures materialize in the gloom, first the older man, slight gut hanging over his white pants, then Bower, the sullen ex-Navy diver, balding, his orange hair combed to hide the port wine stain on his forehead, finally Denny Lara. Lara was the youngest, and fittest, but it was mere appearance and didn't give him any advantage over the other two. His face was angularly handsome and weak, like a catalog model. They all had their arms held in the air.

Brock let Jimmy jump forward with other agents, Jimmy bellowing at Nelson and Bower to get down on the ground, someone pushing Lara to his knees. Jimmy darted behind Bower, jamming his rifle's barrel against his neck, pushing him to the dirt of the hold's floor. The hold rapidly filled with agents. The three prisoners were swiftly handcuffed, then yanked to their feet. An ATF agent went to their dark corner hiding place to find the gun.

Lila said to Brock, "That wasn't so bad."

"Nelson's not suicidal. He had no cards left." But Brock was subtly uneasy. Nelson never boxed himself in.

Bower, led by Jimmy and two FBI agents, was pulled past him. "See you soon, bud," Bower said with a twist of his tight mouth.

"Sometime in fifty years maybe," Jimmy replied gleefully.

Lara followed, weak, guileless eyes on Brock. "I would like to contact someone," he said quaveringly.

"After you're processed," Brock said. He turned as Ed Nelson was brought forward. He expected anger like Bower's or terror like Lara's. But Nelson was grinning, face damp, but otherwise no more sign of anxiety than if he'd lost a preferred position on the golf green that morning.

"I don't know you," Nelson said, supported by FBI agents. "I know everybody, but I don't know you."

Brock grinned back. "I'm pretty acquainted with you."

"I think I can give you something."

"You just did." Brock gestured at the towers of drums around them. "Gave me a good scare."

"Shit won't go unless you handle it properly. Even then it takes more brains than these assholes I sell to usually have." He licked his thin, dry lips. "Let me talk to you a sec. Just us."

Brock nodded. He had heard enough of Nelson's wheeling and dealing in the last months of the wiretaps to appreciate his capacity for unbounded duplicity. Brock thought Alison would love it if he not only bagged Ed Nelson, but all of Nelson's far-flung illegal arms dealing.

A little professional success might cement the cracks at home, Brock thought. It was how things were between him and Alison now.

He had Nelson taken into a small cabin, the agents leaving them alone inside. Nelson sat down instantly on a low, sweat-damp bunk. Cranes could be seen out the dirty porthole behind him. A stack of Spanish porno magazines was on a table beside the bunk along with photos in cheap frames of a sad-eyed black-haired woman and three young children.

"It better be damn good," Brock said, standing over him. "I've got a ton of evidence against you."

"Let's not fuck around."—Nelson squinted, and Brock realized he was fairly drunk—"whatever your name is. Get these fucking things off me." He shook his shackled hands at Brock. "We'll go to a bar and I'll let you have a couple of the goddamn Syrians and you cut me and my people loose."

Brock couldn't conceal his laugh. "You are quite a character. Right this minute, Nelson, I've got you, your guys, the Syrians, the C-4, months of tapes, videos, and your paperwork on this shipment, including the phony licenses and export crap for drilling mud that isn't drilling mud that's supposed to go to Kuwait and won't."

"I'll help you nail everybody in this deal except my people. Goddamn Syrians made me walk over hot coals to get the deal," he said bitterly.

"Give me everybody," Brock emphasized, "and I might be able to get you under a century in prison."

Nelson swore, stood up. Brock saw a man in late middle age, brick red face, looking like a Saturday afternoon football hero bewildered that he had just awakened much older. It was always strange to finally confront face-to-face mobsters and drug dealers he'd listened to for months on wiretaps and bugs as disembodied voices with violent, rapacious appetites.

But Ed Nelson was even stranger. There was a black hollowness in him Brock had never encountered before. It was unnerving.

"Okay, Andrews," Nelson said, idly glancing at the cover of a porno magazine. "You're letting me go sooner or later anyway."

"Why would I do that?"

"You think I did this alone? Little me? This is your government talking," Nelson snapped.

"I don't think so. We're not selling a lifetime supply of terrorist explosives this season." Brock grinned.

"Want to bet?" Nelson said sharply. "I can still make you come out a hero. Make me a deal right now because you'll get shit later."

"No deal." It was an easy decision. Nelson, Brock knew, existed on boasts and bluster. After some time in jail, with the looming threat of a long prison sentence, he would become more tractable. They all did.

"You're a solid gold dummy," Nelson said curtly. "I'm ashamed my tax dollars pay your salary."

Brock brought him out and turned him over to the waiting FBI agents. "You haven't paid taxes for three years," Brock said. "That's my favorite charge when I get the grand jury to bury you."

Nelson vanished down the corridor. A few minutes later, Brock was on the ship's bridge. A dozen police cars were on the pier below, crime scene vans, explosive transport trucks, and a line of chained Mexican nationals taken away in a heavily armored county jail bus. Helicopters swooped and swarmed noisily over the frantic activity. Brock smiled with relief.

Jimmy bounded to him with Lila. "Man, boss, we've struck the fucking number one jackpot today." He beamed.

Lila held her hair back from the helicopters' turbulence. "We get back to Sacramento tonight, Brock, we have got to party something fierce."

Brock shook his head. "No party for me tonight. Sorry. I'll be occupied." He wasn't afraid of disappointing Jimmy;

Jimmy had his wife and the kids to carry him in triumph. But Lila had just the Three Muscatels to share the moment with. He patted her arm. "We'll do it this week for sure. I've got to make a call," he said a little nervously.

He turned, his cell phone out. Behind him, Brock heard Jimmy say to Lila, "Alison, right? Who else's so important?"

"Yeah. Who else."

First Assistant United States Attorney Alison Andrews was on the phone with the chief judge of California's Eastern District when the call came through and her secretary frantically flapped her arms to indicate who it was.

"I'll have to call you back," Alison instantly said to the judge, then punched up Brock. "Hello, stranger."

"Clean sweep, Ally. Can't talk long, got a press conference in a couple of minutes. But we got it all. C-4, Nelson, a bunch of Syrians. It was beautiful."

"I can barely hear you. What's that? Helicopters? Loudspeakers?"

"Cops are keeping the crowd back. We have a mob of spectators here. I've got to brownnose the L.A. undersheriff on the tube. He almost screwed the whole operation." Brock chuckled.

Alison felt her breath catch. "How? Were you in danger?"

"It wasn't his fault exactly. He used an open radio channel to call for more ambulances, and the media latched on to it and spooked Nelson."

"Then crucify the sonofabitch, Brock," she said heatedly. "He put everybody's life in jeopardy."

"Look, it all worked out. There's enough glory to spread around. The locals are hopping mad I'm here."

"Nelson was developed from our sources, our leads, our agencies, and it was a chance of geography he was moving the C-4 from Los Angeles instead of up here. Brock, I don't think you have a killer instinct."

She listened to him chuckling, and her tanned, toned face relaxed. That amused sound of his always made her feel good. It promised happiness and a clean, bright future. A world of Sunday mornings in bed, country road jogs, sharing wine in front of a fire.

He seemed to know her mind. "I'm on the five-twenty to Sacramento. I'll bring a bottle of champagne."

"We'll celebrate," she said, ignoring the line of blinking lights on her telephone console. "I'll try to get a bottle, too."

"The good stuff."

"The very good stuff."

"Then we'll have two bottles," he said, the warbling rumble of helicopters louder, his voice faint. "What a nightmare."

"We'll manage to get through the night," she said. "Hurry back."

"Got to go. Cameras are ready. Catch me on CNN, Ally." The line was silent abruptly.

I'm never letting go, she thought, no matter what frightening differences have started bubbling between us now. She touched a silver-framed photograph of Brock and her, taken at the Sutter Club party after she was sworn in. Both of them were laughing, holding cake plates. It could be confused with a wedding picture. She got up and started for the door. There were other pictures of Brock and her on the walls, but this was her favorite.

Alison strode down the fifteenth-floor hallway, passed the open doorways of other assistant U.S. attorneys, and barged into the outer office of the U.S. Attorney himself. She kept going.

"He's with the Oregon AG! You can't go in!" the worry-creased executive secretary vainly said as Alison ignored her.

Alison found Porter Ridgeway in polite, quiet conversation with another man. Ridgeway was pointing out his blue linen curtained window at the white butter-creme mass of the California state capitol building, its gold dome gleaming in the April sun.

She said, "He did it, Port. Turn on the TV."

She had almost called Ridgeway Popeye, his office nickname. He was middle-aged, short, and his custom-tailored shirt collars were one size too small, making his already protuberant oyster blue eyes bug out.

"In a meeting, Alison. Give me a few minutes."

Alison snatched the remote, and a large screen TV in one corner sprang to life. "Brock nailed Nelson and the whole shipment, Port. You said he couldn't do it. You said we'd be cleaning up the mess for months." She felt her voice grow cold. "So when Brock comes back tomorrow, I expect you to eat a plate of crow."

"Sonofabitch," Porter Ridgeway whispered, looking at the cloudless blue sky and limitless Pacific behind Brock on the television. He was surrounded by federal agents and local law enforcement. Nelson's scowling face popped into a box over his shoulder. Ridgeway took the remote from Alison and muted the sound. "I had my doubts. But you and Brock always get what you want." He smiled, patting her arm a little shyly. "Congratulations. I'll eat a double helping. If you dish it up."

"With both hands," Alison said. She left as suddenly as she'd stormed in. Only in the hallway, out of sight, did she pause, hand to her mouth, the fear of something happening to Brock still wound painfully around inside her.

The attorney general of Oregon stared after her, as if he saw the tall woman in her mid-thirties, blond hair thick and carefully massed, thin mouth, cool green eyes, perfectly dressed in egg white blouse, mauve skirt, simple silver pin merely by the lingering trace of her citrus perfume. He blinked several times. He said wonderingly to Ridgeway, "Was that . . ."

"My good right arm. Alison Andrews. The Golden Girl of Justice Department legend," Ridgeway said, sitting down behind his walnut desk. The hint of irritation was unmistakable even through his practiced grin. "Now, Brock, her husband, he's a headache or two. Sometimes he jumps first, but he makes cases like a sonofabitch. So what are you going to do when you've got a team like that working for you? I get out of their way."

The attorney general of Oregon sat down on the leather sofa. "So what was all this just about?"

"Office politics," Porter Ridgeway said dryly, snapping off the TV as Brock, over three hundred miles to the south, shook hands with the undersheriff of Los Angeles.

It was nearly seven, the late April evening's brightness softening when Brock eagerly drove home. He parked, waved quickly to a neighbor lovingly polishing an antique Rolls, and hurried inside, clutching his heavy briefcase and vintage champagne in a paper bag.

He heard sounds from the kitchen. The large two-story, high-ceilinged colonial was set in a neighborhood of California's capital city bounded on one side by 40th Avenue and called the Fabulous Forties. The state's old barons and princelings had built solid and expensive homes here, and Brock had always felt out of place in their vanished company.

He found Celeste, the wide-waisted, bustling Filipino grandmother who ran the house, fussily finishing several plates of dainty dishes and putting them in the vast refrigerator. He gave her the champagne.

"You have a little party," Celeste said cheerfully, wiping her hands. "I'm going home so it's just you two."

"Where's Alison?" Brock asked.

"Upstairs, I think." Celeste frowned. "Congratulations, Mr. Andrews, for stopping that bad man. You go look for her; I'll be gone by the time you come down." She gave a tiny laugh.

He thanked her, wondering what the last remark meant, then hurried across the foyer, left his briefcase in the study, and went up the curving, ornate staircase. He didn't find Alison in the bedroom, bathroom, or anywhere on the second floor. He heard Celeste's car start and drive off, a pack of kids on bikes crying to each other on the street.

Annoyed, he came downstairs, calling to Alison. Then, he looked through the open French doors. His breath caught.

In a white robe, Alison stood at the edge of the pool at the far end of the wide, elm-dotted back lawn. She saw him and, with no other acknowledgment, slipped off the robe, stood naked in the fading daylight for a moment, then dove with exquisite form into the pale aquamarine water.

He took off his coat as he walked briskly to the pool. She looked as vibrant and desirable as that first afternoon when they had almost collided on the jogging path around Lake Pontchartrain in the unbearable New Orleans humidity, where he'd taken refuge, like her, from a tedious conference on narcotics enforcement, and his life had changed simply and utterly.

He stood on the cement pool apron watching her. An opened champagne bottle sweated on a glass-topped table. He loosened his tie. He picked up the bottle.

She came to his side of the pool. Her sun-streaked, blond hair was held in the back with a blue silk ribbon, her shoulders lightly freckled. "Do I know you?" she asked.

"No glasses," he said, glancing around.

"Gimme," she said in reply, reaching up for the champagne. He handed it to her, and she took a long, slow swallow from the cold bottle, then offered it to him, wiping her mouth with a finger.

"You're a nasty lady, Ally," he murmured, then drank, staring at her.

She laughed, seeing he was aroused. They had great news to celebrate, and tonight, at least, they could pretend all was as it had been from their first night. "House rules say nobody comes in unless they're bareass," she said.

He nodded, quickly putting the bottle down, hopping to get his pants off, shoes and shirt tossed to one side. "May I join you?" he asked formally.

"Why? Am I coming apart?"

"Dorothy Parker," they swiftly said together, chuckling. Parker's wryness, W.C. Fields' asides, these were pleasures they had in common. Along with a million other things, she thought.

Brock raised his arms, assumed a diving stance and

plunged cleanly into the water, surfacing with a gasp, shiver, and paddling close to her. He grinned, saying, "You're still too dressed," and untied the silk holding her hair in the back. It fell across her shoulders.

They swam silently together, watching each other like aquatic animals, then stopped. He wiped water from her eyes. She touched his chest, then reached lower.

"Aside from that incident, how'd the evening go, Mrs. Lincoln?" he asked like a pompous reporter.

"I'm not buying season tickets for that show." She pulled closer to him. "Celeste made some fantastic things to munch on."

"I'm a lot hungrier," he said sharply.

She turned to swim away coyly, the play resumed, but Brock abruptly moved against her body, hands on her shoulders, breasts, ass. He kissed her, pulled back and said, "I love you so much, I don't want anything to happen. I want you so much."

She held on to him tightly, fiercely, as if the embrace insured they would rush ahead together. Linked in velocity, speeding with the same momentum, toward the same dreams.

It was her deepest fear. Perhaps they no longer shared the same dreams.

They began in the water, moved up to one of the chaise lounges around the pool, then ended on the lime green sofa in the living room. A balmy delta breeze blew through the French doors.

"It would be so sexy without protection," he said, unwilling to break the mood if they had to prepare for lovemaking like surgeons.

"Another time, Brock. We'll talk about it again," she said.

So she went to the upstairs bathroom, returned and was ready, too, but the short interlude reminded Alison of one of the great fissures starting to divide them. Brock wanted children. She did not.

They cradled together on the sofa later, the breeze drying their sweat. She listened, questioned him about the raid, hand on his chest. His enthusiasm and pleasure at this success seemed to spark through her fingers.

"Nelson tried to deal," he said, grinning. "I think he'd double-cross himself if he got the chance. He's the crookedest puke I've ever met."

"It's a very big bust. You looked terrific on TV, and I think we'll just take this all the way to trial, no plea bargains, no side deals."

"Shall we go to court together, ma'am? You kill them on opening statement, I bury Nelson with the evidence, we both do closing argument? Stick a fork in him, Bower, and Lara. They're done."

She leaned back against the sofa. "No joke, Brock. The two of us putting them on trial would be the frosting on this cake." She told him about Ridgeway's grudging congratulations. "I want to watch him grovel tomorrow. He'll be completely nauseated when I tell him the good news you and I'll do our first trial together."

"My wife the boss," he said, hugging her. "Only, who leads off in closing argument?"

"You do, of course. Then I finish it. Always save the best for the very end."

"We'll discuss that." He frowned. He kissed her just as the phone in the study began ringing clangorously.

"Christ," he complained when Alison took a deep breath and got up. "Don't go," he said grumpily.

"It's the hotline. I told the office not to use it tonight, so something big's blown somewhere." She walked with unaffected sensuality, but Brock could tell her mind was back on the job. Their personal and professional lives were too interwoven.

He closed his eyes, and then she was back, robe on, arms crossed. "That was Chris Metzger," she said, naming the third-ranking official at the Department of Justice. "He was very enigmatic. But you know Chris."

"No, I don't know Chris," Brock said, sitting up. "You know Chris. You've got the D.C. contacts."

"It's not worth getting mad about."

"I'm not mad. What did he want?" Brock stood and rubbed her arms, hoping the gesture might defuse their sudden mutual annoyance.

"I've got a four o'clock meeting with him tomorrow. He just said I had to present myself at his office."

Brock took a breath. "This has got to be it, Ally. They're finally giving you the Criminal Division. Jesus. That's going to change everything." They had debated, without resolution, what would happen if Alison were offered a high-level job in Washington. Neither of them liked the idea of a bicoastal marriage. Especially now.

"Maybe he wants to pat me on the back for your raid, Brock. You should come, too. Nelson's your trophy as much as mine."

He opened her robe. "If Metzger wanted me in the throne room, he'd have said so. Ally, this is your big step. Go to town." He kissed her breasts.

"I've got plane reservations to make," she said, sliding with him back to the couch. The April night beyond the French doors was fired with violet piping at the horizon.

"We've got a couple hours left to ourselves," he said, voice muffled against her.

"A couple of hours," she whispered.

CHAPTER THREE

Alison had the cab let her off on the Pennsylvania Avenue side of the Department of Justice's formidable stone bulk. It always reminded her of visiting powerful and secretive relatives. She passed quickly through the security station in the vast lobby, mixing with the ceaseless tide of people moving in and out of the elevators even at four on a Tuesday afternoon.

She wore a light teal outfit; but Washington was unusually humid for April, and she felt damp and a little disoriented from jet lag. Yet by the time she stepped out on the fourth floor, slim briefcase in hand and purposefully headed down the marble corridor toward the associate attorney general's office, no one could have discerned what she felt or was thinking. It had taken years to cultivate that implacable exterior.

What's coming? she wondered. It's got to be good news. The last few days she and Brock seemed to be on a roll of private and public success. She smiled recalling last night.

Chris Metzger showed her in, complimented her, apologized for the emergency meeting, then ushered her to a comfortably large sofa under the oil portrait of an eighteenth century statesman. She spent an obligatory minute admiring the newest photos of ducks and sleeping lions on the walls where his predecessors had hung actual trophies.

She pointed at the splayed newspapers on his desk, all blaring headlines and photos on their front pages from Brock's raid. "We took care of business yesterday," Alison said proudly.

"That you did. Yes. You did. It's on every news show."

"You look fit and satisfied." She was puzzled by his dull tone.

"I look like the harried public servant I am, Ally." He waved a dissenting hand, then sat down opposite her in a fragile antique chair. He offered her a bag of sunflower seeds, which she declined, and began cracking and chewing on them himself. "You're the bright star in the room."

She returned his bow. He had thinning hair, and was casually tieless and wearing Topsiders without socks. He ran the Justice Department for the administration and let a venerable aged lawyer play attorney general.

She noticed that even with two computers the large office smelled quaintly of lemon oil and old paper. "I came three thousand miles, Chris," she said. "What's the surprise? I think I've guessed."

"I'm sorry, Ally. It's not the Criminal Division this time. Although," he said hastily, tossing sunflower husks into the wastebasket at his feet, "that is very much in the pipeline."

"I'm not going to tell you I'm not disappointed." She slumped slightly, then straightened. "Well, so what could be more important?"

"We've had a very intriguing offer. Somebody wants to work for us." His small brown eyes stayed on her as he sucked a seed.

"Who?"

"Edward Nelson."

"Brock said he made noises about something like that yesterday. Good. Put the bastard to work."

"But with who, Ally? Who should handle a major arms dealer and turncoat spook like Nelson?"

"You are joking."

He wiped his hands, a smile fracturing his face into sharp planes. "Not a bit. We bring Ed Nelson in as our guy, the bait for terrorists who want weapons, and *you* give him his marching orders."

"I've never handled a snitch before"—she stood up, startled at the suggestion—"well, never one at Nelson's level. I did the usual dopers and low-grade hoods, Chris. This is more up Brock's alley. He's the snitchmeister in our office."

"I'm afraid it would be impossible for Brock to do it."

"He's the best in any office in the country."

She watched Metzger get up, crumple the bag of sunflower seeds and put it in a recess of his enormous oak desk, then study her coolly. Alison thought, the hammer's coming down.

"Ally, to make it convincing, to make it fly"—he raised his short arms—"Nelson's got to get a clean bill of health. We have to cut him loose very publicly."

"I can't sign on to that," she said hotly. "It took six months and a lot of dangerous investigation to bag him on this C-4 deal. It's not worth losing all of that."

"But it is, Ally. Trust me. The decision's already been made by the higher beings you and I serve."

"I don't want any part of it, Chris," she said angrily. "Brock's task force risked their lives. We've got a great case against Nelson and his pals."

"Okay, Ally." Chris sighed and sat down behind the desk, clasping his hands together. "Here's the way of the world. You are entitled to walk away from using Ed Nelson as our biggest and best net to catch terrorists. But we *will* use him. I want you to get the credit, the promotion, this kind of major, major undercover operation will inevitably produce." He leaned back. "Nelson's current case will be dumped. We will publicly eat shit to give him enhanced credibility with future purchasers of his product line."

"I won't help you," she said. It was even, quiet, and intimidating. "Do you have any idea, sitting here"—she waved her hand at the trappings of the large office—"how this kind of humiliation will affect Brock? A lot of dedicated agents?"

"How it affects Brock is entirely up to you," he said.

"What the hell does that mean?"

"If I have to pair Nelson with my second choice snitch handler, Ally, I can pretty much guarantee you Brock will shortly lose his job as head of the Task Force on Organized Crime and Narcotic Enforcement. Firing him will lend weight to the public shit-eating we'll do to give Nelson a boost."

"You are out of your fucking mind, Chris. I've got people on the Hill who'll listen to me if I make noise." Alison hated feeling her emotions straining to run riot. She took a ragged, furious breath. "I will make one hell of a noise."

Metzger looked pained, like one of his big toes had exploded. "And we will lose using Nelson. And Brock will be fired. And transferred. To Georgia maybe. And you will be waiting a very long time for the Criminal Division."

"Screw the Criminal Division. This is a travesty."

He nodded. "There's always a price tag on big investigations."

"Someone else pays it."

"Ally, I know you're mad now. You should be. But you have choices. Come on board and ride Nelson and help your country."

"Don't," she said, pointing at him.

"Brock will get over his humiliation when you're on TV showing everybody our catch of terrorists, enemies foreign and domestic." Metzger's face lit up; his hands gestured broadly. "He'll realize this C-4 investigation wasn't wasted. It got us a damn deep hook in Ed Asshole-of-the-Decade Nelson."

"He'll go through hell until then."

"It's in your hands how Brock and his Wild Bunch—" he snapped his fingers trying to remember—"the Three Muscatels come out at the end of the day."

"You're pretty much of a major league asshole yourself, Chris." Alison picked up her briefcase. "I'll think about it."

"Until Friday. Nelson's got a bail reduction hearing that morning."

Alison left even as Metzger tried to walk her to the door, wishing her a safe flight back to Sacramento. Outside of the building, she felt the enervating damp warmth clamp down. On impulse, she went into a small bar up 9th Street she remembered from her days working in Senator Cantil's office.

Alison sat down in a dark corner, the bar more brass and ale signs than years ago. She drank two martinis for courage to face the future, and to deaden the awful ache of her past Metzger's blackmail had awakened.

Whatever she did next, Brock would suffer.

"Christ," she said, putting her glass down.

Friday morning was cool and clear, and just before nine Brock followed a speeding centipede of black vans and cars. It raced six blocks from the towering block of Sacramento's county jail to the John Moss Federal Courthouse, within a hundred yards of the state capitol. Traffic was halted on all streets as the centipede sped by. Overhead, TV news helicopters rumbled loudly.

A double ring of U.S. marshals and courthouse guards at the entrance parted only slightly as Brock saw three huddled figures bundled rapidly from the largest black van and hustled inside. A shouting throng of reporters and cameras was held back by Sacramento police officers behind barriers.

It took several minutes for Brock himself to push up to the third floor, followed by more reporters, blandly smiling for them, saying he would talk to them all after the bail reduction hearing.

He found Jimmy Yee and Lila Martin sitting at the front of the carpeted, tensely crowded courtroom. He put his briefcase and files on the counsel table.

"Nelson, Bower, and Lara just got here," Brock whispered. "Their lawyers are outside spinning for the media."

Jimmy's mouth turned down nervously. "Boss, any

chance the judge is going to lower bail? Maybe let Nelson out before trial?"

"No chance. I brought some of the wiretap transcripts you guys sweated for." He grinned. "I'm going to get Nelson's bail revoked after the judge reads them."

Lila nodded happily. "I can live with that."

As the clock on the courtroom wall touched nine exactly, Nelson, Bower, and Lara, with their trio of trim suited lawyers and marshals surrounding them all, were brought in, seated, handcuffs removed. Nelson snorted, as he leaned to talk to his lawyer. He wore a rumpled blue seersucker and red tie.

Brock stood confidently. Judge Benjamin Cedillo, tall and owl-eyed, took the bench, the Great Seal of the United States behind him. Brock winked at Jimmy and Lila. Every seat was filled by spectators or reporters.

Brock sensed the astonished rustle in the courtroom before Alison was suddenly at his side. She looked ahead, putting a thin file folder on the counsel table. Her mouth was drawn.

"Ally," he whispered. "You here to watch me in action?"

"I've got something to say to Cedillo before you jump in," she said with a sad smile.

Brock nodded as the judge cleared his throat self-consciously. Alison only went to court on the most important and public cases, and this one certainly met those requirements.

"We're here on a defense motion on behalf of all defendants for a reduction in bail," Judge Cedillo began and Alison interrupted.

"Your Honor, the government has a statement to make which will bear directly on whether you hear the motion."

"Mrs. Andrews, it's a pleasure to see you again, but I was under the impression the U.S. Attorney's Office would be represented by your husband today."

"Extraordinary circumstances have compelled me to step in, Your Honor."

"Ally," Brock whispered, looking up at her. He twisted in his seat. What the hell was going on? Jimmy and Lila wore bewildered frowns. Across the courtroom, Ed Nelson shook his head sharply as if bugs were prowling his scalp. Otherwise he looked bored.

"Well, make your statement, Mrs. Andrews," Judge Cedillo said a little uncertainly, unhappy a surprise had been added to his carefully planned hearing in front of so many reporters.

Brock watched Alison step toward the bench. Every eye followed her lithe figure. In front of the bench she seemed less a supplicant and more the sovereign of the proceedings.

"An exhaustive review of the case against these three individuals has been undertaken in the last seventy-two hours," Alison said firmly, "here and in Washington. The government has concluded that the case is fatally defective and the defects cannot be repaired."

Brock's fist slammed down involuntarily as Lila gasped. Cedillo snapped for order and commanded the ranked marshals along the courtroom's walls to remove anyone causing a further disturbance.

"This is startling, Mrs. Andrews. Have you told defense counsel?"

"They are learning of this just as you are, Your Honor."

"I see. Let's cut to the chase. What is the government proposing?" Judge Cedillo leaned toward Alison.

In disbelief Brock heard her say, with only a slight tremor, "I'm moving to have all charges against these three individuals dismissed immediately and with prejudice, Your Honor."

Brock jumped to his feet. "Your Honor! I would like to know what's going on!" His heart raced, and his mind felt mired in confusion, anger, and frustration.

"So would I," snorted Cedillo, standing up. "All counsel in my chambers. Now. Court's in recess until called."

The murmuring and excited chatter almost drowned out Jimmy Yee beside Brock. "It's got to be some kind of joke, boss."

"Something's happened," Brock agreed, hurrying to join the others in chambers. He walked in, Alison already

standing by the bookshelves of Supreme Court Reports.
She looked away.

The three defense lawyers, older men with pink, smooth
faces, had identical hungry, anticipatory smiles.

Cedillo was on the phone angrily shouting at the head
of the marshal's courthouse detail for more men. "Do not
argue," he snapped. "I've just had a bomb go off in my
courtroom. Not a *bomb*. A bomb. There's going to be pandemonium in about five minutes." He glared at Alison. "So
you get me more people!" He slammed the phone down.

"Judge, I'm the sole representative of the government
in this case," Alison said. She looked at Brock with a coolness that shocked him like a blow.

Cedillo flicked up his robed arm. "That's it, Brock.
Vacate the premises."

"Your Honor, I've got overwhelming evidence against
these guys. I brought transcripts for you."

"You've been unplugged," the judge said with lidded
eyes. "Get out or the boys will throw you out."

Brock wandered back into the half-filled courtroom,
reporters jabbering and darting in from the corridor. He
vainly tried to sort out what was happening. Why hadn't
Alison said something that morning as they dressed? Sat
eating breakfast together? Last night as they lay in bed?

Lila gripped his arm. "This is bullshit, Brock," she said.
"It's got to be. We didn't step on any cracks in this investigation."

Jimmy nodded vehemently. "That asshole Bower was
shooting at me!"

Brock said, "Okay, settle down. Alison's working some
angle. I trust her. Maybe she's got a plea coming."

But even he doubted that, and fifteen minutes later, he
knew it was not so. At Cedillo's stern request from the
bench, Alison carefully laid out a damning succession of
mistakes, sloppy investigation, and incompetence in
Brock's handling of Nelson's case.

Jimmy and Lila hissed in impotent fury in his ear. He told
them to shut up. Agent Yee precipitated a confrontation.
Other suspects were ignored during the investigation.

Legitimate purchase of explosive for use· in Kuwaiti oil drilling. No clear evidence the explosives would be diverted.

Alison didn't falter when Jimmy Yee, cursing loudly behind her, was yanked out of the courtroom by three marshals. "The government's conclusion, Your Honor," she finished, "is that there is neither a reasonable likelihood of conviction at trial nor of sustaining any conviction after appeal. The case is utterly compromised. I ask that it be dismissed."

Brock felt thick, rancid sweat down his back.

"I don't have much choice after that recital, Mrs. Andrews," Judge Cedillo said somberly. "Motion granted. The defendants are released and bail exonerated."

Brock jumped up at the whooping, back-slapping, exuberant handshaking among Nelson, Bower, and Lara. Nelson glanced at him, shrugged, then was gone.

In an impenetrable mass of reporters, Alison passed by him, and then he, too, was crushed by dozens of shouting and gesturing people. He didn't encompass what had happened. It couldn't have occurred.

Lila, her face a mask of rage, yelled at him, "We've been screwed, chief."

An hour later, in the fifteenth-floor conference room at the U.S. Attorneys Office, Brock and Alison faced each other across the barren table. Their shouts carried easily through the closed doors to the stunned lawyers' staff in the hallways.

"You should've told me," he said tightly.

"You'd have tried to stop me."

"Goddamn right. You know there's nothing wrong with the case."

"Everything's wrong with it."

"This is why you've been on the phone every goddamn night to Metzger? Plotting this one?"

"Brock." Alison folded her arms, lowered her head for

a moment. She looked at him. "You can't see how mishandled the investigation's been. You're too close."

"Don't insult my intelligence, Ally! Christ Almighty. Tell me Nelson paid you a million bucks, tell me he's leaving the country. Tell me you're balling him," Brock stopped. "But for God's sake, don't give me any crap about the quality of my team or this investigation."

"Because I haven't been in the trenches?" she shot back sarcastically.

"You would not know what you're talking about. And that weasel Metzger couldn't find a courtroom if you stuck it up his ass."

"You don't have to shout."

"Like hell. I had to listen to the nonsense you said in court, at that press conference." His face was rigid. "Do you have any idea what you've done to Yee or Martin? The rest of the task force? You told the world we're fuck-ups. World class."

Alison looked out at the sparkling skyline of Sacramento spread across the wide windows. It was going to be a bright, beautiful day. She said, "You're reacting like this was a personal decision, Brock. This is purely professional. By the department."

He drove his hand flat onto the table time after time. "No, Ally. This was personal. You and me. You could've warned me at least. Come out of the shower this morning and said, 'Oh, Brock. I'm going to shitcan your investigation and let that asshole Nelson go back to his horses and estate in Virginia.'" He walked toward her, stopped; his voice fell. "You could have done that, Ally. That much."

"It wouldn't have changed anything."

"Between us it would've. Yeah." He turned and left the room.

She waited until she could walk out without trembling, then went to her office and took calls about the dramatic morning for most of the day. When she went home, Alison had Celeste fix a light dinner for her and Brock. He didn't come home then, and Alison carefully wrapped his dinner and put it in the refrigerator. It was still there in the morning. The following night, Alison told Celeste she would only have to make one dinner. Alison resumed taking the moderately powerful sleeping pills she'd given up months earlier. She continued using the pills to sleep when Brock did come home two days later, but moved himself into the guest room down the hall.

CHAPTER FOUR

On a Friday morning a month later, Denny Lara turned again to Bower at the wheel and said, "I can't do it."

"Yes, you can and you're going to."

"For once I'm serious. Swear to God, I cannot do this."

They sat in a rented four-door blue sedan. The engine was running and sending short exhaust plumes into the cool San Francisco May morning. Shoppers and traffic moved steadily around them.

Bower sighed. He reached into his loose overcoat and put a gun in Denny's lap. "Pick it up. Don't wave it around, Christ Almighty, you'll scare some citizen out there." He laughed.

Denny lifted the gun. He wore a tailored camel hair overcoat and a pale silk scarf. "Christ, it weighs a fucking ton, Bower."

"I thought you're the weapons expert."

"I don't know anything about anything that fires less than six hundred rounds," he tried joking. "Look, I do bullshit about weapons, electronics. I can't do this." He nudged the gun back to Bower.

Bower didn't move. He said, "Listen, anybody can do

this crap. It's in the news every day. What you've got is a nine millimeter Lorcin. Barrel's a little longer than I'd like, but it's still a two-incher basically. It's a couple pounds, that's all. Kids use them. That's how this'll look. You got a ten-shot load in there, Den. You keep pulling the trigger and that's it."

"How about you handling this all the way, Bower? I'd owe you."

"Not my call. You know that. Ed says you. And you it will be."

Denny slumped. His tan face was oily with sweat. "He wouldn't know. I wouldn't tell him. We could just go back to L.A."

Bower looked impatiently at his heavy diver's watch. "Don't beg, okay? You know the way it'd go. Someday you get jammed up. Or you get bombed drinking with Ed and some score. Maybe you feel mad at everybody and start talking about how I took care of business and suddenly Ed's knowing I'm lying to him." Bower stared at Denny. "How long do you think you or me would hang around when he knows that? How long?"

"He could get somebody else for this. We don't have to be sitting here."

"Yeah, we do. And it's time. Fucker takes his morning walk at ten-fifteen, right?"

"Look, Bower, when I was a kid, even before my first honor farm, my old man broke my jaw when I wouldn't shoot our dog with a .22. Dog was really sick, but I couldn't do it."

"I'm not your old man. I wouldn't break your jaw. You know what'd have to happen."

Denny's head slumped. "Oh, Jesus," he said slowly.

Bower tapped the wheel. "This guy Kelso trusts you. He'll feel okay. That's why it's got to be you." He ran a slow hand over his thinning hair. "Den, you don't do this, I'm flying back to L.A. alone, and that dark meat you're boning is going to be all by herself."

Denny thought of how beautiful Mandy looked that morning as she stood at the closet, dressing and sighing while she tried to close her flowered blouse. She was six months pregnant with their child.

There was silence in the car for a moment. Denny grunted as if hit, and Bower looked again at his watch. A stylishly dressed woman dragged a wailing little girl up Montgomery Street's shadowy skyscraper canyon. A trio of chattering employees started building a display of swimsuit dummies and beach umbrellas in a department store window near the idling car.

Bower repeated, as if to a dull child, "You bring Kelso over to the car. You and me are going out for a drink. He'll join us. We go down to that nice, quiet dead-end alley and you shoot him, use up the Lorcin's whole mag. Then he loses his wallet and obvious jewelry and we go back out to San Fran International, drop that fucking cheap gun and the other shit in the bay on our way. Noon, we're on a plane to L.A. What's the goddamn problem?"

They both watched a forty-story bank building across the street. Well-dressed men and women bustled through its revolving doors.

"I'm a set-up man, Bower. Not a shooter. I make people buy equipment."

"So that changes right now," Bower said very low and intensely.

Denny got out slowly. He had the gun in his overcoat pocket. It felt like a hook yanking him violently to the ground.

Bower said, "Do it, Den. I'll buy you a double vodka at the airport." It sounded like a father bribing his son with a milk shake so he'd mow the lawn.

Denny moved across the street almost blindly, blinking furiously. Cars honked at him, drivers cursed, and he smiled because smiling had always worked before for him.

He got in front of the Transnational Bank building and saw Bower watching from the car. He turned away and felt almost giddy, as if he was going to black out. Then coming through the revolving door amidst the other bustling people was a small man with thick glasses, pulling a glove on, holding a newspaper folded in quarters under his arm.

"Jesus, Ray Kelso," Denny said as if startled, arms opened wide. "I was coming up to see you."

"Lara? This is a damn surprise." The man lowered the newspaper. "I thought you were out of the country. Singapore, Bangkok, some place. Still in the import business?"

"Oh, yeah. But, something's come up about our last deal, last month? You absolutely need to hear about it."

"I certainly got fucked over royally by Ed Nelson. You, too. Swore up and down I was just drawing up export papers for oil drilling mud. I didn't know he was shipping high explosives! I'm still up to my ears in lawyers." Kelso scowled. "I thought the charges were dropped."

"Something sensitive's come up, more problems. I can lay it out for you in your office." Sweat dripped down his face.

"Five minutes. I've got to buy some damn fancy cheese down the street. The wife says we have to bring it as a gift to a dinner party in Sacramento." Kelso tapped his newspaper with his hand. "Old friends of yours, Denny. That U.S. Attorney Alison Andrews, one that saved your bacon. I don't want to go; but it's a big political do, and the wife says it'll put me in the clear after you bastards hung me out."

Denny improvised quickly. "Something bad's come up about this party, Ray."

"What? You want to do me a favor? Ed wants to do me a favor?" Kelso snapped as they walked into the building and up to the line of elevators in the cavernous lobby.

Denny said something, but he couldn't hear himself; the words simply tumbled out. He'd seen Bower staring back from the car like a shark in a tank. His hand clawed around the gun in his pocket, and he felt the muscles start to cramp. He thought of Mandy and Bower's threat about her.

"This is some scam Ed's pulling, isn't it?" Kelso demanded suddenly. People around them tensed at the sharp tone.

"Wait until we get upstairs."

"Like hell. This is another bullshit scam, isn't it? You and goddamn Ed Nelson are running a scam on me."

"Ed's got nothing to do with this." Denny pulled the gun out. A woman to his right yelped, and a man carrying a small spotted dog skittered toward the revolving door. Everyone backed away.

"I'm going to save your life," Denny gasped. "I'm supposed to shoot you." He turned the gun, pushing it toward Kelso, offering it to him, pleading. "We got to get out of here."

He dimly heard a shout, and a large black security guard bolted from behind a desk at the far end of the lobby. Kelso stared at Denny for a moment, cursed, then fumbled as he pulled a shiny steel gun from inside his own coat. His newspaper fell to the floor.

It's not fair, Denny thought furiously. First time someone really cares and she's waiting for me and I'm going to die here. It's fucking not fair. Even so, he couldn't move.

The security guard ran toward them, calling out. Denny saw Bower charge through the bank's revolving doors. He had a bulky automatic aimed at Kelso's back.

Bower fired four times, still coming ahead. Behind him, Denny heard resonant shots from the security guard. Bower yelled to him, but the words seemed distant and incomprehensible. Then Bower stepped to Denny's side and fired past him at the guard.

In front of Denny, Kelso blinked, fell forward, and his gun slid across the polished marble floor. Denny watched as if through a haze. The guard was facedown halfway up the lobby. Bower lay on his back a few feet away, head jerking like he was trying to sit up. His shoes beat lightly on the floor; then he stiffened and was still.

A ripe, acrid stench like burning wood and wet leaves stung Denny. He turned several times, his ears echoing, aching from the noise. I'm okay, he thought incredulously.

An alarm bell rang incessantly. He saw staring faces, open mouths, behind the glass walls of the bank on his left. Everyone pointed at him.

He stumbled toward the revolving door, but people were

massed outside already, and a few bolder men were coming in. Denny spun to his right. He ran toward an expensive Italian restaurant off the bank building's lobby. He raced past startled late breakfasters, glasses frozen, forks poised. Someone screamed, and a man yelled like a frightened child.

Denny pushed by waiters, through double steel doors into the kitchen, through a mist of steam and smoke. He saw a blur of cooks; then he was at the loading dock doors, surrounded by crates of lettuce and tomatoes, drums of olive oil. Frantically, he shoved open the doors, standing outside for an instant on the dock. He jumped off, landing badly, and pain spurted up his leg. He ran awkwardly down the alley, away from sirens already coming closer.

He still clutched the Lorcin, his fingers feeling like the gun had become part of his hand. He couldn't get rid of it, and he cried out in frustration.

Nobody, not Bower or even Ed Nelson, was going to screw up his life with Mandy anymore. He wouldn't let anybody do that again. He had to get back to her, to see her face again.

Limping out of the alley, he forced himself to slow down and, even though it was agony, to walk naturally on his injured ankle. People remembered limps.

He flagged down a cab and rode to the St. Francis Hotel, and went into the dark paneled bar which was almost empty at that hour of the morning. Denny put on a serious, impatient glare. He told the maitre d' he was expecting two guests for drinks, then left his coat carefully folded at a secluded table in the dimness and went to the nearest public phone.

Easy, he told himself. Take things in order. It was a continuation of an inner monologue he had carried on since he was eleven, unbroken until he met Mandy. He had escaped from homes, honor farms, juvenile detention centers, a dozen times before he was fifteen and once got all the way from Racine to Chicago before he was caught. I can do it again, he thought, dabbing at the sweat on his face.

He called Mandy. She was surprised, then scared.

"This is going to be quick, honey," he told her. "Don't use my name. Don't tell anybody, anybody who asks, that we talked. I'm coming home fast as I can, but I won't be sure where or when we can get together until later today."

"Something's happened, Den. Is it bad?"

"It's going to make some changes." He bit his lip because he didn't want her to hear how frightened he was for them both. "So listen, pack our things. I'll call in a couple of hours. Don't open the door for anybody, don't go out until I tell you."

"Nelson's involved. I know it. I can hear it."

"I'm going to talk to him right after I hang up." Denny controlled his trembling. "But what I just said goes for him."

"Fat chance I'd let Ed Nelson near me," Mandy said. "Damn. He's still your trouble and you've been keeping something from me."

He could almost see her delicate mouth, warm dark eyes bright with anger. "Never again," he said, like an alcoholic taking the pledge.

"Be safe. Hurry back," she said more softly.

He hung up, wishing a kiss to her and the unborn daughter she carried.

Denny wore his impatient businessman's face when he went back to the table. He sipped a double scotch and water and thought about what to do. When the maitre d' inquired about his absent guests, he snapped that they must have mistaken the appointment time.

He went out to the telephone again, ready to leave right after the call. He dialed a number, spoke his number, and hung up. He wiped his hands. Two minutes later, the public phone rang.

"Bower's probably dead," Denny said without preface. "It was a big screwup and he started shooting. Kelso's dead, too. I think."

Loud almost asthmatic breathing. Denny wondered where Ed was calling from, what place anywhere on the face of the earth. "Christ, Den. Christ Almighty. It was an easy deal,'' Nelson said in his raspy, booze-thickened baritone. "Oh, Christ, is this some fucking mess or what."

No questions about me, Denny noted. Hurt, scared, dying? It's not part of the deal how Denny Lara's doing except for one thing.

"Okay, okay, Den. You still in San Francisco, right? You got people on you, local cops?"

"No, I'm clear. I got my ticket and I'm coming back, Ed. I'm really fucking shaking here."

"Sure, sure, this'll do that to you, but it's just a reaction. Look, Den, I'll have somebody meet you at LAX and I'll talk to you later." Long pause, heavy panting inhalations. "You okay about leaving the country for a while?"

"Yeah, of course. With Mandy."

"I'll do my best, like I've done for you before."

"I'm grateful, Ed." He wiped a smear of fear sweat because he knew his fate was being decided in those soothing lies. "Jesus, I'm sorry about Bower."

"It's a hard life we picked, Den," Nelson said by way of an epitaph.

For me and Bower, Denny realized. One down. One to go.

It was nearly noon, the freeways crowded and noxious on the way out to San Francisco International Airport. Denny had the cab drop him at the United terminal. On the way in, rendered invisible by hoards of people and cars, he tore up his Delta ticket and left the pieces in three garbage bins.

He strolled into the gift shop and bought two plastic United flight bags and eight newspapers. He stuffed the newspapers into the bags, put the Lorcin carefully into one, and left that bag in a locker. After talking to Ed, Denny believed he should hold on to the gun.

He went into the lounge nearest the shuttle gates after studying when the next afternoon flight to Los Angeles took off. Then he closely watched the people who went to the gate desk, got checked in early, and lugged carry-on baggage to the lounge for a lingering drink, a bracer to persuade themselves it was feasible to miraculously rise thirty thousand feet into the sky.

He tagged three possibles quickly, and made a certain selection of the brunette who kept looking at her watch, touching blouse and purse, nursing a beer, unable to concentrate on the TV game show over the bar.

How many times had he practiced the engaging smile, walk, attentive gaze in front of mirrors as a kid? He had it down perfectly. Mandy called it The Look. "You're going to sell me a moonbeam," she said once. He smiled grimly because with Ed he had sold things nearly as outlandish. Now I've got an hour to get off Ed's screen, he thought.

He dropped the flight bag into a chair with a heavy sigh. He shrugged off the overcoat, then ordered a beer like the fidgety brunette sitting at the next table.

"You'd think because I work for the airline, I wouldn't mind flying," he said to her, smiling. "But I hate it."

She looked up and hesitantly smiled back.

Fifteen minutes later, Denny stood at the United counter in the main terminal, excitedly saying there had been a sudden change of plan with the baby-sitter and he could join his wife for the day in Los Angeles. He paid cash for the ticket, like the one in the name of Sylvia Golabeck he waved at the clerk, on the one-thirty flight, and checked a single United flight bag which he had retrieved from the locker as his luggage. "I hope you and your wife enjoy yourselves, Mr. Golabeck." The young woman clerk beamed.

Denny walked back to the lounge, handing a grateful Sylvia Golabeck her ticket. "I told you I could expedite your baggage handling at LAX," he said, repeating his excuse for borrowing her ticket. "Besides, us nervous flyers have to stick together."

He picked up his flight bag, which he had asked her to watch, and settled into a seat at the gate. Always give the mark something to do, Denny had learned early. Make them a part of the scam and they won't even mind they've been had.

He stared out at the fuel trucks and baggage handlers on the tarmac, desperately plotting his next moves.

The lifesavers, he thought.

He had two more scotch and waters on the flight south, knowing he was drinking far more than usual or prudent, but like Ed, he needed it bad when he was frightened. Denny didn't remember when he had been more frightened. His ankle burned, too.

Okay, I've got a gun, got myself on a plane under a different name, but I've got to move fast, got to get Mandy and me someplace far away fast. He gulped a third drink.

The key problem was Ed's lethal cunning.

Only eight months ago, he had observed it close up. Ed and Bower were stuck in a Lebanese government guest house, the best supposedly on the Beirut beachfront. The Syrians actually controlled everything. But Denny's clearest memory of the place was the stinking garbage pile beside it, the mangy cats running around, Ed sitting on the porch, bare chest and graying hair baking pink in the Mediterranean sun, drinking pitchers of orange juice and vodka that started being three-quarters juice and ended up mostly liquor. "The striped bastard, side pocket," Ed would mutter, then shoot his pistol at a cat until he hit it. Bower joined in for grins, but mostly he defiantly scubaed in the bottle- and can-flecked ocean.

Denny made four trips to where Ed and Bower were essentially kept prisoner by the Syrians. "They've got my passport; they've got me guarded here," Ed complained every time Denny arrived, sweating and nervous, trying to lighten the tense mood. "They won't let me go until they get the damn C-4."

Days Ed spent phoning, faxing, cursing, drinking. Denny was allowed to travel in and out of the country to speed things along, the gathering of 60,000 pounds of the military high explosives into one shipment. Ed's companies were the buyers. Kuwait was the destination for the drums of oil drilling mud, really C-4 underneath and headed for Damascus.

Denny and Ray Kelso set up the *Ramon Esquivel* to take the cargo out of the United States because the ship followed a barely noticed milk run. Poor Kelso was just larcenous enough to buy Ed's story that the Kuwaitis were buying over-priced drilling mud, and take a fat cut of the profit.

Then there were the Syrian guys, dark, mustached, cold, in black cars, stopping by the Beirut beach house every day or so while Ed shot the garbage pile cats and drank to hide his fear. "You're my lifeline, Den." He grinned lopsidedly. "They're squeezing me to get this stuff *soonest*. You don't get that rust bucket to sea, I'm as dead as those cats."

The whole Syrian deal was supposed to be the start of a major new market for Ed's companies. Why the Syrians wanted very traceable American C-4, he didn't ask about. Not part of my play, Denny thought. I was there to keep those sour, cold guys in the black cars jolly. Keep them from deciding Ed Nelson, bad boy who married a very rich playgirl, whispered to still be with the CIA, was blowing smoke out his ass and stringing them along just to get $15.75 a pound for the explosive. Grand con all the way.

Denny did work it out one of those dank hot nights at the house, the ocean lapping, Ed shouting into the phone, Bower humming and cooking beef stew again because for high-power arms dealers, he and Ed lived like bums under the Syrians' gaze.

U.S. military thinks Ed's CIA, so the C-4 is some op. Kelso thinks it's oil drilling crap for Kuwait; ditto Commerce and State which sign off; ship's owners think it's kosher. And the Syrians buy enough terrorist explosive for anybody who uses it to credibly blame the United States.

That was when, precisely, Denny determined it was time to back out soon. Ed was out of control.

Things got very taut when it looked like the ship was held up. Ed took Denny to the stale, disordered bedroom, fax machines everywhere, unwashed clothes and liquor bottles. "Look, Den, go back to the farm." Ed's wife owned a large working farm in Virginia. "I'm going to give you the accounts. Make sure Josie and the girls are taken care of." He had two daughters in a private school in Connecticut. "I'll swing something here. If I can." His lopsided grin was back more fiercely.

And Denny promised, certain he'd never see Ed again.

Then the call, rush to the farm ten days later, and there was Ed, Bower lurking at a discreet distance, very much alive and in charge.

"How the hell did you get out of Lebanon?" Denny asked the first night with Ed and his family. "I had your memorial service lined up."

Ed, fleshy lips pursed, looked at his stolid, plain, formerly beautiful wife. Her money hadn't faded anyway. "I had someone to come back to," he said. He kissed her, and Denny didn't remind Ed of the afternoons at the Largo in Beirut when the Syrians had allowed him a little recreation by lining up eight attractive young women from which he could make a selection.

"Okay, Den, now let's move that damn mud," he growled.

Josie Nelson giggled. "Ed hates to swear in front of me."

"No," Ed said solemnly. "I really am selling mud this time."

The plane started to bank coming over the glittering Pacific, turning toward Santa Monica for its final approach into Los Angeles. From this height, Denny marveled that he could see everything, the San Bernardino Mountains, Catalina Island, the vast gleaming sprawl of the city. For an instant the clarity was so pure it made him want to cry.

Because he understood Ed finally.

The Kelso thing. Remove the export lawyer. Then Bower takes care of the gofer who arranged the ship. Then Ed Nelson goes on to pursue whatever deal he made to get his ass out of that crumbling guest house on the shell-pocked shores of Beirut.

The plane descended, Denny's mind roiling with what he'd drunk and his unclouded vision. No matter how he worked it, the situation was so bad for him, he and Mandy would have to pull one of the neatest disappearing acts ever in the next couple of hours.

If they were going to survive at all.

CHAPTER FIVE

Right after he called Mandy to pick him up outside the baggage area at United's LAX terminal, Denny limped to a second telephone booth, dialed, hung up, and spoke for the last time to his employer, stand-in father, and certain killer.

"I hit a few snags, Ed," he said carefully. "I won't be able to get out of San Francisco until tonight."

"Jesus. You better get out tonight. You can't hang around when these things happen."

"I'm okay for the moment."

"Give me your flight, Den."

Denny recited a Delta flight leaving San Francisco at eight and the phony name he had used to reserve a seat.

"Someone'll meet you in L.A., drive you someplace safe for the night; then I'll give you the travel schedule myself. I've got to be down that way tomorrow. You better have a couple sweaters, Den," Ed chuckled hoarsely, "because it's ass puckering cold where you're going."

"Anyplace that's quiet," he replied, playacting, too. "I can't stop thinking about Bower."

"Things happen," Ed said. "Important fact is you were

loyal when I needed it last year, and I'm going to get you what you need now. I don't forget."

It sounded, Denny thought, hanging up, as if Ed genuinely meant what he said.

Which was his greatest talent.

Glad I studied under the old master himself, Denny stood gingerly on his painful ankle, watching for Mandy's car. *Always tell the truth, Ed says, especially when you lie through your teeth.*

Driving south on Pacific Coast Highway, surfers riding white waves, tankers hanging at the edge of the blue horizon, Denny put his hand on Mandy's leg and closed his eyes, wondering where they would be in twenty-four hours, and exactly how much time he had bought with the story he told Ed.

Mandy wore white muslin, tiny gold earrings, dark brown, strong legs showing at the edge of her dress, the fullness of her pregnancy scaring him. So much at stake now.

She had a multitude of questions. She had been a legal secretary when he met her, cool and efficient, working at a large downtown firm, daughter of a liberal black Episcopal minister in St. Petersburg, Florida. Denny saw blending, exploitable soft curves in human affairs and she only knew hard lines, fixed truths.

Ain't we the oddest couple, they would both agree, nuzzling heads in bed, whispering so anyone in the world who wished either of them harm would not hear.

He must have dozed because Mandy found the Surfcrest Motel just north of Manhattan Beach. He saw a white, elongated cinder block invisible in a raucous sea of gas stations, Mexican fast food stands, and biker stores. It was a perfect sanctuary.

Into a small room, air conditioner turning it icy, the bolted-down TV loudly braying a talk show, Mandy laying him out like a wounded soldier on the stiff salmon-colored bedcover, undressing him, the questions persistent.

"What haven't you told me, Denny?" she asked, taking off his pants. "What've you done for Nelson now? It's come to Jesus time for us."

She slipped out of the muslin, shoes kicked away, firm body pressed to him, swelling breasts peaked in the cold air.

Because he was not a strong man and because he loved her more than he understood, Denny began crying and then told her everything. Except about the gun still in his flight bag.

Later, darkness making the blinking colored lights on signs and headlights outside more garish through the tightly closed window curtains, they ate Chinese food from cartons she'd brought over from a nearby take-out stand. "You're staying out of sight," she said. "My God, I'm starting to think like you."

In the past he had jokingly told her, "You're making an honest man of me," and now he was afraid the moral tide had turned.

"How about Mexico for a start?" he suggested after changing into light poplin slacks and maroon sport shirt from the suitcase she'd brought. "I can get us someplace very hard to find from there."

"How far are we going to run, Den? How long? Ed Nelson isn't God Almighty."

"He knows a lot of people, and a lot of people do things for him." Denny tightened his belt. It was nine at night, and the motel's pool echoed with squeals and shouts from people drinking and groping. "I want to make it as hard as possible for him to find us."

"Can you make a deal? Can you promise him something?"

He held her, searching that intelligent, oddly innocent, now shaken face. "I told you everything. He's anywhere he wants to be because he does things people need. If he could get himself out of Beirut with the Syrians on his back, he can reach for us."

"So it's the end of our lives." She broke away, arms folded. "I can't go back to Seymour and Clay in the morning. Mandy just disappears."

Denny nodded. "Yeah. We have to start brand new," he said. "I was going to make a break soon; I had the moves all laid out." He stopped when she glared at him.

"Moves. Plans. Damn it, Denny, you haven't been honest with me," she snapped, getting up, pacing, head darting to the blithe lusty pool games. "We have to get one thing crystal clear now, not later, not someplace we've been forced to run to. You ready for *that* change?"

"Yeah," he said, hands in his pockets.

"No more moves, no more plans, lies, scams. We're going someplace together, and we're going to raise our family there if I'm going to make it through with you," she breathed.

Denny nodded, facing her, acutely conscious of the bucket of melting ice she'd tenderly used on his ankle, smells of Chinese food, stale cigarette smoke of the room, the whole complexity of reality. Here it all changed, he realized and felt relieved and uneasy simultaneously.

"I'll make any kind of commitment you want," he said, answering her ultimatum. He reached for her hand, touched it. "Just one more thing, something that'll let us make the break, hon."

He took her car keys from the scarred bureau.

"Whatever you have to do, let me go, too," she said. "Or you shouldn't be going anyway."

"I'll be careful," he said, and they held each other. "Look, I'm in, I agreed, I'm a new model." He spread his arms. "This won't take long, one call, set up a few." He paused. "Things will be different, Mandy, swear to God, but tonight let me get us in the clear."

On the way out, driving north to anyplace busy, frantic, where he would be unnoticed and unremarkable, Denny figured even Mandy's stern deity couldn't expect an instant transformation.

Just one more deal, he thought, speeding up the brightly

lit highway, the ocean darkly sparkling on his left. One final call to the manager of his personal retirement plan.

He didn't think Mandy would approve of their salvation coming from a high-flying, high-living drug dealer named Lennox Chandler.

CHAPTER SIX

Alison finally got off the bed, smoothing her silk print dress. She slipped her feet into thin white sandals, cocked her head at sounds outside.

"One of us will have to go down, Brock. I hear the early birds."

"One of us means me," he said from the bathroom at the other end of the large bedroom. He spat mouthwash into the sink and came out.

"Somebody's got to keep them from pestering the buffet. I'd like to leave something to eat for Val. She's the guest of honor. And Jesus, someone's got to keep the warring factions apart."

"I'll make sure the pols don't swing at the actors, and the lawyers don't make everybody sick before dinner." He heard the faint, almost ghostly marimba band in the backyard. An obscure, profound sadness mixed with anger touched him abruptly.

Alison sat down at a teak bureau, glancing at the long mirror beside it. She frowned fastening a delicate gold chain at her throat. "Try to keep the mob from driving Val crazy until I come down," she said.

"Sure wouldn't want some drunk bothering the senator before tonight's anointing."

"It's just to introduce me to her major contributors, Brock," Alison said evenly. "Is it going to be a bad night?"

"As far as I'm concerned, we'll do the dog and pony show and knock them dead as usual."

"I'm only considering a run for her Senate seat because you said it was all right with you."

"It is," he said. "Go for it. I won't screw you up."

"I'm not fighting that old battle tonight."

His unspoken reference to the Nelson dismissal was obvious. Since their uneasy reconciliation, an undercurrent of resentment remained.

He started for the door, and she went into the bathroom to get a jar of moisturizer.

He paused. "You hear anything new on Kelso's shooting?"

"Nothing except SFPD's courtesy call this afternoon." She put down the moisturizer. "Did your snitches say anything?"

"Nope. I just got the ongoing investigation crap," he said. "It's a possible bank robbery, maybe Kelso was the target, maybe he got in the way. One shooter escaped. One dead."

Alison shook her head. "What do you think?"

He shrugged. "I don't know. I just thought inviting him here was rubbing my face in it a little. You know, his connection to Nelson."

"We keep repeating ourselves." She turned and left the bathroom. "Remember day before yesterday? Kelso is a friend of the Rubins and they're two of Val's biggest contributors."

"Her San Francisco mafia. I remember. I still think bringing him here was a crappy idea."

They both paused, aware another argument loomed. Voices and the playfully syncopated music floated up.

"I better get down there," he said finally.

"Maybe so." She paused. "Brock," she began, then changed her mind.

He had already left.

Brock came down the curved staircase. He hadn't told Alison about the phone call from one of his people in ATF. A curious San Francisco Police Department detective wondered why the dead shooter carried airline tickets in the name Murphy, driver's licenses from Virginia and California for Stone and Thomas, credit cards for Bower, Stone, and Murphy.

Bower's name glowed brightly hot and prompted the ATF call. Did Bower and Nelson connected to a shooting interest Brock?

He strode across the broad living room, the twilight of late May softly shading the paintings, fresh-cut flowers and rich carpet. He had a big operation in Los Angeles the following morning that was calibrated to set another crack at Nelson. Maybe I can wrap Nelson in one big trap, he thought.

He wondered if the sketchy descriptions of the fleeing shooter could really be Denny Lara. It would be incredible. Brock told his FBI and ATF agents to work with the San Francisco detectives. Go all out to find the missing shooter.

A gathering cluster of dinner guests moved across the backyard lawn, between the white linen buffet tables and the red-and-yellow ruffled shirts of the grinning band. Strays strolled the pool apron, admiring the roses and birds of paradise.

Even though crime and theories about crime were usually off-limits at one of Brock and Alison's famous parties, the Kelso shooting would be the prime topic of gossip. As he jauntily made his way toward his guests, Brock realized they would talk about the shooting more openly than he had with Alison.

Sunset drifted into darkness. Around the drinking and dancing guests were paper lanterns, strung colored lights, and propane torches that provided enough illumination to see and be seen by.

Brock, gripping a beer, played straight man for Senator Valerie Cantil and a well-known young actress. In truth he was anxious to get away and check on the next day's complex raid. It was the first time he would be going back to Los Angeles since the Nelson catastrophe.

"So you work for your wife?" the actress said. "How's that go?"

Val Cantil said, "Very well, Tiffany. Like working with your director."

"Sleeping with them, too," she said, studying Brock. She was thin, black-haired, languorous. "But, I mean, can you sleep with your boss?"

"Don't pick it to death," Val Cantil answered with waning patience. "Brock, what was that joke you promised?"

He sipped his beer. He caught sight of Alison again across the lawn. A signal seemed to spark between them. She was in a group that included a senior vice-president at Coldwell Banker, the minority leader of California's Assembly, and various important lobbyists and accompanying spouses. They're all watching her, he thought.

"It's a DEA gag. Two FBI agents are fishing on a lake in Montana. Great fishing. One tells the other, 'Hey, we better mark this spot so we can find it again.' The other agent gets out some paint and puts a big black cross on the boat. 'No, no,' his bud says, 'that won't work.' The second FBI agent nods. 'Right. We might not get the same boat again.' "

As Brock expected, Val Cantil threw her big head back and laughed loudly enough to startle nearby guests. He knew she'd enjoy the DEA-FBI rivalry implicit in the gag and appreciate him telling her. He generally liked her. She and her late husband, who had headed Franklin Industries, had provided the investment advice that bought the house.

"Excuse us," Brock said to the actress, taking Val Cantil by the arm. "We've got to touch base with someone."

He walked her to a shadowed corner of the yard. The party glittered, raucous and familiar before them. No one ever declined a party at Brock and Alison's.

"Thank God," Val said, hand to her large pouter pigeon bosom. She was a stout, clear-faced older woman in a billowing lemon-colored designer dress. "Tiffany's a superb performer and a good draw at fund-raisers, but my God."

"You used to say she's a good argument against progressive evolution." He smiled.

"I'm reforming. Age and political wisdom." A stray breeze rustled through the eucalyptus, oak, and pine near them. "But you convoyed me here for a reason."

"Yeah, I did. I've got a question. Everybody here likes Ally obviously."

"She can charm a stone. They'll write checks until their hands hurt."

He laughed sourly. "Okay. She runs next year for your seat. Suppose I sit the campaign out? Too much work chasing bad guys."

She looked at him with penetrating intelligence. "Are you going to sit it out?"

"It's a possibility."

"Brock, you and I don't agree on any number of things. Poverty and crime. Rehabilitation. The misdirected drug war."

"You've managed to get a lot of things wrong. But that's not my question."

"No. You're right." She smiled. "What we do agree about is Alison. The two of you. Have I gotten that wrong, too?"

"I can't make any commitment to campaign next year."

"I wish there was something I could do for you both."

"You've done a hell of a lot. I haven't forgotten either. Look, maybe Ally'll get the Criminal Division spot at DOJ. Maybe none of this will come up because she won't run."

"It would break my heart," Senator Cantil said. "The country needs her."

Brock nodded, wondering where he would be if, twenty years ago, a shrewd new congresswoman hadn't taken a gangly, driven, blossoming young woman onto her staff for the summer? Not here, that was certain. Without Val Cantil's maternal guidance through college, then to Boalt

Hall for law school, the right words to get Alison into the U.S. Attorney's Office in L.A., he never would have bumped into the stunning, self-assured jogger on that lakeside trail in New Orleans.

"I wanted you to know, Val. In case you have to explain why Ally's out there campaigning alone." He looked toward the party. "Coast's clear. Tiffany's got a bunch of new fans."

They walked back and Val said, "Everybody's whispering about Ray Kelso. It feels tacky to talk about it openly. But, I don't give a damn. What did happen?"

"You've got sources as good as I do." He grinned. "You tell me."

"I hear rumors. The dead assailant was one of the defendants in your big case last month." She was calculatedly casual. "Wouldn't that be something?"

"I hadn't heard that," he said. "It would be something. It's the kind of rumor that shouldn't get spread around without corroboration."

"I won't tell Alison, Brock. One thing I've learned about the business you two are in—" she stopped and looked at him fixedly—"it's possible to step on a lot of toes without realizing it."

"Rumors do a hell of a lot of damage," he agreed, startled again by Val's ability to cut to the quick of any situation. "And you don't know who you'd be hurting."

"No. You don't."

He and Val went to Alison and her latest boisterous, charmed circle of guests. The marimba band swayed and the pool water rippled gently.

Brock said hastily, "Look, I've got to make a call. You'll have to hold the fort yourself." Impulsively he took Alison's hand. It was dry and hot. She had been drinking white wine steadily.

"I can manage with the senator's help."

The minority leader in the Assembly burbled, "I was just pointing out, look around here. Movie people. Media people. Business people. The occasional public servant." He bowed, laughing to Val, and his wife smiled. "You live in Sacramento, Alison, and I bet there aren't two people between you and anybody. The governor. Wino. Killer.''

"Ray Kelso," Brock said, glancing at Val as the others nodded.

Alison said, "Half a degree of separation between us all." She dropped her hand from Brock's. "The human daisy chain."

He caught the ever-present undertone of her suffering. He registered the smallest pain she felt, even after the pain she had caused him. The others chattered on obliviously.

"I'll be right back," he said to her. As if that erased whatever haunted her and relentlessly divided them.

Brock passed guests admiring the house, shook hands, kissed lightly, made quick jokes. It was hard now to keep the act going.

He went into the study, closing the door, and dialed a new number on the secure telephone. Since both he and Alison were senior in the U.S. Attorney's Office for the Eastern District of California, they got this essential piece of equipment as a home perk.

"Jimmy?" Brock said, when the phone was answered. "Give me a status down there."

"Hey, boss. Here we are, five lost souls, sitting across from the target's palatial mansion in beautiful downtown Pico Rivera. Asshole's having a goddamn big party to celebrate his dope deal tomorrow. Limos. Ladies. Hey, I guess it don't matter. Even with big dealers like Chandler," he rolled the name, "it's still chicks and muscle for dopers."

"I can hear the rap music."

"Lila and I put it on the surveillance speakers just for you."

"Lennox making any changes? The deal's still going down ten tomorrow at his warehouse in Torrance?"

"All he said tonight, all day, chief," Lila chirped in, "is how he's going to ball four chicks tonight, boom, boom, one right after another. I'm going to love busting his lying black ass."

Dewane "Lennox" Chandler was the biggest cocaine

distributor in east and central Los Angeles, and he had arranged a major purchase from the Tijuana cartel. During the Nelson wiretaps Jimmy had overheard the one call in which Chandler talked to Denny Lara about a bank account. It had been peripheral to the Nelson investigation. Until now, Brock thought. It made Lennox Chandler a prime target.

"The warehouse covered?"

"We've got an FBI, ATF, DEA surveillance team on it," Lila assured him. "We'll close up here for the night as soon as it looks like Lennox's in with his chicks," she snorted again.

"Negative on that," Brock said. "I want us up and listening to him from now until the buy. Every second. I don't want to miss any changes. Get a back-up team to relieve you and hand off to them. I want you both fresh tomorrow."

"The locals are much more cooperative this time," Lila said. "I haven't heard one squeak about feds being on their turf."

"They got burned like us last time," Jimmy said soberly. "We're golden on this one, right? No defects?"

"Wiretaps are solid, surveillance all approved, yeah. Pass the word that we're sailing."

"No chance we get shot down like the Nelson deal?" Lila asked.

"No chance." Alison didn't know about Chandler's call to Denny Lara. She had no idea there was any connection. This was simply a major doper he was taking down. "I'm coming in on the six-thirty shuttle and we'll go ring Mr. Chandler's doorbell at ten."

"Knock, knock, motherfucker," Jimmy said merrily and hung up.

Brock left his office and mingled outside with people, grabbing an abandoned scotch in a foyer alcove. Tomorrow would rebalance the world Alison had upended last month, he vowed.

*   *   *

Later, Alison made the goodbyes as guests drifted away.
She strolled out with Val Cantil. Val said, "I haven't seen
this crowd purr so much since I announced my candidacy.
Congratulations. We can do the formal announcement
back in Washington later this summer. Have a big party
someplace to celebrate."

"Don't rush me," Alison said. "I need time to make up
my mind. Thanks for giving me the choice."

"Be well, Alison. Things will work out." Val gently
touched her cheek.

It was midnight black as Alison walked alone toward the
pool, wineglass in hand.

She looked at the house. Brock never understood how
she could still feel claustrophobic in a house that size. How
could she, after all those years with her mother and three
brothers in a single-room, tin-roofed shack at the edge of a
vast tomato field?

Situations generate claustrophobia, confinement, she
thought. She and Brock were in one. She was in one.

Alison switched off the underwater lights in the pool, and
the turquoise rectangle became black, only the wavering
reflection of propane torchlight on it. The strung lights
were off, the band and people gone, even Celeste.

She put the glass down on the concrete. She unzipped,
wiggled a little, dropped the dress. She took off her bra and
panties, the thin shoes, then stepped purposefully into the
shallow end, moving until the cool water was up to her neck.

She moved her arms, making almost phosphorescent
wavelets. The situation, she reasoned through wine and
the night's excitement, was caused by her velocity. I'm
streaking ahead and maybe Brock can't keep up, she
thought.

She began swimming slow laps, head above the water.
Metzger's blackmail last month lit the fuse. That's why she
felt this deceit so keenly. The old ugliness bubbled up.

She had told Brock about what had happened one afternoon in San Dimas years ago. Backgrounded it like a good trial lawyer. Father killed in a car accident when she was eight, mother and three brothers forced to accept the offer of father's brother to live on his large farm in Riverside County. Work with the Mexicans in the fields. Cotton one year, tomatoes or lettuce in others.

By stern edict she never went into her uncle's big ranch house. And never, ever at two on Wednesdays. That certain afternoon in San Dimas, she had come in, gone to the sound of people near the back bedroom. Opened the door.

Saw her mother bent over the bedstead, dress up, her uncle, pants barely opened, behind her, eyes squeezed shut. Grunting.

Alison slowed in the water, legs treading, head high, looking at the stars. Her mother had sensed something, briefly turned her head, then without a word, put a hand over her eyes.

Later, at dinner, had come the sad, determined explanation. *It's not what it looks like, sweetie pie,* and for some long time afterward Alison had bitterly assumed the wrong answer.

She started swimming again, legs foaming the water, arms easily pulling her, feeling her momentum, the velocity drawing her from that place, time, to this one.

My mother, Alison thought, was in a situation. She was telling me that situations bred necessities. Things that had to be done. Metzger put me in a situation. I will do whatever I have to do.

But I can't make Brock understand, even if I told him. "You tell him, we lose that outrage he'll have," Chris Metzger had said over the phone before the Nelson dismissal. "No bastard's going to suspect we flipped Nelson if Brock's chewing the walls because you dumped his case."

She slowed in the water, gazing at the dark house, except for one light in the study where Brock was working. To get out of this situation, I'm going to make Ed Nelson crawl.

She swam faster, alone in the black rectangle sparkling with the shattered reflection of torches.

CHAPTER SEVEN

Mandy had restlessly waited for hours until Denny came back to the motel after midnight. She blurted out, "Did you get it done?"

"Much as I could tonight," he said wearily, wincing as he took off the running shoes, touching his puffy ankle. "I've got to make a couple more calls tomorrow."

And because she was frightened and he was obviously exhausted, Mandy decided to let it go tonight.

Near dawn, she restlessly got up. Denny snored lightly. The room's air conditioner was on high for her, and it creaked and grumbled. She crossed her arms, standing, watching him; then as she had often done in the past, she quietly began checking his United flight bags. It was not so much distrust, but the need to know as much as she could. To protect him.

The two bags stuffed with newspapers made her frown. Why was he carrying all that useless paper? Then, swaddled in one bag, she found the gun, took it out, and examined it in the pale light bleeding through the curtains. She sat down in the room's lone chair, the gun beside her on the bureau.

Denny woke up an hour after daylight. He stretched. He looked like a teenager, carefree and smug in his own invulnerability.

"How long have you been up?" he asked, patting her side of the bed. "Come on back."

"What's this for?" She nudged the gun an inch across the bureau.

He scrambled out of bed, half pulling the covers with him. Naked, he looked even more juvenile. He took the gun and pushed it back into the flight bag. "I told you, Bower gave it to me. I was supposed to use it."

Mandy stood up. "You didn't tell me you still had it."

"Why should I? I didn't shoot anybody; I haven't done anything." He sounded almost childish.

"How am I supposed to believe you?" she gasped at the frustration and fear. "I told you yesterday, this is it, you have to be straight with me. About everything. That's the only way it's going to work. You're still doing it, still trying to put one over on me."

"I was just trying to—" He shook his head, sitting down on the side of the bed. "It's not like that at all," he finished.

She had been thinking for hours. "Who've you been talking to then? Who's our savior?"

"There's no point in your knowing. It's better you don't know."

She rummaged through her one suitcase. It was time to resolve all questions.

Denny lay back on the bed, pulling the sheet up protectively. "What are you looking for?" he asked softly.

She held out statements from the Bank of Korea, Olympic Boulevard branch. "I found these two days ago. I didn't know you had an account there." She threw the papers at him. "In three weeks, forty thousand dollars, eighty thousand, two hundred thousand goes in, goes out. Is this Ed Nelson's money? It's not ours. Unless you didn't want me to know you had that kind of money."

He slowly gathered the statements. "It's not Ed's."

"Then whose is it? Why have you kept it secret?" She yelled at him, "Tell me, Den. Tell me something."

"I can't," he said, sitting up completely, head lowered, then raised defiantly. "It's for us, Mandy. I've got to take care of you and me and the baby."

"With this money?"

"A lot more than that, if you'll just let me take care of it," he said. He folded his hands, clasped as if in prayer. "It's going to work out. I've got to make a few more moves."

She stood over him. He wouldn't look at her. Mandy felt a great sickness lying on her thoughts. "You can't tell me because you're scared," she spat.

His eyes were nervous as he glanced at her, and he tried a sly grin. "I'm afraid you'll leave me. Just don't ask any more and I'll get the money and we'll start clean from then. Cross my heart. Okay?"

Sitting in the dark as the day appeared, watching him and reviewing her own reluctant admissions about him, she had marked out her decision, and it made her physically sick.

"I am leaving, Den," she said, grabbing the suitcase, snapping it closed. She had taken the car keys earlier. She moved quickly, through the motel room door, getting into her car and driving south. The day was blue, clear, cool, the Pacific frothy white near shore, people carefree on the beach.

Mandy saw Denny break from the room in her rearview mirror. He clutched the sheet around himself, one arm waving frantically, and he was shouting something, perhaps her name; but she didn't hear it.

CHAPTER EIGHT

"**H**ere we go," Brock said to Lila. "Say a prayer."
From across the street, they tensed as the uniformed, heavily armed FBI tactical squad rushed forward. It was nearly ten and hazy in Torrance, a grimy city enveloped by Los Angeles. A few minutes earlier, Lennox Chandler and his favorites, swaggering and loud, had driven up in expensive black cars and gone into the bilious green, old ice-making plant they had converted into a warehouse for the sorting and selling of cocaine in quantity.

Lila hesitated. "Don't go near there until they've got it locked down, chief," she said.

"I wouldn't miss this for anything," Brock said, snapping orders to the FBI technicians in the mobile communications van, then jumping out. The van was blue, a twenty-four-hour locksmith sign on it. A myriad of other police cars and vans rapidly surrounded the old ice plant, sirens echoing and screeching.

Brock had a Sig Sauer pistol, ballistic vest on, as he and Lila trotted forward, following the swarm of Los Angeles County sheriff and police SWAT teams pushing into and encircling the ice plant.

He saw Lila watching him anxiously. Not for herself, he knew, but concerned for his safety. Jimmy, of course, had gone in with the first rush.

They reached the rusted, wide doors, exploded open by a battering ram, dust still thick and falling. Now Brock heard the shouts and running inside the plant, chaotic and reverberant against the peeling, high walls. Ancient refrigerant motors and cracked ammonia tanks lay scattered, and then beyond them, the shiny bright glow of new lights and steel tables, Lennox Chandler's additions.

Lila tugged his arm. "Over here, chief. They're back here." She, too, was caught up in the excitement, darting ahead of him toward the focus of noise, running, and confusion.

Brock bumped into a black-uniformed sheriff SWAT team member, a brown-haired kid clutching a black rifle with a scope. The kid stared at him balefully, then raced past.

Brock ran, turning down a warren of corridors with low ceilings, dirty floors, and suddenly he was in a larger room, a tremendous new fan turning lazily over it, huge fluorescent lights blazing. Stacks of neat translucent white bricks shimmered on the tables. Figures swirled by him, men yelled, and he heard the first shot.

Instinctively, he ducked, crouched as he had been taught at Quantico when he and Jimmy and Lila had gone through their training, always moving, eyes casting rapidly for the source of the danger.

But his mind exploded with one terrifying fear. Christ, not Chandler. Don't let Chandler get shot. I need him.

He came around a sickly green concrete pillar, gun at the ready. Ten yards away he saw Jimmy. The other agents and cops were arrayed behind pillars, the steel tables, whatever concealment they could find. But Jimmy had risen from a crouch, pointed his pistol with almost cold steadiness, and fired four times.

There were more shots, all aimed at a rude barricade of tables, crates, and metal chairs against one wall. A stocky black man lurched from the barricade, a gun wavering up and down in his hand. Brock saw Jimmy fire again and the man fell forward.

"Motherfuckers! I give up, I give up!" a screaming man called from the barricade.

Brock shouted orders, and the massed agents and cops engulfed the barricade, dragging out five black men in elegant pearl gray suits. Lila crisply gave commands, keeping men away from the body on the concrete floor. Brock stared down, amazed at the depth of his fear at what he might see, then the rush of exultation. The bent, bloody body was not Lennox Chandler.

He holstered his gun, swiftly checking the five prisoners now handcuffed, jerked back to their feet. The third in line, taller and sharp-featured, mouth spewing obscenities continuously, was Lennox Chandler. Brock smiled, his blood still pumping.

Lila supervised the transfer of Chandler and the others outside to waiting vans. The crime scene investigators moved in smoothly and began the elaborate chronicling of what had just happened in a matter of a few minutes.

Brock and Jimmy stood apart. Jimmy's breath was short; then he steadied himself. "The fucker was shooting at me, Brock," he said. "The guy shot at me and I wasn't going to let it happen again."

"It's a good shoot. It'll come out all right."

Lila returned. Even though the room was large, the atmosphere was stifling with so many people milling around, boosted by the furor, relieved to be safe and unharmed. "The crime scene guys want to keep everybody here for a while," she said. "It could be a long time before they call the shooting righteous or not." She patted Jimmy's arm.

Brock shook his head and started for the door. "I'm getting what I want from Chandler right now. Come on."

CHAPTER NINE

Alison sank into a first-class seat on her flight south from Sacramento to San Diego.

She sipped black coffee from a china cup and saucer and studied several papers from her slim, oxblood leather briefcase. She glanced out the window into a bright, cloud-cluttered vastness, weightless and without memory. The image calmed her a little. It was going to be a tense, important meeting, she knew, and she had to be prepared.

When the plane passed over the Central Valley's desert fastness, the man-made green fields, Alison once more felt elation and pride because she had escaped that limited, stultifying life. Two of her brothers were still down there, farmers always teetering on ruin. The calls came with mechanical regularity either to her office or home: *Hey, hey Ally, it's been really tight this month. Three hundred would be a big help. The kids say they love you.* Both of her older brothers used the same ploy. She always wrote a check.

A little after ten, she landed in San Diego. The sharp edges of blue sky and ocean just beyond the airport made her blink. She looked at her watch quickly as she strode to the car rental counter. In theory she could call the office now, find out if Brock was set up for the raid in Los Angeles. She wanted to hear that he was all right, happy. But the last thing Alison had done before flying out was tell her secretary she'd be unreachable for three hours, until she reported in for Senator Cantil's public subcommittee meeting. Better wait, she thought. I need the cover of those three hours.

She got a car, white, four-door, and when she picked it up, she was aware of covert glances from the men and women around her. They all think I'm somebody famous, Alison knew. The celebrity whose face you never quite place.

She drove out of the sprawling airport, heading south toward the city center. Maybe, she thought, letting the ocean wind rush past, that cover is the best one I have. She wore a teal silk scarf on a tawny cotton suit, and it fluttered as if alive.

Only Brock saw through her carefully layered existence. When he held her hand and scolded her for the ragged, bitten nails, he'd say, "Come on, Ally. Next time you shake hands with the AG or the president, they'll wonder why you're so nervous." Then he'd kiss her fingers tenderly because he knew. She retained a residual terror of ending up back on that farm. Failure in anything was her gravest fear.

A city map spread on the car's passenger seat flapped in the sea-scented wind from her partially open window. She glanced again at the streets she'd marked out in red, and when the freeway signs for the civic center appeared, she turned, watching carefully. The traffic was heavy for a weekday. She turned again on Manzanita, slowing. Her eyes roved along the storefronts; jewelry jammed against electronics, a Spanish restaurant sharing the same building with an Irish pub. She was close. Her snitch had caustically said to look for the "one damn place a bunch of Basque dummies and IRA dummies can buy each other rounds. No pun." He had laughed.

At the corner of Manzanita and Wilmott she spotted the bird dropping spattered mailbox. A frizzy-haired woman with a tiny black dog paused to mail a letter. Two unshaven men argued in the doorway of a nearby week-to-week hotel, a flickering swordfish sign above them. The woman suspiciously watched Alison; one of the men whistled. She ignored them. She looked closely over the mailbox, then found it. Below the letters "U.S." was a small white-chalked cross.

Alison instantly spun the car back into traffic, onto the freeway again, annoyed at this elaborate invitation. She wondered if Brock had the same irritating problems with his snitches. I can't just ask him, "Gee, how do you keep a snitch in line? Is it like housebreaking a puppy? How do you set up the rewards and punishments?" she thought. Secrets could bind people together as much as divide them. We could share insights on the care and tending of undercover operatives over warm wine in front of a fire, she imagined with a small smile.

She put on sunglasses against the glare. But what are the risks if your snitch knows the game's moves infinitely better than you do? Who's breaking who in when that happens, Brock? What I can't do is tell him what I'm doing.

She found the house number in scrolled brass on a stone pillar. The chalk cross meant, *Come ahead, it's safe. I'm waiting*. She parked in the long, fake cobblestoned driveway of a large plantation-style mansion set on several acres. She walked to the colonaded door. Sprinklers sent rainbowed arcs of water across the plush deep green lawn, and an Hispanic man dug singlemindedly in the far end of large, colorful flower beds.

The door opened after she rang. Alison smiled slightly, holding her briefcase lightly in one hand.

"I hope this place isn't on my tab," she said to her snitch. He wore white duck pants and a yellow polo shirt that didn't fit him well at the shoulders and left a small gut at his waist. His fleshy, regular features creased into a smile as he whipped off reading glasses that had sunk halfway down his broad nose.

"This is strictly from my ill-gotten profits, Alison." Edward Nelson grinned, bringing her inside.

* * *

"I don't want the grand tour," Alison said. They walked through a high foyer. She was cool, commanding.

"It's a comfy little shack," Nelson said. "The admiral and his wife are getting melanoma in Grand Cay, so he let me have it on short notice. You and me weren't scheduled to meet again for a week."

"I thought a meeting on the fly would keep you honest, Ed." She took off her sunglasses and gazed at him.

"One of Brock the jock's snitch handbook maxims, I bet. Throw the untrustworthy informant a curve."

"No. It's my own idea."

He chuckled. His voice was hard, rubbed raw from drinking, and his breath caught every few seconds; but he projected strength anyway. "You've got me by the short hairs, Alison, my love. We both know it. I'm always honest with you." He gave a little bow and pointed toward the living room.

"I've got to be at the Convention Center by noon to make my appearance, so this is going to be very down and dirty, Ed. Who's the admiral? Am I supposed to have him on my list of your buddies?"

"No, we did some business ten, fifteen years ago, but he's out of it now, just on a couple boards of directors killing time." Nelson swung his reading glasses by the stem. "I did get him a vice-presidency at this outfit that makes special fire extinguishers for commercial airlines. Might work on submarines. He's strictly retired military. Boring."

They came into a broad, pale blue carpeted room with thick, dark sofas, deep polished oak tables. One wall was filled with hunting prints in elegant gold frames, another with scenes around Coronado at sunset. Alison tossed her briefcase onto an antique, spidery chair. "If he's just retired military, he's made a goddamn fortune. Don't give me your bullshit."

Nelson twisted his heavy torso languidly. Over the fireplace was a formal portrait of a slender, silver-haired man and woman against a palm tree. He wore a gold-braided

naval uniform. "I don't want to cause Freddie Rusher or
Monica any trouble, Alison. He's not involved in anything
you and I are working on."

She studied him. Every informant shared certain quali-
ties, she knew, whether they were dopers or officials or
oddities like Nelson. Self-preservation mattered above all
except for the few with martyr complexes. But dissembling
was universal. Lie and the world loves you, she thought.

"Are you recording this session?"

"No," he said, slipping his glasses on. "Are you?"

"Maybe I should."

"Maybe I am wired. For insurance. You want to check
me?" He spread his arms for a frisk, leering.

"I don't want games when I ask a question," she
snapped, uncomfortable for some reason. "I don't like
our arrangement, and I won't take any crap from you
today. There's too much to cover. Understand?"

He feigned contrition. "Excuse an old cocker's playful-
ness."

"I'll be back in a few minutes. Make some coffee and
then we'll get started."

"Why don't I make some coffee?" he repeated, pointing
to the left. "The powder room's over there, I think." He
padded away toward the kitchen.

Alison closed the bathroom door. Lilac wallpaper, *Town
and Country* magazines in a rack. She stared at the mirror.
She was losing her concentration, worried about Brock
and his raid, Brock and her. She steadied herself slowly,
inch by inch. Ed Nelson's worried, too, she realized. The
demeanor was bluff, carefree, but unlike their earlier meetings, she spotted his underlying anxiety. About what? It
was a lever to keep him in line now.

She walked out to the kitchen. It was white-tiled, with
brass and steel fittings, and turquoise fleur-de-lis designs
on the walls as a royal afterthought. Nelson busied himself
with a large, complicated coffee machine, nervously whistling an old marching tune.

A few months ago, she had casually probed Brock about
snitches. Never write their names down, not in drop files

hidden in your office, or on computers. Never keep records linked to your snitches. Brock had said, "Last six years, Ally, I kept all the names up here"—he tapped his temple—"what we pay them, everything. It's the only safe place."

Nelson swung around when he heard her. "You look fantastic, and I'm sorry Andrews is such a lucky bastard, Alison. Really. Second-rater like him doesn't deserve you."

"Who does?" she answered abruptly.

"Me, of course. You and I have a lot more in common. We want to get ahead, work hard at it." He poured coffee, then rummaged in the cabinets for sugar and spoons. "On paper I've got an impeccable pedigree. Like you. But we're both pretty much self-created, aren't we?" He handed her a cup. He knew she didn't like milk or cream.

At every meeting she measured his reflexive attempt at seduction. Running Brock down, army brat whose father was thrown out for allegedly stealing money, tires, sheets, and typewriters from supply stores. Scholarship student. Nelson always ended with the same blunt accusation: You're carrying him, Alison. He's the dead weight.

She stirred her cup. Nelson can't reach me, she insisted. He's just a snitch lying to improve his situation. "The coffee better be strong, Ed. You'll need it."

Outside on the covered patio, they drank coffee while sitting at an elegant glass-topped table. Across the perfect broad lawn were artfully placed miniature fruit trees, pears, oranges, and limes. It was vital to make Nelson obey disagreeable orders. It was also vital to find out exactly what he was doing.

Alison had her briefcase opened, and she wrote cryptic lines of figures on a legal pad as she questioned him, often making him recite figures several times to make certain he wasn't obviously concocting them.

"So Applied Microavionics is doing about twenty percent better business than Century Technologies?" she asked, looking at the pad.

"About," he growled. "I got a couple of the old contractors from my Agency businesses in Century Tech. But you wanted Applied Microavionics started fresh, so I've been creative. Look at it this way, Alison, you've got two government undercover companies that are showing a real profit this quarter." He blew on his coffee. "Now, that's something in this world."

"Creative means what?"

"I charge the assholes more," he said simply. "You're Johnny Sue Bob Nuthead and you want two, three hundred AK-47s with nightscopes, well, I have a freer hand with Century Tech's price structure." He chuckled. "My old customers, the ones you're going to nail with Applied, want the same old prices whether it's guidance systems, black box shit or whatever tech transfer's the flavor of the month."

Alison sat back, watching Nelson chew on the stem of his glasses again. Definitely nervous about something. But he was providing her with easily verifiable amounts flowing into the two front companies she had him set up as part of the complex sting she was running. Applied Microavionics, headquartered in Alexandria, Virginia, dealt with all things that flew. Century Technologies in Oklahoma had a wider reach. Ostensibly it sold legitimate explosives and mining equipment. But it also dealt, with Alison's approval, in the clandestine sales of illegal weapons.

"Okay, Ed," she said finally, "this is where I wanted to be about now. You're up and running, openly established as a persecuted sonofabitch."

"I am persecuted," he said pensively.

"Which means there is a little justice in the world," she said, sitting forward. "I've read the transcripts of your meetings with the militias and I want to go to the next stage."

"What would that be?"

He knew, of course, but he seemed to take an infantile pleasure in making her spell everything out. "Set up meetings with the Cobra militia leaders and introduce our FBI agent as your associate; then you drop out and we do it again with the next militia and the next."

Nelson coughed, spat, tossed the remainder of his coffee onto the grass. "You probably want to do the same bullshit with Deng Li and the Chinese boys and girls, right?"

"Ed, someday I'm going to get search warrants and then indictments against these people and I don't want to name you. The FBI undercover is the only person I have to blow in public."

Nelson shot to his feet, shaking his head. "Listen, lady, I've been doing this business for years. For the Agency, no matter what crap they put out in public. I know the business. I know the people who want to *do* business. Your fucking Bureau guy won't know, and it won't matter if he's the greatest bullshitter in history." Nelson braced himself on the alarmingly frail glass tabletop. "Because I will be burned. Big time. And I've had a little experience with these folks. They will come after me. They will go after my family."

"We've gone over all this. You'll be protected. I will cover for you in any open proceeding. In court, in front of Congress."

"I'm the one who's going to get nailed by these wackjobs no matter how you try to cover it up, so I'm the one who'll make the deals. I can look out for myself and your fucking sting," Nelson said. "That, as my former Columbia classmates on Wall Street say, is the bottom line."

Alison put her pen down slowly, eyes fixed on him. He was scared and he meant it, but she wasn't convinced he was afraid for those reasons.

For the next half hour they argued, outside in a light breeze, then back in the living room where Alison took a seat on a long sofa while Nelson went to the mirrored wet bar by a pewter dry sink, pouring a stiff scotch.

"You will bring my FBI undercover agent in, Ed. I don't care if it breaks your balls. You're starting to make me think you're hiding things."

Nelson drank, then poured another. He folded his reading glasses carefully. "Alison, my one true love. Listen.

Herr Professor Nelson is telling you that his playmates are
suspicious, nasty people. Just like him. That's why we get
along so well. When your fucking agent shows up, even if
I make him my long lost brother, you will one"—he raised
a stumpy finger—"send our potential buyers running for
the hills in panic"—he stuck up another finger in a plainly
obscene gesture—"and two, certainly make them feel
threatened or pissed off enough to take me down. As in
blow my head off. Now, from both of our perspectives,
these certainties are not happy ones. How about we just
forget it? Let me set up the buys, you get all the video and
audio and whatever other crap you want for court, and we
both go away very satisfied? I'll make them sign goddamn
confessions if that'll melt your chocolate bar."

She made a show of looking at her watch. There was
merit in what he said, but he still had to take her force
card. She shook her head. "I'm your only friend on this
side of the fence, Ed. We're doing it my way."

He snorted, staring at the tranquil landscape. "What
the hell did I do to end up with you?" he asked, turning
with maudlin bemusement. "Twenty-three years I gave the
Agency, fresh kid from college, all eager and full of every
dumb-ass patriotic idea. Did deals here, did business there,
ran their front companies and made profits with every
damn one, and then one fine day, one fine bunch of new
bastards comes in and decides to have an agency scrub
and out I go." He prowled toward her, stopped, then thrust
his hands into his pockets. "I'm okay, Alison. I got stuck
in some power play, some penny pinching, but you check
me and you'll find I am okay. I did my job. Just like I will
for you."

She smiled. "No, Ed. You are not okay. You're a street
kid from Brooklyn who forged a high school transcript,
forged letters to get a scholarship at Columbia, washed
cars, waited tables, sold dope for all I know through college.
You lied to poor dumb, rich Josie Fenton of Newport,
convinced her you were a rich son of privilege, blue blood
CIA type. She'd crawled through enough scandals before

you showed up, I assume her family was ready to marry her to someone who looked as good as you did. On paper."

"Fair assumption. From one self-created survivor to another."

She went to him at the doorway to the spacious backyard. Her voice was hard, quiet. "Next week, Ed, you'll call for a meeting with the Cobra militia. Make it on a neutral field, Boise maybe. You've got a great deal on grenade launchers, okay? And then you introduce our guy as your army source. He'll put the actual deal together, get them on tape, set up the bust when the time comes."

"And arrest me?"

"Of course. You'll keep your cover. It'll enhance your reputation among the foreign arms dealers." She looked at her watch again. "You're going to make some really big deals with the Chinese buyers before that side of the operation wraps up."

She began gathering her papers and putting them in the briefcase. "Are we clear now? I've got to go. I'm due at the Convention Center."

Nelson shambled to the bar, made and quickly threw down another drink while she watched impatiently. He seemed to be hoping for an infusion of courage. He smiled awkwardly, glass still in his hand. "Well now, Alison, darling. You've kind of forced me to put something on the table now."

"Make it fast."

He took a rasping breath and said sheepishly, "I may have a slight reputation problem in the making."

Sitting so close together on the long, curved sofa she could see the bristly dark hairs on Nelson's forearm, Alison took in the news that could shatter everything.

"Ray Kelso," he said throatily, "worked a little on the C-4 thing, legal work"—Nelson hunched forward, eyes hooded—"and Richard Bower was an old friend, went way back."

"I know about you, Bower, and Lara." This was very bad.

"He was the best if you needed a chore taken care of, bill paid quietly." Nelson raised his hooded eyes to her. "Someday I'll tell you about Senator Cantil and Bower."

"What the hell does that mean?" she snapped.

"Sorry I brought it up, but if I were Senator Cantil, I wouldn't look too closely at contributions from the Asian-American Civic Society, and a couple others. Bower handled a lot of money matters, bringing money and people together so the people could bring the money to other people. Like your senator."

Alison again felt the repulsion and fascination Nelson aroused in her. Deflecting his own iniquities by inventing or reporting the sins of others, especially those who threatened him.

Or simply trying to dominate the situation, she thought, by making me worry about Val.

"Don't even think about blackmailing Val Cantil," Alison said, "because I will cut your throat. Now, what about Ray Kelso and Richard Bower? What's the danger to you?"

Nelson put a hand to his mouth. "I thought by now that someone, some cop in San Francisco, had put Bower and me together. Because that will put me in a very exposed position, won't it?"

She got up, folded her arms. The stealth interrogator, Brock had once dubbed her, coming in invisibly and deadly. "I haven't heard anything like that. Which doesn't mean it won't happen in the next fifteen seconds. So, what happened? Are you involved?" She leaned down to him. "Are you lying to me right now?"

"I do not know what happened. I do know Bower was taking Denny Lara to see Kelso. Kelso loaned Denny money, didn't get it back, bad history there. I think it's possible Lara created a volatile situation and Ray acted."

"Over some deal? Is that what you're saying?"

They both paused, watching as the gardener loped into the yard, tossed a burlap bag of tools onto the lawn, shook his head, and loped back around the side of the house.

Alison tensed. Nelson was certainly trying to persuade her of his innocence, and that alerted her.

"I believe you should find Lara, because he's the one who either shot Ray or did something that made Bower think he had to defend Ray." Nelson shrugged in confusion. "Lara's the key. I think I can help you find him."

Alison paced. "Did you know about this meeting yesterday? Did you set it up?"

"You have the list of people I keep in touch with, Alison. Bower's been off my screen since you and I started working together. And Lara"—he waved dismissively—"who the hell is he? He poured drinks, made small talk, kept the guys laughing and the ladies charmed."

She knew disaster loomed if any provable recent tie existed between Nelson and Bower. Soon she might have to confront how far she was willing to go to protect Nelson and this undercover operation.

She opened her briefcase, tossing a pad and pen to Nelson. "Write down every phone number, name, address, anything you have on Lara. I'm going to give it to SFPD; then I might find some rationale for the FBI to pick it up. We will find Lara."

"Perfect. That'll keep me out of it." Nelson scribbled. "I'm surprised with his cop buddies and narc pals that Brock didn't turn up Bower." He glanced at her. "You'd think he'd make the connection almost immediately"— he grinned harshly—"good buddies that we are."

He handed her a page with a multitude of names, one circled and underlined as girlfriend/live-in. Alison would start there.

She took the briefcase, holding it tightly, and went to the kitchen, Nelson following. She poured a glass of chilled white wine from the refrigerator.

"When did you find out about Bower and the shooting yesterday?" Alison asked. He leaned against the countertop, raptor's eyes on her. "Did you talk to Bower before or Lara after?"

"Oh, Christ, Alison, I'm not going anywhere near a situation that could, well, screw our deal up completely.

No. I read about it in the paper today. Made the connection just before you came.''

She finished the wine, carefully putting the delicate stemware down on the counter. ''We're going to resolve this one way or the other and move on,'' she said. ''I'll stay in touch and you better pray this checks out all the way down the line.''

They walked from the kitchen, through the living room littered with signs of its absent owners who had threads binding them to Nelson just as Val did apparently, and I do, Alison thought. I'll have the Navy and FBI run backgrounders on the retired admiral. The expensive wine left a sour aftertaste.

''I keep telling you I'm okay.'' Nelson stood in the home's doorway as if he owned the property. ''You should start listening to me.''

She drove away, sunglasses only cutting the outer glare, leaving an inner, bright and terrible certainty.

In a little while she would face TV cameras, inquisitive citizens, a panel of senators, and she would have to hide deep inside herself. Like she did with everyone except Brock.

Last night before the party, Brock had known about Kelso and Bower and Nelson. Of course he'd made the connection. Or a cop had made it for him. He must have known when she'd asked. And he'd lied to her.

Now she knew he'd lied.

She believed Nelson knew as well. It was the reason he brought Brock up.

Self-preservation is the dominant drive in snitches, she recalled. Nelson was only doing what came naturally.

When she drove up to the vast steel and palm-fronted Convention Center, two smiling young men in blue blazers were waiting to escort her inside. She heard the gulls above her. She walked by three TV reporters, all calling out.

Implications, she thought. Terrible implications. A pain bloomed riotously in the center of her mind.

Brock was lying. Perhaps about everything.

CHAPTER TEN

A few minutes later, Alison sat beside the mayor of Baja, and beside him were the mayors of San Diego, Tijuana and Newark. She stared at her watch. How was the raid going in L.A.? She felt like a defendant waiting for a fearsome verdict.

"I'm going to explain how we licked drugs with more cops," the New Jerseyite whispered, reading her name tag, as if she needed an explanation for his presence among West Coast drug warriors.

Alison nodded slightly. She was in a roped-off section near the front of an enormous room on the center's second floor. High intensity lights bathed the entire space in a whitish, pitiless blaze for the bank of TV cameras scattered strategically among the carefully chosen "citizen" audience. A curved dais was set at the front of the room. Six United States senators, aides behind them, sat at the green-cloth-draped dais. Val Cantil was questioning a tall, distinguished, white-haired man sitting at another green-draped table in front of her.

After forty minutes, Val called a recess. The fierce lights

overhead dimmed. The audience of several hundred stood and stretched, buzzing.

Alison went to the dais. Val stood and walked around to her.

"How many do I have ahead of me?" Alison asked, gesturing at the large gathering of witnesses in the roped-off section.

"I think three," Val Cantil said, frowning. "But I've got to take the czar next. He's pleading big business back in Washington." She used irony when naming the chairman of the President's Council on Drug Enforcement, the familiar tone she and Alison preferred after years of sharing triumphs and defeats. "Probably another hour's wait for your pep talk."

"Then I'll go get something to eat. I've seen the show before."

"I'm surprised you volunteered last night for our little tribal dance. It basically means a whole wasted day for you."

"Face time, as Brock says, is never wasted." Alison pointed toward the entrance. Time to get away.

"Well, get a drink or something or a lot of coffee. You look like someone dropped a ton of bricks on your head." Val chuckled, but she was plainly concerned.

Alison took an elevator to a small seafood restaurant on the street level. There was certainly a hospitality room for the witnesses, but she didn't have the stamina to trade gossip and small talk with the assorted politicians, scientists, and senior cops assembled as props for the subcommittee's public forum. And I needed the forum as a prop to hide my meeting with Nelson, she thought. Great way to use Val's friendship.

She did not know what to do about Brock or her own growing resentment toward him. I'm doing all this for him, she thought. He's deceiving me for his own benefit. Nor did she feel assured of controlling Nelson in the next most difficult stage of the undercover operation.

She got iced tea, a shrimp salad, and sat at a table facing out toward the almost glowing blue Pacific. People paused at her table, then moved on when she refused to acknowledge them.

She nursed the iced tea for a while, then rose to find a telephone. Standing in an alcove off the lobby, holding the phone, Alison was both furious and tired of delusions. She wanted to move, and move so fast she outran moral exhaustion.

It took a while to track Brock down. He was either lost in the overlapping tangle of police agencies at the converted Torrance warehouse or on his way to the federal Metropolitan Detention Center in downtown Los Angeles.

She paced the large lobby. The forum had resumed, and every so often applause, laughter, and the booming words of a witness drifted out. "Resources to fight must be augmented," "a multiplicity of tactics and strategies," "new thinking," "the interplay of education and interdiction," the phrases expressing hope more than actuality. She often used similar incantations. They were armaments in the long drug war.

She dutifully checked in with her secretary in Sacramento. The usual crises loomed: a judge threatened one of her prosecutors with contempt, an Indian casino case was overheating, staff needed to see her immediately about budgets, witness immunities.

Alison dispatched problems, set up meetings, and put off others until she got back. Jillie, her longtime secretary, said nervously, "Oh. Porter *has to see you*. He said to bring you in in chains."

"Tell him I'll be back by five-thirty. I'm sorry if that keeps him late. Did he say what's so urgent?"

"No, he didn't, and I will not make that overtime crack," Jillie said cheerfully. Alison inspired respect but not blind obedience. "He did rant about something you should've told him."

Alison hung up, then walked to the wide doors of the conference hall, peering in. Val sat, leaning back and rocking while a jolly senator from North Carolina slapped a chart an aide held up for him. Face time for everyone. No one lost even if their views did.

She closed the door, the public phone ringing. She hurried to it.

She grabbed the phone quickly. Seeing Val just now cemented an unpleasant task. I've got to ask her for a favor because she's the only one I can trust who has pull, Alison thought. So be it.

"Brock?" she said, turning inward to the alcove, shutting out everything else. "I can barely hear you. How'd it go?"

"Are we on an open line?" he asked, sounding like he was in the middle of a raucous party.

"We're a couple of paranoids broadcasting to the world," she said. "It's all right. The FBI cleaned all the phones just before the forum."

He took a deep breath. "Well, in that case, Ally, we made a great score. Sixteen arrests, including Chandler. I'm at the Metro Center now. I'm going to chat with him. That's the good times rolling you hear."

She knew the incessant cries, shouts, and chaos of even a well-run jail. "So what's wrong? You sound funny."

"I do? Damn. I'm on top of the world. Lila Martin probably wins my ten-buck bounty on the coke. It'll come in about twenty-one-five street."

"I hear bad news, Brock," she said, growing uneasy.

"Nothing that beats popping a lot of high-level dopers and grabbing their buy money and over twenty million bucks' worth of coke." He laughed, as if pleased by something unsaid. "I had one fatality. But it's a good shoot by Jimmy Yee," he said defensively.

"I'm sure it is. Congratulations," she said, adding as if it had just occurred to her. "Before I left Sacramento, I got a fingerprint confirmation on the dead shooter yesterday." It wasn't true yet, but she waited for his answer.

"Who was it?"

"Richard Bower. Nelson's Richard Bower."

"Now that breaks my heart."

"Why?"

"It should've been Nelson." Pause. She yearned for him to say he knew all about the shooting. But he only said, "When are you coming home?"

"I thought you'd want to know everything about the shooting. It's Bower, Brock."

"I'll read the reports or the newspapers, Ally. Bower's been off my plate since last month."

"You don't see any link to the old case here?"

"Not particularly." His voice tightened slightly. "Is there one?"

Alison hesitated. "No. Just speculating." The circle of lies was complete. It was going to be silent, secret war between them, she thought. For a flickering instant, that seemed right. It expressed their true situation together. The Nelson case had only underscored reality.

"So. When are you getting home?"

Alison suppressed her deepening anger. "I have to see Porter about something. I'll be on the ground at five."

"I'll pick you up at the airport."

"It's all right. I can get around."

"Ally, I'd like to do it. Look, I've got to work on Chandler now. I'll see you in a couple of hours. Maybe we'll have a drink, you know, celebrate." It was a breezy almost carefree goodbye.

She hung up, going inside the conference hall, sitting down beside the mayor of Newark while the mayor of Baja testified. What are we doing? she wondered. How bad was it going to get?

The mayor of Baja finished his testimony, stood, waved to the audience, got applauded, and Alison was called. She sat down without notes, facing the dais of senators. Val winked at her and gave a laudatory introduction.

Three still photographers crouched down before her like worshipers and began snapping shots. Alison spoke clearly, firmly, automatically. She had done this forever, and she received applause at the right moments. Val smiled contentedly at her.

Alison sat straighter, looking at the senators, then the TV cameras. "And finally, I want to announce that the U.S. Attorneys Office, in cooperation with many federal and state law enforcement agencies, has just seized nearly twenty-two million dollars' worth of cocaine and arrested sixteen suspects in Los Angeles."

Someone whistled, low, at the booty. Alison thought Brock would like the reaction.

She nodded to Val. "This operation by the Eastern District's Task Force on Organized Crime and Narcotics Enforcement is one of the biggest victories in the war against illegal drugs."

Senator Cantil's smile faded. "I'm sure, Ms. Andrews, as a prosecutor you share my concerns. It's impressive to make arrests, but arrests won't stop the flood of drugs . . ." and she began a canned repudiation of law enforcement alone as the way to end the societal failings that forced people to take drugs.

Alison stood, shaking her head. The cameras had swung to her as if she were magnetic north. "No, Senator Cantil, I do not agree. The war on drugs is winnable if you and your subcommittee and Congress will give us the money and support."

A smattering of applause and hissing swept through the audience, most of whom hewed to Val Cantil's views, unsurprising since her staff had selected each person there.

"I'm glad we have your opinion on the record," Val Cantil said with a practiced smile that did not fool Alison. "Nevertheless, when my late husband and I began working with substance abusers in California's inner cities . . ." and she was off on the prepared text.

Alison sat down, aware of people whispering about her. The mayor of Newark abruptly shook her hand. "Jesus, I thought this whole deal was stacked against locking the bastards up," he said.

Politics and public service. Talking to Brock always brought out an idealistic streak in her. Even now, she thought. Alison lowered her head in momentary vertigo. Too many discordant demands to stay stable, she thought.

"I'm not arguing with you, Val. You'll either do it or you won't," Alison said.

"First you asked me to let you appear today. Then you stand up in front of everybody and throw the whole forum back in my face." Val Cantil stared ominously at a frothy iced coffee drink in front of her.

"I can't hide my professional opinion."

"You damn well have to! People know our connections. You just made me look stupid and weak, Alison. After I helped you."

They sat in a cleanly modern coffee shop just down the street from the Convention Center. It was the closest place Alison could find where they would have some privacy. A parade of jaunty men and women in beachwear or expensive fashions passed by the window. It was as tense a meeting as she anticipated.

"Look, Val, I'm sorry. Maybe I can make it up to you," she said, taking out a piece of paper.

"With another favor? Right now is not the time to ask me to pull strings. When you've got enough of your own available."

Alison sat back. She looked solemnly at Val. "I need you to use your connections at the FBI or maybe Senate investigators to find these people." She pushed the paper across the tiny table.

Val Cantil picked it up. "Lara? And a woman named Mandy Hayes? Why? Who are they?"

"I've given you all the information I've got. I need to find these people right away."

"The logical question"—Val folded the paper and put it in her purse—"is why you aren't utilizing the FBI yourself. Or your own investigators. How would you answer that question?"

"The U.S. Attorneys Office can't be tied to any request to find these people."

"Why?"

"Trust me." Alison felt anger that protecting Nelson's information required blindsiding an old friend like this. There was no choice. Brock would find out quickly if she moved to find Lara or his girlfriend.

Val took a tentative sip of her iced coffee, grimaced. "In

the summer we used to hike around Mount Tam or sail down San Francisco Bay; I never could stand this junk. Coffee should be hot enough to peel your tongue." She frowned, gazing at the oceanfront, then said, "All right, Alison. You're as bad as Brock with secrets. But it must be important."

"I wouldn't ask otherwise."

Val stood. "I've got a couple of eager reporters waiting for me. I can still make this forum sound like a call for sanity. Most of my witnesses said the right things." She smiled. "I'll chalk this up to your home problems."

Alison walked out with her into a May afternoon of sun and palms. "I said I'd make it up to you. While you're trying to find Dennis Lara and the legal secretary he's with"—Alison took Val Cantil's slim, dry hand—"you better take a hard look at contributions you got in the last election. Look at the Asian-American Civic Society."

Val Cantil's hand squeezed back. "Funny money? It's serious?"

"Very funny. Very serious."

CHAPTER ELEVEN

Brock and Lila Martin were in the Spartan office of the senior U.S. marshal in the Metropolitan Detention Center. "Thanks for your help," Brock said to the smooth-faced Hispanic marshal. Turning to another man he said, "I'd like to see Chandler now if you've got him ready."

The man he spoke to was silver-haired, leathery, in a fastidiously buttoned blue suit. "Oh, he's ready. We can't shut him up," said Stofan, Brock's counterpart in the Central District's U.S. Attorneys Office, which was based in Los Angeles.

The three of them headed across the new jail's rubbery-floored lobby toward the elevators. Although only a few years old, the federal Metro Center already showed distressing signs of age: vaguely dirty drinking fountains, smudged walls, the odor of unwashed bodies sinking into the concrete. It was an eight-story sandy pillar off to one side of the federal courthouse in downtown Los Angeles, and within a short distance from the famous outlines of city hall.

After they got out on the sixth floor, walking briskly down a brightly lit, dun-colored corridor, Brock asked Stofan, "What's Chandler been saying? Exactly?"

Stofan buzzed at a steel-bolted, vaultlike security door. "Same thing, Brock. Over and over. He wants to talk to you."

"It's so nice when things work out. I want to talk to him."

Lila followed him and Stofan, the door electrically bolting shut behind them. She said to Brock, "I wish I wore my waders. We're going into deep bullshit with this guy."

"There's a silver dollar in the crap," Brock said cheerfully. "I'm going to make him hand it over."

Lennox Chandler had been changed from his supple, hip fashionable clothes to a stiff white T-shirt, faded jeans, and the jail's soft slippers. MDC was stamped on his shirt. He sat with one wrist handcuffed to a metal table's heavy ring.

It was a small, barren room: four green plastic chairs, flat white acoustic tile on the ceiling and walls and the low hum of an air conditioner through a high vent. Stofan locked the door behind them. Three guards, all armed with rifles, caustic sprays, and large caliber guns, waited grimly just outside.

Chandler grinned when he saw Lila. "You didn't have to bring me take-out. It's okay. I eat it here."

"You couldn't afford this combo," Lila said evenly. "Believe me."

"Maybe I get a taste, see if I like it?"

Brock listened, watched, weighed. He and Lila had discussed Chandler's possible responses, assuming he even agreed to see them. His high spirits now were intriguing. He was a brutal, intelligent man, up from the crumbling houses and wolf pack mercilessness of Lennox, a city lost amid a dozen others in L.A.'s sprawl.

"Okay, Lennox," he said, waving the others to the chairs, "I'm going to take notes of what we talk about. These people are going to be witnesses, you understand? You've gotten your Miranda?"

"I signed the form. I'm very cooperative." Chandler leaned back as far as he could, handcuffed in the plastic chair. Brock noted the exaggerated gangster cadences faded in and out as required.

"Lennox," Stofan began earnestly, trying to assert some status in an operation he should have directed, "what we need from you is a complete—" and Chandler cut him off.

"I don't talk to anybody but him." He pointed at Brock. "That's what I been saying. And I want any fucking recorders you got—" he jabbed his finger up at the air vent— "there or anyplace else in this fucking kiddie school turned off or I ain't talking to him either." He sat back, tight, hard face set.

"How about me?" Lila asked, arms folded. Even with only the barest trace of makeup, dressed in functional unflattering clothes, she was a desirable, attractive woman. "You kicking me out, too?" Brock liked the performance.

"Not now, sweet stuff. You take it outside with Mr. Stofan. Later you and me'll get down and personal."

Stofan nodded brusquely and buzzed to get out. He waited for the guards to identify him, and then he and Lila left. Brock heard a faint undertone in the rush of air through the vent go silent. The recorder was off.

"I give you my word there are no recording devices functioning now, Lennox," Brock said. He wanted to add, *But I listened to your lying, murderous garbage for weeks on the bugs we had in your house and office.*

He didn't say any of it. He blanked his face, pulled his chair around the table so he was opposite Chandler. Chandler rattled his handcuffs with a grin, like a tiger teasing his trainer. Brock said, "You do understand where you are right now? You've got a murder. You've got a couple hundred pounds of coke. You've got a bunch of very upset Mexicans ready to roll over on you. And"— Brock grinned—"I've got you on tape, hours and hours of it, laying out this whole shipment. I could tell you what you had for dinner last night. So," he said coldly now, "do you see where you are?"

"I see. You be surprised how good." Chandler's voice was so soft it was nearly a whisper, and he leaned far across the table. Brock assumed he was trying to be hard to hear, in case anything was being recorded.

"All right. First. I won't promise you anything. You give me your honest, full cooperation, I'll give you my full cooperation."

"Can I get that nice piece of ass you brought?"

"Don't start, Lennox. You want to talk to me, right? Let's look at where you are. I've got you on murder."

"I didn't kill anybody," he said indignantly, as if offended. "You motherfuckers shot Tyrell."

"The law says any homicide during the commission of a felony is on your tab, Lennox. You're the one who goes down for murder."

But Chandler didn't seem fazed by the threat. "Well now, how about I don't care you shot his ass because I find out Tyrell's taking a buck here and there? I get a bunch of Vuitton suitcases with cash and I say, 'Wallace, I trust you, you watch these tonight so's I pick them up fresh in the a.m.'? And that night he goes through these suitcases, takes a hundred, two, from every fucking bundle in every suitcase, gets himself one hundred thousand fucking dollars. And then"—Chandler stabbed the air, his voice cruel, low—"he wraps that money, that money that is *mine*, in a diaper bag and he give it to his old lady and then the next day, I get these suitcases short? And he buy a new car, a Lotus? And I get a whole lot of shit from some people because they are saying, 'Lennox, we got short! They's money missing' and I say, 'You are lying fuckers' and I have to kill a couple of very, very good business partners, all because Wallace Tyrell got the money in a diaper bag and I believe him, not them."

Brock waited, a small notepad from his coat pocket still virgin on the table. Pasteboard people like Chandler, he knew from long experience, were hollow at their center. They delighted in manipulating others above all.

So play him, bait him, then find out what he's hungry for and dangle it just out of reach, Brock thought.

"The best deal is the first one. Your buds are going to give you up maybe in the next ten seconds. Then you're

the only one who goes down behind murder, Lennox."
Brock's face hardened. "You give me the sun and moon
now, I'll help you out." He thought Chandler's next, anxious question would be a plea to find out what Brock
wanted. Then I'll mention Denny Lara, he thought.

Chandler unexpectedly laughed. "The best deal's when
you got something, Mr. Andrews."

"I'm ready to dance."

Chandler still smiled. "What I get is a pass. All the way.
I walk right out."

Brock smiled now. The lunatic audacity of people like
Chandler continually astonished him. When Alison asked
about informants and snitches, he vainly tried to tell her
about this separate world. The posturing. The macho senti-
mentality. Or the bone-melting abject terror. The world
of informants and snitches from the inside. She said she
needed to know more for a quarterly DOJ report.

He said to the man opposite him, "I don't think that's
in the cards. A federal murder rap means the death penalty
now, Lennox. You been keeping up with changes in federal
law? We're serious now."

"So you offering me, what? Life in the joint?"

"If you've got gold for me."

Chandler broke into a gut laugh. "Big fucking deal,
motherfucker." Chandler stopped laughing abruptly and
jangled his chained wrist. "I don't give a shit about murder
or any of that shit and you can tell the Mexes to kiss my
ass. You"—he pointed two rigid fingers at Brock—"are
giving me a pass."

"Why?"

"Well. How about Mr. Edward fucking Patrick Nelson?"

Brock stood up slowly. He could not entirely hide his
surprise. A fluttery sinking feeling hit him, like the morning he had opened the front door at Fort Carson post
housing and four men had pushed by, grabbing his father,
a piece of breakfast toast still in Master Sergeant Terry
Andrew's startled hand. His mother had screamed.

All I've learned since that moment, he thought, is to

play the opposite. Don't show your real feelings. Chandler had already made the connection from Denny Lara to Nelson to him. So he returned Chandler's triumphant laugh.

"What the hell could a sorry asshole like you tell me about Ed Nelson? Something you read in a magazine on the crapper, Lennox?"

Lennox Chandler relaxed in his chair, licked his lips as if sated. "Now I got your attention. Now I got it."

A few minutes later, Brock buzzed out, mind churning. He took Stofan and Lila toward a water fountain. The guards watched, then stared hard at the interview room door, leather belts festooned with ammo and Mace canisters creaking as they shifted their feet.

"Are there any recording or open mikes working in that room now?" Brock asked, their three heads bent together.

"What's up?" Lila asked.

Stofan shook his head. "Not unless you've got one up your ass. You are definitely not Memorex in there."

Brock straightened, then took another drink. "No joke, Frank," he said, putting a hand on Stofan's shoulder. "If I ever find out you've been eavesdropping, you'll be working in Montana."

Banter didn't disguise the sting, and Stofan stiffened. He knew Brock could do it. As they walked back to the interview room, Lila said, "What's the deal with my boyfriend?"

Brock thought for a moment. From somewhere the smell of burnt lasagna made him long for the exotic ripeness of the Cafe Tanjore. He said to Lila, "He's making interesting noises all of a sudden. I'm setting him up to drop a hammer on him. We're on a four-forty out of Burbank, right?"

Lila nodded. "Our people are all on it." She sensed his restrained excitement.

"Get hold of Jimmy, Lila. We may miss the flight back to Sacramento."

* * *

For twenty minutes, Brock went over Chandler's tale again and again. It was short, simple, and if believable, very tempting to him. He walked the bounds of the small room, hands on his hips, like that prehistoric, seemingly earthshaking basketball championship against Cornell when he had been sidelined with a torn ankle ligament. The whole game was right in front of me, Brock thought, listening to Chandler, but just out of reach.

Like Nelson had been out of reach after Alison jerked him to safety. Now, Brock thought with a tingle, maybe I'm back in the game. Ready to score.

"So what I said before"—Chandler grinned—"is you give me a pass on everything today. I go home."

"I can turn and walk out the door and you are dead. I'll get Nelson sooner or later."

"Lot later the way your old lady got you whipped. You ain't getting anywhere near Mr. Edward Nelson without me and you know it now."

"I'm almost out the door."

"Yeah. I'm almost Bill Clinton."

It was galling that his marital upheaval could be flung at him by a thug like Chandler. It was more galling because Brock felt it was true and people like Stofan or a hundred others thought the same and simply didn't say it aloud.

He said, "Maybe I could sell this. You'd have to do some work for me." Brock avoided the obvious. If Chandler's claims were true, a grant of immunity even for murder would be hard to resist. It made Brock enraged, mingled with his longing to get at Nelson. "I could maybe drop down to straight murder. No midnight injection for Dewane." He mimed the executioner's lethal needle going into his arm. He looked up. Chandler wanted a deal as badly as he did. He felt it. This was his gift. Brock had a nearly instinctive perception of when a tug on the spider's web indicated a meal was ready.

Chandler swore, turned, spreading his fingers on the

table. He said, "I don't do no work, Mr. Andrews. I don't have to work. I can bring you Edward Nelson."

"Because you can bring me Denny Lara."

"That's right," Chandler said calmly. "I been in business with Denny now for, couple months. We got this account at a bank on Olympic. I'll even give it up to you. He's holding some money for me, I pay him some money, I set up some little side deals, and he gets paid off. For his retirement, he says."

"Drug deals?"

"No." Chandler was puzzled. "Wouldn't go near anything like that. Clean graft is what he wants. I mean, I don't understand it, money's money, am I right? But Den wants it that way, so for services, I let him have the cash from a couple restaurants in Bell and Commerce I'm disposing."

"How much money?"

"Clear for Den about four hundred."

Brock nodded. "Retirement? He's leaving Nelson? Why?"

Chandler sighed, as if he'd been trapped with a slow-witted child. "As I been telling you. Den says to me, 'Ed's gone nuts. He's doing stuff I can't do, blah, blah.'"

Brock didn't think a crisis of conscience, if that's what happened to Lara, was something Chandler could comprehend. "What stuff? What frightened Lara?"

"Guns going to white boys who like to shoot things up here, I mean, *downtown.*" Chandler grinned. "Maybe even like this place and free us political prisoners. Den thinks Nelson's getting tired of him, got something else going and he don't want him around."

"That's why Lara was with Bower yesterday in San Francisco?"

"I think Ed Nelson was going to close out Den like I might've closed out Wallace Tyrell. Den think so, too." Chandler grinned, secure in the unshakable belief he had Brock salivating for his deal.

And, he's right, Brock thought, fighting to control his anticipation. Let him think if I want Nelson, I need Lara as bait. I have to make a deal with the killer who can give me Lara.

"Tell me again about last night," Brock said, making notes, looking Chandler in the eye.

"Well, there I am, partying, all happy and such for this little sweet thing I worked so fucking hard to set up and you fucked up." Chandler scowled briefly, then brightened. "And I'm enjoying things when about ten, eleven, I get this call from Den. He's all nice and easy, but I know the man." Chandler shifted, groaned, contorting his face, his voice pleading. "He says, 'Look, Lennox, I got to move fast. I got Nelson on my ass. I got to get away. I got to get my money right away. Tonight.'"

"You couldn't get him any money last night," Brock said, nodding, smiling like they were old friends. "Too much partying."

"So I go, 'Den, hang tight, and I get you your money, maybe little more for a going away present. But I do it tomorrow.' Which is today." Chandler stared hard at Brock.

"Lara is waiting for your call? Where? What time are you meeting?" He paused, as if only vaguely curious.

"Well, now, that's our deal. You want Den, I got to make a call, tell him the time and place is okay. You can have it all, soon's I get my pass on everything you motherfucking messed up for me today."

Brock closed his notepad, thinking rapidly, trying to keep his fury apart from his rationality. He was playing this one perfectly thus far. Deals were part of his world, the good ones and the monstrous ones, and this one was truly monstrous. A stray cry welled up inside: Ally put me here.

"Okay," he said finally, "I'll write up our agreement. You sign it, I sign it, and you give me the time and place you're meeting Lara. If it holds up, I show the agreement to a judge."

"Then I'm clean?" Chandler gloated.

"Then you're clean," Brock said bitterly, rising, about to be buzzed out, Chandler merrily chattering. Suddenly, as he was about to push the button, he acted as if something just surged into his thoughts and he swung around to Chandler.

"Shut up," Brock said. The change in demeanor bewildered Chandler into momentary silence.

"Listen to me, Lennox," Brock went on, standing over the handcuffed man, pointing at him slowly. "You got a call from Lara last night, eleven maybe? Worked out the details for his payoff, told him you'd call?"

"Yeah, yeah."

"He's here in L.A."

"It's a big city. You going to find him yourself?"

Brock leaned closer, letting his exhilaration shine out. "I've got it all on tape. I've got the time and the place because I've been listening to your shit for weeks."

Chandler breathed hard, sat straight, shook his head.

Brock straightened, too, buzzing the door so the guards and Lila would know he was finished. In truth, he realized, I'm just getting started. Thank God. He said, "Lennox, you are going to work for me. You are going to call Lara today and if you're very, very good"—Brock pointed at him—"you get a chance to spend your life in a federal prison. Think about it. Your decision."

Brock and the others moved back to the senior U.S. marshal's office. He was conscious his shirt had sweated tight to his chest. He was deliberate and sharp, though. "We've got a meeting set. I let Chandler think he had me over a barrel; then I bagged him. He turned into a 'reliable informant' just now and he's going to bring Lara to us." The inescapable order of Brock's world clicked into place. Chandler was absolved of a homicide, Lara set up, and Nelson the pig was in the slaughterhouse chute.

"Oh, my," Lila managed to say. Her eyes gleamed.

"Lara's going to be at MacGregor's in Santa Monica, the restaurant parking lot at eight. That's what he and Chandler talked about last night."

"He won't run if he sees Lennox on time," Lila said.

"No, he will not." Brock said to Stofan, "I'll do up the paperwork for an arrest warrant based on what Chandler told me. Do you have a magistrate on call who can sign off on it?"

"I can round somebody up," he said, hands in his pockets. "Brock, you've got fans down here. So does Alison. Everybody remembers the way she whipped through the office leaving a trail of headlines."

"If I bust Lara, are you going to have a problem?" Brock said quickly. He didn't want a recital of Alison's controversial rise in the U.S. Attorneys Office here.

Stofan shook his head. A bell clanged in the jail. "There's too much infighting in our outfit. You're going after Ed Nelson, and I'll make sure you get the help you need."

Lila grinned. She and Jimmy loved the rush, Brock knew, and that was coming fast now.

Brock thanked him. "I want to cover the area around the parking lot, in case Lara spooks and runs."

"Will do."

He went over to the aging marshal, who smiled, looking up from his cluttered desk. Brock had a great regard for U.S. marshals. They were young and old bloodhounds, seemingly exempted from the rivalries and political storms that battered other agencies. This guy's got parabolic ears, Brock thought delightedly, like all the good ones. They heard and took in everything and were ready.

"I'm assuming everything goes all right tonight," Brock said to the marshal. "I'd like to have a plane ready to get us to Sacramento as soon as I've got Lara run by a magistrate down here. Can you have a plane, maybe from six o'clock on?"

The marshal stood up. He was lankier than Brock, hipless, his white shirt and blue tie hanging straight down his torso. "Oh, I think so, Mr. Andrews, sir. I think I'll have a fine government jet for you at the Imperial terminal out at LAX. How's that?"

Brock impulsively slapped his bony shoulder. "That's

what I was thinking." He said to Stofan, "How about letting me have someplace to get this warrant ready?"

On the way across the busy street, a Santa Ana drying and making the air seem crystal clear, Brock walked ahead with Lila. A harried black city traffic cop flapped his arms at the intersection to get the crush of one-way traffic moving past the deafening jackhammers breaking up asphalt.

Brock had to shout near her ear. "Chandler will turn around and bite us in the ass if he can tonight."

"It's in his job description."

"I'm not going to let him cause trouble. Would you mind if I set you up with a blind date?"

"A one-nighter?" she asked, obviously enjoying the prospect.

"Unless you have conjugal visits with him in the joint."

CHAPTER TWELVE

So that he wouldn't miss the most important meeting in his life, Denny dressed and quietly went into the Surf-crest's parking lot at seven that night, an hour in advance of when he was going to see Lennox Chandler.

He wore stonewashed jeans and over them an elegant and loose guayabera shirt that Mandy had bought because she said it made him look dashing. He hid the gun in his waistband under the shirt, as he had seen Bower do sometimes when guarding Ed.

He casually walked among the cars, then compared rooms to see which were silent and dark. People probably out eating nearby if the cars had California license plates. Sunset had just gone, and an orange glow lit the sky at the horizon. Cars rushed by on the highway; music clashed from motel rooms and the fast-food places lining the highway. People shouted and laughed, and at that moment, Denny felt cut off from the whole world.

He finally found a pea green two-door sedan with out-of-state plates and a very quiet room. A long-distance traveler, he hoped, getting an early night. Have it back in a couple hours, he thought.

In a few moments he was in the car, working beneath the steering column, and then driving out, heading north on PCH toward Santa Monica. It was amazing how quickly it all came back to you, he thought. His brief pleasure was buried almost at once under the weight of shame and loss that had paralyzed him all day.

Since Mandy left, he had barely stirred from the room. She would come back. He repeated that idea. Wish hard enough, it will come true, one of the kinder keepers at one of the gentler state homes had told him. Mandy. You've got to come back.

For hours he hadn't dared to get far from the motel phone. Nor did he want to miss Lennox's confirmation call. Because he was so positive Mandy would not desert him permanently, Denny had a fierce determination to get his money and provide for their joint security.

By now, he had thought fearfully, Ed's figured I'm gone. By now he's checking, beating around. Putting the word out.

That was at ten or eleven in the morning. As the day wore on, his panic and loneliness grew until he thought he was going crazy. He only saved himself by minutely plotting his moves that night.

He drove the stolen car off PCH, up into Santa Monica, passing the floodlit remodeled pile of the Miramar Hotel, the strip park along the street filled with palms and derelicts who shuffled, grumbled, or sat bleary-eyed on the curb. The streetlights had just come on, and the place had its usual garish vigor as Denny turned east along Wilshire.

He soon found the aging restaurant, a grinning Scotsman, pipe clenched in his teeth, outlined in broken blue neon over its quaintly shingled roof. Denny slowed, circled, eyes on the cars, the few older couples drifting in and out. He went around the block, repeating the process. What truck or van looked out of place? Which bum seemed too studious picking at the trash in his shopping cart? Slight signs that the place was under surveillance. By who? Ed? Lennox Chandler? Denny hadn't sorted it out very specifically. He was intensely distracted, worrying about Mandy.

Finally, he thought the scenery looked safe enough. He drove through the parking lot toward the rear, slotting his car between two others, switching off the headlights, able to see who came in. He was forty minutes early.

He put his head back. The gun dug into his side, and he shifted in the seat.

On the eve of falling off Ed Nelson's screen forever, he suddenly recalled their first meeting five years ago.

He sat in Ed's eighth-floor Washington office, not far from the Dupont Circle Metro station. It was raining. I was pitching gold futures, big find in Borneo, Denny thought. Working with Petto's crew, taking the hottest leads from them. Dressed like a solid winner, Euro-cut charcoal pin-stripe, a little gold here and there, silk tie.

Modestly, Denny knew he was good. He wouldn't be working with an old pro like Petto on the scam if he wasn't. He was therefore stunned when this guy Nelson started laughing.

"Borneo fucking gold?" Nelson cackled. "Oh, man. Oh, Christ. Listen, my old man lost his hump forty years ago in the Indonesia gold scam. Samples were all salted, so they came out looking rich as hell. Hosed a lot of little investors. My old man put everything—" Nelson was abruptly stone serious—"every cent on these phony gold strikes. So I worked my way through college washing dishes, pumping gas. My sister. Well, let's say sudden not-so-genial poverty didn't agree with her. Maybe she tripped over the railing on the roof of the Plaza, but I've got my doubts." He smiled again. "We used to go to the Palm Court for our birthday parties."

Denny had cleared his throat, inwardly cursing Petto roundly. This was exactly the kind of screwup a pro avoided, entirely by doing research on a lead. "I'm sorry to hear about that, Mr. Nelson, but I was led to believe . . ." and Denny plugged away at how *different*, how sound, these latest strikes were.

Nelson, shirtsleeves rolled up, a mountain of disorderly papers and plastic cartons of fancy take-out dinners stacked on his desk, gave Denny a kindly look. "Led to believe? Listen, kid, never be *led to believe*. You do the leading."

Before Denny could try again to salvage something of this debacle, Bower came in, tapped his diver's watch. Nelson rose, nodded, rolled down his sleeves. He looked tense. He led Denny to the door. "I've got a very important deal, Mr. Hall"—it was the name Denny used at the time— "but don't go away feeling like you struck out here. Nobody could've found out much about me. I've made a kind of career out of making up careers."

"I understood you were interested in investing," Denny said, relying on the hot prospect Nelson supposedly presented.

Nelson, coat shrugged on, rumpled but ready to wrestle alligators, said, "I was looking for people who try to sell things. I'm looking for a certain kind of ambitious individual. I can spot them. Somebody like you." He nodded again to an impatient Bower. "You want a job with lots of opportunity? Be all that you can be? Come see me."

That was Denny's introduction to Ed's recruiting technique: conning the con men. Hooking the wiliest fish with bait they couldn't resist. The name of the Washington company was, at that time, Universal Polytechnologies. Denny came back for his new job a week later.

But when he sent me and Bower to San Francisco yesterday, Denny thought, now staring at the parking lot in front of him, Ed still knew I could be led to believe. Led to believe somebody else was the sole target. Not me. Others could be led to believe I was a killer.

A little before eight, Denny slid lower in his seat, almost hidden behind the dashboard. He put the gun beside him. Denny did not really consider using it, but with Lennox Chandler, displaying a tool he frequently used himself tended to make him more tractable. Like showing a plumber you knew your way around wrenches, Denny thought wryly.

He tensed as a long, sleek black car pulled into the

parking lot, slowed, turned and reversed itself so it pointed out toward Wilshire again. Denny sardonically thought Chandler, a flamboyant figure, would stand out among the staid diners here. But he concluded Chandler probably owned the restaurant and felt secure on his property.

Nothing happened for what felt like hours. Then at last the black car's interior light flicked on. Denny recognized Chandler, dressed for success in muted perfectly draped silk, step out, button his jacket, motion, and a young black woman came out, standing beside him. She seemed to have her hand nestled amorously at his lower back.

Denny relaxed a little. Lennox Chandler had brought one of his women. He would not do anything extreme. Denny put his own gun in his waistband again, straightening behind the wheel. Chandler and the woman turned and turned around, trying to see where Denny would appear.

He opened his car door slowly, knowing it would instantly attract their attention. Denny carefully walked toward Lennox Chandler and his woman.

"On time," he said cheerfully. Both of them turned to him. Denny saw Lennox's oddly droopy stance as he got closer. "I almost went crazy today trying to get hold of you." He put out his hand. He and Chandler had always been friendly.

Chandler didn't move. The woman, young, athletic, finefeatured oval face, followed Denny's steps with what suddenly looked like hunger to him.

Chandler smiled wanly. "On time is right, Den. On the dot."

Denny heard the incredible mechanical roar of the helicopter swooping down on him at the same moment its blinding searchlight blazed over him and a voice boomed at him to lie flat on the ground.

He instinctively fumbled for the gun. Chandler was shoved to one side, and he saw that the young woman had held a wicked heavy gun at his back, not a lover's hand. She screamed at Denny to get down. *"Do not move or I will shoot."*

Denny raised his arms like the terrified, ecstatic worshipers he used to see at Pentecostal churches as a boy. Suddenly, two agents hurled him to the asphalt, hands jerked so harshly and quickly behind his back that he yelled in pain. Two bums abandoned a bottle and ran over to help. He saw they had guns, too.

He was hauled to his feet, the gun torn from his waistband so roughly his pants started to fall. Someone held them up. Handcuffs agonizingly squeezed his wrists. He couldn't see, or react except to blink, then shout incoherently himself. He was held fast by many hands it seemed. The restaurant parking lot was alive with dark figures in armor, vests, assault rifles. The noise was deafening.

Denny glimpsed a lanky, almost handsome man coming toward him through the pandemonium. He wore a dark suit, and a badge gleamed on his coat pocket. He spoke to the young woman, and she smiled widely.

The man came to Denny. I know you, Denny thought madly in the tumult of his shocked, terrified mind. Andrews. The U.S. Attorney.

The man seemed startled when Denny struggled wildly to twist free of the heavily armed figures restraining him. Denny, as though far away, heard his own frenzied yells.

The man made a nearly imperceptible gesture, and Denny found himself half dragged along the asphalt toward a black van. "Shut up, Lara," the man named Brock Andrews said calmly. "We've got a lot to talk about."

The last thing Denny saw was the huge smiling neon Scotsman, vivid as in the noonday sun when the helicopter's light swept back and forth over it.

CHAPTER THIRTEEN

For the first half hour after they were airborne, Denny pretended to be asleep. It wasn't difficult. He was truly exhausted.

It was nearing midnight, he guessed. He was handcuffed to a hard plastic seat, alone in the rear of the small twin engine turboprop, probably a King Air from what he had hurriedly seen of it at the Los Angeles airport when, with cops, guns, shouts, he was shoved inside. The plane belonged to the U.S. Marshal's Service and was obviously used to transport security prisoners. Separating Denny from the front portion of the aircraft was a heavy steel mesh gate. The plane smelled of holding tank disinfectant, as cloyingly familiar to someone raised in state homes as a broken lavatory.

Denny tried his wrist. Barely enough room to wiggle. The hard plastic seat cut into his legs. Andrews was up front with the young black woman from the restaurant, an Asian guy, and about a dozen other men and women. Laughing. Having a high old time. Paper cups of coffee passed around.

Denny was too tired, still too distracted about Mandy,

what was happening to him, to digest everything he'd just picked up. The strange thing was that Andrews, after first saying they had a lot to talk about, barely allowed him three more words during the processing through booking at Metro Detention, hasty appearance before a puffy-eyed, sullen federal magistrate, rushed back on the freeway, out to the airport, up into the night. Denny didn't even really understand where he was being taken.

Andrews, holding two cups of coffee, left the other merrymakers. He had a uniformed marshal open the steel gate. He came in, sat down by Denny, one cup of coffee held out.

"You're awake, Lara," Andrews said. "Drink this. It's a short flight so there's no dinner and movie."

Denny sat up, took the coffee. It was thin, bitter, scalding. He was hungry and light-headed. "Where are we going?"

"Well, if you'd been listening in court tonight, you'd have gotten that. We're due in Sacramento in about forty minutes. We'll be landing at McClellan Air Force Base and then you get a return ride to the new downtown county jail." Andrews sipped, stared ahead boredly.

Denny glanced out the tiny window beside him. Below, the land was black, scattered pinpoints of colored light slowly passing, then gone. It reminded him of the rare, but terrifying flights he took with Ed. When their personal appearances were required somewhere. In a small plane, like this. At night, too. Drifting across radar in the Gulf, apparently just part of the constant helicopter traffic from oil rigs; landing at strange dark airfields in jungles or deserts. Wondering if they would be allowed to fly away, even as they roared down some airstrip hurriedly torn into the earth, even if the deal had gone down smooth as silk. Ed was a real white-knuckle flyer, and he took endless hits from a silver flask until they were back in the U.S. For a man who was temperamentally so jumpy, Denny always thought it funny Ed had chosen one of the most inherently perilous and risky occupations imaginable.

"Sacramento? I was arrested in L.A.," Denny said, trying to sound irate. "What's the bullshit?"

Andrews didn't answer. Denny repeated the question. Then it hit him. Always disorient a subject prior to interrogation, lots of movement, noise, lack of food. Bower used to gloatingly reprise interrogations he'd taken part in, South Africa or Uganda, Denny recalled. The bloody ones Bower liked best.

Surprise, Denny thought, clutching his coffee cup. I am disoriented and scared. The old gags were always the best, just like Petto and the pros used to tell him.

"Well, Lara"—Andrews crumpled his cup in one hard motion—"you are such a leprous individual, my associates in L.A. let me have you. And I will use you. And I may even tie you to that O.K. Corral thing in San Francisco yesterday. I'll stack so much time on top of you, you'll see daylight just before they throw dirt on your face. I'll be interested what your gun has to say."

"It's not mine. You'll find out."

Bored. Worse, amused. "Okay, I'll be interested what the gun you were holding onto for someone has to say."

"What am I being arrested for? Being in a parking lot? I want a lawyer and I want him now." Denny rattled his handcuffs, and the shrillness of his voice appalled him.

Andrews stood up, rubbing his eyes. He seemed anxious to get back to his pals who were congratulating each other, already telling tall tales of their day's exploits.

Andrews had to talk loudly for Denny to hear him. "Lara, you want a lawyer, I will personally drag the federal defender himself over to represent you." He turned toward the gate. "But you won't want him."

Denny tried to stand. He felt the same blind, deep fear Ed fought on those airplane rides in the night. Yet, there was a quality about Andrews, almost as if he empathized with a man chained to a chair, who was being dragooned hundreds of miles to face long imprisonment.

Years of judging, using, conning and trying to con men and women in the system as a kid had taught Denny to rely absolutely on his instincts about people. His instinct about Andrews, against the evidence of the man's posed boredom, the overwhelming show of force, the brutality of the other feds on the plane, said to trust him.

This one cares. This guy has the weakness. Denny could spot that no matter how cunningly it was hidden beneath a tough carapace.

So he blurted out, "What do you want? You said you had a lot to talk about. What do you want to talk to me about?"

And this fed, with the wound somewhere he hid from maybe everyone else, grinned slowly. "I want to talk about Ed Nelson, Lara."

I knew that, Denny thought, sinking back in his unyielding seat with despair. All he wanted to do was put as much distance as possible between Ed and Mandy and him. The danger Andrews posed was simple. I'll be pinned down like a bug in federal custody. Ed will come for us.

Andrews opened the steel gate, and the young black woman was coming toward him, smiling and doing a little dance step. Everyone was in high old spirits. He said to Denny, "So that's who we'll talk about. If you feel like it. Your girlfriend? Mandy Hayes, right? We'll find her pretty fast, see what she feels like saying."

He stepped through the gate. The woman wagged her finger in the air, chiding and beckoning Andrews.

Maybe it was the sight of her that shot Mandy's face through every fiber of Denny's awareness because he suddenly wanted something more than anything else he had ever lusted after, lied for, connived to get in his life.

"Yeah!" he shouted, lunging as far as the handcuffs tethered to his seat would permit. "You find her. I'll help you. Christ, you find Mandy for me."

He knew by their expressions they didn't fully understand.

Better this fed gets to Mandy before Ed Nelson does.

Mandy rolled back to the Surfcrest Motel a few minutes after midnight and nearly ran right into the four men who were cleaning out Denny's room.

She was ready to march in and say to Den, "All right. Let's start again. I've thought about this all day," because she saw the window lights streaming from the room. Then the door opened and the men started coming out, lugging suitcases, bedding, towels, even some of the furniture. At first Mandy blinked, thinking this was a burglary. But she noted the stout lady motel manager standing and excitedly talking with a tall older man in a tweedy sportcoat who gave quiet directions to the men going back into the room.

Mandy spun the wheel in panic, screeched the tires as she backed up. Something had happened to Denny. She had to get away, think, reason it out.

She didn't go far, parking in the small lot of a surfing equipment store separated by a chain-link fence from the motel's lot. She could just make out the men as they purposefully emptied the motel room, everything going into a large blue or black van without markings. The ocean waves hissed ashore. There was a jaundiced quarter moon in the sky. A salsa beat pulsed from the Mexican restaurant to her right.

She felt queasy and sour from the junk food she'd thrown down all day, anxiously brooding, trying to decide what to do. Mandy unconsciously put a protective hand over her stomach. It was up to her, she realized, to safeguard the baby and Den.

I can't choose one or the other. I can't walk away from either one, she thought.

Who the hell would want everything in Den's room? What were they looking for? She'd dealt with a few cops when her law firm handled LAPD promotion discrimination cases. She didn't recognize this behavior, midnight wholesale looting of a motel room, as part of the police work she'd encountered. Was it Ed Nelson, Denny's elusive boss? But the manager seemed quite at ease, as if the whole surreal event were unremarkable. Official.

Less than five minutes later, she saw the large van drive away, the curious guests drift back to their rooms or the pool. I've got to find out what's going on, Mandy thought, heading for the motel's registration office.

She walked in boldly. A TV blared in one corner, sounds of someone rooting in the rear apartment where the manager lived floated out. She hesitated.

It was an unsettling end to a turbulent day, from the moment she found the hidden gun and stormed out until now. Mandy had gone home. She had an apartment on Orange Avenue, the building a white stucco Spanish-Moorish Southern California relic, with slightly warped hardwood floors, leaded windows, and a persistent reek of turpentine and boiled cabbage. It was just a few blocks from the Los Angeles County Museum of Art, so she had gone there to struggle through the day's wreckage. She often sat in front of Impressionists or the solid portraits, whispering to the baby, as if alerting her to the wonders of the world. Denny didn't know about these visits.

Nothing came to her this time or later, and so she'd ended up driving back to the motel, willing to give him another chance. She was always willing to give him one more chance.

Now she stood in the motel manager's office, as the stout woman reappeared holding a yellow plastic bucket with brushes and sponges in it.

"Something's happened to my room," Mandy said angrily. "It looks like everything's been taken out, including my luggage."

The other woman stared, then smiled. "Well, I thought we'd lost you there."

"What about my room? Where's the man I came in with?"

"Oh, my honey, he just stepped out, he said he'd be right back. You probably just missed him. We had a terrible leak in that showerhead in your room, flooded everything, but I got all your stuff in my place, dry and safe," the woman went on, setting the bucket down, coming around toward Mandy, who backed away. "He told me to give you something very important. I got it in back, if you wait here a second, okay?" She pressed Mandy's hand between both of hers like a piece of dough.

Mandy felt the clammy hands even after the woman

disappeared back into her apartment, chattering, then going silent for a moment. The TV expelled strident music, and Mandy started, her glance falling on a white card shoved near the office's cash register. She read it and trotted for her car, heart racing, yet her mind stayed almost frozen.

The fat lady was calling someone, Mandy thought, driving away fast up the highway. Calling whoever had taken Denny away, whoever left cards around for an excitable, obviously forgetful motel manager. Mandy saw the words she'd read: *Brock Andrews, Assistant United States Attorney.* Followed by phone numbers, including one scribbled in, probably a private line.

When she got to her apartment, Mandy locked the door, closed the drapes. She smoked one of the very last cigarettes and drank what was left of an expensive burgundy Denny had brought back from some secret trip. Experimentation with more harsh and exotic stimulants was long in the past.

She ground out the cigarette. Bad to smoke, bad to drink now. But one thing was clear to her. She went into the bedroom, throwing aside clothes in the closet until she got to the elegant European-cut dark suit Denny cherished. She fished in the smallest pocket in the coat and found the scrap of paper.

She sat on the bed and dialed. Denny had left her one phone number guaranteed to reach Ed Nelson. *Just in case*—he'd grinned boyishly—*I really need a hand. Ed can give me a hand, no matter what's happened.*

Mandy held the phone so tightly her fingers ached. The feds had Denny somehow. Stripped his room in case he'd put notes, names, information anywhere. Now they were looking for her, too. Left little cards. Maybe even at Seymour and Clay by now.

So, she smiled grimly, the irony is that Ed Nelson is the only one who can help us suddenly. The enemy changed instantly into their lone friend. He's the only one strong enough to reach out and help Den.

I can make some kind of deal for Den and me with him because Brock Andrews, whoever he is, can squeeze a poor, weak man like Den dry, and that's the end of all of us.

Someone answered at the other end of the line and she tensed.

CHAPTER FOURTEEN

Earlier that afternoon, Alison had flown back to Sacramento, landing after five. There was a message from Brock waiting for her when she got off the plane. Questioning Lennox Chandler was going slowly and he was taking a later flight. He apologized for not meeting her. Their cruelly insincere phone conversation bothered her deeply. It was better not to see him now.

She took a cab downtown to the tall, blue-black glass building on Capital Mall that housed most of the Eastern District U.S. Attorneys Offices. Spiky modern fountains decoratively sprayed water into a reflecting pool on the plaza as she crossed it. People from various law firms, state agencies, and companies left the building for the day.

Alison took the elevator up to the fifteenth floor alone. Everyone else was going down, going home. When she got out, she pushed through heavy simulated-oak doors, the burnished brass seal of the Department of Justice on the wall to one side. In the cramped, makeshift lobby that had been hastily constructed to accommodate new security measures, she gave a slight smile to the two beefy retired marines, in gray uniforms now, who manned the metal

detectors and sometimes scanned the endlessly roving surveillance camera displays on a TV near their station. Usually they were preoccupied with arguments about boxing
or football.

She showed her identification badge to the receptionist
sitting dully in a booth behind bulletproof glass, was buzzed
in. The gray padded cubicles for staff were silent, empty
after five. She said a few words to various attorneys working
late, raised a warning hand when a few tried to corner her.

Her office was at the far end of the floor. She tossed
her briefcase on the desk, then dropped her head for an
instant, fatigue and irresolvable thoughts troubling her.

"Popeye's been waiting, Alison." Her secretary, Jillie
Lawrence, entered at once. "He's got the SAC in with him
and you are *expected.*" She had a glass of iced mint tea
ready, without being asked, and handed it to Alison. Jillie
was fifty, wide, shrewd, and unflappable. With five kids,
Alison sometimes recalled bemusedly.

"Why's the FBI here?" she asked Jillie, taking the tea,
drinking with a grateful moan. She went to her double-
locked, reinforced steel file cabinets, opening the first and
putting her briefcase inside. Better not to leave Ed's pearls
of wisdom lying around even here, she thought.

"Popeye does not confide in lowly creatures," Jillie said,
taking the empty tea glass.

Alison strode down the short corridor to the U.S. attorney's office at the corner of the floor. She went in without
knocking.

"Hello, Porter," Alison said equably. "I'm back from
the publicity wars with a couple of good sound bites on
my belt."

Porter Ridgeway was in the middle of a wide-mouth
laugh with another man when she came in. He closed his
mouth, then moved from the worn leather sofa back to
his black walnut desk. Behind him, through open linen
drapes at the window, the white butter-creme mass of the
state capitol building was floodlit at dusk.

"Alison, this is Special Agent in Charge Merical. This is

my first assistant, Cubby," Ridgeway said by way of introduction. "I make the policies. She runs things."

Merical, Alison saw, was new. She didn't realize a reshuffle of the FBI regional top management was in the works, and that blind spot rankled her. She shook hands. He was a brown-haired, late middle-aged man in a solid dark blue suit. His shirt collar, like Ridgeway's, was one size too small. She idly wondered if the FBI would nickname Merical "Popeye," too.

"I've got a lot to do, Porter." She turned to him. "There are ten fires burning that you don't want to get worse."

The FBI agent sat down. "We watched you on TV just now. I love it when someone stands up to Senator Cantil."

Ridgeway sat down, adroitly rolling a silver pen around one thick-knuckled hand. "Yes. Terrific speech, Alison. Alison's a close personal friend of the senator, Cubby." He smiled thinly at her. "Wish you'd told me you were going to go after more funding, Alison. Like to coordinate that kind of thing."

"Since when does an opportunity to yell for money need staffing out, Porter?"

He shrugged. "Cubby's got some important news. For you especially."

She was bored with Cubby and Porter, and the obvious old boy connection, which had probably facilitated the change of SACs for the region. Something old Popeye kept from her. He would, she thought, have to pay for playing his own games. "I'm always interested in important news, Cubby," she said, one hand on the back of a leather chair. "But give it to me quickly please. I've got a lot to clean up, and I want to go home this week."

Merical's geniality flicked off. "I told the U.S. Attorney that we've done a full backgrounder, investigation, canvass on this bank shooting yesterday," he said coolly.

"What do you know?" Porter Ridgeway involuntarily ran a finger inside his too tight collar. "Seems the dead shooter is Richard Bower. You know, the bastard you convinced me we had to dump last month. Along with his boss, Edward Nelson. So guess what, Alison? Cubby's going to give us

all the cooperation we want if we go back after Nelson.''
He steepled his fingers, blinking at her. ''And do you know
what else?''

''Cut the twenty questions, Porter,'' she said. ''Just tell
me.''

But it was Merical who answered, watching her reaction.
''The other civilian victim is Ray Kelso.''

''Old news,'' she said. ''As a matter of fact, Senator Cantil
and I briefly discussed this last night.''

Porter Ridgeway grunted, pursing his lips. ''I'm of the
opinion this is all Nelson's deal, Alison. This Kelso bastard
did the licenses and whatever on that C-4 thing.''

''I briefed you extensively on the fatal problems we had
with that case,'' she said. ''None of that's changed.'' She
raced ahead. Had Porter stumbled onto her new undercover operation? Was he making the requisite noises for
Cubby, obviously an old pal, who'd brought this information to him? Had the associate AG slipped it to him? She
didn't know. She took a breath, realizing she had no idea
what was going on suddenly.

''I don't agree,'' Porter Ridgeway said. ''This shooting
changes everything.''

''Maybe this is a break here, Cubby,'' Alison stalled. ''I'll
talk to the head of our task force. He handled the original
case.''

''Brock Andrews,'' Porter Ridgeway prompted cheerfully. ''Alison's husband. You know him, don't you?'' he
said to Merical.

''Heard him at a couple conferences. Sounds like a good
guy. Read about the two of you in magazines.''

''Don't we all,'' Porter Ridgeway added, and Alison
caught the envy. ''But I think we've got to move immediately. Bower was Nelson's right arm.''

''Nelson's especially vulnerable,'' Alison said. ''I agree.''

''So what I want to do, with Cubby's blessing, is put the
bastard under twenty-four-hour surveillance and catch him
the second he steps over the line.''

''I haven't been apprised Nelson's doing anything criminal. He's been on good behavior since we cut him loose," Alison said.

"Well, he's dirty. He's been dirty since he learned to talk, and he's doing something now and we can catch him in the act if he's got to handle things himself because Bower's dead." Porter Ridgeway glanced at Cubby Merical. "Wouldn't that be great? We finally clip this gentleman."

"I don't want to start something as intrusive as round-the-clock surveillance and risk alerting Nelson," she said. "Let me talk to Brock first. We can meet in my office tomorrow at nine." Nelson was her snitch, and to protect Brock she had to protect him.

Merical nodded. She turned, hoping to get back to her office. Think it through. Get answers quickly.

Then Porter said sharply, "Well, I don't like it, Alison. We looked ridiculous last month. This is a fresh, hot lead on Nelson." His eyes bugged. "I don't want to look ridiculous again by losing this opportunity."

The pent-up frustration and worry exploded from her when she wheeled on him. "I will not be stampeded again and run the risk of another embarrassment." She spoke directly to Merical. "Don't begin any surveillance on Nelson unless you get it from me. In writing."

Merical nodded. "Hey, I'm not getting between you two. I only want this guy."

Alison sensed an agenda between Ridgeway and Merical. "So. Nine tomorrow?" she said, more a declaration than question.

Porter Ridgeway agreed sullenly. "No surveillance right now. Fine. But since you're so sure he's clean, where's he now? What's he doing, Alison?"

She faced him. "I have no idea."

"See how she orders me around?" he grumbled to Merical.

Working in her office, rapidly typing at her computer, Alison entered all of Nelson's figures on his front companies. She hid the information in several innocuous files.

Unlike Brock, she couldn't keep so much information in her head. She also wanted a detailed trail in case someone, sometime, called her to account and Chris Metzger at Justice was nowhere to be found.

Which will happen if Nelson is uncovered or goes out of control, she thought.

She finished entering the information, then wrote out the rough draft of something Ed Nelson had been pestering her about for months. It was a letter, in her official capacity as an assistant U.S. Attorney, acknowledging his good works, help to the government, and giving him an unconditional promise of no prosecution for criminal acts as part of their bargain. She stored the letter deep in her computer. These documents were called "Queen for a Day" letters, rare and very valuable. Like the letters of transit, she thought, switching off the computer. She and Brock could recite lines from *Casablanca* effortlessly, as if imaginary romance and intrigue were more compelling than reality.

Alison put her handwritten pages through the shredder mounted on her wastebasket. She had a burn bag for especially sensitive material, but suspected that ingenious prying eyes might be drawn to a burn bag rather than mere daily garbage.

On the drive home, she wondered if concentrating on the problems she and Brock were having had put her off her game. Overlooking the change of FBI SACs, even if a boob like Ridgeway tried to conceal it, was incredible for her. Out of character.

She got home, the streetlights reassuringly burning bright, a few well-behaved kids on bikes, a neighbor who owned a major construction company lovingly waxing his antique Rolls.

Something bothered her, though. She picked up the pile of mail Celeste had put on the foyer table when she went into the house. One certainty existed. Alison headed for the kitchen. Porter Ridgeway could never be involved in an undercover operation with Nelson. He'd either blow it or try to take complete credit for any successes.

Alison sorted through the mail, and found Celeste singing along with a sitcom rerun's bouncy theme coming from the little color TV on the sink counter. She was washing dishes.

"It'll just be me for dinner, it looks like," Alison said. "Mr. Andrews won't be back for a while."

Celeste frowned. "That's too bad. I make chicken grande because you both like it."

Alison smiled at the goodwill. "I'll make out, Celeste. You go home when you're finished." Celeste took care of three grandchildren. It struck Alison, with more force than she thought it would, how unbalanced a life she and Brock led compared to so many people around them. Her secretary. Celeste.

Brock yearned for a different life, she knew. I tried, Alison thought, consigning the memory of their worst moment again to a recess more secure, more closed than any vault or locked cabinet at work.

She went upstairs, keenly aware of how a relentless silence and emptiness prevailed in their bedroom.

Celeste called up, "I fix you a little dinner plate? You hungry. I make it tasty."

"All right," she replied, "thanks, but don't go to too much trouble, please." She realized that aside from a very light breakfast and light lunch, she hadn't eaten much all day. She was hungry now, a little faint even.

Alison undressed, showered for a long time, then sat on the bed, a towel on her lap after she'd opened the doors to the small balcony and a delta breeze fluttered in. Suddenly much of what she was doing seemed desperate and futile, and she had to fight the impulse to dive into that locked vault and its pain at the back of her mind.

She dressed hastily in sandals, tan shorts, and a pastel yellow blouse, combing her hair with hard, abrupt strokes.

"Dinner's ready, Mrs. Andrews," Celeste sang. "It's hot for you."

Alison stopped, lowered her brush. She knew what had bothered her ever since she left Porter Ridgeway's office.

Celeste called out again. Alison answered automatically.

They never mentioned Lara, Alison thought. The FBI did a thorough shooting investigation, and Merical never said anything about Lara being there or a third gunman at all.

Neither did I. I shoved everything Ed told me to one side. A trick Brock once told me. You can't trip up if you've deliberately forgotten.

Under normal circumstances she would have mentioned or wondered aloud about the mysterious third gunman. Both Ridgeway and Merical hadn't remarked on this singular omission from a seasoned, savvy prosecutor.

Alison put the brush down slowly. The breeze felt icy on her scented skin. Did Ridgeway and the FBI suspect her of working for Ed Nelson? Was the whole meeting this evening a security check?

She looked down from the balcony. The green lawn and turquoise pool merged with only slight pause into the yards, streets, and fine homes of the Fabulous Forties.

But was it all right and normal? Alison counted the parked cars, then darted to the windows on the south side of the bedroom. Were there any unusual vehicles? Strange people surreptitiously watching her? She stared at the kids blithely riding their bikes.

Celeste called again.

Am I being watched? Was I watched today? Alison moved back from the window. She was no longer hungry.

The noise, half-heard, half-remembered, woke her up. She was sitting in bed, the DOJ manual on electronic surveillance open, the light still on. A nearly empty bottle of pinot grigio sweated condensation like fear on the night table.

Unsteadily, Alison wobbled downstairs. The lights were only on in the kitchen, Brock at the microwave. He had stripped down to his underwear, his white shirt half-unbuttoned, tie off and he was barefoot.

"What time is it?" she asked, coming next to him.

"Two. I tried to be quiet. I was dying and I found this

in the fridge.'' He took her uneaten chicken dinner from the microwave. "Want some?"

She licked dry, thick lips, trying to focus. "Had mine. It's late, isn't it? You have trouble with Chandler or something?"

He sat down at the table covered with a gaily red-and-white cloth and began eating rapidly. "It was a madhouse, Ally, but a terrific operation. I couldn't get out any earlier."

He was exhilarated and yet subdued somehow. She sat down. "We were on the news and in the papers today," she said, touching his hand, then sitting back. "I'm thinking we should start charging admission for these performances." The depthless night pressed in, and she understood that only the magic circle of light with Brock kept it at bay.

"Couple of hams." He grinned, belched. "I am so damn tired. Just so tired. You must be, too." When he got up, he put his arm around her waist. They left everything and went upstairs.

He saw the wine bottle. She tensed, knowing he disapproved but wouldn't say so. "I had a rough day at the office," she said as he used the bathroom. "You want to hear about my rough day?"

"The highlights maybe," he replied. "That's about all I can handle tonight, sweetheart." He used a movie drawl.

"I'll have to leave all the good parts out."

Brock came out, changed into the T-shirt and shorts he wore at night. When they both were in bed, she turned the light off and pulled closer to him, the sensation of unseen watchers and judges very powerful. But it was Brock who clung to her, his head lowered to her stomach, drawing his body tightly alongside hers.

She told him about Ridgeway and Merical. He sighed deeply. "I don't think Popeye could find his ass with both hands."

She started laughing, and Brock said, "You ought to get blitzed more often, Ally. You're a great audience."

"I am not drunk," she said solemnly. "I am heightened. I hear a pin drop. I see a spider on the wall."

"You're drunk. But I'll go in with you tomorrow and

tell Popeye and Merical to shove it. Nelson would make surveillance in ten seconds and lead those clowns around by the nose."

She was surprised Brock opposed the idea, too. Probably because it would interfere with his secret effort to snare Nelson. The thought was stale, sour to her. He put his arms around her waist again, and she began stroking his hair slowly. "What a funny life," she said softly.

"Lots of kicks," he said lightly. Another line from some old movie they had once enjoyed together.

She felt reckless, rebellious. "Suppose Chandler was a snitch."

"And I was going to use him to run up the ladder for his suppliers?"

"Yes. He's lying to you. Could you keep an investigation using him together?"

"They all lie. You start with that. I've got a better one. Think about Ed Nelson as a snitch." Brock chuckled at the idea.

"What's funny?" she asked, recklessly pushing to the very brink of admitting what was going on.

"I don't feature Nelson undercover. He's got zero credibility so you couldn't use him in court as a witness later. He'd also burn you before you ever got to court."

"What do you mean?"

Silence, the faint sounds of a nightingale, a door slamming distantly. Brock didn't answer for a moment, as if pondering a new possibility. "Okay, this is another lesson in Snitch 101."

"Before I fall asleep." Although in her heightened state, she felt hyper alert, wakeful beyond fatigue.

"What you always have to watch out for with snitches," his voice was fading, his breathing slowing, "is their games. Chandler, Nelson, doesn't matter. They all play games. The trick is to keep them playing your game. Or keep whatever they're doing on the side from screwing up your game." He was nearly asleep. "If I was using Chandler, I'd make sure he wasn't turning my investigation to his suppliers. Nelson," he snorted, "if he was a snitch, you'd never know which way the burn was coming. But he'd burn you right to the ground."

Alison sat very still in bed. A collision of disquieting thoughts disturbed her. Ed Nelson could easily be playing his own game and she would never know until it was too late.

Plots could be in motion against her personally. If she was being watched, perhaps Brock was, too.

The second unsettling recollection struck her; that worst moment locked away broke free again. It was two years ago. She and Brock had just passed their fourth anniversary and she lost her biggest trial. Twenty thousand elderly people from Eureka to Fresno had been swindled by a telemarketing scam that induced them to join one regional telephone company and then, without notice, switched them into another company for much higher payments. It was called "slamming." This was the grandest slam that ever hit the Eastern District. But her key witnesses grew frightened, changed their testimony between grand jury and trial, went into hiding. Day by day in court, in full view of everyone, her case came apart.

Brock knew how badly she took the blow. So many vulnerable people had depended on her, clung to the defiant, blunt vows she'd made to get these scam artists. Alison shivered at the torment of that betrayal.

So Brock, as a surprise, took her to Lake Tahoe. They stayed at a resort right on the California-Nevada border, hiking in the tall pines, dinner sometimes at a casino restaurant, and they passed several afternoons with a light snow falling, just quietly watching the lake's misty gray waters.

She did not know with absolute accuracy if it was on one of those relaxed, healing nights that the baby was conceived. The timing, though, strongly suggested it was so. Brock was beside himself with happiness that she tried to feel, if only by reflection.

In bed now, Alison heard the nightingale's haunting, misleading cries again. Imitating any other bird, drawing victims to it.

Three months later, in the midst of a pretrial hearing, she'd had a miscarriage. It was over.

She'd gently stroked Brock's hair. *It's just the two of us, Ally,* he'd said to comfort her, *the two of us against the world.* And so it was, she thought. She'd bought him a silver ring to memorialize that pledge. *Aeternus,* she carved inside.

But the guilty, despairing secret she'd locked away and yet couldn't keep locked away was not losing their unborn child.

It was the scalding relief I felt, she thought, when I was lying on the examination table at the hospital. It was over. I was glad.

The memory couldn't be shredded or burned. It was impervious.

She tried to see Brock in the darkness. Even trying to explain her relief eluded her. It was something about those years in San Dimas, her mother's grotesque bargain to keep a roof over their heads. Or maybe, like the endless inventions of informants, it was something entirely different.

Compared to that, Alison leaned her head back against the wall, keeping Ed Nelson a secret is a piece of chocolate cream pie.

CHAPTER FIFTEEN

Three days later, Ed Nelson bumped and jounced along eleven miles of unpaved forest road in a four-wheel drive van. The driver was squat, tight-skinned, ink black hair cut down to his scalp. On his pale right wrist was an elaborate prison tattoo of a cross. His name was Vernon and Ed hated him. Neither of them had said a word since they turned off the last paved surface and vanished into the pines, elms, and barely restrained underbrush that threatened to inundate the dirt road entirely.

Ed took another drink of scotch from his flask, squinting out the window. It was cold in southwest Idaho even in May. He wore a scarlet ski parka. Vernon glared at him, seeing the flask.

"It'll kill you, man," Vernon said in his oddly high pitched voice. He'd lectured Ed on the evils of liquor, narcotics, alcohol, and dope during their drive.

"What won't?" Ed replied. It was at that instant he felt Bower's loss most deeply. Bower normally would've been the rider on this little jaunt. Bower would have been the negotiator back in Boise that morning in the relative comfort of the downtown Sands. Bower understood people like Vernon, like the rest of the Cobra crew. Christ, Bower might've joined some militia himself if only to steal them blind. Ed chuckled.

Ed sipped again. Bower, though, is dead. I've got to do everything myself.

"Hey, Vern, how much farther? I want to take a pit stop," Ed demanded. The tall pines, reaching into an impossibly blue crystalline sky, cast flashes of light and shadow over him as they drove at high speed deeper into the forest.

"No stops. I told you back at the hotel, Mr. Nelson."

"Mother Nature won't mind me leaving a little something." Ed stowed the flask in his parka. "Pull over, Vern."

"No way. The president said to bring you right away. We compromise our security if we stop."

Ed cursed and started to open his door. "I said pull over, you moron. I can cover the security myself."

Seeing his passenger's determination, Vern slowed, tiny black eyes bouncing in his head like angry ants. "I don't know if we were followed leaving town," he said, hand going down to the nine millimeter with sound suppressor at his waist.

Ed nimbly hopped out, trudging into the woods. His feet crackled over dead pine needles. It was so quiet he heard a bird calling as if it was in his ear. He stopped behind a towering pine and relieved himself. Jesus, for dealing with this crowd of monkeys, I should've given Bower that raise I kept promising him.

He finished, zipped himself, the four-wheel drive van's engine revving with Vern's tension.

Ed leaned against the pine. He took another long pull from the flask. He had a lot on his mind.

Mandy, Lara's girl, for one. What was she doing? First came the anxious, very insistent call three nights ago. She'd meet with him, work out how best to help Lara. Who, Ed knew for certain, was now in the custody of that number one asshole Brock Andrews, mate of the lovely and ambitious Alison.

Give me the hungry ones every time, he thought. I'll

make them drool. And lovely Alison was one of the hungri-est he had ever run across. Even Bower, whose taste in women tended toward the quick and dirty, confessed to heavy duty lust for the elegant, intelligent Alison.

Vern honked his horn twice, then sat on it. Ed cursed again. So what was going on with Mandy Hayes? Two meet-ings he'd set up, gotten down to the wire on each, and she'd backed out. He pushed away from the tree. "Cut the crap, Vern," he spat angrily. "Don't make me any more pissed off than I am."

She hadn't shown in Los Angeles at the Dorothy Chan-dler Pavilion, a nice crowded site that an amateur would conclude was safe right after a performance of the Mormon Tabernacle Choir. Nor had she appeared at their next try the following afternoon. Ed had stood outside the Wilshire Regency for an hour past the meeting time.

Something's spooking her, he thought as he got into the van again. I've got one more try day after tomorrow.

He wanted to have hold of Mandy Hayes in case Denny began to talk to Andrews. With Mandy on a leash, Ed calculated he could keep Denny from saying anything at all.

"Step on it, Vern," he said. "I don't want to keep the president waiting."

He tried not to sound too sarcastic. Although, as he glanced at Vern's taut, reformed substance abuser features and scooped out forehead, he doubted whether sarcasm of even the broadest kind would filter to the few remaining viable brain cells.

In the last couple of hours they had barreled out of Boise heading south, passing magnificent cascades and black basalt formations and postcard perfect farms, flash-ing by Twin Falls, crossing the Snake River's turbulent, spring-freshened rush, speeding through Hollister, and finally turning into the bleaker, more deserted forest not far from the border of northern Nevada. At the dirt road, Vern slowed, then jumped out long enough to swing aside a locked gate posted with a sign: AMERICAN NATIONAL PROPERTY. *Keep Out.*

The imbecile arrogance of the warning sign made Ed shake his head. Then they were off toward the hidden compound of Alison's first target, the Cobra militia.

Ed hoped the FBI was vigilant enough to keep this crew of clowns under surveillance. He hoped, as he bounced down the dirt road, some FBI camera was recording his passage. He very much wanted Alison, and the others who would later critically scrutinize what was going to be the biggest law enforcement failure in American history, to have a very clear photographic record.

Always leave trails. Ed learned that from his own father, the petty deal maker. People love trails. Paper ones, pictures, bread crumbs. It didn't matter. Leave a trail and people have the fuzzy warm illusion they can find their way out. They can find the truth.

A trail leads people where you want them to go, Ed thought.

Vern slowed. The trees around the dirt road were so high and interlocked that their branches provided a deep, purple shadow. Ahead was another gate, this time with a skinny sentry in flannels and hip boots. He held an assault rifle at port arms.

Ed had a terrible urge to laugh. Behind the sentry, who spoke in solemn, clipped phrases to Vernon, was another sign. It was large, green and white, and only slightly crookedly lettered: COBRA MILITIA: FREE AMERICA UNIT #1. There were, to Ed's sure and certain knowledge, only two other "units," both in mobile homes in the southwest.

Still, even if the Cobras had only about thirty members, even if the Davidians and the employees of an average-sized McDonald's looked like armies by comparison, it was possible to make the Cobras appear a vast, potent, devastating force.

If used correctly. If revealed correctly. If positioned correctly, Ed thought, getting out of the van. The sentry saluted. He was about twenty-two and didn't shave. He led Ed past the gate and off to the right, toward a cluster of small wooden and aluminum-sided buildings. Twenty or so men, women, and a few dirty children watched him pass. A generator rumbled nearby. Ed smelled stale grease from the flat gray dining hut.

Still, appearances were deceptive, as he knew and hoped. Before he was finished, the Cobra militia would be the greatest threat to national security since Pearl Harbor.

He was stopped outside a slightly larger gray wood building, its roof thick with pine needles. More goofy sentries, salutes, military pantomime. The flaccid flag hanging outside the building depicted an aroused cobra surrounded by thirteen sparkling red, white, and blue stars. Inside, Ed was saluted; he brushed away attempts to frisk him, and hoped the FBI hadn't gotten so close to this bunch that the building was bugged.

Hell, so what if it is? he thought. Everything I'm doing is sanctioned by First Assistant U.S. Attorney Alison Andrews.

That's where all the trails lead.

"He'll see you in a minute," a gawky older man announced. Ed sat down on a spindly wooden chair. The rude wood walls were garlanded with posters of menacing cops, minorities, and a stylized floating eye. He heard the clicking of computer keyboards. He sighed. If these loons weren't so essential to what he was planning, both for his own future well-being and lovely Alison's destruction, he'd be out of here instead of politely sitting down, reading what the head loon had written in the latest issue of their newsletter, *A Free People's Chronicle:*

> We believe that freedom is God's gift, not the political whim of GOVERNMENT. If Christ, meaning God, the ANNOINTED word of truth returns tomorrow and finds HIS creation without faith, HIS servants howling and drunk, HE'S going to wipe those people out with the hypocrites, liars, government servants, idol worshipers, tax men, agents of ATF, FBI, and etc. in a CLEANSING blast of the end time.

Ed folded the newsletter carefully.

Couldn't have put it all better myself, he thought.

Ten minutes later, conducted into the next anteroom

and then into the shrine itself, he faced a man in his mid-thirties, medium-sized, with a deeply creased face and a six-inch scar from his right nostril, down his lips, partly to his chin. His orange hair had been clipped to a stubble, making him look to Ed like a popular cheese-flavored snack. He had on a sweatshirt from a motel in Kona, Hawaii. When Ed came in, the man stared up from a fax sheet he held in trembling hands.

"Ed," the man said in a hollow, unearthly croak, "do I look like a psychopath?"

"Christ, no, Lyle," Ed said with unabashed duplicity. The man stared back, seemingly enraged.

"No, you don't look like a psycho, Mr. *President*," Ed added, wishing again that Bower stood here, pretending to be reasonable.

"It's just this letter." The man got up from a card table desk on which several phones, a red-shaded lamp, and papers were balanced precariously. "I did this interview with the Boise paper last week, and now I get this letter and someone's alerting me that the article's going to say I am a psychopath hiding out in the woods like" he spluttered, reading, "'a crafty, crazy, cartoony Robin Hood of the Right.'"

"You should see my PR," Ed replied, sitting down. "Forget it. That's my advice. Move on. We've got important things to do. You wanted to talk face-to-face?" Ed felt barely in charge of his annoyance.

Lyle Flecknoy, president of the unborn Free America, took up several more minutes by pacing, shaking his head, spouting intricate lines of conspiratorial links between Boise's major daily, the federal government, and unholy spiritual forces.

Finally he said, "So they got Dick Bower."

"They got him," Ed agreed. It was always best to agree with someone who had the bounds of creation discerned. "But I'm still going to make delivery of the AK-47s, Lyle. Mr. President. I'm going to let you have first crack at a new source, too. Grenades. Launchers." The Cobras had placed an order for four hundred assault rifles. Ed suspected they intended to become retailers.

Lyle Flecknoy chewed the scarred side of his lip. "We paid you a lot of money already, Ed. I haven't seen one gun. One bullet. One sniper scope."

"Our contract's pretty specific. You make the up-front payment to bind the deal. I provide half the shipment. You make final payment at the time of delivery. I'm telling you the first shipment's coming in two weeks."

"Bower said it would be later."

"Well, I'm moving the schedule up. You want these items sooner, right?" Ed ached for a drink. Lyle's croaking voice grated like fingernails on a blackboard. Two comic opera sentries patrolled outside the room's lone window, framed by the trees and militia members bustling around the compound.

"It's not my schedule, Ed," Lyle said. "It's God's. God is guiding this fire out of the west."

"So get the delivery payment ready. This's your heads up. I'll have planes flying. I can't just put on the brakes in midair."

"I want the rifles for three hundred per."

Ed snorted, nearly coming out of his chair. "You agreed on five. You're going to sell a lot of them, right? Make your money off that end."

"God wants this done. For five hundred dollars, you get us grenade launchers, too. And M-16s with silencers."

"Look, Lyle, I set stuff going in places. People have made commitments. I can't change the price now without taking financial punishment myself."

"Then you'll have to stay here."

Lyle Flecknoy's fingers danced over several buttons. Five men, armed with assault rifles, handguns, and Bowie knives stomped in. Ed noted that the oldest wore a cap from Waterworld, USA.

Surrounded by the soldiers of Johnny Sue Bob Nuthead, as he had described Flecknoy to Alison, Ed sat down slowly, the Waterworld man's eyes following him every inch. Ed spread his hands on the chair's armrests. Well, if the circumstances changed, you had to change your plans, too. He would have to advance a few things to buy time.

Alison wanted an FBI agent next to these bozos. So it shall be done now, Ed thought deliberately.

"All righty, Mr. President. We'll go your way. I'll tell you what. I will bring my associate, the guy who will personally service your needs for guns and ammo, to our next meeting. Set the two of you up. Now, this guy will make sure you get some antipersonnel weapons, too. How about that?"

"What antipersonnel weapons?" Flecknoy asked suspiciously.

"Mines. I will make sure you get a selection of Czech and Italian land mines. I'll palletize the shipment, no extra charge. From my plane to your trucks."

Flecknoy sat back. The guards flicked their eyes to him. Outside, a woman sang sweetly, the words indecipherable. Ed forced a smile. He suddenly realized how valuable Bower and Denny had been, running interference, smoothing the waters. He cursed Alison and Brock for so disrupting his life.

Finally, Flecknoy rose. He said, "Got this scar when a bomb I was making four years ago went up by accident. They got me in the hospital, they did some surgery on my vocal cords, make me talk funny, try to silence me. Didn't silence me."

"I hear you. That's why I'll get you my new associate, some really fine equipment."

He put out his hand. Lyle Flecknoy straightened his shoulders and shook the hand slowly. Flecknoy said, "So you're real clear here, Ed. I know you don't believe in what I do. But I want you to believe I am not, and none of my people are, afraid to die for God's cause."

Ed repressed disgust at the dry, cold handshake. "I think that's the basis for our very successful partnership, Mr. President."

As Flecknoy smiled, the guards lowered their guns a little, the tension seeping from the scene. Ed decided this was the moment to dangle the biggest, reddest piece of

meat before Lyle Flecknoy and get him to start snapping
at it.

"There's a huge society party outside Washington in a
couple weeks, June 17. Lots of celebrities, media. I get
invited every year."

Lyle Flecknoy gurgled, listening. The sweet singing woman's voice floated over them angelically.

Ed said nonchalantly, "You guys look like party animals
to me. How would you like to go to this year's shindig? As
my guests?"

He loved the president's puzzled, then wolfish grin. "Yes.
A flaming spear in the beast's belly. Are we bringing gifts,
Ed?" he asked, chortling as he watched the faces of his
followers.

"A good guest always brings a suitable gift," Ed said,
and not caring at last whether this collection of reformed
drunks, methamphetamine mainliners, and freelance
delusionals objected, he pulled out his flask and drank a
hearty toast.

Afterward, to show there were no hard feelings, Lyle
took him out to the new shooting range, and they practiced
firing various automatic weapons at targets drawn crudely
to resemble the president of the United States, a stereotypical Jew, and rampaging Hispanics and blacks.

As he shook with the gun's recoil, Ed thought with satisfaction that he had one more wheel to set spinning and
then there was only Mandy to bait, hook, and reel in.

Lyle and his militia would provide the manpower to do
that.

CHAPTER SIXTEEN

Several mornings later, Ed violently argued again with his wife Josie. The usual theatrics. He stomped out. He was in a hurry, a plane to catch out of Dulles so he could make a parents' day at his daughters' school, and the most important wheel of all to be set in motion.

And Mandy would be met that night by four of Lyle Flecknoy's goofballs.

It usually took Ed some time to get away from the farm anyway. Josie owned ten thousand acres in the Virginia hunt country, and driving along the winding, tree-shaded road, he often stopped to chat with the foreman about the horses or how the duck blinds were being maintained or whether there were enough deer for his guests when they all went on wild midnight shoots, spotlight on the lead Jeep stabbing ahead into the darkness.

Josie had been a rare, wild beauty when he spotted her years ago on the Washington party circuit. Now he couldn't divorce her. She had the money. She knew too much about him.

Today, driving swiftly down the road, the silos, barns, and outbuildings receding in his rearview mirror, he was more restless than those dark days waiting in fear on the Beirut beach.

By the forenoon, Ed had flown north and landed, rented a car, and driven to New Canaan, Connecticut. He admitted he'd gotten a little morbid since Bower's death, recalling the bad old days as a kid refereeing the drunken brawls and flung insults between his parents. The old man had been a minor league schemer, penny stocks that folded, novelties that went unbought. And a drunk who had ended up at Bellevue after the gold scam failure. Two years later, Ed had brought the old lady there, too.

His sister had by that time gone to the rooftop of the Plaza Hotel in New York, site of many happy childhood memories, and perhaps with a wide smile, jumped off. Alone among his family, he loved her.

Maybe she'd still have jumped, had I been there, he thought.

Maybe I'd have had the guts to jump with her.

He slammed the car door when he got out, taking a short pull from his flask. He wondered if the drinking and fights with Josie meant he was turning into his father.

Who never had the guts to jump when he should have.

The three men came into Gigi's Grill in Darien, off a busy, humid street, and sat near the back. They ordered lamb chops and salads and beer and tea in less than two minutes.

There were important matters at hand.

"I'm here talking to my kids' class," Ed told the other men. He chomped noisily on a bread roll. "In case anyone asks."

"Who would ask?" asked a slim, dapper Asian man of indeterminate age who had almost no hair. He seemed all slashes, lines and angles.

"Yeah, who'd want to know? You got some interest we should hear about?" The remaining diner was stocky but soft, young, in an open-necked pink dress shirt and brown sportcoat.

Ed finished the roll, wiped his hands. "Pretty soon now, I'll have the FBI following me everywhere."

The Asian man sat back. He drummed skinny fingers on the plastic-topped table. There were only a few people in the restaurant on a weekday afternoon. A light drizzle fell outside.

"Ed," he said, "you seem very casual about this situation. I take precautions, of course. Connor here does, too." He waved at the young man who nodded. "But why are you so certain the FBI will be tailing you? And. Are you certain they did not follow you here and have us all under surveillance now?"

"Shit. What is going on?" Connor asked.

Ed leaned forward, shoulders hunched. "Let's just say it's to our mutual benefit that the feds know exactly where I'm going and who I talk to."

"Not sure I like *that*."

"Well, I got a deal going with the U.S. Attorney," Ed said. "And I guarantee she will either put a tail on me herself or her boss will put one on. So what I'm supposed to be doing is selling military equipment to you bastards, and that is what they're going to report to her."

"Pardon me, Ed, old friend," said the Asian man slowly. "We've done a great deal of business together. So I can ask, what kind of arrangement do you have with the government?"

Ed saw the bloody fate awaiting him behind the studied courtesy. He'd get past his own nerves only because of the big payoff. He wore his most persuasive expression. He took another roll. "The deal is, I'm a snitch."

The young man blew out an expletive, started to rise. Ed put a hand and shoved him back down. The waitress brought their meals, and they waited until she left, the plates cooling untouched in front of them.

"Listen, you dummy, like Deng said, we've been in business a long time. I just made a deal to keep the feds off my back while we do some even bigger business."

"While you inform on us," Deng Li said, slight hand shaking a little.

"They're going to see what they expect to see, me talking to arms dealers. Then I've it worked out so they'll have to get nine million miles away from me forever." He glared at them, daring contradiction. He began eating quickly.

"How the hell you doing that?" young Connor Lake asked.

"I'm going to drag them through so much shit they won't come near me again. It's the perfect insurance."

"Very risky, Ed," said Deng Li, finishing his tea.

"Yeah, well, things got hot with that Syrian thing and they'll get hotter, and my way gets us clear."

"So what the hell do we do?" Connor groused.

"Not a fucking thing, you moron. Just act the way you always act."

Now Deng Li smiled, a slash across his tight-skinned face. He was buying it, Ed saw with relief. "Did Dick Bower's incident have anything to do with your idea, Ed?"

"I've got that taken care of."

"I've always told my superiors to respect your audacity and your intellect. If you were willing to sacrifice Bower, then I think you're sincere. But don't deceive me, Ed."

"Me neither," Connor Lake said, ravenously eating his chops. "I got a family."

Deng would make sure I was welded into a barrel dropped in the Atlantic or I fell out a window. Or maybe I'd just end up on a plane that landed in Beijing. Now that would be fun for sure, Ed thought grimly. Beirut a million times worse.

"I wanted all the cards faceup," he said. "Now we can do some deals. Connect some dots." He grinned at Deng Li.

"Can you get the items I asked for yesterday?"

Ed ordered another beer. It was now raining hard. The rain beat on Gigi's Grill.

"Deng, old pal, I can get, and I say this unequivocally, any fucking piece of hardware in the United States military inventory. Hell yes, I can get your black box equipment. But it's going to cost a shitload more."

They spent two hours arguing. Their voices were low,

then angry, finally murmurs. Glasses and bottles came and went. The rain ended, and shafts of weak sun spotted the sidewalk outside.

Prices were raised, lowered, then compromised. Shipment points arranged, shifted, then agreed on. The legal department at Applied Microavionics would draw up contracts, at Ed's direction, for the purchase of certain specified automotive and electronic scrap from Connor Lake's New Jersey company, Atlantic Industries. Then, on the same date, Applied Microavionics would transfer ownership to the seagoing containers of scrap to Deng Li's company, China Resources. The containers, loaded on shipboard at Long Beach, California, would sail for Manila and Hong Kong without customs or security inspection.

They would not, of course, hold automotive or electronic scrap. Nor would their true destination be Manila or Hong Kong.

The three men shook hands, raised toasts. Although later contracts and documents would memorialize that something had happened at the table that afternoon, what Ed truly traded was his handshake. His coming fortune and life depended on it.

"Connor," Ed said, "you're worried about getting hold of this stuff, aren't you?"

"Some of it's pretty hot," Connor acknowledged with a tiny grin to Deng. "Tech transfer like this's harder than most."

Ed sat back, feeling at ease for the first time since Lara called with the news of Bower's death, the details of that monumental screwup. "I'm going to nail down every item tonight, okay? I got a guy staying with me, guest. He's *embedded* in the DLA. I'll have the items recoded, ready to go by this weekend."

Connor nodded. He understood DLA to mean the Pentagon's Defense Logistics Agency which operated the vast military surplus sales apparatus called the Defense Reutilization and Marketing Office or DRMO. He also understood that Ed had contacts in almost every branch of government. The first time he visited Ed's offices, he was startled to see a dozen retired admirals and generals sitting at desks, working the phones like stockbrokers. "They make deals, I get a fifteen percent cut," Ed chuckled.

Ed could make things happen.

Connor also knew that before Ed and the late Richard Bower showed up at Atlantic Industries six months ago, the foundering machine tool import-export company was within a week of bankruptcy. Ed bought the company for almost nothing. In cash, too.

"All I'll ever be buying from you is scrap," Ed had told Connor, "and nobody gives doodly about scrap. You're buying stuff the military wants to sell."

"So why don't you buy it?" Connor, briefly defiant, had asked.

"Because I sell to people who don't want to be anybody's business."

Connor was left with the distinct impression, underlined by Bower and that joker Lara with winks and nods, that Ed Nelson was doing some sort of intelligence work for the government. There was certainly enough new money coming into the company to keep Connor quiet and sated.

They concluded lunch at nearly four-thirty, getting up stiffly. Deng had been vaguely puzzled by Ed's insistence on certain delivery dates. The scrap containers had to be at sea soon after June 17. They must not, under any circumstances, leave earlier.

"Trust me on this," Ed said, putting an arm around the other man's small shoulders as they strolled to their cars in the thick, pale afternoon air. "After June 17, we could box up the fucking White House and sail away and nobody would touch us."

Deng agreed to the dates because he was requesting, on behalf of his government, sophisticated American military equipment that was otherwise unobtainable, certainly at the comparatively cheap price Ed Nelson was demanding.

The Stealth tactical electronic warfare suite, the magical black box that took over when Stealth technology failed and kept the aircraft flying. Inertial guidance systems for fighters, bombers, and cruise missiles. Shoulder-held anti-aircraft missiles, and machine tools for manufacturing the complex curves of high-performance wings. Guided bombs. Computers with encrypted intelligence still intact on the hard drives from Kelly Air Force Base's "Security Hill" where battle plans, war game telemetry, and flight plan profiles were kept.

Deng paused at his modest black two-door sedan. Connor picked his teeth. A fire truck roared by and they watched.

"Can you tell me the significance of June 17, Ed?" Deng asked without pressing.

"It's a party," he answered by way of complete explanation. "So listen, we're straight on the payments? I don't want to get jammed on my money again."

Deng bent to Ed so Connor could not hear an agreement decided before this meeting. "Sixteen million dollars into your Cayman accounts on delivery of the scrap to Long Beach."

"No sailing without payment. I'll shut you right down."

"No sailing," Deng agreed.

Connor, who was content to let them talk to themselves, now smiled, shook hands. "Well, I got to ride off. Pleasure doing business as always." He got into a customized luxury sedan and honked on his way into traffic.

"There goes a prime reason I love what I do," Ed said wonderingly. "He'd eat a dead horse if I told him it was roast beef."

"I, too, must hurry, Ed. The embassy's putting on a cocktail party and my presence is commanded. I'm a prime example of the very successful Asian-American entrepreneur."

"Life's tough." Then Ed said sharply, "All this other shit aside, you going to deliver the forty-sevens on time? I'm going to have the guns before the end of the month?"

"Yes, yes," Deng said. "Four hundred AK-47 rifles. Cost deducted from your fee on this latest contract." He got into his car. Ed stared at him, with a look that was hard to fathom. At times, although he found Ed a pleasurable challenge to bargain with, a sense of hidden agendas and subterranean worlds in the man's mind disturbed Deng. "Buyer troubles?" he jokingly asked, engine started.

"I'll worry about the buyers," Ed said, turning away swiftly. "Just get me the goddamn forty-sevens."

Deng did not press this man who had created the most productive military equipment supply line from the United States to his country. And all, he thought, so obvious and trivial no one cared.

Ed got back to the farm after dark. He ate a hasty dinner so he could spend time laughing and joking with his guests and join them for the deer hunt later that night.

Josie stayed in her room. He knocked hard on the door and got ringing silence in return. These long-term sulks following fights were becoming routine, Ed realized.

The phone call at nine jolted him. Lyle's goofballs had missed Mandy Hayes. He cursed them. Then a second call came immediately.

He closed the study door. He wiped his sweating hands. He took deep breaths, then picked up the phone again.

"Mandy," he said carefully, "there were people, good people, waiting for you at eight. You didn't go to meet them?"

A huffed, nervous gasp from Los Angeles. "I don't know. I don't know. It didn't feel right."

"Mandy. I told it was all right. I told you these people would take you to a safe place and then we'd get Den cut loose from the feds."

"I didn't feel safe going to a taco stand, waiting for your friends. Suppose this U.S. Attorney and the FBI were there?"

Ed used one hand to take out a nearly empty scotch bottle from a lower drawer in the desk, untwist the top and pour a shot. "How could Andrews be there?" he said with feigned patience. "He does not know where you are or where you would be meeting my people."

"Listen, he left cards everywhere, the motel, my office. He got Den. I don't know anymore."

"I will handle Brock Andrews. But I need you to make one meeting we agree to. You wanted help and I will help, but we've got to work together. Okay?"

He heard the silence, like Josie's cold fury. He cajoled, explained. He was the epitome of reason.

Mandy finally said, "Okay. I guess I'm just nervous. I'm sorry for causing all this trouble."

"It's no trouble if we get together, get Den clear."

"I'd feel better if I was meeting you. I'll meet you someplace," she said firmly.

So Ed agreed to a final attempt, tomorrow afternoon at three. "In front of the Peninsula Hotel in Beverly Hills?" he said, making notes. "I'll buy you a drink, too."

"I may need it. I don't sleep very well since Den was arrested."

"Listen to old Ed," he said, downing the scotch quickly, his jaw tight, yet his voice light and sincere. "You work with me a little, Mandy, and I guarantee, I promise you, we will set you and Den up and you can have that child in safety and security."

"All right, Ed. I'll see you tomorrow afternoon. I guess I just need your personal touch." She sounded relieved.

Ed sat still after hanging up. He heard his guests, who had been freely liberating his liquor stocks since mid-afternoon, loudly talking, laughing riotously in the living room.

Okay. If the woman wanted him there personally, he would be there, and he would bring Lyle's goons in the back of the car; and when they had her they would duct tape her fucking stupid mouth. At that Ed stopped, his rage spewing nakedly. Control. Control, he thought. He got up and went to his guests, outward calm repaired. He took Colonel Buckland aside.

"Bucky," Ed said, "you with me? You sober enough? If you aren't, I'll sober you up." He yanked the man's shirt halfplayfully.

"What's going on, my old friend?" said the colonel. They were alone in an alcove near the front door, unseen and unheard.

So Ed said somberly, "You're going back to work tomorrow, Bucky. I saw people today. We've got to move some merchandise and meet some delivery dates.''

It was pleasing to note how rapidly Buckland's pickled brain locked on to the central idea drummed into it. Ed and he were invisible warriors for their country. "We're going in black,'' Ed had once told Bucky at an early meeting, "right under radar, right under everybody's nose.''

A DLA drone like Buckland thirsted for the spook bravado, secret ops, magical signs that Ed flashed around him.

"You tell me when and what, Ed,'' Buckland said, struggling for sobriety's facade. "I'll get your goddamn shit ready.''

Near midnight, still hollering, waving glasses, eight men and women clung to careening Jeeps that tore up and back along the edge of the woods and through pastures, spotlights mounted on the hoods lancing ahead of them. The men and a couple women carried rifles Ed supplied. When a champagne bottle was tossed from a Jeep ahead, he reflexively blew it apart. He grinned at the outraged shouts from drunks who thought he was shooting too close to them.

Ed's Jeep leapt over gullies, roaring ahead of the pack of Jeeps behind him. Suddenly, he yelled to the driver to slow down.

Caught in the spotlight's white beam was a tawny doe, white-tailed, running in frantic, futile terror. The other hunters saw it and let out whoops.

Ed had his rifle out first. This was his kill. He indulged in a satisfying image of Mandy Hayes trapped in an inescapable spotlight like this one just before he pulled the trigger.

"How did I sound?'' Mandy asked as she went on quickly stuffing clothes into an open suitcase on her bed.

"I believed you,'' Lila Martin said. "He believed you. Nelson's going to get a little surprise when a couple U.S.

marshals and me"—she handed a clutch of blouses on hangers to Mandy—"show up for the meeting."

They had been packing with rude, rough haste for ten minutes. Only take the absolute essentials, Lila said, making an instant inventory of the Orange Avenue apartment. "Whatever you're missing, we'll pick up for you."

Three suitcases, a smaller bag for the various medications Mandy took as an expectant mother, stood near the door. The lights were on in every room. She'd packed as much as she could of Den's clothes, toiletries, and several pictures they'd taken on trips.

"I feel like the bad guys are galloping through the gulch toward me," Mandy confessed. She was tired, feeling heavy and inert. "I'm not entirely sure who the bad guys are."

Lila picked up two heavy suitcases easily. "You know who the bad guys are, Mandy. You wouldn't have called us if you didn't. Wait here until I come back."

Mandy sat down on the sofa. She thought it might be the last time. Last time to visit the museum today and the day before, sitting in front of Monet and Cézanne, talking to the baby, trying to sort out what she should do, who she could trust.

She got up, glanced around to see what else might be necessary to take. It was only a short flight north to Sacramento, but she had the sense that it was like transitioning from one world to another. Brock Andrews had said to her this morning, "We'll take care of you and Denny. Ed Nelson's not your friend, he won't help you, he'll probably try to harm you."

Which, once she thought clearly at long last, was the one thing that made perfect sense. Then Brock Andrews had said, "Someone will come to help you make the move. It's just like stepping across the street, that's all."

Lila Martin returned, hefting the remaining luggage. Mandy shook her head. It was definitely not like stepping blithely across the street. It was traveling an immeasurable distance from the known to the unknown, the familiar to whatever lay in the dark.

But her hope was with Den. And Brock Andrews had Den.

Lila Martin said cheerfully, "All right, it's clear. Let's go, if you've got everything."

Mandy wanted the baby and Den. "I've got it all," she said. Lila Martin regarded her with intensity, as though with a sudden, profound understanding of the situation.

They walked quickly to a waiting sedan parked just outside. There were two marshals standing watchfully beside it.

Getting in back with Lila, Mandy confessed, "I've been jumping every time I hear a horn or loud noise."

Two cruising cars passed, and Mandy saw the marshals stiffen, then hurriedly bundle into the car and drive west toward the airport. The marshals were obviously apprehensive as well. The city's lights, hard, bright, colorful, seared her eyes. Lila chatted. Mandy was still wary about her. The empathy was there, the professionalism, too, but Mandy caught an unnerving detachment in the other woman's brusque manner.

I'm a job. Keep me happy. I'm not a human being to her, Mandy decided. I'm a package to deliver undamaged.

To interrupt the soothing, glib patter, Mandy said abruptly, "How's Den? You said you'd tell me. Now I want to know before I get on that plane."

Lila Martin stared ahead silently, as if trying to frame an answer.

CHAPTER SEVENTEEN

Early the next morning Brock and Alison sat in a simple cafeteria in a state office building just up the street from their own offices. He thought their conversation had been guarded, off-kilter. They both had important meetings in a few minutes, but he'd been deliberately vague about his.

Alison asked abruptly, "Have you gotten any unusual requests from Porter in the last couple of days?"

"Like what? He just came in and gave me the old hearty handclasp for the Torrance raid. Nothing else."

She silently stirred her tea. "I think Porter's running a security screen."

"On who?"

"Me." She said, mouth tight. She looked strained. "I'm not sure he's doing it. I don't know if it's his idea, the new FBI SAC, some directive from Washington. I just don't know."

Brock poked at the remains of his congealing eggs. "You have any idea why he'd run a check on you?"

"No. Unless he's worried I'm getting too much attention. I don't know. I really don't."

They got up and went to the car. He drove the short

distance down the street and turned left. The late May sun was up, a warm, dry day forecasted, all the state agencies starting to come to life. Live with someone long enough and you can hear things in their voice, their choice of words. Words turn in on themselves, become their opposites. Alison had just said, "I don't know," but he'd heard certainty instead. The games went on, he thought. She knows precisely why Popeye's candling her, seeing where the shadows fall.

"Something I did the last couple days bother you?" he asked irritably. "You mad about the Torrance raid?"

"Why would I be mad about that?"

"I don't know. Ever since I got back, you've been mad about something."

"No, I haven't. And if I've been a little preoccupied"— she was irritated herself—"I've got a few things on my mind. Like whether Porter's bird dogging me."

He nodded, wondering again why she acted wronged around him lately when he still bore the shame of the Nelson dismissal. I haven't done a damn thing to her. But he said, "Forget it then. I'll keep an eye open. If there's a security investigation going, I'll find out."

Alison got out in the underground garage, in the slot reserved for the first assistant. "I'll shake him out of his tree if this is a power play," she snapped. Then she whispered to him because there were people nearby as they waited for the elevator, "I think it really might be us against the world."

They were his words to her that day in the hospital when he'd still believed he knew her hopes and dreams.

"Yeah, sure," he answered when the elevator arrived.

He didn't tell her he was making a last attempt to flip Denny Lara into a snitch against Nelson later that morning.

Brock sat at the head of the long table in the spacious fifteenth-floor conference room. The biweekly meeting of his task force had gone on for an hour when he stood up at the lectern, DOJ seal on it, and announced, "We're going after Ed Nelson again. We're going to burn him to the ground."

He let the startled chatter build. Twenty men and women from the FBI, DEA, IRS, Customs, and ATF had applauded him at the beginning of the meeting because of the recent raid's success. Now they watched him with astonishment.

An FBI agent said quietly, "What do we go for this time?"

"Arms dealing. Drug dealing maybe. He's into a lot of things now. It's got to be a very strict need-to-know investigation. Don't put anything in writing unless you personally clear it with me." He noted the raised eyebrows among these career bureaucrats who created protective memos as naturally as breathing. "And you will only discuss this case with people in your agencies as you require their assistance. No office bullshitting. No staffing things out. We'll do all of that on the task force."

There wasn't much enthusiasm, he saw with dismay.

How could there be? None of them relished revisiting a failed investigation. Brock stood beside the large screen TV near the table. He had to fire them up. He told his task force about drawing a tight trap around Nelson. They would use wiretaps, surveillance, down and dirty searches of his businesses.

The ATF supervisor sucked air loudly through his teeth. "Tell me, Brock, how you figure this will work now? We all busted our backs for months, as I recall it. Overtime, missed meals with our nearest and dearest." He grinned at the chuckles around the table. "We'd do all of that crap again. For you. No question."

The man's face was stony. "But we went after the bastard and his plastic explosives, his people, the whole ball of wax. And he still got away from us."

Brock knew what was coming.

The supervisor's paled face tightened further. "Why the hell is this time going to be different, Brock? Why the hell should we go to the mat this time?"

Brock walked back to the head of the table. They were waiting to hear his justification for another run at Nelson, something beyond personal pique or the desire to restore his damaged reputation as an imaginative, successful prosecutor.

Unspoken, he knew, was the charge he might be going after Ed Nelson again simply to resolve some marital dispute with Alison, whose office was just down the hall.

He did not have a completely untainted answer to that last charge himself.

So he said firmly, "This time is going to be different. We will have an infinitely better shot at bagging Ed Nelson and shutting down his operations than we did before."

Lila and Jimmy Yee's superior at ATF broke in, "What gets us a better shot at him?"

"We've got a snitch close to Nelson this time," Brock said.

He desperately hoped it would be true.

Twenty minutes later, Brock met Jimmy Yee outside the concrete russet tower of the new Sacramento County Jail. They went through the special security station for cops, judges, and lawyers, showing their badges and getting slightly jaundiced stares from the deputy sheriffs sitting on metal stools. There was an electric buzz of voices, metallic clanking, and hard-soled footsteps in the vaulted lobby.

At the elevator, Brock said, "How's Lila doing with Mandy, Jimmy?"

"Things are tense but under control," Jimmy replied. He seemed in high spirits, as usual. "You know her. She'll be hard mamma or the lady's slumber party best friend."

They rode up to the eighth floor. Brock shook his head. "I do know Lila. I don't want her making Mandy angry."

"No mas, boss. She knows you need her to bargain with."

They stepped out into a corridor made apparently of stainless steel, and walked quickly to the security station at the far end. Leaner guards with more guns stood outside a series of electronically controlled barred gates.

Brock nodded, recasting his mind on the immediate problem about to confront Lara. He'd made very little progress thus far with Lara. *I went out on a limb just* now, saying I had a snitch near Nelson, Brock thought. The reinforced steel door to the jail's most secure cell opened. He saw Lara lying faceup on the flat bunk bolted to the metal wall. He made a silent promise.

I turn Lara right now or I lose Nelson for good.

Brock had no intention of imitating his predecessor in the U.S. Attorneys Office, carted out on a stretcher, consumed by the fire of impotent rage at unreachable goals.

He glanced at Jimmy Yee, who made a slight acknowledging nod.

"How are you doing, Denny?" Brock said as the steel door closed and the electronic bolts clanked behind him.

Lara looked up. He wore a white cotton shirt and beltless jeans and his feet were bare. His thick sandy hair was unkempt. The morning's sunlight slanting through the steel shutters on the cell's lone high window fell on his tense, boyishly handsome face. Several floors below them, there was a boisterous basketball game, and other inmates used the rec time to stare down at people on the sidewalk, whistling or calling obscenely to women.

Brock sat on the bunk. It was hard, one thin blanket over a mattressless pad. Jimmy leaned against the far wall.

"I said, how are you, Denny?" Brock repeated.

"Ask me again." Lara closed his eyes. His arms were crossed over his stomach, almost as if he were laid out in his coffin.

"Agent Yee of the ATF is present for the record, Denny. Like he's been for the other four visits we've had. He's my witness."

Lara blew a small breath, eyes open.

Brock went on, "And like the other visits, you can have your lawyer any time you want, you can tell me to go to hell, you can just lie there and go to sleep. I can't make you do anything or say anything."

Jimmy shifted, folding his thick arms. He wore a Dodgers windbreaker and lent a quiet, subtly menacing presence, as Brock intended.

Brock stood. The seamless, metal shell of the cell reminded him of being inside a giant aluminum toaster. He did not envy Lara spending the last three days here. Or the prospect of spending many more.

"Listen to me, Denny," he said. "I hope you've been thinking about our talks. How I can help you."

"I've been thinking," Lara said, swinging his feet to the floor. "Except when I get my fifteen-minute dog run in that tunnel for exercise, that's all I've done."

Every day, for just fifteen minutes, Lara was taken by three guards to an enclosed concrete tunnel on the roof and allowed to walk back and forth. That was his only time outside the cell. It was just possible, Brock knew, to see a square of sky, perhaps a slice of sun if the day was clear, through the one barred opening overhead. Then the guards would pass over the opening, and the sun would be covered by their boots.

Jimmy strolled to the shuttered window as Brock talked.

"Well," Brock said, "I've got another thing for you to think about. Have you heard of the National Tracing Center?"

"No."

"The ATF runs it. NTC can tell you where almost any gun in this country came from, right from the time it left the factory to the time you request the information."

Lara watched him now with growing interest.

Brock said, "I told you I'd find out about your gun. I ran the Lorcin, Denny. It's got an interesting history. Made in 1988, sold legitimately four times. Then used in two unsolved homicides last year in Los Angeles."

"What kind of homicides?"

"Jewelry dealer and a convenience store manager coming to work."

"It's not my gun. I've said that over and over. Who's it registered to? Ed Nelson? Bower?" The sardonic laugh was short, tinged with fear. Lara blinked quickly. Brock had had daily reports of Lara's restless, nearly sleepless nights, the muttering and bouts of crying. The meals left uneaten on the cart brought to him.

He's ready to go, Brock thought. I know the signs. Come on, come on.

"Denny"—he put a foot on the stainless steel toilet also bolted to the wall—"you're missing the operative fact here. The Lorcin was reported stolen two years ago. Then you say Bower gave it to you. What was supposed to happen? Have you worked that out? I bet you have."

Jimmy smiled very slightly when Brock waited a second before going on. "Bower gives you this gun with a bad history. You don't come out. We run you and the gun, and it looks like you tried a shakedown and you and Ray Kelso killed each other."

"That's an Ed scenario," Lara agreed slowly.

"He set you up. You don't owe him anything." Brock stood close to Denny Lara. "He will try to wipe you out until he's stopped. I'm the one who can stop him."

Brock watched the complex play of conflicting emotions over Lara's face. Lara stalked to the cell's far wall, near Jimmy, shaking his head. In a moment, Brock thought. It will come in a moment, as easily as giving birth to a second child.

Denny had already passed the first and hardest hurdle for a conscripted informant. He was letting himself be shown the way. He hadn't kicked Brock out.

Brock felt trapped, just like Lara. Maybe it was a bond Lara sensed. An old scene had intruded in Brock's mind: his father trying to talk to him from in jail. The same fixed smile, uneven twists of his body as he sat down on the other side of the visitor's room table, military police flanking him. The futile attempt to act normally, to carry on a normal conversation with his young son like they were still sitting in the living room or out camping and they were alone, the fire low and stars multitudinous.

But his father, face leaning close to the smudged plastic screen between them, only said, "You've got to be the man now. You've got to watch out at home if I'm gone."

Brock now put his hands in his pockets, feeling the currents in the cell as Denny Lara prepared to make the last leap across his own river chasm. "Your father's protecting them," Brock's mother had said bitterly that night, "and they won't lift a finger to help him. They're officers." She spat in teary fury.

He never copped out, never gave up anyone, just took the two years in prison after the court-martial, Brock thought.

Some men can't cross the chasm between betrayal and loyalty. My father confused betrayal and loyalty. I know Lara's churning that inside himself. And he's scared of Nelson, too.

Lara put a hand on the steel shutters, as if trying to grab the sunlight. He spun on Brock, and Jimmy tensed.

"I want to see Mandy. I've got a right to see her."

Brock realized he had to use his last and harshest bargaining chip. "You don't have any right to see her," he said, glaring at Denny Lara. "We make a deal this minute or you won't see her again."

"You can't stop her from coming here."

"Lara, I've got a federal grand jury standing by to indict you on fifteen counts of wire fraud, money laundering, banking violations. Chandler was very comprehensive in his statement to me. All I have to do is add Mandy as an accomplice."

Lara lunged forward, and Jimmy grabbed him. "She didn't have anything to do with it! She's not involved."

Brock let Lara struggle in Jimmy's implacable grip. This was the worst part of the care and handling of snitches. Convincing them there was no other way but his, no path but the one ahead. Nothing behind but burning ruins.

"You think I'm a fucking asshole, don't you?" Brock said quietly.

"You are a goddamn motherfucking bastard." Lara's head snapped from side to side, then slumped. Jimmy raised his eyes inquiringly. Brock nodded and Lara was let go. He stayed rooted to the spot, arms limp, head down.

"Den," Brock said firmly, "I will indict Mandy. I will send her and you to federal prison if I have to. That's how badly I want Ed Nelson. I am willing to do that if it forces you to help me nail the sonofabitch."

"You're the sonofabitch," Lara said, going to his bunk. He sat there. Jimmy went to the side of the bunk. "You're just like Ed. Bottom line guys. Fuck anybody on the way."

Brock whispered to Jimmy, "Don't grab him unless I say so."

Jimmy nodded. He'd seen this, too. They either exploded with rage or caved in. It happened in a split second, and you were never sure until the moment passed whether your new snitch was going for your throat or curling into a ball.

"I do care," Brock sat down slowly on the bunk. He glanced every so often at Denny Lara. Just a little further, a twist more. Lara was almost hooked. "I want to help you and Mandy get started in a new life. We'll write out a contract, and you'll testify for me; you'll provide information to my investigators, and I'll get you and Mandy to a different state. New identities. I do care." He paused. "When's the baby due?"

"Late August. If everything goes all right."

"I envy you."

Lara looked at him, puzzled by the words and their sincerity. "Sure you do," he said coldly.

"From now on, believe me when I tell you something. I do want you to have a new start. I do wish I was in your place."

Lara studied him, seconds painfully passing.

I need you. You need me, Brock thought.

Jimmy surreptitiously held up five fingers. He's betting five bucks Lara tells me to go to hell, Brock thought.

Then it happened, like passing from one side of an opaque membrane to the other. Lara scrunched up so he was propped against the steel wall, legs dangling over the bunk. The basketball game had obviously broken up suddenly because there was an almost preternatural silence muffling the eighth floor.

He started talking. They always started talking about whatever scared them most. "Ed told me once how he met Bower. We'd all been celebrating some deal," Lara said softly. "High-tech radar to Argentina. Anyway. Ed said he

was kicking around Ghana, getting some rusty old guns
down to guys in Monrovia. The Liberian liberation, he
said. He's in a dive outside Accra and he's going to order
from the menu."

Brock found himself smiling, partly with relief but Lara
was also a good storyteller, voices and gestures perfect.
Even Jimmy crossed his arms and listened with a grin.
Ed Nelson couldn't figure out the menu. Bower helped
translate. Bower had been in the jungle building heliports
with pygmy labor. Pygmies were salt of the earth workers,
Bower told Ed, unless you piss them off. He'd somehow
done just that and woken up to find himself deserted by
his workers, half-finished heliports stuck in the middle of
the Ghanian jungle. Week and a half trek back to Accra.

Ed was intrigued by Bower. He liked resourceful people.

"So they get along great and Bower orders the food.
The menu only has three things on it. All pidgin English.
All meat is 'bif,' for beef. There's 'bif what fly' which was
probably chicken or some bird. 'Bif what swim' Bower told
Ed was probably fish. And 'bif what crawl' you never order.
Bower'd ordered it on a dare and still wasn't sure what
he'd eaten."

The three of them, in Lara's security cell, laughed at
the recounting of that long-ago meeting.

"I mean," Jimmy spoke for the first time, "that could
be snake or worm, right?"

"If you're lucky," Lara agreed, and they laughed again.
Jimmy peeled off a five-dollar bill and slipped it to Brock.
There was no doubt which way Lara had jumped.

Brock got up. There was a great deal to do to cement
this deal in place. Nothing could disturb Lara's belief he
was doing the only possible thing.

Lara put his hands on his knees. "Ed's got some things
going right now with a bunch of crazies in Idaho that'll
curl your hair, Brock." He said the name crisply. "Ed's
got some fucking big things cooking soon. You better not
miss him this time."

Brock shook his head. "You've got my word Nelson's
going down."

Denny Lara half nodded, as if he didn't believe it yet.

"Agent Yee and I are going to get Mandy," Brock said.

Outside the Best Western Motel at the main north-south intersection of I-5, a small procession moved from room 258 down concrete stairs, across the parking lot, to Brock's government car. He walked a little behind Jimmy and Mandy Hayes.

"She's acting up," Brock said, low, to Lila beside him.

"Don't blame me, chief. I been sweet to this spoiled bitch ever since we brought her here. She thinks I'm one side of a Nazi," Lila said.

Jimmy got Mandy into the backseat, and kept a vigilant eye on the cars and people nearby. The motel's huge blue sign stuck out against the spring sky like a sore.

"Something's got her going," Brock said. "She hasn't stopped complaining for twenty minutes."

"This lady thinks she's a gift, Brock. She's smarter, better, you name it, and we're all after her and that precious con man boyfriend. Last night, she was all gushy over me; now she's making these demands."

"I don't want her tipping Lara over again," Brock said.

"Then you better watch out."

They had an uncomfortable short drive back downtown. Mandy Hayes, with makeup and a fresh dress, looked determined and mad. "I want to know exactly what you told Den," she said to Brock in the car. "I will not have you threatening him into doing something dangerous."

"Mandy, I don't have any surprises. I'll lay it all out for you."

"Just remember it's not Den alone here. You have to deal with me."

"I'll keep that in mind."

Underneath the bluster and demands, Brock spotted a frightened, disconcerted young woman. She would require delicate handling.

They proceeded through the jail's security, up to the eighth floor, and Brock watched with Jimmy and Lila as

Mandy gave the cell a quick, hard survey before taking
Denny Lara's hand. Lila muttered something acidly when
Lara and Mandy abruptly held each other tightly, entwined
as though main force would be needed to tear them apart.
Even Lila quieted when Mandy had tears on her face.
"What have they made you do, Den?" she asked.

"I'm going to give them Ed," Lara said sheepishly, hand
on her wrist, swinging it back and forth slowly.

"No, Den." Mandy Hayes loudly replied, then turned
an accusing glare on Brock.

CHAPTER EIGHTEEN

"Jillie," Alison buzzed her secretary, "get me Senator Cantil, please. Right away."

It was ten in the morning and her anger at Brock's blind selfishness was diminishing. Things had to be done to keep the Nelson secret right now.

It took some time to track Senator Cantil down. She was on the Senate floor, then perhaps in the cloakroom, finally snared as she came into a meeting of her subcommittee.

"Have you found anything, Val?" Alison asked.

"Too much, depending on your viewpoint. I've only got a moment or two, Alison. We're about to go into executive session."

"Tell me what you can now."

The voice Alison heard hissed and crackled over the thousands of miles. "Well, I'm a little disturbed. Frankly. Your information about my campaign contributions has opened a whole can of worms. There's talk of an ethics investigation."

Alison closed her eyes. "What turned up?"

"So far," Val Cantil said sourly, "it looks as though five major contributions came to my campaign committee from people who died several years earlier. Or who were so broke they were being chased by collection agencies.''

"I'm sorry, Val. But you've got to be in the clear. You didn't know there was a problem with the contributions.''

"My opponent, the one I beat?'' she said irritably. "He's filed a formal complaint with the Senate ethics committee. It should hit the papers any day.''

"I can tell you as a prosecutor''—Alison stared at the picture on her desk, wondering if any of them had ever been that unfeignedly happy—"unless there's some evidence of a tit-for-tat, Val, you giving something in return, this'll just be a nuisance. Sloppy bookkeeping during a hectic campaign at worst.''

The prolonged stillness across the country made Alison's throat tighten. She heard, as if distant and playful, the voices of other senators in the background, trading laughs, the easy comradeship of power. "Val?'' she asked firmly.

"We're about to be called to order. I'll get back to you in a little while.''

"You don't have anything to worry about.''

"From a certain perspective,'' Val Cantil said slowly, "some of my votes about certain Chinese companies might look suspicious. Like the money bought a vote.''

"That's ridiculous,'' Alison said hotly, sorry she'd even passed on Ed's toxic information. Or, the thought rose in her mind, maybe this upheaval was precisely what Ed counted on happening. But if so, why? "Val, did you find anything about Lara or his girlfriend?''

Someone was talking to Senator Cantil. "That's the other thing. Then I've really got to go for now. My investigators did their homework, talked to old acquaintances, you know the deep, dark club these people love to be in. Yes, coming right away,'' she spoke briskly to another person. "The natives are doing a war dance. Alison, Dennis Lara is in your county jail. Brock put him there under the name James Lynch. God knows why. About four days ago.''

Abruptly the line went dead. Alison hung up, sat back.

Porter's secretary called imperiously. Alison ignored her.

She got up, feeling a dull ache spread through her shoulders.

The shock of Val's news made her writhe inside her skin. For days, Brock had kept this information from her. It was not like the flash about Ray Kelso's shooting. This was planned, well-crafted. How could he carry off that intricate ballet of the last few days, their mutual courtesies and politeness, and still hide this from her? Maybe I don't know him at all anymore, she thought with mixed fear and outrage.

Alison left her office, passing the open doorways of other attorneys, clericals burdened with stacks of papers nimbly stepping out of her way. Brock had deceived and would go on deceiving.

Outside, she headed up the sidewalk. It was a warm, slightly cloudy morning. On the other side of the broad street with its wide, neatly tended grassy medians were state departments built in the formidable, numbing style of East European agricultural ministries. Alison rolled her head, trying to loosen the tightening, angry grip at her neck.

On impulse she bought a pretzel from a stand outside the mustard yellow Department of Education. Nelson was the center of her dilemmas. Got to ensure his reliability, she thought. End the games. End the fear of his games. She also had to guard against whatever Brock was doing, because it would certainly affect her undercover activities with Nelson.

The indistinct outlines of a bold idea appeared in her mind. It solved her Nelson problem and Brock's threat to the undercover operation. She walled away what Brock must feel toward her now. The necessities of the situation came first.

On the way back she nearly ran into Cubby Merical in the hall. He came from the direction of Porter Ridgeway's office.

"I've been looking all over for you," he said. He held a buff-colored file tightly.

"Here I am," she said, continuing past him to her own office. "I'm swamped, and unless what you've got is very important"—she sat down, pushing aside papers and files on her desk—"you'll do a lot better seeing me some other time."

"It's important." He put his file in front of her. "I'd hold all your calls." He closed her door.

Alison suppressed the desire to throw him out. Her new idea loomed perfect and insistent, and Merical was an unwanted delay. "You've got five minutes," she said.

He showed a wintry, empty smile. "After our little talk the other day, we've stayed clear of Nelson. Like the four of us agreed."

Alison watched him. He had splotches of hectic red at his cheeks, as if tension boiled inside. She and Brock had given Merical and Ridgeway a rough session several days earlier. It's ironic, she thought, how great a team we are. A real bureaucratic snowplow. She didn't think either Merical or Ridgeway forgot or forgave. "Four minutes thirty," she said.

He opened the file. "There's been no surveillance of Edward Nelson, Mrs. Andrews. Period." He splayed the large highresolution color photographs like a winning hand at poker. "These were taken thirty-six hours ago about a hundred miles south of Boise. Right near a national forest." He grinned emptily. "We've been doing some fairly intensive surveillance on the people at this location recently. There's a very reliable threat these people are getting a shipment of AK-47s soon. These are not people you want having any more firepower than say"—he opened his hands—"a water pistol."

Alison picked up the topmost picture.

Ed. Her snitch. Holding an automatic rifle, smiling and shaking hands with a stubbled, scarred smaller man in rumpled fatigues. Other oddly shaped, heavily armed men around them also in fatigues.

Jillie buzzed suddenly, and Alison started. "Senator Cantil on one," she announced.

Alison went from picture to picture. "Tell the senator I'll call back." She looked at the FBI agent. "Where were these taken? Exactly where?"

"Inside the compound of the Cobra militia. The funnylooking guy with Nelson is Lyle Flecknoy. He's the head geek."

"Do you know why Ed Nelson is with this group?"

"I can speculate."

Alison shook her head. "Then you don't know."

"Nelson's a gunrunner, Alison." He was neutral, reportorial. Definitely not friendly. "The Cobra militia's getting access to a large quantity of illegal weapons. It doesn't take a rocket scientist."

Alison saw the blinking red lights on her large phone console. Never make mistakes, even when you're wrong, she thought. Old advice from Val. She made a decision swiftly. "How do you know this militia is getting illegal weapons?"

"We've got a source in their compound," he said flatly.

"Your source is mistaken." She stood up, pointing at Merical. "I know you were listening when we went through all of this the other day." It was a cold, hard reminder. "Nelson is off-limits for now. Go back to your source and get the information more fully because it will not involve Ed Nelson."

Merical touched his jacket handkerchief as if he could make its folds more sharp. "Pictures don't lie."

"Go ahead and keep an eye on this group. I remember something about them from a DOJ threat bulletin." She waved a hand as though it was only a minor piece of information. "But, Cubby, if you go tromping around Nelson, you will put your foot in a giant hole and you will never get it out."

She reached for the phone, pressing the first of the blinking lines. "You don't need me to spell that one," she said.

He realized the meeting was over. He gathered the pictures back into the file. "I think I understand," he said. He studied her for a moment, then swept his gaze around her office. The plaques and carefully chosen pictures. Law books in one antique glass-fronted case and behind her desk on the wall. In a place of honor, a framed program for a long-ago basketball championship between Amherst and Williams, inscribed, *"To Ally. I would've thrown this game if you'd asked. With all my love, Brock (you know who)."*

She saw Merical nod, clutching his file. "Yeah, I do understand," he said. He left.

What he understood, she knew, was false. Brock was not running an operation with her, nor were they pursuing Ed Nelson together. But it might convince Porter Ridgeway and Merical to drop a security check on her, if one was going on.

Might as well let them all think Brock and I are still a dynamic duo, she thought. The shining pride and joy of DOJ.

It was Val Cantil again. "I'm sorry I was short, Alison," she said.

"I've had better days, too."

"Well, I've got good news for a change. Paulette Lurel's a major giver of mine. Old, old money. She's got a lovely place in Chevy Chase, and she volunteered it for any formal announcement we might want to make."

"I haven't even thought about the Senate race," Alison said truthfully.

"Think about it now. Seriously. Talk to Brock. Paulette has a big party every early summer. Everybody comes; the media covers it. The time and setting would be ideal, Alison."

"I don't know. When do you have to have a decision?"

"The party's June 17. A few days advance notice would help. Frankly, you've got to come no matter what you decide. Rub elbows with the Beltway crowd. For the cause," she said sarcastically.

She must mean my spontaneous outburst for more drug war funding, Alison thought. Val loves to get her little digs in. "I'll think about it."

"Talk to Brock definitely. See if he's changed his mind from the other night."

"Changed his mind from what, Val?"

"Talk to him. Please. I've got to go."

Val hung up. Alison thought again of those damned pictures of Ed Nelson, grinning clownishly as if he'd just won the lottery.

Val's ambitions for her could wait. She had much more immediate emergencies to handle.

CHAPTER NINETEEN

Alison swiftly made a series of calls before noon.
She was uneasy about what she'd find.

Using her title as a pry bar, she first called the watch commander of the Sacramento County Jail. "Do you have a federal prisoner in protective custody now?" she asked levelly.

"We do, Mrs. Andrews. May I ask why you want to know?"

"No. Is his true name Dennis Lara?"

Pause. Alison imagined the commander, veteran of departmental politics, not the bravest or brightest deputy sheriff if he was doing time at the jail. He was quickly trying to calculate who he'd offend least with his answer. Or how many points he might earn by being very forthcoming. He would need a favor himself someday. Alison guessed correctly because he began talking without hesitation.

"Lara's in the PC section on the eighth floor, ma'am. Been there continuously since he was brought in. Paperwork shows he's got federal charges pending. Rough stuff. Explosives and smuggling—"

"Who has access to him?" she interrupted. This was vital.

"Just the deputy in PC. Meals are inspected before he gets them. He eats in his cell. Gets an escorted exercise period."

Alison made notes. "Who's visited him since he came in?"

"Just a second here," a wheezy grunt as a too large body bent over an armrest reaching for a keyboard, she surmised. "Getting it up here on the screen for you right— now. Well." Silence.

"Who're his visitors?"

"Three. Two come in this morning, different times. Matter of fact, the three are upstairs with him right now. We've got an Agent Yee, ATF. Been in four times and currently. And an Agent Martin, also ATF."

Alison glanced at the framed photo near her hand. "The third visitor, who's that?"

"Assistant U.S. Attorney Brock Andrews, ma'am. He's the one who signed Lara in."

Alison nodded to herself. Of course he was. Brock had herded and roped Lara himself and was even now converting him into a snitch, she thought. And Brock's snitches were premium, patented. No guesswork about their loyalties or lusts, and if there was, Brock knew how to deal with it. "We've been having a confidential conversation—" she began, and the watch commander interrupted.

"Ma'am, I assume Brock Andrews is some personal relation of yours."

"He's my husband," she said icily. "That doesn't mean anything. You are not to disclose to him or anyone else that I've discussed your prisoner or any of his custody arrangements. There are lives at risk," she said. Ed, for one. Me. I'm certainly at risk. "If you discuss this conversation," she added, "I guarantee there will be severe repercussions." She was ready for the next important call.

"Say," the watch commander grunted, "excuse me, ma'am. I misread the screen here. Lara's had four visitors. Fourth's a new one; she just came in with the ATF people and your husband about thirty minutes ago."

"Who's the fourth visitor?"

"Signed in as Mandy Hayes. Signed in with your husband. Anything I need to know about here?"

"No."

"I didn't ask."

Alison felt the angry tension in her body flow away, replaced by a tingling rush of urgency. She got up, holding the phone, making sure her door was closed and locked. She stared through the large window at the city. She dialed Applied Microavionics on a direct line that did not go through the switchboard.

"I want to talk to Ed immediately."

"He's unavailable." The snotty young office manager. Alison had always wondered, given Nelson's cultivated reputation for adultery, if he was screwing the brittle, beautiful woman. Stupid. Of course he was.

"It's very important. Tell him it's his federal tax accountant." That was the emergency signal, and Alison disliked the necessity of using it.

"Financial trouble?"

"He's got to deal with it right now."

"Give me your number. I'll try to reach him." Blithe, careless.

"Tell him," Alison said bluntly. Few people ignored her.

It was nearly noon. The direct line phone rang less than three minutes after she'd called Applied Microavionics.

"Christ, Alison," Ed growled, "you put the fear of Jehovah in Bonnie. Why'd you do that?"

"Where are you?"

"Is this on the record?" Joking.

"There've been developments, Ed," she said. "I need your location."

"Seattle. I'm taking care of some of our Century Tech business. What's up?" Now he sounded concerned.

Alison turned her chair so she faced the glassed-in law books and tangible proof of her achievements on the wall.

"Stay low for the next little while. Don't go anywhere unless you go back to Washington, all right?"

"Can do, my love. For you. For a good reason."

"Two good ones. The FBI has the Cobras under surveillance and some great candids of you holding a 921 sub thirty weapon. That's what the law calls an Uzi."

"So it was. Your second reason?"

"Brock's got Dennis Lara and Mandy Hayes in county jail, and he's probably going to twist Lara." She waited for his usual burst of expletive-laden fury, but only a deepening silence came from him. The FBI surveillance news didn't seem to faze him, she thought. But Lara and his girlfriend and Brock together, that slowed him up. "The FBI has information the Cobras are getting AK-47s. I hope those are ours."

Nelson was irritable. "Shit, yes, forty-sevens, Alison. This's the deal we discussed two weeks ago. I set it up through Century Technologies, and the bastards think they're buying a truckload of functioning guns. What they get are forty-sevens without complete firing mechanisms. Duds. You've got to keep the fucking Bureau dickheads from stepping on our thing or I'm setting up all this for nothing."

"Let me work on it. But stay clear of the Cobras for a while. I don't want the FBI linking you to them again." She paused. She could hear secretaries, going to lunch a little early, passing outside and laughing about a popular TV star. "Ed, this is the time to bring a federal agent in. Let him handle the Cobras. It'll make things much easier at my end."

"Glad you mentioned it," he snapped. "I've got the inbred sonsofbitches in Idaho primed for it already. Yeah, let's put your guy in and keep me out."

The first step in her grand idea had just been taken. The next step was much harder, she knew.

"Listen, Alison," Nelson went on, cooler suddenly. "I'm counting on you to keep Lara from messing me up. If you want me to do good things for you, well, I've got to be available for the job, don't I?"

"I'll take care of Brock and Lara," she said. It was unavoidable. She had known that from the moment the watch commander told her Brock had Ed's former jester. "There's nothing here, Ed? Lara's solely responsible for the Kelso shooting?"

"Well, yes he is. And if he wasn't—" the slightest break—"would it make any difference now?"

"If you were the problem, I'd abort the operation."

"Now? Really? When it's all coming together?"

"You bet." And she believed it.

Then with a chuckle, Ed Nelson spoke softly. "Oh, yeah. You would. You're a huntress, a tigress on the prowl. Christ you're perfect. Tell you what, after this is over, and you're riding so high we'll all be down here waving up at you, you dump Brock, okay? You and me'll take on everybody." He spoke more softly, his voice lustful, then obscene, the images and acts brutal and sensual.

For a moment, she was startled. The crudity didn't bother her. A jailhouse wiretap once fed her daily atrocities far worse. It was Ed's inner intensity that came through. He's trying to say he loves me, she thought with amazement.

"Cut it," she replied suddenly. "I've got your 'Queen for a Day' letter. I can dump it in a heartbeat. I'm not aroused and not amused."

"Give me my letter, I'm a happy guy."

"Just stay out of sight until I set you up with the agent to put next to the Cobras."

When she hung up, Alison had an odd feeling. Ed Nelson repulsed her in many ways, but his ferocious energy was intriguing. She got up, making sure the drapes were tightly closed, shutting out the sun, giving her office a dark, cave-like quality. Saw too much of the sun you could never shut out or escape, she thought.

She wondered if Ed was lying about Lara. I've got to have my eyes and ears next to him, she thought.

There was one more person to talk to before she went ahead. She called Chris Metzger in Washington. She stood at the window.

"There's a problem," she said. "The FBI knows Nelson is talking to that group of crazies in Idaho."

She heard Metzger cracking sunflower seeds. "Great. This's the Cobras, I assume. Let the FBI play it out. A character like Nelson would naturally be under suspicion."

"They could trip over what I'm doing."

"No chance. I've put a memo on the operation and your Nelson reports in the safe. You're covered."

My Queen for a Day letter, she thought without irony.

Metzger went on, "As long as the FBI keeps you informed, what's the damage? You know where to steer Nelson to keep his skirts clean."

She turned from the window. "I think Brock knows, too. He's hiding something and he's going after Nelson."

"How can you be sure?"

She wouldn't list the dozen little hints at home, Brock's moods she knew so well. "He's targeted Nelson. I know he has."

"Well, again no problem. Actually, Alison, a gain for us. With Brock chasing him, Ed Nelson's going to have to stick to you for protection."

The final question. "I want to tell Brock."

"No. Under no circumstances. You are not to inform him. For all the reasons you know already. Look at it this way, Brock will do his damnedest to catch Nelson, won't he?"

"No question about that."

"Good. What makes Nelson's bona fides more believable to bad guys like the Cobras than your badass husband on his trail?"

"It's a mistake, Chris," she said.

"It's my decision. Got to run, sorry. But Brock stays in the dark." He hung up.

Alison nodded alone in her office. The last obstacle to what she planned had been removed. I can't talk to Brock, she thought, because a dumb office jockey like Metzger won't allow it.

But I can tell someone else.

"Jillie," Alison said to her secretary, "I'm taking a long lunch." She took a small black purse. She had to hurry.

Alison walked out of the building just as the Cathedral of the Blessed Sacrament several blocks from the capitol tolled the noon hour. The bells sounded pure and implacable.

It was only a five-minute walk, across L Street's moving throngs spilling out for lunch, past the malodorous carnival on the K Street Mall of wandering guitar players, aging immigrants sitting and smoking on decorative planters outside week-to-week hotels, spindly kids with agate eyes looking to score too many ugly things, and the state workers and well-tailored and barbered lawyers and lobbyists from around the capitol, and into a purple-black glass tower. The lobby was glowing rosy stone, and she took a slow elevator up to the tenth floor.

The Bureau of Alcohol, Tobacco, and Firearms was not listed on the building directory in the rosy lobby. Nor did any plaque or sign announce that the regional offices were behind two large, blank doors. Alison walked by three bulging black plastic burn bags stacked in a corner near the doors, on the tenth floor's silent corridor.

She pushed into the offices. She heard laughter, then a soda can popping open somewhere in the back.

At the reception desk the frosted glass partition was slid back halfway. A middle-aged woman in a thin red sweater looked up.

"I'm here to see Agent Yee," Alison said, reaching in her purse, pushing the badge and DOJ identification to the woman.

"Do you have an appointment?"

"No."

"He's not in." She glanced at the chalky, smudged sign-out board to one side of her desk. "OTF. Out to the field. He should be calling in very soon."

Alison nodded. She saw the glimmer of nervous recognition on the receptionist's face. "I can wait a few minutes."

She sat down on the single blue plastic chair. She looked at the sign-out board. Lila Martin was also OTF. It didn't matter if they both came back from the jail. She'd talk to Jimmy Yee alone, and if she was persuasive enough, he wouldn't repeat anything to Lila Martin. Or to Brock. Or to anyone.

One lesson she'd absorbed from informal seminars Brock gave on undercover work when they'd both had a cocktail or two before bed, when they lay alone by the pool on rare, sparkling weekends, was that everybody parceled reality. Life went into boxes that never crossed, mixed, or spilled over.

The perfect insurance against ever making a mistake, even when you were wrong.

The receptionist asked tentatively, "Would you like a cup of coffee?"

"I'll just wait, thanks."

Alison took a quick, clinical inventory of the office. Ansel Adams prints, clipboards of bulletins on the walls. A dank, encrusted coffeemaker on a small plastic table. A black battering ram in a corner was decorated with plastic holly and balls from some Christmas past.

Two older male agents passed her. They dropped their voices, then sauntered on. Alison sat back tensely. If she could pull it off, Jimmy Yee would be hers.

Along the walls, in every empty space between brass plaques commemorating dead or retired agents, were OPSEC exhortations. They look like those World War II posters, she thought. Loose lips sink ships.

The operational security warning directly across from Alison said in large black letters, ARE YOU AWARE OF THE THREAT?

Oh, yes, she thought.

She wondered how she'd put the proposition to Jimmy Yee.

She wondered, eyes shifting to the doors just opening, what she'd say to Brock tonight. Or tomorrow night. Loose lips and threats, she thought.

* * *

Ridgeway and Merical went to a crowded Mexican restaurant down the block from the California Water Resources building.

Although there was a long line of chattering people standing under the trees or shielding their eyes from the sun as they waited to get in, Ridgeway knew the owner. He and Cubby Merical were quickly seated outside, their orders of beer and carnitas brought instantly.

They ate and talked low, sitting close together. No one noticed them.

"I told her we've got somebody inside the militia," Merical said, wiping a rim of beer foam off his upper lip.

"She buy it?"

"We'll see. If it comes back and those peckers start looking under mattresses for a snitch." Merical shrugged. "Then she's spinning information to Nelson." He attacked the tenderized pork in red sauce, mopping his face with paper napkins that soon piled up around his plate.

"Oh, damn," Porter Ridgeway said, burping, stretching his neck in the tight shirt collar. "I'm not going to let her bust my balls like she did the guys in L.A."

"Let's go slow, Port. She's got friends, and this might be some screwup Nelson's backing."

"But she is a ballbuster." Porter Ridgeway pushed his plate aside roughly.

"One hundred percent."

"She's got her Inaugural speech written, I bet. First woman president. My God. Not on my back, lady." Ridgeway took out a tiny bright blue case and from it a gold toothpick. He worked the toothpick around in his mouth. "Got another call this morning from the same State Department fag. They remain"—he rolled his eyes up—"interested in any situation involving Edward Nelson and the government of mainland China. His name's popping up. Weapons are going to move. Big money."

"I told you it's not just those refugees from *Deliverance*." Merical leaned in. "Look, Port, if Alison Andrews' is bought and paid for by Ed Nelson, it ain't for some two-shit deal with a bunch of peckers in the Idaho woods.''

"Damn right it ain't," Porter Ridgeway said as they both got up. Porter Ridgeway took the restaurant's owner by the arm, one hand at his elbow, the other shaking his hand vigorously, and the two smiled and laughed loudly.

Ridgeway and Merical walked back to the U.S. Attorneys Office. At a long light, Ridgeway said, "I would expect that bagging a couple big ones like Alison Andrews and Nelson is going to make waves in this country like you haven't seen for years.''

"If there's something to bag and if we have it on all fours with tapes and videos. That's how this puppy's got to go down." Merical put his hands in his pockets. "I'm not totally happy with the thing.''

"Why the hell not? Why the hell do you think I broke my ass getting you here now, Cubby?''

They briskly walked across the broad street. The sun was hot on their backs, and state gardeners were mowing the medians and grass on the other side of the street so the air was heady with a musky, clean smell.

"I don't have a problem with glory." Merical grinned lopsidedly. "I feel very uncomfortable about Alison Andrews. She could go down hard over a mistake, an innocent mistake.''

"Or she's working for and with one of the biggest assholes we've ever had.''

"Yeah. That's what bothers me the most." Merical shook his head sadly. "Brock's a good guy, too. People'd cut their arms off for him.''

They rode the elevator up to the fifteenth floor, the conversation growing more circumspect and quiet with other people nearby. Porter Ridgeway faced Merical in the hallway just outside the law library. Clerks inside bent over computers and books through their lunch hour.

"So I want to know if Alison and Brock are in business together. Show him your Kodak moments and let me know what happens," Porter Ridgeway whispered hoarsely.

Several minutes later, Cubby Merical walked into Brock's

empty office and sat down. It was a small room, barely large enough to contain the square solid oak desk, two leather chairs backed against a wall, and a bookcase filled with an assortment of law books, manuals, awards, and honorary caps from various law enforcement agencies. Merical noted the dusty basketball trophies on top of the bookcase. The window was undraped, showing the city's panorama.

There were no photos other than a framed head shot of Alison, her honey-colored hair glowing as if lit by a halo, placed beside the telephone console. Brock would have to see it every time he was on the phone.

Merical crossed his legs. He held the file folder and stared thoughtfully out the window.

Brock's secretary peeked in. ''Mr. Andrews is still out, probably at lunch, Mr. Merical,'' she said with a slightly nervous smile.

Merical shifted his legs, laying the file on his lap.

''I'll just wait,'' he said without turning away from the window.

CHAPTER TWENTY

At the same moment, Ed Nelson stood at the window of the Beverly House Hotel in Beverly Hills, California. He brooded looking across the street at the huge frosted stone and marble sprawl of the Peninsula Hotel. He had just told Alison he was in Seattle.

His room was on the small hotel's top floor, the third. He could see the Peninsula's curved entrance drive off Wilshire Boulevard, scurrying valets snagging cars, and militarily costumed doormen opening the glass doors for guests.

Vernon barged clumsily into the room with a small chipped tray covered by cheap paper napkins. "I brung all they had, Mr. Nelson. Just some old doughnuts and bananas left over from that continental breakfast."

"Close the door," Ed said, still looking out the window. "You're letting the air out." The small hotel's cramped halls were stifling, and he'd turned the room's air conditioning up.

"Did I miss anything? Has she shown up yet?" Vernon dropped the tray onto the round table pressed nearly against the double bed. He crowded eagerly next to Ed at the window.

"Get back," Ed said.

"I just wanted to see," Vernon complained. "My people are down there waiting for her and you made us come up here."

"That's right. Be quiet," Ed said. His hands were deep in his pockets. He could see a dung-colored sedan parked just to the right of the smartly tiled entrance drive. There were three members of the Cobra militia sitting inside, making a poor pretense at reading newspapers.

"All you been doing is ordering me around." Vernon sat on the bed, lifted a napkin and plucked at a stale doughnut, then peeled a banana. "Phone rings and you tell me to go get something to eat. I think you don't trust me."

Ed turned from the window. "I don't," he said, smiling. He went to the tiny bathroom, tore the wrapping from around a glass, and poured an inch of liquor from his flask into it. He certainly had not wanted this throwback in the room, listening to his conversation with Alison and the various filigrees and frauds he'd attached to the truth. Mandy Hayes had apparently set him up, too. Which meant he had no handle on Denny either because Brock now had both of them.

Well, he sipped slowly, I've still got Alison.

"Isn't she supposed to be outside there by now?" Vernon glanced at his watch nervously.

Well, Mandy Hayes sure isn't making an appearance today, Ed thought. Let's see if Alison's got the situation scoped accurately.

"Listen to me," Ed said, taking Vernon by an elbow, hauling him to his feet like a bag of sand, pointing at the telephone. "You call 911 now. Say you've just seen three guys acting suspiciously outside the Peninsula Hotel. They've got guns, too. It's an emergency. Repeat that to me."

Dutifully, like a child reciting for a capricious relative,

Vernon screwed up his taut face and repeated Ed's instructions. Then he made the call. He spoke in a falsetto.

When he hung up, Ed said, "Why did you sound like that?"

"I thought it'd be scarier from a woman." Vernon smiled awkwardly.

Ed shook his head and poured out another inch of scotch, then stood at the window. He didn't wait more than a minute. From four parked cars across the street and in front and behind the dung-colored sedan, he counted eight men, in slightly bulky suits and ties, which indicated some kind of bulletproof vests, swarming out, guns drawn.

"Oh, my Lord," breathed Vernon, also at the window.

Ed approvingly noted how speedily the sedan was emptied, the three Cobra militiamen thrown to the asphalt, hands behind their backs. Two more men, holding stocky rifles with sniper scopes ready, appeared on the rooftop of the Peninsula Hotel. Three black-and-white Beverly Hills police patrol cars screeched up, and the shouts, slamming doors, flashing red-blue lights, had already drawn curious people. It was hard to tell whether something was going on or another movie was filming in town.

"Rapid response," Ed said, finishing his glass. "Okay, fella, time to check out." He put on his suit coat. There was nothing else of his in the room. He'd registered using one of several useful names. He wiped the glass with a paper napkin.

"What about our guys?" Vernon demanded angrily, darting toward Ed, who stopped him with a fierce, awful smile.

"Unless they were really stupid, Vernon, they followed my instructions and they don't have anything on them more dangerous than a ballpoint."

"You don't leave your people behind."

"Christ. They'll be cut loose. They're just some guys minding their own business, right?"

"I don't know why you done that to them."

"I'm sure you don't," Ed said, stepping into the stuffy

hall, moving with surprising speed as Vernon struggled to stay with him. "You get back to Lyle and tell him everything's just fine. I'll be bringing our new supplier to meet him very shortly."

"Everything's gone to shit! My people are under arrest; that nigger you said we'd get, she's loose."

Ed went down the faded carpeted stairs at a half run. He avoided the small lobby and headed for the back of the hotel and his rented car. When Vernon still wouldn't settle down, Ed stopped suddenly and put a finger very lightly in the center of the other man's sunken forehead. "Everybody makes sacrifices. It's the nature of the world. I learned a great deal just now from the very small sacrifice your guys are making."

I learned, he thought, that Alison's right. I now have an attentive audience for everything I do.

Which, as every magician knows, is exactly what you want.

He turned and gently opened the rear door of the hotel, then stepped into the parking lot. The swelling crowd and amplified voices giving commands filled the adjacent street. Ed figured he'd take the alley out.

Vernon's pinched face had gotten tighter, more confusedly angry. "Why'd I have to make that call?" He gripped the car door.

Ed slipped inside the car. "They tape 911 calls, Vernon. Now, go back and do what I told you."

Ed slammed the door, shaking off Vernon's grasping fingers, and backed into the alley, then sped away. The noise, lights, and confusion faded behind him.

A small convoy of three cars rolled up to the less used Peacekeeper gate to McClellan Air Force Base near twelve-thirty. When the convoy was stopped by guards, a major in uniform scampered from a light blue car parked inside the gate.

Brock got out of the second car and spoke to the major, who walked down and stared briefly into each car, counting. The major returned to the guards, said something to them as Brock got back in his car. A moment later, they were waved through. The major's blue car now led them to the right.

"Like every honor farm I was ever at," Denny said, sitting in the backseat of Brock's car beside Mandy. He hugged her tightly, blew out a slow breath. "Except much bigger."

"I feel like I'm coming home," Brock said.

"Were you raised in the joint?" Mandy asked waspishly.

Brock said gently, "It's not a prison for you, Mandy. Neither of you. It's the safest place you could possibly be."

"We'll decide that ourselves," she said, eyes forward. The base spread out expansively around them, and the car shook abruptly from the roar of a great C-5 Galaxy transport lumbering off a nearby runway. Denny watched it rise into the sky.

"Bring back old memories?" Brock asked.

"The places I've been with Ed," Denny said almost regretfully. "Things I've seen."

"I want to hear all of them."

Mandy pulled Denny closer, as if to shield him from Brock's influence. "We'll decide that for ourselves, too," she said, voice trembling a little. Her display of defiance was mostly show. "I'm not jumping off any bridges until I have our guarantees all down, signed, witnessed, and then signed again in blood."

Brock turned and looked ahead. The major's car had gone right again, then left along what appeared to be a narrow, too perfect street of identical compact 1930s white brick, art deco homes, each with one large leafy elm in the yard, little brass plates near the door. An airman was unscrewing the plate at one house, and the major's car stopped there and he bounded out. Brock was beside him, taking in the street, the quiet, the world within a world here. He felt an ache of nostalgia. It was indeed like every post he'd lived at as a child.

"Here we are," the fidgety major said. "Balboa Drive. Base officers' housing."

Brock supervised Mandy and Denny being shown to the

house. He stayed a little behind. Jimmy and Lila, along with three U.S. marshals, got out, and Brock held a hand up. He wanted Mandy and Denny to enter the house on their own, not be forced into it.

Lila came to him as the couple vanished inside and the airman finished taking the plate off, giving it to the major.

"I don't want to play referee again," Brock said to Lila firmly. "She's important because he's important, so just ease off."

"That one's a piece of work," Lila said, hands on her hips.

"She's scared. She's got a baby to worry about. Plus Lara."

Lila had not calmed down from the rowdy, bitter shouting match back at the jail with Mandy.

What Lila doesn't catch, where she's tone deaf, Brock thought, is for the sound of fear.

"Okay. They've gotten the smell of the place. Let's tuck them in," he said.

As they walked into the living room, Jimmy said, "I can come back to baby-sit any time you want, boss. But I got a couple hot spots back at the office."

"Take off, Jimmy. Thanks for dropping everything to watch Mandy at the motel this morning."

Jimmy grinned. "I'm loving every second of Nelson's payback." He wiggled a finger at Lila. "Need a ride to the barn, darlin'?"

"I'll stay," Lila said coolly. Brock nodded. She was a solid pro. "The sweethearts are upstairs."

Brock looked around. The living room was basic, an upholstered sofa, several covered chairs, flat beige walls with flower prints, a pristine brick fireplace. The only oddity was a drooping enormous fern in one corner. Brock bent and picked up a very small slipper with a bunny face at the toe.

He handed it to the major, who grimaced, and quickly stuffed it in a pocket. "Oops. I'm very sorry," the major said. "I thought we went through the place."

"I'm going to have it checked for electronics anyway,"

Brock said. He headed up the stairs, Lila and the major following.

The major said to him, low, "I thought the uniform was a good touch, don't you? Normally we don't wear them."

"Very impressive. Very official," Brock said. The major was second in command of the base's Office of Special Investigations detachment. He had been eager to help arrange housing for a federal witness. Brock looked in the master bedroom, then went farther down the hallway.

"It's still a prison cell," Mandy said fearfully, walking the bounds of the second bedroom. "Call it anything you want." She touched the neatly made bed, a colorful afghan spread over it. "You throw somebody out to get us here?"

Brock thought of the child's slipper. "We're all lucky. A colonel was transferred to Turkey with his family last week. You need a secure place near the federal grand jury."

He glanced at Denny Lara, who looked quietly through the empty closets. Brock had an instant insight about Lara. He always lets Mandy do the important talking if she's around. Probably did it with Nelson, too. Lara's definitely back in the dog team. He needs to be led. I can use that.

Mandy groaned, holding her swelling middle, and sat down on the bed. Denny hurried to her. Lila turned away, as if it was merely a play for attention.

"Are you all right?" Brock asked.

"I'm just fine. Thank you. Now before we start in with grand juries or this nice little jail cell, I want this witness here"—Mandy pointed at the major—"to hear your promises, Mr. Andrews. We are not under arrest, are we?"

"No," Brock said, "you're not. I dropped everything when you walked out of Denny's cell." He moved his head slightly, and Lila closed the door. The bedroom was filled with them and two small teak bureaus, white-shaded lamps, and a large mirror on the outside of the bathroom door. It looked as though Brock was talking to an audience in the reflection.

"In return for his full and truthful testimony before a federal grand jury and in any prosecutions which follow,

Denny will get complete immunity. The only thing he can be prosecuted for is perjury. I want the truth."

Denny Lara chewed his lower lip. "Maybe you don't."

"I do, Denny. You can take that to the bank." Brock strolled past Lila and the major, both standing in front of the bedroom door. "The U.S. Attorneys Office and the Justice Department will provide protection for you during any trials. Afterward, we'll put you into the Witness Protection Program if you want. New names, new homes."

"Starting when?" Mandy asked, slowly moving a hand over her middle. "For how long?"

"Today. I'll come back at four with a written contract for you to sign, Denny. Tomorrow we'll get into the information you've got, what we started talking about back at the jail this morning."

Denny Lara stood up, head low, hands in his pockets. "Then what?"

"I'm going to put you in front of a grand jury here as soon as possible. I want indictments."

Mandy trembled more. "Well, we're in a fine bargaining position, Mr. Andrews. You grab Den. You put him in jail. You threaten him."

Lila suddenly snapped, "You came to us. You begged for help."

"It's all right." Brock put his hand up, giving Lila a hard stare. "Denny knows what he's done and how he can help himself."

"But you've always got me and the baby over him," she shot back.

Brock was impassive as Denny Lara raised his head, chewing his lip more worriedly. In a blink, it could all go sour. Yet Lara's got to realize I'll never lie to him, Brock thought. "That's right, Denny's always going to know his family's at risk," Brock said, seeing his own stolid image in the mirror. His voice dropped. "You both made a bargain with the devil, not me or the Department of Justice. Ed Nelson's your problem, with or without me. I'm offering you the only way to get clear and get clean. That doesn't sound like such a crappy arrangement."

Before Mandy could say anything, Denny nodded.
"Maybe it isn't." He sat down beside her again, taking her
hand, turning it, letting it go. She looked at him, the
tremble tugging at her face, and he touched it, as if to
quiet her. "Lie down, Mandy. I'll get these people out of
here, okay?"

She nodded, lying back. She still had on her brown
sandals, and Denny carefully took them off. She said to
Brock, "You didn't get this place this fast. I don't care if
the people went to Turkey or Timbuktu. You had it ready
back when Den was in jail."

Brock looked at her sympathetically. "I figured you'd
make the right choice."

Downstairs, Brock sent Lila and the major outside. She
lingered in the doorway as Denny Lara started down.
"These two are trouble together," Lila said. "They'll play
you back and forth. Good puke and bad puke."

"I'll be careful," Brock answered. Lila closed the front
door. The nameplate of the departed officer lay on a small
coffee table where the major had left it. Brock pensively
picked it up. Denny Lara pointed at two U.S. marshals
roaming the kitchen, then the backyard. "What are they
doing?" Denny asked sharply.

"You'll have protection inside and outside," Brock said.
"Another team will relieve them tonight."

"Shit. Mandy's going to hate that," he said, as though
worrying about an item he'd forgotten to buy her at the
grocery. "If I promise to be good"—he smiled ingratiat-
ingly—"how about letting us be alone. Maybe just
tonight?"

"Not possible, Den. You know Nelson, too. I don't want
to take chances." Brock nodded to the marshals,
motioning them over. They were middle-aged, calm, their
holsters concealed beneath wide-cut suit coats. They shook
hands with Denny.

Brock walked Denny Lara out to the yard. Lila leaned
against the first car. "We'll bring some personal stuff for
you tonight, too, Denny. I want you and Mandy to feel

comfortable here. Before we get someplace else worked out, you'll be here for a while."

"But not under arrest," Denny said sardonically. He looked at the front yard, the lush tree and trim lawn. "So suddenly I'm an average guy in the 'burbs with a kid on the way, two-car garage and grass to cut. Amazing."

Overhead another C-5 appeared to hang momentarily motionless in its slow ascent. Denny put his hands on his ears. Resupply for somewhere in the world, Brock thought. Trouble near and far.

He was startled by Denny Lara's quick, unpleasant smile. "The white race militia guys and the guns I told you about at the jail? It's the tip," Denny Lara said, smile gone, eyes drifting to the government art deco house, the street of quiet homes and order, like they would all vanish in the next moment, "just the tip of the iceberg. Ed's got something much bigger cooking on high heat. Maybe before you come back tomorrow, you should find out about DRMOs." He correctly pronounced it, like it had to do with skin. "Ask him." Denny motioned at the major chatting with Lila. "I bet he knows a hell of a lot. Kind of an hors d'oeuvre, Brock, before we have the main course."

Brock waited until Denny was back in the house and one of the marshals gave him a high sign at the picture window, drawing the drapes. He handed the brass nameplate to the major. "You forgot this. Maybe the old family needs it," he said with more force than he intended.

For a moment Brock again saw the brutal, swift expulsion of his own family from their base home after his father's conviction. A soldier had ripped out their cheery nameplate near the front door. He'd indifferently tossed it to the grass.

"They'll have a new one made up," the major said, puzzled at Brock's tone.

"Where to, chief?" Lila said, holding open her driver's side door. "I'd like to scrape those two off my clothes."

"I think I want to have a little lesson in military surplus first," Brock answered. "Let's go to your office," he said to the major.

The two-car convoy swung out of the artificial enclave, onto a flat wide road, passing huge warehouses and hangars. "It's like a slice of Norman Rockwell pie back there," Lila said. "Just don't look too close."

"Everybody needs little con jobs to get through the day," Brock replied. He wondered what Denny and Mandy were thinking back in their strange new illusion of a home.

When Alison said she wanted to talk to him, Jimmy Yee hesitated, then asked, "You mind driving a little? I feel better going someplace."

"I hear rumors my lawyers think their offices are bugged, too," Alison answered with an ironic smile. Jimmy Yee remained suspicious she was waiting for him at the office.

He drove them out of the city center in his government car, across the Sacramento River and then over a levee highway. It was only two lanes, and Alison realized it allowed him to easily see if anyone was following them. This's going to be a rough sale, she thought. He indeed sees threats.

Neither of them spoke for twenty minutes. A fair delta breeze had sprung up, sweeping in from the west through the Carcinas Straits, scattering dust high into the sky, giving the sunlight a faint orange tint. The full eucalyptus and elm along the levee shook and rustled. Jimmy Yee, with a burst of tire-squealing speed, rushed by a slow tractor pulling a hay wagon.

The brief excitement roused him. "You like burgers, Mrs. Andrews?" he bit off.

"Of course I do," she said, smiling. "Who doesn't?"

"You never looked like a burger person," he said.

They pulled over shortly, parking on the land side of the levee. Alison looked across brown and green fields of wild mustard and corn, dotted with small farmhouses. Dusty roads were wrought in the fields like leather carvings.

The sight of the farms and fields steeled her, an echo of her past. "I'll bet you're wondering why I asked you here," she said to Jimmy Yee as they strolled across the levee highway.

"You'd win that bet," he said.

You're mine, she vowed.

They walked down rickety wooden stairs to a packed dirt space planted thickly with dirty white-topped tables, lines of broken colored lights strung from the trees ringing it. The cold spring river gushed noisily to their left, a few power boats and skiers slicing white-foamed wakes in it.

She sat down and they ordered hamburgers and coffee. There were four other people eating, two river rats arguing and a well-dressed couple talking quietly.

"Bet that's the current office romance." Jimmy Yee grinned, sizing up the couple. "Everybody comes over to this side of the river for a little privacy."

"Brock says you, Lila Martin, and he are the . . ." Alison started.

"Three Muscatels," Jimmy Yee finished it. "All for one."

"You can help Brock and yourself."

"Doing what?"

She didn't answer immediately or directly. Their coffee arrived in cracked, inch-thick mugs. A greasy mist hung over the restaurant's kitchen nearby. Alison saw his coiled intensity. "I assume I'm not one of your favorite people," she said, sipping the coffee. "I said some tough things about the way you handled the search warrant on Ed Nelson five weeks ago."

"You did say some things." He studied her.

"There was a very good reason."

"I was doing my job and I do it pretty well."

Alison looked at the overlaid initials and vulgarities scored into the tabletop. "I was doing my job, too."

"Can I call you Alison?"

"I'd rather that than what you're probably thinking."

He smiled a little, sniffed, crossed his thick arms on the table. "What the hell's going on? If you wanted to talk to me about something, you just call and I'd have come running to your office."

His interest is keen, she realized. And he's guarded around me. That'll work. She put her hands carefully on the table. One of the river rats jumped to his feet and pointed a quivering finger at the other, his voice shaking with indignation. "I ain't giving you none of my pruno again, you goddamn thief," he swore.

A burly waitress came over and smoothed the waters quickly. Both Jimmy and Alison shook their heads and grinned.

"You ever tried pruno?" he asked her.

"Once. When I took a tour of Pelican Bay. The warden had a jug of it he'd just confiscated from some lifers."

"Smooth brew, right? Goes down nice." Again they both grinned. Prison-made liquor had the ability to strip the roof of your mouth raw.

Suddenly, Alison said sharply to Jimmy Yee, "I need you to help me. I need you to work for me."

"Put in a request, Alison," he said, grin gone. "You're first assistant United States Attorney in this district. Unless I wanted to get my retirement ticket punched by refusing, I'd be assigned to your office."

"I want you to work for me, Jimmy," she said. "Not the U.S. Attorneys Office directly."

Their hamburgers came in ancient plastic baskets, wrapped in oily paper. When the waitress was gone, Jimmy Yee started eating and said, "I don't understand that last one. How does that do squat for me or Brock?"

Alison kept her face blank. "I need you to go undercover."

"Sure."

He's losing interest, she saw. Figures. I'm offering a bureaucrat's chore. Spy on some clerk stealing paper clips. Outside agencies were brought in for these monumental investigations.

She said, "Ed Nelson's working for me."

He stopped chewing, hamburger frozen in his hands. "Say again, please."

"Ed Nelson is my informant, Jimmy. He's been working for me ever since your case."

She picked up her own hamburger and took a bite. She was surprised at how hungry she was. She looked at Jimmy Yee, still sitting stiffly, astonished.

"I bet pruno would hit the spot right now," she said to him.

"You'd win that one, too."

CHAPTER TWENTY-ONE

Sunset came just as Jimmy got the barbecue coals glowing and the marinated chicken sizzling on the grill. He and Lila hauled citronella torches out for the first time that summer and stuck them around the small backyard. Two Bureau of Narcotic Enforcement agents and their wives sat drinking half glasses of Wild Turkey at the picnic table. In the lemony fading light, Jimmy's little daughters romped and yelled until Trisha called them back inside. Lila wondered why Jimmy's wife was so edgy and almost rude tonight. It was unlike her.

"It's not you," Jimmy said, like he heard the unspoken question. "We had some, you know, disagreements before you got here." He went on turning the chicken, sipping a beer.

"Verbal altercation?" Lila joked.

"There you go. Verbal altercation," he said. He wore a silly red apron that said YOU THINK IT'S HOT NOW? in melting letters. He finished the beer, deftly popped another bottle open, and went on turning and drinking, never raising his eyes to her. "Not quite a domestic dispute. No punches thrown and the furniture's okay."

One fixed point in a changing, unhappy world, Lila knew, was the mystical, uncritical love Jimmy and his wife shared. Sometimes he'd be on the phone to her five, six times a day if the task force had an out-of-town operation going. With good nature, he took a lot of crude humor about it from others on the task force. Except Brock, of course.

"I bet I know what it's about," Lila said soberly. "Your visit from the Ice Queen."

"I'm changing my opinion of Alison Andrews," he said flatly.

Later, the girls tucked in bed after ice cream, the night's breeze rattling stiff palm trees in the backyard, Jimmy took Lila into the garage, closing the outside door. Trisha sat at the picnic table looking into space, nursing another large glass, while the BNE guys and their wives grew rowdy.

"She's putting away more than I've seen," Lila said to him.

He waved angrily. "She wants to cop an attitude, okay. Great. Trisha won't even talk to me about it. I told her it's a chance of a goddamn lifetime, and she just does that." He waved again toward the closed garage door.

"What's so red hot?" Lila asked, leaning against the van. "You guys shouldn't be doing this. You got a great life."

He didn't answer, but bent down slightly to open a waist-high old safe. "I got this one last weekend," Jimmy said. "Colt. Cherry, right?"

He held out an antique Colt six-shooter, the handle still deep brown, the metal gleaming as if new. Lila admired the workmanship. He put the gun back into the safe. "How come you ain't married, Lila? Woman who appreciates fine weapons?"

"You were taken," she answered.

Jimmy grunted. "I thought you had the hots for Brock."

"It's always been you, babe," she said, looking away quickly. He hadn't caught it, just smiled at her as always. Around the spotless garage, partly filled by the family van,

were sleds and skis, tool benches and carefully racked saws
and hammers. Lila said, "What did the Ice Queen want,
Jimmy? How long did you take to tell her to go to hell?"

"I didn't tell her to go to hell."

"Is that why Trisha's worried?"

"She ain't worried."

Lila shook her head. "You are one dense fucker sometimes. What's Alison's scam?"

He slowly swung the safe shut, and spun the combina-
tion. A single bare hundred-watt bulb blasted the garage
brightly. Jimmy's expression was almost truculent. "No
scam, darlin'. She's got a job lined up and it's going to help
Brock. Shit. It'll help the Three Muscatels." He grinned,
hoping she would join in.

"Alison fucked us all over, so I'd like to know how that
works."

"I can't tell you the whole deal," and when Lila snorted,
he went on angrily, "but it's a straight deal. I looked it all
over because I was thinking just like you, like we've all
been thinking since she threw out our C-4 busts."

"I've been wrong? All this time?"

"Damn straight. Couple weeks, you'll see how wrong."

"Shit, Jimmy. She did some great sales job on you."

He slammed a hand against the safe. "It's no sales job.
You think I couldn't see that?"

"Let's find out what Brock says about it then."

"I can't tell him. You can't either."

Lila pushed away from the van. "Then as far as I can
see, she's just blowing smoke." But Jimmy's zeal couldn't
be dismissed. "Okay," she relented, "how much can you
give me?"

"Just a little. Between us. Alison's going to put me next
to a bunch of militia assholes with AKs."

"BFD," Lila said. "Task force could set up an undercover like that."

Jimmy smiled, an infectious delight spreading from him.
"But even better, she's got a way to get me in with a crew
of Chinese arms smugglers, darlin'. Big timers. Moving
big-time military hardware out of this country."

"How's Alison doing that? The woman never ran an undercover operation in her life. She just looked pretty."

"Well, she's got a fucking perfect way to do it now, and with me on the inside, lying and buying, making the right moves"—he bobbed his head exuberantly, hoping Lila would see the perfection of this plan—"I will serve up one hot steaming platter of fried motherfucking gunrunners and white punk pukes."

But Lila couldn't digest the implausibility of Brock's wife reaching out for Jimmy and persuading him to join her in some harebrained undercover scheme. Outside, one of the BNE guys clapped wildly, and someone's wife tried to quiet him because "the kiddies are sleeping." Trisha never said a word.

"It's going to be great, Lila," Jimmy promised, blowing out a breath, swelling his chest as if to beat on it. "Maybe I got to tell these slobs to keep it down around my family." He moved toward the garage door.

Lila put an arm on his rocklike shoulder. "Trisha's got it right. It doesn't work out right. That's why she's scared."

He had a hand on the door. "She says it's dangerous. She says everything I do is dangerous."

"Yeah, Jimmy, I bet that's how the Ice Queen nailed you."

"Say what?"

"Alison sold you on how dangerous this deal was."

"Give me a break," he said disgustedly, barging into the backyard and pretending to curse his guests. Lila got another beer and sat down next to Trisha Yee, but neither said anything.

Lila felt very lonely and suddenly afraid.

"I can't find anything. I don't know where anything is," Mandy complained, slamming cupboard doors in the kitchen. "Is there a plain drinking glass in here?"

Denny strolled in, dropping a plate of dinner scraps in the sink. "If you can't find any, they'll buy a set."

She turned on him. "It's not funny, Den. We're prisoners and you made one bad deal for us.'' She found a plain glass, filled it from the faucet and carried it into the living room. The television was on in the tiny family room to the left, one of their guardians watching a medical drama. Mandy stared thoughtfully out the sliding glass doors into the twilight shadows in the backyard. "See him?'' she said softly, "just sitting back there?''

Denny stood beside her, hand low on her back, barely touching. As if they were spying on a rare bird or animal, they looked toward the darkest shadows underneath two apple trees. A small red glow appeared when their other guardian took a deep drag on his cigarette.

"Be fair,'' he said to her. "They stayed away, as much as possible. It's like they're not here at all.''

"Oh, they're here,'' she said, drinking the water. "Now what? Do we go kick the other one out of the TV room? Sit in there with him like he's a friend of the family and watch shows? Maybe have some popcorn?''

Denny didn't answer. The marshal left them in the TV room, and they tried to be distracted by the medical drama.

Mandy held him close. Chairs scraped in the kitchen; the door to the backyard creaked open and closed. Another bulky body settled into a groaning chair in the living room.

Denny knew what Mandy was thinking, as she knew what went through his mind. They thought of his ride to the courthouse tomorrow. They both thought of the unseen shape again in the shadows beneath the apple trees, only a sporadic red dot in the darkness indicating anyone was there.

Denny said to her quietly, "Ed Nelson's the enemy.''

"I hope he's the only one,'' she answered.

"I can't find the little gold necklace,'' Alison said, carefully sorting through her jewel box. "The one you gave me last anniversary?''

"Wear something else. You'll look terrific.'' Brock swiftly

knotted his burgundy tie in front of a tall antique mirror. "Reservations are for eight, Ally. Got to hustle here."

She glanced up. "You gave me that necklace and I feel very much like wearing it tonight."

"Don't make yourself crazy. You don't have to put on a show for anybody. It's just me," Brock replied, snatching his gray tweed sportcoat from the closet. "Tonight's going to be a great time, so take it easy."

"Why are you rampaging around here?"

"Because we will be late and we will lose our table at one of this world-class city's best restaurants." Brock smiled, but it had a tinge of insincerity, the same taint their conversation had carried since they started showering and changing.

"Let's go out," he'd suggested suddenly when he got home. "We could use a night together." She'd agreed readily. There was a sense this was a last chance. They both felt it.

He now looked at Alison's slim, tapering back, tan skin glowing in her moss green, low-cut dress as she sat in front of her bureau mirror. Jesus God, he thought, let us get through this night unharmed.

He went to her, tenderly massaging the rigid neck and shoulders. His hand moved down to her round breast, gently cupping it until she slowly rolled her head against his arm.

"We don't have to go out," he said.

"I'll find the necklace," she replied, shuffling through the jewel box again. Brock stepped back.

"I'll wait for you downstairs," he said, turning. They talked to each other, but the words had become foreign, as if they had lost the gift of understanding. And today he'd seen Merical's photos, grasped part of their meaning. Heard Denny Lara fill in more pieces and the OSI major's droning, almost winking delight as he explained the crimes of military surplus sales.

That's a whole lot to ignore, shut away, he thought. A lot of secrets one night together has to keep at bay. We've got a lot we don't want to say out loud to each other anyway.

He poured a small glass of merlot and carried it to the kitchen. Celeste swabbed the countertops with flourishes of a huge cloth.

"I hereby set you free," Brock said. "Take tomorrow off, too. Get a start on the weekend."

She wiggled her eyebrows excitedly. "You look so nice. For you both I have little gifts."

He protested, then stood grinning as she returned with a stiff, freshly starched handkerchief she expertly slid into his coat pocket. "For Mrs. Andrews, you give her this." Celeste handed him a bloodred rose, perfect as if sculpted. "You two got to enjoy yourselves like this every night."

A moment later, Brock heard Alison coming down the stairs. He finished the wine and pecked Celeste on the cheek, then marched to the foyer. "I'd have thought of this myself," he said with mock gallantry, presenting Alison with the rose, "but duty to my country occupied me too much." There was a faint, absurd touch of Ronald Colman in his voice and bow.

She bowed. "It's lovely. I found your necklace." She touched her throat where the slender length of gold hung.

"You were right, Ally. That's the only one to wear tonight." He held out his arm for her, feeling pleasure and sadness and fear mingling at once. "You didn't give up."

"I don't surrender," she corrected him.

Dinner downtown, at the sparkling restaurant incongruously across from the city's bus maintenance garage. A faint constant rumble of buses coming and going played underneath the music and energetic conversation.

Alison lifted the first cocktail. "One dry martini at the most," she intoned.

"Two at the most." He wagged a finger. "Three puts you under the table."

"Four under the host." Alison smiled, touched the glass to his. "Thank you, Mrs. Parker."

The owner came by, effusively greeting them, recommending the veal. She was a broadly gesturing, well-known woman, and every other table watched with envy as she bestowed time and attention on the elegant, yet somehow melancholy couple.

When she left, Brock and Alison both chuckled. "After martinis, I feel like a beef haunch," he said. "Something solid. Real."

"I was going to say lamb or beef." Alison sat back. "You look tired," she said.

"You do, too."

"We could both quit."

"Write books. Paint. Take up sailing."

"I could brush up," she reminded him. "I did a lot of sailing after law school. We should've done some." There was a small, hard regret lodged in her voice.

"Yeah," Brock feigned jealousy. "Sailing with that prick you met at Stanford. Christ, Ally. Think of that. Tonight you could be sailing around some polluted lake with a fat-assed partner at Pillsbury, Madison." He drank deeply of his martini. She shook her head at another. She touched the gold necklace again.

"I knew what I wanted."

"Me, too." He took a quick drink. "Well, sailing's out. What else could we do? How about raise some kids?"

"Okay. We can talk about that."

But instead of plunging into that dangerous subject, they lapsed into awkward silence for a few minutes, eyes on their silverware or drinks.

Then Brock said brightly, "Six years. It's gone by so goddamn fast."

"It's not our anniversary. You sound like tonight's history."

"I feel kind of epochal this evening," he said with a smile, voice husky. "Looking at you."

"The look," she said softly. "I know that look."

He thought instantly of Alison at poolside one past sum-

mer afternoon. He'd come from the house and she was
half-asleep. She was stretched full length on a chaise, long
hair splayed like a pillow around her head, eyes closed,
legs open, her deep blue shorts tight between them. Her
bare feet rested on her running shoes. Her arms, pulling
her compact breasts taut, seemed to reach toward him.
She was utterly relaxed, uncharacteristically at ease, and
utterly desirable.

It was a cruel thing to make such a moment, and even
the languid lovemaking later, so evanescent.

They ordered finally. Alison settled on braised lamb,
and he suddenly had little interest in the food. He picked
a steak.

"Martinis and steak," Alison teased. "Reckless, Brock."

We won't survive, he thought clearly. We're sparring
beneath everything, and one of us has to land a blow.

"My day," he said, poking at the cold salad when it
arrived, "was nuts, Ally. But informative."

"I'll trade you information for the meetings and noise
I went through."

Brock ate mechanically. "I found out everything I ever
wanted to know about DRMOs."

"Enlighten me."

"Well, you know, Ally. We do these cases, undercover
cases from McClellan or down in the Bay Area, one of the
defense contractors. It hasn't been anything spectacular.
Civilians carting away paper or desks or computers. Sell
them at flea markets."

"I don't remember any big cases." She dabbed at her
mouth with a stiff cloth napkin. "What intrigues you suddenly about military surplus?"

"It doesn't have to be desks and tires, Ally," Brock said,
marveling at her coolness. Lara hinted that Nelson was
into DRMO crimes. Merical had photos of Nelson. Alison
didn't want surveillance of Nelson. Alison cut Nelson loose.

Maybe it's all wrong, he thought hopelessly. Maybe she
doesn't know.

But he went on, the words forced from him like water
through a too narrow pipe. "Ally, a DRMO is the wrong end

of the cow. Everyone looks at the front end. Procurement is where you find whistle-blowers and scandals. All the money and glamour is at the front end, big planes, big ships, smart weapons. But here's the kicker. Exactly the same equipment comes out the other end as surplus and no one notices."

"Cow shit," Alison said. "Is that it?"

"I'm not joking. Somebody could move every sensitive, top secret piece of military equipment through a DRMO."

"You'd need a network."

"Not necessarily. A few people in a few places and they wouldn't even have to know what they're doing is illegal." He sliced roughly through his hardly touched steak.

"Could you put a jet through this system?"

"Misclassify it as nonsensitive. Lose its coding completely. Maybe certify it was broken up for scrap as required when all you did was dent up the fuselage. Ally, nobody checks." He chewed, pushed the plate away. "The easiest way, you just take the jet apart carefully, mix it in with scrap, put it in with lots up for public auction and buy the lots. Ship them to some bogus port, then on to the real destination, and pick your jet parts out from the scrap again. You can do the same thing with computers, guns. Missiles."

"Maybe this is something the task force could look at. Maybe Customs, too."

"Customs and a couple other agencies are already hot. The biggest DRMO west of the Mississippi is just up the road at Perrey Air Force Base. Very much in our jurisdiction," he said. "So what do you think?"

"Sounds like a national scandal waiting to happen."

Brock glanced around the crowded room. Three tables over, holding court, was the speaker of the California Assembly. Next to him, a local TV anchorman and his current girlfriend, the other tables filled with successful more anonymous doctors, legislators, lawyers. Who knew what any of them were really talking about over their food and drinks?

Who wonders what we're talking about? Do we? he thought.

Alison drank a little of the wine they had ordered. "We don't have to talk cases now," she said. "That's why we're out tonight."

With a sullenness that he hadn't anticipated, Brock flared. "The Stanford prick probably'd have more exciting conversation, wouldn't he?"

"Almost anybody would."

Brock stopped himself. He had much more, but he saw the way she flinched. He could not bear causing her pain, even knowing what he did. He reached over and took her hand. "Forget it, just put it all someplace else."

She nodded, squeezing his hand. "Let's go dancing."

They had a drink and danced for an hour or so at a fashionable restaurant, but then both of them grew restless. They drove north out of the city into a countryside smelling like cinnamon and roses from the already drying hay, underbrush, and dust. There were only rare lights, streets glimpsed hazily through trees.

"I know where you're heading"—she held him—"but it's so late, they've got to be closed." A chilled champagne bottle from the restaurant nested between them.

"I called and made them an offer," he said.

She chewed a nail, flooded obviously with memories of days past when the two of them had sneaked out here from the office early in their relationship, when it was still not quite sensible to be openly together right after she transferred from L.A. Like I pulled strings for personal reasons, she thought. Which was, of course, true.

A few moments later Brock parked. They strolled across the deserted highway to a padlocked boat yard gate. He fished around the ground, brandished a key hidden there, and opened the gate. Alison felt overwhelmed as they went down the gently rocking dock to the river. It was dark all around them, only the sputtering neon of the rental boat yard's sign against the sky.

"Alberto retired," Brock said, as he helped her into a small metal, flat-bottomed motorboat. "But his kid said he'd do all this for old times. And a modest fee."

"It would be nice to go back, wouldn't it?"

"It might," he agreed. "If you could."

They pulled into the wide, sibilant running river's current. Along the banks, trees started up like ragged hands. Alison sat holding the champagne and her small purse. It was a very mild evening and she wasn't cold.

"You want to open this?" She held the bottle toward him. He gripped the tiller lightly. She could barely see him. A low insect hum surrounded them. Alison tucked the bottle on the boat's bottom. They couldn't go back, she knew. Nor could she admit mistakes. There were only threats to confront.

"I know you've got Dennis Lara," she said.

"Yeah, I do," he said calmly.

"He's the shooter in Kelso's case."

He swung the boat slowly, almost effortlessly to avoid a looming fallen tree in a river shallow. Brock idled the engine so his voice echoed against the dark banks, over the dark water. "I've got SFPD working flat out, Ally. The cops'll tell me what happened, but for the record here, Lara swears it wasn't him. He's not the kind of guy who goes for guns."

"He'll use you, Brock. You're head of the task force. He'll lie to get immunity." It was coming, she knew, only a few words, seconds, thoughts away, but bearing down on them after they had struggled so hard the last weeks to hide, deny, survive it.

Brock sat forward a little. "I saw the FBI pictures of Nelson, Ally. That's why you didn't want surveillance on him."

"My mother said things aren't what they look like."

"Shit," he shouted. "Popeye and the FBI think you're working for Ed Nelson."

She laughed spontaneously; then a hand covered her mouth. "Anybody can hear us." She waved at the dark land.

"There's nobody. That's why I brought us out here. Like talking to a snitch where it's safe."

So it has arrived, she thought. The blow was so terrible it hit her and left a painless cold.

"I thought you were being sweet," she said. "Wrong again."

"We don't have the luxury of being coy or cute. The FBI has persuasive evidence you're working for a high-grade asshole."

"They're wrong. I know you think so, too."

"It doesn't matter what I think. Popeye and his old bud Merical are probably convinced you and I are in on this together." He shifted, the boat rocking, water slapping roughly against the sides. He slid close to her, eyes clouded, smelling of lime aftershave and stale wine. "What the hell are you doing with Nelson?" he demanded, but it came to her almost as a plea.

They came back to the dock, and he secured the boat. They stood at the railing, inches and miles apart from each other.

Alison told him some of her arrangement with Ed Nelson. Brock had provoked her too far with his suspicion and deceptions. It was sanctioned at DOJ, she said. She didn't tell him why she'd agreed to run Nelson. It was deep undercover, and it would yield up a treasure trove of convictions. Nelson could go places no one else could. "You always preached the value of good snitches," she said. "I've got one of the best. One of the biggest. A solid gold reputation in his world."

"Christ, Ally," Brock said. It was quiet, awful. It maddened her.

"So he's the worst, Brock. All right. Agreed. But I can turn a bad actor like Ed and make him do things we could never do otherwise." She was evasive about exactly what kind of operations he was involved in for her.

"Nelson's somebody you just stop. Period."

"Pure romanticism. There isn't one evil individual or

even a whole group," she snapped. "It's a process, what we do. It goes on. There aren't final battles." She faced him like an antagonist at the office.

The champagne bottle sat on the railing, like it marked out a border dividing them. She touched it. They would never drink it.

"No, goddamn it," Brock snapped back, turning from her. "I'm talking about pure practicality. Cut out a top, smart bad guy like Ed Nelson, and the ones left in his business or the ones who follow him are stupider, easier to get at."

"Drop the condescension, Brock! You don't have the right."

"You don't know what you're doing. The idea here is to knock off the other side's leaders, not get in bed with them."

He threw an arm wide and accidentally pushed the champagne bottle off the railing. She made a grab for it, but it splashed heavily into the dark water, sinking instantly. "What's the use?" She spun on him angrily. "Cut Lara loose. He's going to cause trouble for everything I'm doing."

"I won't give him to you. You've got to prosecute Nelson."

"Screw you," she said, walking to the car. "I'm not letting you near Nelson."

Behind her, Brock called out, "He's going to turn you inside out. You'll be working for him."

"I said, screw you!" she shouted. I did it for you, she wanted to fling at him. But that admitted he was right to deceive her, and right to stand in judgment.

"Remember the other night you said there's only a half a degree of separation between bums and our friends?" He trotted up, taking her arm, and she shoved him away. "Ally, there's only a half a degree between us and Nelson. It's nothing. He can reach anyone. You don't make deals with him; you step on him hard."

"You're letting a lot of personal, shitty feelings screw

up your judgment." She got into the car, holding her hand out for the keys.

He gave them to her, and they drove back along the empty, dark highway. Their headlights were like the lights of a speeding, runaway train. A sick, cold ball filled his middle. She was partly right in her brutal assessment of him.

"You've been sneaking around me for weeks," she said tautly. "At home, this morning even. Hiding Lara. You don't trust me, Brock. That's abundantly clear."

"Can you hear yourself? You dumped a major explosives case, one that meant a hell of a lot to me and a lot of other people and not a damn word why. Not a word of truth in anything you said, Ally."

"Because I know you and you'd take this exact attitude. You're right. Everybody else is wrong. My world doesn't run that way," she said angrily. "Brock the holy man isn't the only righteous human being."

"I never said I was." He leaned back, anger and frustration running through him. He lowered his voice. "Ally, okay. Maybe I am blind. Maybe we'd both have a little perspective if we had kids. Something more than the two of us and our ambitions." He looked at her shadowy profile.

"We won't. I draw the line with us."

"You don't want children? Why the hell not?" He said loudly, then realized he already knew the answer.

"I'm not inflicting on someone else what happened to me growing up." It was a declaration. Immutable.

"Christ Almighty, Ally. What the hell does that have to do with anything?"

"It's me. And you. Who we are. Not who you want to twist us into being. For once, Brock, just look at things as they are." She turned. "Look at me."

"We're fucking strangers," he said, hurt and trying to hurt.

They flared from time to time until they were in the house, the raised angry, bitter voices reverberating across the street. Alison went upstairs, tossing her shoes and purse, the sheer dress flung to the floor. She fumbled furiously with the necklace, then tore it off. She heard Brock downstairs for some time while she lay in bed. She turned the light out.

He came up, still dressed. He had something in his hand.

"I'm going someplace else tonight," he said. He put what he'd been holding on the covers beside her.

"I don't want you here."

"Yeah," he said. He filled a small sport bag and then left. She heard the car start, the sound fade, and a silence more perfect and terrifying than she imagined settled monstrously over the house. I can do this, she thought. It was a clumsy lie.

Alison cried. A line from Dorothy Parker's attempt at serious poetry, something she and Brock had grimaced reading, floated into her mind: "Secrets, you said, would keep the two of us apart . . ."

Brock had laid the evening's doomed rose on her bed. He must have brought it in from the car.

Here lies Alison Andrews, she thought, rose clasped in her hand. Dead inside.

But I've still got my snitch. How goddamn great.

CHAPTER TWENTY-TWO

Mid-morning in Porter Ridgeway's office. Brock surveyed a gloomy, cloud-heavy sky outside, and a chill dampness crept even through the building's climate control system.

"She's got Nelson," Brock finished painfully.

"That's what she says," a puffy-eyed Merical replied. "Could be just the opposite."

"Alison's not a fool," Brock snapped. "Get her in here and ask her what she's running with Nelson."

He spoke to Porter Ridgeway, who sat with arms outstretched along the sofa like a crucified Pilate. "Not so fast," Ridgeway answered. Brock went on.

"The simplest thing to do here, is for Alison to lay it out for you. Like she did for me last night. Then we can decide how to pick up the pieces."

Cold untouched cups of coffee sat before each man. Brock couldn't understand Ridgeway's hesitance about confronting Alison, especially given Merical's persistent insinuation that she was tethered to Nelson criminally. He had the ugly impression they had been gleefully talking about him and her just before he walked in at nine.

"Well, Brock, the problem here is that if she tells me

everything, well"—Ridgeway's bulging eyes seemed to start out farther—"I may be obliged to do something."

"We've got to get a handle on what's happening." Brock got up, hands in his pockets. He felt ready to punch Merical.

"Maybe I don't want to do anything," Porter Ridgeway said. "Alison's a high-flyer, and some patron back at DOJ is bankrolling her."

"Find out who. What the parameters of the operation are supposed to be."

"And then old Porter's got to pull the trigger. Shut her down. Get in bed with her. Get her money. Make whatever she's doing this office's business."

"Shit," Brock said, "you better find out because Nelson's busy out there."

"I know, I know." Ridgeway waved his hands soothingly. He got up and sat down behind his desk. "Cubby? Insights?"

"I think we let Mrs. Andrews run for a while."

"Me, too. See what happens. Always time later to move in."

Brock swore futilely. "There might be a fucking mess to clean up."

"Yeah." Merical scowled out the window.

"But it'll be Alison's mess," Ridgeway said with clinical finality, as if pronouncing a terminal diagnosis.

"I want full surveillance on Ed Nelson. Starting now," Brock said.

"We can do that," Ridgeway almost purred. "But you're her husband. Didn't she tell you what Nelson's up to?"

"No," Brock said simply and walked out.

Windshield wipers on high, Ed Nelson squinted at the glossy black streets and fuzzy-outlined people on the sidewalks. It was early afternoon but looked like early evening in the downpour.

He'd gotten lost twice, circling around streets, stopping once at a gas station for directions. He always waited a few moments before driving on as though he was concerned someone following might lose him.

Cursing to the sound of the oldies rock on the car radio, he turned into a large shopping mall in Sacramento's north area. The vast, glistening parking lot shimmered in the rain. It was half-filled. He swung to the rear of the shopping complex, stopping near the loading dock for a giant toy store. He switched off his windshield wipers. His cheap translucent plastic raincoat crinkled as he peered around him. He appeared to be looking for cars passing by the loading dock.

After ten minutes, just as he'd restarted his car and was about to drive away, a cobalt blue sedan cruised by him, then parked in an empty employee slot.

Ed smiled. He assumed the FBI was using a box surveillance technique, keeping him in view on four sides. It took a lot of manpower, but he'd never spot them. He hoped he'd allowed them enough time to stay with him now.

He got out, one arm over his head, vainly trying to keep the rain off, and trotted to the blue sedan, rapping his knuckles sharply on the rear passenger window.

Jimmy Yee rolled it down. He had a stony, bemused look. "I thought you were joking about him," he said to someone in the driver's seat.

"It's all a fucking joke," Ed rasped. "Now open the goddamn door and let me in."

This is cozy, Alison thought.

She sat in the sedan's driver seat while Ed and Jimmy feuded verbally in the back. The rain spattered endlessly on the roof. Jimmy apparently didn't believe Ed about anything.

"I was in the city," Ed said again. "Taking care of business when I got Alison's call for this meeting. That's why I got here so fast. End of story."

"Pretty convenient," Jimmy said, unconvinced.

"Alison knows I come running when she calls." Ed

grinned. "So. Interrogation over? I assume you've got something important." He spoke to her.

It was hard, she realized, to concentrate fully. There was a thin film over words, people, actions. Shock, she thought, from last night. Brock was gone, and she understood he might not come back.

"Jimmy's going to be your associate, Ed," she said, half-turned to face them. They looked like truants. Ed, hair stuck down his head, red-jowly face damp; Jimmy, tight, tense, uneasy. "We're under severe time pressures now. Brock's going to move with indictments, and the FBI's got the Cobras under surveillance. You've got to get Jimmy near them, deliver the AK-47s and then stand aside so Jimmy and I can roll them up."

Ed wiped rain off his forehead. "Okay. Here we are June third. I'll call a meeting," he spoke to Jimmy, "and you meet me at the Sands Motor Lodge in Boise on the fifth. We'll work out the time and rooms and all that shit."

"How's the gun deal supposed to go?" Jimmy asked.

"Century Technologies, Alison's and my baby"—Ed smirked at her frown—"has made the arrangements with Norinco, okay?"

"Chinese guns?"

"Coming in on the eighth and we'll do the deal on the ninth. We'll work it out, okay, Agent Yee? Maybe we'll do it in Boise, long as we're there."

Alison didn't like Ed's sarcastic reference to Jimmy Yee. She knew him well enough to spot the menace. "We'll move in on the Cobras, catch them with the guns. Ed's going to put you near the Norinco suppliers at the same time, Jimmy. Right, Ed?"

"Sure, sure. I've got enormous respect for Agent Yee's abilities. Saw how he scooped up my Syrian deal."

"Nailed you," Jimmy said a little boastfully.

"And I'm grateful," Ed growled, stark grin stuck on his face, "because otherwise we wouldn't be sitting here chatting on a rainy day. I wouldn't have had those little tea times with Alison either."

"Cut it, Ed," she said. "You can bring Jimmy up to speed

on the Chinese military smuggling. The Cobras," she said to Jimmy Yee, "any other militias, whatever domestic terrorists Ed can set up later, are big catches. But this Chinese network smuggling military equipment is the biggest."

"Right," Jimmy said, excited by the prospect.

"I've got this nice story for you," Ed said to him, "what you tell these clowns. You're unhappy in the army. Racism. Family troubles. You need cash fast and you've got access to relatives in the old country who get you things like the forty-sevens. And from our own warehouses, you can get grenade launchers, all kinds of fun shit."

"I provided Ed with your background. It saved time," Alison said when Jimmy looked at her. "Jimmy's going to keep me posted on a daily basis so I can set up the Cobra raid with locals and people up north."

Ed sneezed suddenly. "Any chance Brock's going to drop Lara? Can you put your foot on that?"

Alison shook her head. "No. We have to get the arrests first. That's the one way to stop any indictments. Brock's bought Lara's lies, Ed."

"Well, Den always was good at them. I spotted it." He abruptly clambered out of the car. "Can't hang around with so much to do."

Jimmy slid in beside her as Ed Nelson's car drove into the rain-obscured gray distance. "He's for real," Jimmy said. "I wouldn't have believed you turned him."

Alison started the car and moved carefully down an alley toward the main street. She listened to Jimmy Yee's barely contained excitement, but like Ed's undercurrent of resentment, it didn't register on her fully.

Jimmy said, "I'm going to keep him screwed down, Alison. What about letting Brock in?"

"He doesn't want what we want. He'd shut us down," she said bluntly. "I know for sure."

Jimmy nodded, disliking it. But he was a good agent and he'd accept the decision.

She might, if she wasn't distracted, have warned him not to tread hard on Ed. Or she might have even pulled

Jimmy back entirely because something didn't seem right at all in Ed Nelson's demeanor.

But as she drove through the rain that afternoon, all she said was, "We're running against the clock," meaning Brock and his looming indictments.

And something more personal than she dared to acknowledge.

Brock had kept the abruptly called task force meeting sharp, brisk. "What about Nelson's companies?" he asked the IRS agent down the conference table.

"We're working on that closely," the thin man answered. "Applied Microavionics is new, just like Century Technologies, but they brought over elements of his businesses before."

"The ones I shut down after the C-4 arrests?"

"Correct. Now, both of these new entities are filing quarterlies; they've gotten the paperwork in on time for employees' withholding, Social Security, and so forth."

"Ed Nelson does not just set up new businesses. Where's the bad news?"

"Brock, we're only starting to look at their contracts and income streams."

"By Monday's meeting, you've got to find how these companies are rotten." He felt the crush of time, a sliver of ice in his middle. Sheets of rain beat against the conference room's wide windows, then stopped as if shut off. He went down the list of tasks on his legal pad.

"Give me the latest on shipping points, where military equipment could be moved out of the country." He pointed at the Customs agent halfway down the table. A dank odor from raincoats and umbrellas stowed beside the door filled the room.

"Well, Brock," the Customs agent said almost shyly, "are we going to get more specific leads from your source? I mean, right now, there's too much territory to cover."

"Yes. There will be specific information. Today, with luck," he said, hoping Lara would be talkative in a few hours. After Alison's revelations last night, he'd put off taking Lara to the grand jury before knowing more himself.

"Well, here's what so far," the Customs agent sighed. An overhead projector was flipped on. They all sat forward, looking past Brock's head at the screen showing bright blue spots along California, the underbelly of the Gulf, and on to the Atlantic seaboard. "If we can tie some kind of contracting together"—the agent gestured at the IRS rep—"and your source narrows things down, we can go right for possible shipping points."

Brock shook his head at the number of ports and border crossings. "Best guess now?" he asked curtly.

"Well, since your information relates to DRMO sales"—the agent's pointer moved across the screen touching spots—"these are the best bets. But I've got to tell you, Brock, this is one humungous chore. Take the DRMO in San Antonio. You've got crates and containers on the harbor up the kazoo. Or if equipment's being shipped through some secure port facility"—the pointer jabbed across the country to southern California—"we'll need an army just to check it out."

"Why?"

"Take the volume of business at two ports, Long Beach and Los Angeles. Every month one hundred thirty-two thousand containers come in. One hundred twenty-five thousand go out. Assuming your source is right, six hundred to a thousand declared shipments go to China. That doesn't count ones under the table."

"We'd have to crack every container of scrap, take every piece out," Brock finished. "Okay. I'll squeeze my source so we can narrow it down." He wouldn't reveal even to his task force who Denny Lara was, until he took Lara in front of the federal grand jury.

And that, of course, would be the acid test of whether this whole effort to snare Ed Nelson was going to succeed or not.

Brock said, "Perrey Air Force Base's got the biggest DRMO around here. How about an unofficial look around tomorrow?"

"Saturday?" the Customs agent said, dismayed.

"Yeah," Brock replied. "Call me when you've got a time we can do a walk through."

The FBI agent to Brock's left raised his hand. "What about search warrants for these companies?"

"Not yet. The worst thing for us would be to go in, come up dry, and try to put a case together after that." Search warrants, based on Denny Lara as a Confidential Reliable Informant, would be worse than useless if he could not also face a grand jury, and then Ed Nelson in a trial. I need answers to those questions first, Brock thought wearily. "Did you bring the arrest reports from Beverly Hills?"

"But of course." The FBI agent smiled, pushing a quarter-inch stack of stapled pages toward Brock. "Arrests for loitering, citations for vehicle defects, no current reg., bad rear taillights."

Brock swore, and got up. He waved, the lights came on and the overhead projector went off. Across Sacramento's skyline, a bright blue line appeared between the receding cloud bank. "At least the weather's cooperating," he said and got a nervous laugh from the men and women around the table. He said to the FBI agent, "Look, three members of a militia group advocating violence are picked up outside an expensive hotel and that's the best anybody could do? A bum taillight cite?"

"As of ten o'clock"—the FBI agent checked his watch— "the muni court down in Beverly Hills dumped all other charges. Insufficient evidence. We're keeping tabs on the three Cobras. FYI"—he glanced at the rest of the table— "B.H. police and the city are screaming they'll bill us six thousand dollars in overtime and equipment for the busts."

"Do we know why these turkeys were hanging around the Peninsula Hotel? Was it a target? Were they doing recon?" asked the ATF agent at the other end of the table.

"They didn't say a damn thing," the FBI agent replied. "There was a lot of pissing and moaning about God's wrath, the New World Order. Demon rum."

Everyone but Brock laughed. He flipped the reports

open to one suspect's statement. "Here it is. You told me about this crack," he said to the FBI agent. "What did one of these pukes mean that 'a cleansing spear will plunge into the beast's belly very soon'?"

"He didn't say anything else. The other two only talked about how the white race is oppressed."

Brock said, "We better find out what kind of spear these guys are getting ready to throw. And I mean by our next scheduled meeting on Monday. I want answers."

We all want answers, Brock thought, driving too fast on the rain-slicked streets toward McClellan. Sprays of water spattered against the car, and he weaved almost recklessly through the mid-afternoon traffic.

I've got to get at least one answer. Nelson sent the Cobras to meet Mandy Hayes outside the hotel. An anonymous call brought down the concealed snipers, city cops, and FBI agents. Mandy had set the meeting with Nelson herself. Was it simply great good luck that an alert citizen spotted those Cobra militia buffoons?

Or did Nelson know Mandy wasn't coming to the meeting?

He swerved to avoid a slow pickup truck, a horn braying angrily behind him. And if Nelson knew Mandy wasn't coming . . . someone told him. I can't face that now, he thought.

He impatiently sped onto the air force base, parked outside the house on Balboa Drive. A marshal, strolling across the lawn, cigarette cocked in his mouth, nodded as Brock strode inside.

The other marshal sat in the kitchen, beige raincoat water speckled, drinking coffee by the stove. It was quiet.

Denny said softly to Brock, "Mandy's lying down. She's having a rough time. New places, new faces"—he rubbed his jaw nervously—"old shit for me, but she's a solid type, likes to be on firm ground."

"Let's talk in the TV room," Brock said. He pulled out a small pad and minicassette tape recorder. The implacable routine of working a snitch would tap down the relentless, ugly questions about Ally forcing themselves into his mind.

He pulled the thin, louvered doors closed behind Denny. "How's she feeling otherwise? Physically all right?"

"We were both up most of the night."

Join the crowd, Brock thought. I sat up in a motel. He sank into an easy chair. "It'll pass once she gets used to the routine. Which we start right now."

Denny sat down on the couch. He wore loafers and jeans. He nervously patted his hands together. "I feel like I'm taking a test here."

"It's not enough for you to tell me what you know about Nelson's deals. You've got to tell nineteen people on a federal grand jury. Then you've got to sweat out a trial on the witness stand, with Nelson trying to stare you down. His lawyer's going to work you over, then do it again, and I may not be able to prevent all of it."

"I've got to make it myself, don't I?" He giggled nervously.

Brock nodded, switching on the recorder, pad on his knees. "I'm counting on you and so is Mandy."

For the next two hours, with only short, awkward breaks for coffee in the kitchen, trips to the bathroom, walks around the small backyard while a vigilant marshal stayed close, Brock probed, repeatedly asked, even taunted Lara about Edward Nelson's life seen close up.

Brock was pleased that Lara barely bridled at his jabs, the boring repetitions. It was a far distance though, from a couch in the TV room to the grand jury and then a crowded courtroom.

"Okay. Again," Brock said, flipping a new page on his pad. "Five weeks ago, he's back in this country. Looking at prison, right? Then the charges disappear overnight."

"Your wife," Denny Lara said.

"What did he do? What did he say to you about her or the explosives smuggling charges?"

Ed, Denny said, was wild for the first couple of days back at the Georgetown office. Swearing at everybody, even running Bower out. Closed doors. Lots of drinking alone.

Then he'd take Den drinking, close down restaurant bars.
He stopped seeing his office manager, the one he kept as
a lay on the side. He was, Denny Lara told Brock, a very
scared hombre.

But one night, one interminable night of drinking at a
fashionable Georgetown restaurant, almost being thrown
out, the two of them failing to get a cab back to the office,
Ed started talking as they stumbled along Eighteenth
Street. "Knowing the guy," Denny said to Brock, "this was
major league odd. I mean, Ed talks a whole lot. But he
hardly ever says anything, you know? It's a trick he made
me learn." He grinned. "I was fairly good at patter, but
Ed is beyond the canned spiel. You hear promises that
aren't promises, facts that float away. Dots."

"Dots?"

"Ed loves dots. Connect them. Make a picture. Let your
target make connections." Denny Lara grinned boyishly.
"The connections may or may not exist."

"What did he say that night?" Brock asked calmly. No
point in tensing Lara. But Brock felt sweat down his own
neck.

They passed a block of ethnic restaurants, Mexican, Ethi-
opian, Italian, Chinese, and Nelson had a war story about
something or someone in each country. Then he started
talking about the Syrian C-4 debacle. "True story will come
out someday," he said. "Lots of fat asses get shot out of
their chairs around here." He swept an arm to indicate,
Denny thought, the Washington area. "Meanwhile. Mean.
While. Old Ed has to watch out for himself and his own."
He took Denny Lara's shoulder in a clumsy hug. "Wife
and kids. People working for me. Can't even let Bower in
on this one."

Brock got up. Denny watched him anxiously. As if I'm
displeased, Brock realized. Christ, can this guy take it in
front of Nelson and the publicity? "Bower was the strong-
arm business associate. What would Nelson hide from him
and tell you?"

"Ed said things about the Syrian deal before it went
sour. Like the whole deal was somehow scammed."

"Don't shorthand, Denny."

"I believe Ed had something else going on when he made the Syrian deal."

"Or he wanted you to think so because he's a duplicitous, screwed-up asshole." Brock let out a breath. "What do you think he was doing in Beirut?"

Denny Lara swallowed, clearly unhappy he wasn't pleasing Brock. "Okay. My impression was that the C-4 deal was an intelligence sting. CIA, I guess. Ed's old pals. Like he never really got thrown out."

Yeah, Brock thought in horror. That's the way the dots would connect, true or not.

That's how Nelson would play his defense. A winning defense.

Maybe that's what Alison knew, too.

They walked on the slippery, wet grass. Denny was jumpy and smoked. The marshal in the beige raincoat stood near the fenced backyard's gate. He scuffed his shoes in leaves from an avocado tree.

Brock didn't pursue Denny Lara's devastating suspicion about the Syrians and the explosives. There was a more urgent question. "How did Nelson get out from under my charges?" Brock asked, stopping beside a dripping elm.

Long drag from Denny. "He got to your wife."

"She got him," Brock said impatiently. "Alison dumped the case. She's got approval from the Justice Department."

Denny lowered his voice. "Couple days after our night out in Georgetown, he's in the office, and when he comes over to me, he's happy. He's seriously bombed, but very, very happy. Like he'd figured it all out. He had one of those news magazines and he kind of waved it at me. 'The shape of things to come,' he said and later a couple other things."

"What's the significance?"

Denny Lara sucked on the cheap cigarette again. "There was a big picture of your wife and Senator Cantil in the magazine." He avoided Brock's bitter glance. "So he wants company again that night, so we do the long dinner with lots of beverage routine again, and Ed says, 'You know the trick of making a woman happy?' I shake my head. 'Simple trick,' he says, 'just give them exactly what they want.' "

Lara started walking slowly, looking up to the second-floor bedroom window behind which Mandy lay sleeping. Trucks passing and a flight of jets overhead noisily punctuated the dying afternoon. Lara said, "I go, 'Hell, Ed, that's no trick.' I'm thinking of his pretty, pissed-off wife and the mistresses I know about who don't regard him as the most caring guy."

"His answer?"

"Well, Ed throws back another double whatever. 'You're not listening,' he says to me, smiling. 'The trick is finding out *exactly* what they want and giving it to them. I've got a lady and I'm going to find out what'll make her happy.' "

They passed the marshal on their way back inside the house. "Nelson approached my wife? Is that what you're telling me?" Brock asked as dispassionately as possible. His controlled anger made Lara flinch even so.

"You know Ed. He knows everybody. He got the word to someone who could get the word to your wife that he wanted to make a deal. Maybe somebody else approved the deal, but take my word for it. Ed picked your wife to handle it."

Before Brock could say anything, they both heard Mandy in the living room talking to the marshal. Denny hurriedly crushed his cigarette and headed for her. Brock grabbed his arm. "What did he find out? What the hell did Nelson think my wife wanted so badly she'd dump the case?"

Denny Lara looked at Brock steadily. "Ed told me your wife wanted to make you proud of her. She'd do anything to protect you." Lara tugged away gently and went into the living room.

Brock came in a moment later, still trying to absorb what Denny Lara had repeated. True or false? Something so intimate about Ally he'd missed and a bastard like Nelson had spotted?

Mandy wore a loose housecoat and tangerine open-toed slippers. She moved with unsteady, heavy steps, the marshal helping her with one hand. Denny immediately took over.

"I was going to make his afternoon coffee," she spoke to Denny, pointing at the docilely nodding marshal. "But I got the swimmies for a minute."

Brock said, "Do you want to see a doctor?"

She peered at him, hand on her stomach. "Can you get me a personal physician? Not a military guy at the base?"

"I'll take care of it," Brock said. She nodded, whispered to Denny and slowly disappeared into the kitchen. The marshal opened his hands wide to Brock, showing he had become the object of her forced hospitality.

Brock looked at Denny Lara, his prize snitch and linchpin of his case, and disliked him intensely. It was petty, derived entirely from what Denny claimed Nelson had said and done with Alison. But, I need him, Brock thought.

He went back to the TV room, retrieved his pad and switched off the minicassette he'd carried outside. Denny Lara smiled expectantly.

Brock said, "You did very well today. We'll work harder over the weekend. Monday afternoon, I'll start you in front of the grand jury. We better find out right away if you can handle testifying."

Denny Lara's smile froze, and he murmured either an obscenity or a swift prayer. Mandy began humming an old show tune in the kitchen. "I guess she's getting into it," Denny said unconvincingly.

"I'll find a doctor over the weekend. That's one thing you won't have to worry about anyway."

Denny Lara grinned tightly, hands trembling as he pulled out another cigarette. "I've got a couple other things to worry about, don't I?"

I'm the one who's got to make it through the next forty-eight hours alone, Brock thought. And maybe all the hours and days afterward.

"And that one," Lyle Flecknoy said, pointing at an older panel truck. "I think that makes six."

"Yep. Six trucks," agreed the salesman. He glanced nervously at Vernon beside him. "Great vehicles. For the money."

"I'll make a cash deposit today," Flecknoy said as they walked toward the grimy glassed sales office. *BEST BUY USED TRUCKS, FALLS CHURCH, VA. Miles to Go. Guaranteed*, was painted in chipped green. "I'll give you the rest when I pick them up."

"Cash?" the salesman asked, chewing gum rapidly. "You sure? We take plastic."

"I'll pay in your country's currency."

The salesman frowned momentarily at the strange reference.

Vernon grunted, and they sat down on the cracked chairs. Two other salesmen argued on the phone. Flecknoy looked around disgustedly. Their salesman chattered as he wrote up the purchase agreements for the trucks. "You picked the cream," he said, handing a pen to Flecknoy. "We grabbed them babies when the furniture factory in town went under. You could pack couple tons easy in these babies."

"Don't you ever shut up?" Flecknoy signed the forms. Vernon grinned.

"Sure," the salesman said, slowly chewing his gum. "I get your final cash payment on June 16. Or you don't get the trucks."

Flecknoy opened his worn billfold and counted out unused hundred-dollar bills. He motioned impatiently to Vernon that they were leaving.

"Why you guys buying these fine used vehicles?" The salesman recounted the money.

"We're going into the moving business," Flecknoy said.

Outside in their rented car, Vernon excitedly pointed down the highway. "We're right here. I don't believe it, sir."

"A little over six miles from Chevy Chase, Maryland," Flecknoy said hoarsely. "Across the Potomac River."

He started the car. "Let's go see where the swine are going to gather. I want a feel for the land around the house."

CHAPTER TWENTY-THREE

Brock didn't get away from the office until nearly seven that night. He was scheduled to meet with the civilian head of Perrey Air Force Base's enormous surplus yard the next day at eleven.

When he got home, it was as though he'd been on a very long journey. Yet the street looked unchanged. Lights glimmered behind curtains and the air was rain freshened. But it was not the same place he'd left the morning before. He took a jittery breath. Alison's car was in the driveway.

He went inside. He half smiled at the familiar sounds, smells. Celeste talking sternly to herself and lemon furniture polish. Where was Ally? He was hesitant about even seeing her.

The irony is that Denny Lara gets a house and family because of this investigation, Brock thought. I've lost mine.

Celeste caught him at the foot of the stairs. "You back, Mr. Andrews? Mrs. Andrews will be very happy. Me, too."

"No. I've got to get a few more things and then I'll be gone again."

He turned, shocked at having spoken it. Celeste said, "Mr. Andrews, maybe you both need a little time away.

My husband, we stay away lots of times"—she giggled—
"and we got kids, twenty-eight years together."

"We're trying a different way," he said with his usual
bounce. He went up the stairs. What expectations had she
married with? he wondered. When she and her husband
sat around a dinner table with their energetic brood, what
did she see in him?

The problem with Ally and me is that we never saw each
other. We only thought we did.

He was relieved to discover she was showering and he
might not have to face her. He hastily grabbed more
clothes, stuffing them into a suitcase. He felt like he was
running away from school, guilty and irredeemable.

Alison's office work was strewn across the bed, an open
bottle of dry white wine and a half-filled glass beside the
telephone. Her diaphragm, in its shell pink case, was beside
the glass, as if she'd started drinking and brought it from
the bathroom. It was too private and too revealing. He
began poking among the papers slowly, then almost frantically, as if a definite answer was at hand. He only came up
with an engraved invitation.

Alison's shower stopped, and she came out of the bathroom with a pastel, ornately patterned robe on, her hair
wet, tugging a heavy towel around it. Brock straightened,
like he'd been caught cheating.

"Thought I heard the car," Alison said. She finished
wrapping her hair in the towel and took a drink from her
wineglass. "It's just you."

"Just me," he said, putting down the invitation and
forcing more clothes savagely into the suitcase. His guilt
perplexed him.

"Just you and me," Alison said. "You see there's a party
on the seventeenth? Big do in Chevy Chase."

"I'll have to skip it," he said. She'd seen him with the
invitation from Paulette Lurel. She slurred words a little.

"I called the old lady and told her I'd be there alone."
Alison shook with a laugh, like a prank. "I think she was
asleep. Val says I've got to go." She bobbed her head, then

drank again. "You won't see Val give me her blessing for the Senate."

"Is that where you want to go?" he said, closing the suitcase.

"At the moment. I know I'd be happier than staying with Justice."

"Yeah, you would."

Alison nodded, sat down on the bed, propped up. Her legs were rigidly before her, the robe falling open to her naked crotch. She irritably pushed away the papers around her. "Where are you staying?" she asked him with a bright fixed smile.

He named a moderately priced hotel a few minutes from downtown. She noticed him looking at her and pulled the robe's edges tightly closed with a fading smile. "How long are you going to be there?" she asked.

"I don't know. I really don't, Ally."

"It's thrown Celeste into a tailspin."

"She got me on the way in. She's playing marriage counselor." He said it to gauge her reaction.

"You know what I was thinking about just now? Going to the Benbow Inn up north like we used to do. Friday getaways. You turned your pager off. I left mine here." She winced, again like it was a prank. "All day Saturday, walk around those terrific gardens."

Brock glanced to see if he was forgetting anything. He could not come back feeling this anguish again. "I remember sleeping on the lawn chairs that time and getting a second-degree burn."

"What about the ten thousand Harleys the other time? We drove all that way for some quiet and got stuck in the world's biggest motorcycle race."

"Bad timing," he agreed.

"Bad timing," she said, drinking.

She watched him stiffly open the suitcase and cram two more dress shirts inside, like he allowed himself only the one piece of luggage as a penance. He stared around, almost like she wasn't lying in front of him. It bothered her and she got up. "Whoop," she said, feeling for the bureau, then standing upright. "This is going to be more than a weekend." She picked up the glass, facing him.

Brock completed whatever memory he was carefully creating. "I don't know, Ally. Probably."

"It doesn't have to be."

"You know it does. In fairly short order we'd start picking at each other; then it'd get worse. Nelson's just a catalyst. We'd get here again eventually." He sounded so certain, she slammed the glass down, breaking its frail stem.

"You're always right," she said bitterly. "Like hell."

"Last night was just a taste," he said sadly. "We know where all our skeletons are."

As he turned, Alison said blandly, "Ed Nelson wants me."

As she said it, she was disgusted for doing so. Brock swore and started down the stairs. She followed him, holding the robe, bare feet slapping on the cool foyer tiles.

Brock stopped and said savagely, "See how it's going to go, Ally? That's what we've got in store for each other. Christ, I will not do it to you, and I sure as hell won't let you do it to me."

She was ashamed when Celeste came smiling from the kitchen, heard the last exchange, and turned around. Brock waited, poised to bolt, for her to deny his prediction.

Alison straightened, hands in the robe's deep pockets. "Sure you won't come to the party? We'd be a hit."

"Goddamn, Alison," he said as plaintively filled with resolve as the first time he'd called out her name when they made love. But now he was determined to leave instead of embracing her.

"Well, at least we'll always have the Benbow," she said, resorting to flippancy as the only defense against her oncoming despair.

Two figures tramped the still-damp golf course at seven-thirty on Saturday morning, June 4.

Porter Ridgeway extracted a long club from his bag, winked at Cubby Merical's gloomy expression, and swung vigorously at the ball. It skidded yards down the verdant, tree-fringed course of the Del Paso Country Club where he and Merical were playing nine holes. It was a routine they had followed since meeting right after law school, interrupted until Merical's transfer to Sacramento. They had left their wives drinking Bloody Marys in the large ranch-style club's dining room.

"Your problem is the slice, Cubby," Ridgeway said as they hiked to the next hole. "You've got the slice."

"I've still got a better handicap."

Ridgeway shot a sour glare at him; then they addressed the ball. "Anything new since the damn pictures yesterday?"

"No alarms have gone off. Nelson's down in Los Angeles, tucked in with some broad he met in France last year. Looks like a weekender to me."

Ridgeway nodded. "I was pretty surprised when you waltzed in yesterday with pictures of Alison, Ed Nelson, and an ATF agent all snug in a car."

"Too bad the buildings and the rain screwed up hearing anything. All the techs were screaming about it."

Merical swung, cursed. He shouldered his bag. A few other hardy golfers trudged the course behind them. "ID is positive," he went on. "James Yee. Been with ATF for eight years. Great record, but he kind of goes off the reservation sometimes."

"Now watch, Cubby. No slice. That's the secret. Eliminate the slice." Ridgeway tensed, swung, hit the ball close to the next tee. "See? What about Alison?"

"Stayed in all night. Brock came by, looks like he just grabbed some clothes and left. I think the split's genuine."

"Been there, done that," Ridgeway said. He frowned, recollecting the upheavals of his married life. "You have any more thoughts about Yee being in with Nelson and Alison? I mean, what's that all about?"

"Trouble. I know that much. If Nelson and Alison Andrews have gotten to an ATF agent, we've got a real cancer."

"Probably should alert ATF?"

"Probably." Merical stepped to his ball, smirked at Ridgeway and swung, sinking the shot. "No slice."

"You're right," Ridgeway said as they walked, the rain-soaked grass soft underfoot. "Got to let this mess develop a little more."

"Wait too long and the cancer's spread too far."

Ridgeway nodded, stopped and selected a club, eying it thoughtfully. "Every crisis offers opportunity. I'll move precisely when it's necessary. She hasn't told Nelson your trick story about us having a snitch inside the Cobra compound."

"It'll turn up soon. This lady's giving that bastard the keys to the store. We'll know for sure when the Cobras start looking for a nonexistent snitch."

Ridgeway swung violently, his ball arcing to the left.

"Nice slice," Merical said with a grin. "Now you got it."

"Shut the fuck up. We've got three more holes. By that time the gals'll have had enough to be bearable."

"No joke, Port. I'm getting more nervous about Nelson and Alison Andrews every day."

"It shows in your game. Hell, I'm beshitting myself wondering what those bastards are doing."

"How about black bagging a couple bugs in her house?"

They moved on, the morning sun broken with high clouds, the remnants of the late spring storm's passage.

Brock was out of bed at the same time, the sheets and covers flung into a ball on the floor during the long, tense night. He dreamed, without recalling images, of Alison. Somehow her pitiless childhood sunburned over his indistinct impressions, as if he'd been with her even on the farm.

He ate a quick breakfast at a twenty-four-hour diner, then came back to his office, saluting the night security man in the lobby, the guards on the fifteenth floor. It usually was strange in the office on a weekend, even with one or two others working. Doubly strange this weekend, he thought, starting to make calls. I've got to think about transferring out.

It was clear he and Alison couldn't work in the same office. He could stand seeing her unexpectedly, like yesterday when he was with Popeye. You can steel yourself. But what he couldn't tolerate was the certainty of growing callous about her presence.

Like she'd meant nothing, means nothing, he thought.

The short-term answer was immersion to the point of exhaustion in building the case to bring Ed Nelson down. All his other cases would have to be set aside.

Brock called several physicians and soon had a name. He phoned Denny Lara. "Dr. Frisch's got great recommendations. I think Mandy will feel comfortable with him."

"I'm worried about her. She's always upset."

"You have to keep a clear head, Denny. Right now your first responsibility to her is getting through the grand jury."

"I know, I know. It's just goddamn hard seeing her cry, listening to her. She's scared, deep down. I mean, if she just had some of her friends, maybe if she talked to her dad."

Brock was firm. "Don't do that now. For this first little while until we get indictments against Nelson, you've got to stay low. The marshals will take her to Dr. Frisch. You can buy whatever you need at the base exchange."

"I'll try to hold on. Thanks. If it's hard for us, I bet it's hard for you, too."

You don't know at all, Brock thought. But he said, "Slight time change. I've got an appointment this morning, so I'll see you about three, okay?" A question suddenly occurred to him. "Did Nelson or Bower mention Perrey Air Force Base recently?"

Pause. Brock heard Mandy in the background, talking to one of the marshals, a surreal domestic scene. Denny said, "Yeah, now that you give me the name. Bower told me something about a trip to Perrey he was taking, two or three months ago."

"Did either of Nelson's companies do business with the DRMO at Perrey?"

"No. Positive. But what the hell does that mean?" He chuckled.

Not much, Brock thought when he hung up. Nelson certainly dealt with intermediaries. The difficulty lay in untangling the trail from each company or individual who bought equipment at the Perrey DRMO and then resold it. Brock sensed there was little time. Alison's fierce, possessory protectiveness about Nelson, the increased activity of his companies that the task force had already detected, all suggested some project in high-speed motion.

He looked out the window. The city was somnolent, resting and restful-looking on a Saturday. He felt odd man out in many ways.

He wanted Jimmy or Lila, both preferably, along on the Perrey tour. First, he called the FBI agent he trusted most on the task force. The man was about to take his kids to Candlestick Park for a baseball game.

"I need a quiet, deep check," Brock said. "It can't wait."

He repeated Lara's incredible suggestion that Ed Nelson had never in fact left the CIA. "It changes everything if that's true," Brock said. "You have a problem doing a little probing of a sister agency?" He said it lightly, knowing the answer.

"I'll hate every minute and I'll hate myself in the morning," the FBI agent replied.

"If you can dig out anything, call me anytime."

Brock hung up, dialed Lila at home, the receiver pressed to his ear. Everything had gone upside down. Alison was radically changed or seemed so.

A traitor might be a patriot. The FBI was spying on law enforcement officers. Alison, he feared, was under surveillance by now.

He was not surprised then when Lila's line, always free on weekends, buzzed a busy signal. He hung up, went to the lunchroom's coffee machine, and got a thin, scalding paper cup of coffee, then rushed back to his office when the phone burred loudly. He grabbed it.

Things were no longer tangible, expectable. Chaos

exulted in all places. He slopped coffee onto his blotter, hastily wiping it up with memos in his in-tray.

Lila said sharply, "Trisha Yee's been on my phone all morning. She's losing it."

"I just tried you," Brock said, uninterested in someone else's marital problems. He swabbed at the staining coffee. "I need you and Jimmy to come up to Perrey with me at eleven."

"Jimmy didn't come home last night. He's gone." Lila was rarely rattled, but she was now.

"Meet me in the Crocker Art Museum parking lot," he said. "Twenty minutes, all right? All right?" he had to repeat over her worried exclamations.

Jimmy never left his family unless he was working, and he never simply walked out.

So, Brock wondered, is he working something at ATF I don't know about? Because he isn't working for me.

CHAPTER TWENTY-FOUR

At mid-morning on Saturday, June 4, the large Chinese cargo ship *Island Princess*, inbound to its company's port at Long Beach harbor, radioed from just outside international waters that it was experiencing difficulties with its electrical system.

Long Beach harbor officials acknowledged the call and inquired if the *Island Princess* needed tugs or other assistance. The harbor officials were thanked by the captain, but informed that the ship's owner, Norinco, was sending electricians out to repair the damage. While the ship would shut down its engines for a short period, the docking time it had announced would be only delayed by an hour or two at most.

The southern California coastline waters were choppy, foam-flecked. A single small ship, riding the swells caused by a retreating storm, pulled swiftly toward the idled cargo ship.

Morosely studying the coast through dirt-streaked windows, Ed Nelson said, "So the FBI's still watching the front of the building. I just walked upstairs, across the roof."

Deng Li, a little queasy from the up and down motion

of the ship, said, "The bags of groceries you carried in yesterday indicated an intent to spend the weekend indoors?"

"Yeah," Ed growled, drinking from his flask. "Claudine and I were all over each other. She's a good girl. Yeah, we looked like it was going to be one long screw. Would have been, too, except I had this little chore."

They stood at the rear of the pilothouse. Both men wore loose gray coveralls stamped with the logo of the cargo ship's company. Deng Li waved a hand with a grimace when Ed proffered the flask. Then Deng Li said something brittle in Chinese to the only other man, who handled the wheel. "We will be on board in ten minutes, thank God." He belched abruptly, closed his eyes. "You're a very suspicious man, Ed."

"Humor me," Ed said, walking toward the front of the pilothouse so he could see the looming bulk of the cargo ship better.

Two electricians were seen clambering from their ship, up a metal stair on the cargo ship's port side, and were met by the captain, who personally conveyed them down tight passageways and more metal stairways to the hold. He used a set of keys, welded to his belt, to open the weightiest cargo hold door, almost like a safe. Ed brushed him aside, leaving Deng Li to repair any hurt feelings, and then shouted for Deng Li to get the fuck in and close the fucking door.

The hold, lit by dim bulbs, reeked of oil, seawater, and rotting food. Crates rose high, covered with oilskin or tarp. Deng Li led Ed through a warren between the crates and stopped at a block labeled *Electric Motor*. He counted, as Ed instructed, two over, one down, pushing crates aside awkwardly as Ed watched coldly. Finally, two crates were pried open with a short, steel claw. Ed peered down. "Yeah. Motors okay. All these crates get unloaded today, you put them on the trucks, make a big show. I'll be there waving for the FBI."

"I understand, Ed," Deng Li said. He'd recovered his equilibrium in the steadier, larger ship. "The ATF agent will meet you and both trucks tomorrow in Bakersfield?"

"He better. Moron." He stepped to the other crate. "These eleven"—he pointed at crates also all labeled *Electric Motor*—"go out with Lake's Atlantic Industries drivers." He swore. "That asshole better get these goddamn crates to his warehouse by the eighth. They've got to be moved south. I've got some nice clean storage lockers in Bethesda. Keep the party favors nearby for the seventeenth." He chuckled.

Deng Li's slim fingers probed delicately among the black, elegant barrels and stocks of the neatly stacked and stored AK-47s. The smell of fresh Cosmoline was pleasant. "A nearly flawless design," he said with admiration.

Ed contemptuously snorted. "If tires paid like this, I'd sell tires and they sure aren't flawless."

"But you sell weapons, Ed. You've always sold death," Deng Li said as they reclosed the crate.

Ed snorted again, but a little uneasily. "Thanks for the palm reading." He counted crates again until he found one with a barely noticeable green dot in one corner. "Those the forty-sevens that can't fire?"

Deng Li nodded. "As you requested, one crate of inoperable guns."

"Let's get out of here," Ed said brusquely. They walked to the cargo hold's massive door, swung it open. They were, Deng Li assured Ed again, the only people on board who knew the true contents of the crates.

They climbed up a metal staircase. Ed said, "So this fed Alison sticks me with, ATF guy, I don't think you'll have to meet him after all."

"What a disappointment."

They were on deck. A clean, sharp wind whipped off the ocean, and the ship's gently undulating bow pointed at the gray and brown city ahead.

Ed smiled for the first time that morning. "President Lyle and the Cobras are going to fall for him like a ton of bricks when I bring him in. The guy who can get them mines and grenade launchers.''

"They'd be quite unhappy if they knew the true situation.''

"You know,'' Ed said, inhaling a great breath of salty air, "I bet they go apeshit when they find out he's a fed.''

Deng Li's slit mouth widened into something like a grin. Their ship bobbed alongside the *Island Princess.* "Once again, Ed, you are the teacher. I'm a lovesick pupil.''

It was the silence, Alison decided. She had to get out.

Saturday morning, after enduring Celeste's chilly disapproval, she bundled up the office work into a briefcase and packed a small shoulder bag. It would be, she thought with mock cheerfulness, an informal working weekend.

Alison drove north on 101, through the dark forests and cool valleys to Garberville. The Benbow Inn's white and brown Tudor juttings and angles at least recalled happiness. Checking in, as the place was starting to fill for the weekend, Alison recognized her quest as a naive belief that someplace where she'd been happy might make her feel happy again.

She left her room immediately. The small blue lake nearby was dotted with rowboats and early swimmers. Alison let a romping family push by in their eagerness to get a good shoreline spot. Heavy white clouds hung over the inn and lake, and people seemed to be laughing or shouting all around her.

She sat in a low-slung cloth chair by the lake for a while. When she got up, a restless, angry loss had soaked through her. Six years with Brock and the best they could do was a petulant breakup. The worst part, she thought, was that he believed it was permanent.

She went into the restaurant's small bar. It was festooned with coats of arms and crossed swords and dark with aged beams. She ordered a gin and tonic. A little man, with a stiff hairpiece, paused as he walked past her. He cleared his throat. She looked away, appalled at his palpable loneliness.

Even though it was cool, slashes of sun and aquamarine between the clouds outside, Alison tried working in her room before lunch. There was nothing she could do until Jimmy called Sunday with his first report. Ed would have introduced him to the Cobras. Then the gun sale would be finalized next week, with Jimmy getting it on tape, and local police moving in to arrest the Cobras at the buy. ATF and FBI agents would take the Idaho compound apart.

Alison sat back in her chair, papers on the tiny brown cedar desk. She wondered again if the price she was paying was worth it. Brock and I could have bumbled along, more or less intact, if Chris Metzger hadn't pulled that stunt on me, she thought.

She ate a desultory lunch, aware every instant of sitting by herself in a dining room filled with men and women together. She walked afterward in the lush gardens. There were other couples, mostly older, in sensible shoes and khaki shorts, prowling knowledgeably among the bright flowers and vines. A few bestowed on her what felt like pitying glances. Such a pretty woman alone. Alison went back to her room. This had been a mistake.

She called Val Cantil at home just outside Washington in Alexandria, Virginia. She looked at her watch, the silvery charm Brock had given her on their second anniversary when they had exchanged watches, like time was a gift. It was late afternoon on the East Coast.

Val was sharp at first, then softened when she realized Alison was calling. "I've been having less and less pleasant conversations all day," Val said to apologize. "I didn't mean to snap."

"Snap away," Alison said. "I've been doing some of it myself. It's salutary."

"I know that tone. What's wrong, Alison?"

Without any preamble, Alison recounted the last twenty-four hours. She only omitted Nelson's special involvement, but Brock was probably right about it. The bastard was only a catalyst. "So that's my story and I'm stuck with it,"

Alison ended. She carried the phone, cradled against one
ear, and looked out the window on the lake and grounds,
and wished serene things had the power to replenish trust
and love. "Brock's at a hotel. I'm staring out at a damn
fish pond. I don't feel tremendous, Val."

"I'm very sorry," Val Cantil said. "Do you want my statement on family values or a woman's right to choose?"

"I know you're trying to give me a chuckle, but I've
passed the chuckle stage."

"And I'm only stepping on your feet. Excuse the feeble
humor. Seriously, maybe this is just a weekend thing."

Alison thought of the months preceding last night. "It's
not. We hit a wall finally." Saying the words made a con-
gealed lump sink through the center of her body. "I look
around and the whole world seems linked up, coping
together. I can see a man and woman on the grass"—she
stared down—"arguing a little. Then they walk away. He
takes her hand. I can't," she paused, afraid her voice would
fail, "understand what's happened."

"You're welcome to stay with me. I've got enough room.
I've avoided my own hot spot, I think, so I won't bite your
head off."

Alison turned from the window and sat down at the
desk. Her solution was there, the work. Guiding Jimmy
Yee and Nelson. The big arrests. "I better try here first,"
she said, moved again by Val's consistent goodwill and
friendship. "Thanks for the offer anyway. What about your
problem?"

"I've made the rounds in person and by phone. I think
I've persuaded everyone on the Ethics Committee that this
campaign contribution accusation isn't much. Technicali-
ties."

"I'm glad."

"So I've got to haul out all the records of my campaign
committee, sit down with the accountants and treasurer."
She laughed wearily. "But, yes, the worst is over."

"I'll see you in about ten days anyway. At Paulette Lurel's
party."

Val Cantil wanted to make her feel better, but misstepped. "There you go, Alison. The party. I guarantee that's going to be something special for you."

I'll be there alone, Alison thought, when they hung up. Is that the unspoken contract? I rise, I become popular, even powerful. I give up six years with Brock. I give him up? What a bargain.

She washed her face slowly, thoughtfully, in the tiny, perfectly decorated bathroom, with a tiny perfumed piece of soap, and realized she had no answers. "Go home," she said aloud.

In mid-afternoon, bag slung over her shoulder, hurrying through the lobby after she'd checked out, Alison presented to the guests and impressed staff the ideal image, made real, of a decisive, beautiful woman, on the run to another exciting destination.

CHAPTER TWENTY-FIVE

"He didn't leave any information back at the office? Where he was going? What was going on?" Brock asked. He and Lila were in his car driving north toward Perrey Air Force Base. They had just spent a rough time with Trisha Yee and her two frightened children. No one knew where Jimmy was.

"He signed out," Lila said, shaking her head again. "The dumb dummy. Took all his sick and overtime. Then he's gone." She was bleakly upset.

"Trish said you and Jimmy were talking at the party last night. About what?"

Lila gave him a sidelong glance. "Jimmy's going to check in soon. We both know he will. Call Trisha, call you or me. Ask him then Brock."

"You're right here," he said. "You tell me."

"Oh, no. You know it never works that way even for us," she said, plainly torn about what to do. "Jimmy's got to tell you. Or you better get it from Alison."

"Get what? What the hell is going on, Lila?"

"Jimmy knows and Alison knows."

Brock swore in frustration. The training about hot

undercover operations was strict, the bars ironclad. Nobody was allowed to know anything unless there was an articulable danger to the undercover operator or specific authorization. Lila didn't think Jimmy was in imminent peril or she'd say something.

"Holding out is not a great idea," Brock said.

"I don't like doing it, but that's the way things go. Anything happens to Jimmy," Lila said, hugging the Raider's jacket and holstered gun in her lap, "people responsible are going to pay."

It was, Brock realized, a pledge as solid as an inscription in marble.

Soon the city faded behind them, and shimmering rice paddies appeared with crows skimming over them like black ash.

Perrey Air Force Base was six miles south of Redding, in a dusty flat landscape bounded by distant, still white-topped mountains. The base dated from right after World War I. It had started growing piecemeal since then, and now encompassed a huge swath of scrubby former farmland.

Brock and Lila drove in and were met at the base's south gate, directed deeper into the sprawling complex dominated by a high acid green water tower, to the office of the DRMO's civilian manager. He was a chipper, slight man named Cavanaugh, and he stammered. Brock wanted to keep this inspection as low-key as possible for the moment. He had nothing concrete to bring the Nelson investigation here except a wordless, intense premonition.

While they waited outside for Cavanaugh to get some papers in the ancient wood office building, Brock told Lila why they were there.

"Nelson's got a grudge. We poked a big stick in his eye on the C-4 busts. I think he'd like to get even."

Lila pointed around at the enormous base. "So? He's got DRMOs all over the country he could use."

Brock nodded. "Lara heard him talk about Perrey. Bower talked about it. It's the biggest surplus operation"—

he faced her with a wry smile—"and it's right in our jurisdiction. I know this asshole well enough to think he'd love
to jam that stick in my eye by running his scam on my
turf."

Lila grinned finally. "I don't think he wants to jam it in
your eye."

For the next ninety minutes, using a small electric cart
to ferry them around, Brock, Lila, and Cavanaugh toured
the DRMO. Brock was stunned at the scale of it. Even Lila
sat shaking her head.

In a space the size of three football fields were vast steel
and tin warehouses, and around them, like beached refuse
left by a great wave, yards filled with machinery. As Cavanaugh stammered, pointed, showed inventories when Brock
demanded, they passed among ceaselessly working cranes
and lines of battered, tanklike trucks that were filled with
boxes, crates, or sometimes just the raw scrap. Each filled
truck was followed by an empty one. The line was endless.
Cranes lifted whole wingless jet fuselages into the air a
final time. "It's a big push, all the downsizing," Cavanaugh
stammered, waving an arm as he weaved down lanes in
the great upraised mountains of equipment. "Got a memo
last week from D.C. They want more profits, profits, profits.
This is one government program that makes a hell of a
profit," he said proudly. "We pooled all the branches here,
soldiers, air guys, navy."

Brock asked him to stop inside one of the warehouses.
There were, like tiny ants, a few civilian and air force
personnel wandering among the stacks of shelves that vanished into a hazy distance. He flipped the clipboard inventories. "Are these accurate? All this equipment's coded,
right?"

Cavanaugh's stammer blossomed. "Listen, you can't
have everything. You want to make money on surplus? You
want lists? You want everything accounted for? Can't have
it all."

Brock started walking. Desks loomed overhead in towers.
Steel filing cabinets by the hundreds. He and Lila went
through a door and found themselves, under a sky that

even seemed abashed by the scene below, in one of the yards.

"Christ," she said, folding her arms. "My tax dollars at work."

There were rows of tanks. On the nearest, a very young airman fiddled with an acetylene torch, vainly trying to cut through the tank's gun barrel. "He can't demilitarize a tank with that." Brock swung around. It was like dismantling a bank vault with a match. Another airman was tossing computer terminals and strange electronic boxes into huge steel Dumpsters. There was a casual indifference to it all. The other end of the cow, he thought. Nobody cares.

They walked on, seeing missiles like bowling pins, ferocious armor-piercing shells in ranks, and the cannon to fire them. Brock kept flipping through the inventory lists. Some things were listed. Some were not. Some were coded like desks even though they were machine guns. It was staggering, an incredible Sargasso Sea of military machinery. He stopped, wiping away sweat. Lila was dazed like a child at a toy store. It was as though some impossible mechanical giant had crashed to earth, sending its pieces everywhere.

On their way out, they stopped in Cavanaugh's office. Brock asked him, "When's the next public auction?"

"About ten days. Sure. The fifteenth. Got buyers coming from all over."

"Do you have a list of buyers in advance?" Brock asked. It would be too good to believe.

"Some. Lots of folks, companies, show up on the day. It's like a big flea market, real friendly." He beamed.

"You have an inventory, some kind of catalog of the things being sold that day?"

Cavanaugh, eager to curry favor because Brock earlier told him a full-scale audit of the operation was possible, quickly shuffled through an unruly stack of smudged printouts. "There you go," he said triumphantly, hands on his hips after presenting the inch-thick list to Brock. "You looking for something in particular? We probably got it."

"I'm counting on it."

Lila glanced at him. Brock held the list as if it burned his hand. Nelson, he believed, was in here somewhere.

Vernon read aloud from a current Washington area guidebook as he and Lyle Flecknoy walked along the boxed hedges and aged oaks. They were on the side of a broad, empty street.

"Slade House was built in 1797 of native brick, black walnut, and yellow pine. It consists of twenty-six rooms. Since the prevailing architectural style required absolute balance, there is a window set in a second-floor storage room and a fake door in the center hallway." He paused. His reading was slow and labored. "What the hell."

"Go on," Flecknoy said. He snapped pictures of the elegant old home beyond the gravel drive. He used a 35mm disposable camera. He had changed into a gaudy sweatshirt that said I LUV NY. The day before, he and Vernon had merely driven by. This was their serious reconnaissance.

They walked to the stone pillars at the gate. "Pleasingly proportioned, the structure has a two-story central core with symmetrical one-story wings connected by hyphens. It is privately owned by the family of former Ambassador Willard Lurel and not open to the public." He paused again. "What the hell?" He shook the guidebook.

"What about the land?"

"Oh, yeah. The twelve acres of gardens and grounds are graced with oaks, elms, and boxwoods."

Flecknoy nodded and snapped another picture. "Some of us will come through the gap in the trees there." He pointed. "At the same time as our trucks come through the gate. A perfect pincer trapping everybody inside."

"Thank you Lord."

"Do you see the trees all around? Camouflage everywhere," he said throatily, face alight.

They left soon afterward, driving back through the upscale stores and well-scrubbed people on the streets of Chevy Chase. Outside the city center, they pulled into a complex of cinder block and metal-roofed buildings beside railroad tracks. Flecknoy and Vernon went into the U-STORE-U office.

"I called," Flecknoy said to the thin older black woman in cross-trainers and fluffy pullover. "I wanted your largest storage room."

"Locker," she corrected. "Oh, sure. I got it," she said when he gave her a false name. "One hundred fifteen a month. You can practically put your whole house in there. I should know. I basically did it after my divorce."

He took the code to the gate keypad outside, signed the rental agreement with his false name, and got directions to the locker. He gave her three one-hundred-dollar bills for the first and last month. When she handed him the change, she asked, "You know it's basically got a door you pull up, like your garage? You want a lock? We sell all kinds of locks." She pointed at a wall display.

"No, thank you. We'll bring our own when we use the *locker.*"

"When might that be?" She stared at his scarred lip, touching her own mouth unconsciously. "You'll appreciate our security. We keep track of who goes in, comes out."

Vernon fidgeted by the door, eyes roaming everywhere.

"In about a week some things will be moved in," Lyle Flecknoy said, folding the agreement and putting it in his wallet.

"I'll mark down the twelfth, thirteenth, something like that," she said. "You know you can't keep explosives, flammables, any kind of controlled substance in your locker." She was staring again at the scar, then at Vernon's jumpy eyes.

"Of course not," Lyle Flecknoy said. "That would be illegal," and he managed to torture the last word into six syllables.

It was nearly seven by the time Alison got home. The house's black, unlit bulk loomed sullen and sad on the sunset bathed street.

She was annoyed to find a florist van parked in the driveway, front pointed to the street as if for a quick exit. She pulled in behind the truck, partly blocking its access to the street. Alison got out, shoulder bag in hand, wondering which of her neighbors was getting flowers.

She unlocked the front door and went inside. Three steps forward, then stopped. Celeste was definitely not here. No singing, none of the reassuring sounds she made. Alison listened. There were thuds, low voices, the quiet creak of a drawer opening and closing upstairs. Heavy bodies moving around.

She calculated swiftly. At least two, maybe more of them. Maybe even another one downstairs she hadn't noticed yet. She decided to get out, call the police from next door.

As she turned, her partly opened shoulder bag slipped, and a clattering cascade of pens and lipstick hit the foyer's tiles with explosive intensity.

She was at the door. She heard an instantaneous silence upstairs, a low obscenity, then loud thudding. Alison bolted through the front door.

She crossed the lawn and reached the hedge, about to vault over it to her neighbor's yard when she turned enough to see an odd sight. Three bulky men wearing short-sleeved khaki shirts and long pants ran from behind her house and jumped into the florist van. One man, she noted, carried a black toolbox. The van surged forward, stopped, tried to pull around her car blocking it, then jumped forward, clipping her car with a crash of metal, spinning the car sideways. The van screeched into the quiet street and roared away. Alison tried to get the license number but couldn't.

The Fontells' two collies were madly barking several doors up because of the commotion, and her car's security alarm whooped like an imbecile calling for help. She went back into the house, hurrying up the stairs. In the bedroom she found chairs overturned, a window open, and the telephone and a lamp partially disassembled on the bedcovers.

A grate had been removed from the air vent near the bathroom.

So much for burglary, she thought in cold fury.

Brock worked in his office until the sun went down, then closed the curtains, turned on the lights, and worked on. He'd left Lila at the ATF office, checking through part of the auction list. He sorted through another half, and the whole list had been faxed to Customs and the FBI. It was like looking for an ice cube in a glacier, but Brock knew for certain that Ed Nelson's next step involved moving sensitive military equipment out of the country as scrap. In this upcoming auction list there was, he desperately hoped, a connection to Nelson. It could be something small, nearly invisible. But he'd find it.

The session with Denny Lara a few hours ago had convinced him. It went well. Lara was more relaxed, even though he still smoked cheap cigarettes as they talked outside. Mandy already had a call in with Dr. Frisch for an early appointment.

Brock questioned Denny Lara as they sat under an apple tree in the backyard.

"He cut you out? Why would Nelson do that?" Brock asked.

Lara sucked on the cigarette. "I've thought about it a lot. My contribution was always gladhanding, bullshitting. Ed didn't need to grease anybody, keep them mellow. It was a done deal. It was also so big he didn't want me to get a piece."

Brock frowned. "You were a pal. He'd stiff you?"

"Ed's a very cheap guy."

"So what kind of big deal, that didn't require your talents, was he working on? What did you pick up around the office?"

Then Lara told Brock what transformed the Perrey DRMO auction list into gold. Once a Chinese businessman came to the Georgetown office, hustled out with Ed and

Bower to a long drunken lunch. Then a tubby man named Lake, whom Ed yelled at, then also took out to lunch. Denny heard Bower and Ed right afterward talking about moving merchandise to Long Beach by mid-June.

"Who's Lake?" Brock asked, alert to a new name.

Lara grinned, ground out his cigarette. "Connor Lake runs a scrap, salvage-type company in New Jersey. Except he doesn't. Ed owns the place. Atlantic Industries. We used them to hide shipments of guns sometimes. Who checks scrap?"

Brock dug deeper as the sun faded and the marshals changed shifts. Denny Lara had been pulled aside by one of Ed's tame generals, one of the telephone men. What, the retired army general wanted to know, was Ed doing with a list of restricted aircraft and military computer equipment? It was, Denny recalled the general fuming, a goddamn shopping list.

"Nobody was supposed to see that list," Brock said, sitting back in his plastic lawn chair.

"That's right. I didn't even get a chance to ask Ed about it. I got dumped out with Bower the next day to meet Ray Kelso in San Francisco." He coughed, lit another cigarette.

There it is, Brock thought excitedly. He said to Denny, "Nelson wasn't trying to clear the decks about the old C-4 deal. He was pissed you knew too much about something coming up, coming up fast. Smuggling restricted military equipment out through a DRMO auction."

Denny Lara had blanched, gotten up. "Oh, Christ. I should've put that one together."

Which was why Brock now worked so single-mindedly on the auction list. It had been so important to conceal this plan that Nelson had tried to kill one of his most loyal inner circle. But maybe Nelson had suspected Lara was no longer loyal. Maybe Nelson even knew about Lara's side deals with Lennox Chandler. The last thing Brock had said to Denny Lara that afternoon was, "Monday morning, we'll start laying this all out for the grand jury. You know enough to be pure dynamite."

Enough to blow a lot of fat asses out of their chairs,

he thought, recalling Nelson's boast. Brock had studied Denny Lara's shaken, jittery face under the apple tree. Pure dynamite as long as you keep your nerve on Monday, he thought.

Brock only left the office for a brief trip to the lunchroom, raiding the refrigerator for someone's leftover vanilla pudding and a half of a salami sandwich. It was the scavenger's way he ate lately. His direct phone line rang after eight. He grabbed it.

"You scared Trish," Jimmy Yee said.

"You scared her, turkey. Where are you?"

"Sitting on my keester in a roach motel again. Big doings tomorrow." Jimmy sounded compressed, tight with anticipation. "I got Trish calmed down. It's all cool."

"Where are you?" Brock repeated. "What are you screwing around with?"

Pause. "Nothing we haven't done before. A sting. I get a look at the merchandise tomorrow morning, we set the buy, I fade in, I fade out. We bust them."

"This is an open line, so I'm not going to say a hell of a lot. I saw pictures a little while ago. You, Alison, another man. You know. I saw pictures of him taken this afternoon with your merchandise. It's all on the record, Jimmy."

"Then I won't need more backup. I'm covered."

Brock thought of smug Popeye and Merical again splaying a range of surveillance photos before him when he got back to the office. The latest, sent by secure fax, showed Ed Nelson on a dock in Long Beach, as trucks were loaded with crates purportedly containing electric motors. The trucks, according to the FBI, were on Interstate 5 heading north.

"Get out right now," Brock said. "Pack up, come on back. This one stinks."

"Personal or professional judgment, boss?"

Brock didn't know anymore. "We're coming at this guy from another angle right now, Jimmy. Big time. He's not right on yours."

"I got to tell you," Jimmy said defensively, "so far Alison and the bad guy've been straight on everything. Look, tomorrow I'll sniff the shit he's moving, check the details. If it feels bad, I'm heading back to Sacramento."

"If it feels okay, how long are you signed on for?"

Jimmy was cheerful, exuberant. "A week. Maybe ten days. We'll come out of this golden, boss. Make up for the crap we got last month."

"All right," Brock reluctantly relented. "But keep in touch."

"Thanks for seeing Trish. The girls love Lila." Then he hung up, and Brock wondered how close or how far Jimmy Yee was at the moment, and how strong the lifeline Alison held on him.

He stared at the auction list. A wild jumble of parts, weights, weapons certified as demilitarized. Like the kid trying to cut up the tank, he thought. So where was Atlantic Industries in all of it? Was this Connor Lake just going to show up on the fifteenth? Brock got up, rubbing his eyes. At least he'd guarantee other interested parties from Customs, ATF, and the FBI would be at the auction and Mr. Lake would have the pleasure of meeting fellow junk metal enthusiasts.

Was Nelson's infatuation with the Cobra militia connected to the DRMO auction? How was cooperating with Alison to break a millenarian militia tied up with arms smuggling overseas? Were they tied together at all?

He picked up the last chunk of the salami sandwich. Answers. Answers. A clock was running, he believed absolutely. But he had no answers and no way to know how much time was left.

When the direct line rang again, Brock snatched it up. He assumed it was Jimmy, quickly reassessing the undercover operation and signaling he was coming home.

But Alison said, "Something's happened. We need to talk."

"I was thinking the same thing," Brock answered, startled by the mix of desire and anger he felt.

CHAPTER TWENTY-SIX

Alison and Brock met at the Hyatt Regency downtown. He wore a sweatshirt with a sportcoat thrown over it, and she thought he looked tired. She pointed up, and they rode the elevator to the top floor, walking out to the rooftop parking lot seventeen stories above L Street. There were three cars parked forlornly in the concrete lot.

"We're alone up here for sure," he said, going to the edge of the roof and looking down at the light traffic.

"For sure," she agreed. She had on a tan leather coat and a casual long dress he once liked.

"You want me to go first?" he said.

"No," she answered. She told him about the phony break-in.

Brock cursed, hands jammed in his pockets. "Goddamn Popeye. Suppose you went for the gun in the study? Suppose there was shooting and then the next thing Popeye's telling the world it was a mistake?"

"I was mad about it earlier. I'm all right now."

"See what's happening, Ally? You've got to end this Nelson crap. You've got everybody chasing themselves."

She smiled faintly. Brock's first reaction was expectable.

It's all somehow my fault. "What I'm going to do is tell Chris Metzger to put his foot down on Popeye. Call him off."

"Metzger's backing this Nelson fiasco?" He blinked, turning to the roof edge again. "That's perfect. Guaranteed failure. So why tell me?"

She came to him. "You've got to drop your investigation, too. Let Ed Nelson finish the cases he's working on."

"He's not working on cases. He's working another scam."

Alison controlled her anger. Back at the house, after the initial shock, it had taken a similar effort to calm down, see exactly what must be done. "No, he's not," she said tightly. "But if you go ahead, you'll screw yourself. If you get indictments against Nelson, that's the end of your career, Brock."

"Says Metzger? Says Nelson? Give me a break. I know why Nelson picked you, Ally. I know." He nodded vigorously. "You don't have to protect me. I can take care of myself."

"No, you can't. I'm giving you the facts of life." She wondered, darkly, where Brock got the idea she was shielding him. "Ed Nelson is handling a very sensitive series of investigations for DOJ. Indict him and you destroy them. Don't be so goddamn stubborn." She walked toward the elevator. The sky was black, starry and enigmatic. Even constellations with names appeared incomprehensible when she looked at them. "Why the hell should I protect you? You scare me," she said angrily. "You're turning personal vindictiveness into a crusade."

"Wrong again. I talked to Jimmy Yee a little while ago."

"He hasn't talked to me yet. I guess loyalty to the Three Muscatels counts more," she said.

They stood inside an enormous silent air vent, a column of warmth rising from it. She felt like they were alone in the world, on a concrete oasis, in eternal night. Brock looked impatient. "Jimmy didn't tell me what he's doing. He's a good agent. But I'm scared of whatever he's into now. It scares his wife and kids."

"You trained him. Rely on that."

"You've got his life in your hands, Ally. You and Metzger. You're betting Nelson's manageable. But you drop Jimmy, he falls, trained or not. Can you live with that?"

We sound like antagonists, she realized. It mystified her how that had come about.

"I know where these crazy insights are coming from," she said. "You're lapping up whatever Lara says, aren't you? You're the one getting scammed. Jailhouse bullshit. And for the record, Ed Nelson did not pick me," she said hotly. "It was my choice. First to last."

"He picked you. He convinced Metzger, and Metzger squeezed you. But Nelson set it up."

"You *are* paranoid," she said wonderingly, pushing the button for the down elevator.

"Doesn't mean I'm wrong," he said. "I'm getting evidence Nelson's selling classified military equipment, probably to the Chinese. One of his companies, Applied Microavionics or Century Technologies, is going to buy phony scrap from the DRMO at Perrey Air Force Base in eleven days. Jimmy said your deal is wrapping up in a week or so. That's pretty close for coincidence."

"I know what the companies are doing. We're nowhere near military surplus." The elevator door opened and she got in. He followed.

"You aren't. He is."

"Lies from Lara, Brock."

He shook his head, angry. "What the hell is Atlantic Industries?"

"I haven't the slightest idea." But she hesitated.

"You better find out. Nelson's buying bogus scrap from Atlantic Industries and shipping it out from Long Beach just about the same time your Cobra deal winds up."

They both fell silent, walking across the lobby, oblivious to the laughter and satisfied people out for a pleasant evening. On the street, they stopped opposite the floodlit state capitol.

"You have documentation?" she asked, voice very low and tense.

"I will."

"So what you actually have is Lara's bullshit."

"Nelson's working the Cobras and he's working the DRMO deal. It's big trouble."

She shook her head. "Oh, I'll see what's there. But stay out of my way."

"We're not in competition."

"Of course we are. We always have been. From the first time we met, trying to see who could run the fastest," she said. "You're jealous now, Brock. So I won't go down with you and I won't let you pull me down either."

"Bullshit, Ally!" he shot back. But she strode away to her car down the block. "It's not true," he finished.

He went into the hotel bar. He had a foreboding ache mingled with regret. If he was going to deflect the fast approaching disaster, he and Alison would have to be in competition. That's the way she wanted it.

One of us loses. One of us wins, he thought. He drank and thought sad, gin-flavored thoughts.

The following morning, June 5, Jimmy Yee watched Ed Nelson say something funny to the two drivers of the aging panel trucks. They all laughed, and the drivers ambled into the busy MEALS FOR WHEELS restaurant topped with a spinning neon radial tire.

Jimmy said to Nelson, "You trust those guys?"

"Always use union drivers. Salt of the earth. Freelance hotshots are too curious anyway."

Jimmy didn't think it was a wise idea to transport illegal weapons in trucks this way, but Nelson seemed content. Their two trucks were parked at the far end of the large truckstop in Oildale, just outside Bakersfield. Across a dusty asphalt lot, a dozen rusting black oil pumps rose up and down with bovine slowness in the flat desert all around.

"Let's get a look," Jimmy said coolly. He did a quick check of the idling eighteen wheelers at the rank of gas pumps, spotting where drivers were. He and Nelson had this corner near the sagging link fence to themselves.

Nelson unlocked the back of one truck, swung it aside and got up, squeezing into the narrow space between stacked crates, and pried the top off one. "This what you came for, Yee." He motioned.

Agilely, Jimmy jumped up, his back shielding the crate from anybody who might wander by. He looked at the AK-47s carefully nestled in the crate. "Can't fire?"

"You're the expert." Nelson grinned. "But these are for show only. Let Flecknoy and his birdbrains get all hot and bothered thinking they've got for real guns."

Jimmy couldn't tell, without closely examining one of the assault rifles, whether it was in fact inoperable. So he grabbed one, quickly did a cold fire and smiled when the rifle remained as silent as an iron brick. The Cobras would never be given the chance to put even one bullet in a rifle. He laid the rifle back, and the crate with a nearly imperceptible green dot was closed. He and Nelson locked the truck and went into the noisy restaurant. It reeked of sour coffee and bacon grease.

They sat at a chipped Formica-topped table, ordered. Nelson was charming, even telling goofy stories about how nervous he got in airplanes. Jimmy, already satisfyingly excited about the sting, found himself grinning.

"The rest of the guns are shit, too?" he asked quietly.

"I didn't look at each one," Nelson said, slurping his coffee and making a face. "But it doesn't do me any good to peddle live guns to the Cobras."

"Fucks you," Jimmy said with a wide smile. "Where are they going from here?" Nelson had warned he'd be reticent about details until after they met in Bakersfield.

"Well, I've got a storage locker in Boise. These dopes'll dump the crates there tonight, tomorrow morning. I'll get in touch with *President* Lyle tonight and we'll set up our first meeting for Wednesday."

"I don't like sitting around for two days."

"Jimmy. My old buddy. The Cobras are quixotic. They may have beans for dinner tomorrow, start farting and decide, hey, let's talk about the guns. We have to be ready."

"The actual deal is on my timetable," Jimmy said evenly. "Not theirs." He drank his coffee and made a face, too.

"Absolutely. You think I'd be working with the lovely Alison and let the Cobra militia make the rules?" They again rehearsed Jimmy's cover story as a disgruntled army quartermaster, stung by anti-Asian racism and little promotion, who was willing to deal weapons for hard cash.

They ate fried eggs. Jimmy remained uneasy about the prospect of waiting in Boise; but the guns were going to a safe place, and he would supervise their unloading, he told Nelson. He'd keep the key to the storage locker. The guns were inoperable and thus perfect bait. Nelson was correct, of course. He stood to lose everything if this sting went sour. He was an asshole and yet Jimmy found him good company. It happened sometimes.

Nelson wiped his mouth with a paper napkin. "Time to hit the road. This segment of the business used to be Bower's territory. He loved traveling, loved the colorful jackasses he met." Nelson fell serious and silent. "So, tell me, Jimmy my boy. What did you like best about ATF training?" he finally asked.

"Lock picking. Blowing shit up." Jimmy smiled broadly. "I guess I have a criminal streak someplace."

Nelson ate and talked. "Bower would've liked you. Christ, you could've worked for me under different circumstances."

"No chance," Jimmy said, a little of his genial feeling for Nelson evaporating. It came back when Nelson, holding a mass of dripping yellow egg aloft on his fork, recounted a very funny story about meeting Bower for the first time in the jungle and ordering a mysterious meal of bif what crawl.

A dish that was never what it said it was. And never the same thing twice.

That night, Jimmy called Trish from his room at the Sands Motor Lodge. He was still humming on high energy, but an edge of fatigue told him he had to take it a little easy.

The girls were unhappy he wasn't there, so he said good night to them both and told Trish to kiss them twice. He felt much better.

He lay full length on his stiff bed and called Alison. Their routine from now on, she said, was to be regular calls every night at nine. In an emergency, he could page her. Backup, she had promised, would be with him as soon as he met with the Cobras. She was arranging it.

"Got the guns locked away," he told her. "Nelson's talking with the militia tonight, maybe we meet earlier, but by the eighth anyway."

"I want you wired for that meeting."

"I think for the second one," he said, wiggling his bare feet. "I want to get the feel of these guys, how paranoid they are first. Maybe they'll strip search me. Who knows."

Alison sounded preoccupied, as if she was thinking about something else. "No, you're right, Jimmy. I don't want Ed on tape. Just you making the sale to the Cobras. I can use Ed again if he hasn't been burned in open court as my guy."

"I got to admit, he comes over okay. Maybe I'm just buying his line."

"Watch him," she said sharply. "He's only working because I've got him on a leash."

"Whoa. Don't bite me." He sat up. He was feeling the strain of inactivity already, combined with the day's frantic driving. "How soon is the Chinese deal coming together?"

He didn't want to sound that eager, but the prospect of snagging international smugglers fired him up like a kid waiting for Christmas.

"Let's wrap this one up, see how Ed performs, then take it from there," she said, again preoccupied. A lot less certain of the Chinese operation, he thought disappointedly.

"Okay, but I am hot to trot on that puppy," he said. He stood up, bunching his shoulders excitedly. "I'll get around the city tomorrow, see what looks good for the buy site."

"I'll have your local backup ready," Alison promised.

When she hung up, Jimmy tried watching TV, but as usual out-of-town, he was too energized. Lila or Brock weren't around to kill time with either. He felt alone and restless. He finally drove to a bar, nursed a single beer, thought of Trish, and was more lonely and frustrated than ever.

Alison called Ed Nelson from the study. The large screen TV was on in its solid oak cabinet, the sound muted. It was past eight, she had eaten a small salad, slogged through unavoidable paperwork, and tried to reckon why seeing Brock the night before upset her so much. It was not merely what he said.

The study teemed with reminders of her and Brock, sterile memorials in paper, pictures, plaques. On the sofa they had hugged and made love after triumphs or disappointments.

"Alison?" Ed drawled into the phone. "You called me. You there? Hel-lo."

"Something on the tube," she said to cover the embarrassing lapse. "Have you set up a meeting with the Cobras?"

"Yep. All set for Wednesday the eighth. Flecknoy's very jacked up about Jimmy the arms merchant." He chuckled. "We might have to meet at the Cobra compound, though."

"Negative on that, Ed," she said abruptly. "Jimmy does not go there. It's too isolated. You persuade Flecknoy to come to you both."

"Tough. Tough. Well, I'll tell him Jimmy's got access to mines. I mentioned it once and Jesus, Ally, you should've seen that nutlog's eyes light up. Oh, boy. Would he love to have a couple mines to spread good cheer."

Alison stared at the TV's shifting scenes: London, Lexington, Kentucky, Rome in the blink of an eye. Real life, beyond the camera's light-speed distortions, seemed so hideously leaden and intractable, she thought.

"What the hell is Atlantic Industries?" she demanded

suddenly. Flush this bastard out or show up Brock's lying snitch, she thought.

"Junk dealer, I think."

"Are you doing business with them?"

"Could be. I've got a bunch of legitimate clients to cover our transactions."

"Ed, if you lie to me, you will regret it. I've got your Queen for a Day letter in my computer. Do you know how fast I can hit the delete button?"

"Alison my love, you're mad. Don't take it out on me."

I am mad, she thought, glancing again at the TV screen, as if it could instantly transport her somewhere else. "I'm going to put Atlantic Industries under a microscope," she said. "I better not find anything."

"Let me know if you need help with records or personnel. I want you to feel absolutely at ease here."

Alison got up, the receiver against her ear. She half imagined Brock was going to come through the door. It was like living in a house filled with live ghosts: unsettling and impossible. Some decisive act had to break this tension.

"I want a face-to-face, Ed. Right after the Cobra arrests. To assess our relationship." Why had she put it that way, particularly after Nelson's crude advance that she had flung at Brock? Get a grip, she thought. "I've got to be in Chevy Chase on the seventeenth. Paulette Lurel's party. We can meet that morning or afternoon in Washington."

Now she was puzzled by the long silence at Nelson's end, like he had gotten caught up reflecting on something else. "Hel-lo?" she said. "Chevy Chase. June 17, Ed? Got it in your date book?"

"Oh, yes," he said slowly, even sorrowfully? "I got it. I didn't think you'd go to that old babe's sideshow."

"It's a command performance. First things, though. I want Jimmy Yee safe and sound."

"I won't let him out of my sight," Nelson said, recovering his momentarily lost focus. "Don't worry about anything, Alison my love."

She hung up, turned the TV's sound on again. Her hands roved over the room's photos and framed praises.

No matter how the Cobra operation ended, she and Brock had already done so. It was a clear and unambiguous conclusion.

Her head jerked to the TV. A young woman, in front of the floodlit United States Capitol, said with the breathless delight of a village gossip, "CNN has just learned from reliable sources on the Senate Ethics Committee that a vote tomorrow will open a full-scale, formal investigation into campaign finance irregularities during last year's successful reelection effort by California's senior United States senator, Valerie Cantil."

Alison immediately sat down, calling Val.

CHAPTER TWENTY-SEVEN

Like the hectic ritual of getting a kid ready for school and out the door, there was much commotion and rushing around on Monday morning. Brock helped Denny Lara choose the right kind of suit, dark, with a cool-tinged striped tie, for his grand jury appearance. The marshals brought cars up, eased an almost tearful Mandy back in the house after Brock gently separated Lara from her.

Then the caravan was off, speeding in fact, to make it to the federal courthouse on time.

"Don't be nervous," Brock said to Lara.

"Man, aren't you?"

"I'm nervous so you don't have to be," he said, and the marshal literally riding shotgun grinned back.

The federal grand jury for California's Eastern District met at nine o'clock that Monday morning in early June, in recently refurbished quarters on the courthouse's third floor. It met behind locked doors with marshals in blue blazers guarding the corridor. Nineteen men and women, drawn by lots from the voter rolls of the district, sat in a pale egg white room, at two-tiered tables, a small pit formed before them for witnesses and the assistant United States Attorneys who would present cases for their consideration.

They had their own bathroom, kitchenette, and access to secure copying machines, shredders, and staff. Brock had appeared before this mixed group of people often during the jury's twelve-month term. A few jurors even smiled at him when he stood alone in the pit, a chart in front of them listing the multitude of charges on which he hoped to indict Edward Patrick Nelson. Denny Lara, who had started to get a cornered, stricken look when they marched into the rear of the courthouse under the escort of armed marshals, waited in the adjacent witness room.

Brock intended to beat Alison by securing indictments and thus putting an immediate end to whatever scheme Nelson had set in motion. He went to the chart. He wanted the jurors thinking about Nelson and his crimes every minute.

"Ladies and gentlemen," he began, the court reporter tapping his words into her computer, "some of you may have noticed the tighter security around the courthouse this morning. There are quite a few additional marshals and plainclothes FBI agents on duty." He had their rapt attention.

He pointed to the chart and Nelson's boldfaced name. "This heightened security is necessary because I am going to present testimonial and documentary evidence to you about a threat to the defense of our country." He looked at each of them. "The threat comes from this man, Edward Nelson."

Brock meticulously summarized for the grand jury the progression of evidence he prayed Lara and the task force would produce.

He stepped back. Several jurors were making notes, and any lightheartedness among them had vanished. "This is the most important case you will consider," Brock said. "It will take a number of sessions to lay out all of this evidence, but I am certain you will return an indictment at the conclusion."

He inwardly took a breath. There was a moment, in any

investigation, when turning back became impossible. He nodded to the juror designated to alert the marshal guarding the witness room.

This was the moment. Me. Ally. It's all now. No going back.

"You will first hear from a former close associate of Edward Nelson, and he will outline, in detail, the crimes the government has alleged occurred."

Brock moved to one side as Lara entered through the side door like a reluctant martyr in the arena. He sat down at the witness table, only a small plastic water carafe and cup before him.

Brock began asking questions, slowly and crisply.

He marveled as Denny Lara shed the tremulant nervousness of the last few days and the ride downtown. Lara's performing, Brock realized. He's the sincere young investment banker, looking at the jurors directly, hands folded, voice firm.

We're going to make it, Brock exulted suddenly.

At noon, an irate Porter Ridgeway and Cubby Merical were alone in a private dining room at the exclusive Sutter Club, just a few blocks from the U.S. Attorneys Office.

Ridgeway raged, coat off. "I won't take that shit from anybody. Anybody."

"What did he say?" a more restrained Merical asked. He snacked on tiny crackers until their luncheon special arrived.

"Metzger calls an hour ago. Edict from on high. Lay off Nelson. In every respect. Lay off Alison Andrews. Give me some reason, some explanation, I ask reasonably." He smacked a hand on a seasoned old table.

"And?"

"No explanation. No reason. Nelson is God's gift, understand? That's all I get. From a half-assed golfing buddy of the president. Jesus H."

"Okay." Merical wiped his hands. "So why're you really honked off?"

"Because ten minutes later, like she's on the other line with Metzger listening to me getting reamed, Alison waltzes in, asks if I'm clear about everything and then waltzes out. Jesus. The arrogance."

"That wraps up keeping tabs on Nelson."

There was a discreet knock on the door, Ridgeway yanked it open and a wide jacketed waiter brought in two plates of broiled salmon and vanished silently.

"Does it?" Ridgeway demanded, sawing violently at his fish.

"Does it what?"

"I'm not pulling the plug on Nelson just because Chris Metzger back in D.C. is doing favors for Alison."

"I don't like that direction, Port." Merical chewed thoughtfully.

"Well, listen." Ridgeway wagged a knife. "If bagging a couple bad apples like Nelson and Alison and maybe this ATF agent is a big fucking deal"—he nodded rapidly—"how big do you think hooking a crooked associate attorney general is?"

"Metzger working for Ed Nelson?"

"Goddamn why not? So keep watching, keep the pressure on."

"Big game hunting. Very risky," Merical said, fork in hand. "What about Brock?"

"He and Alison split? Okay. He's on our team. He gets all the surveillance information, not her. He plays for us." He tossed his knife down. "Damn fish's like leather."

"I assume the CIA volunteered a hell of a lot of information," Brock said at the task force meeting just after one in the conference room.

Down the table, the FBI agent and the other men and women snickered. "The good news is that they insist Ed Nelson was chucked out, part of a general housecleaning. My source," the FBI agent made it sound comical, "suggested Nelson was a particular turd they wanted to dispose of."

"The bad news," Brock finished, "is I still don't know if Nelson went on working for them, right?" He tapped his pen on the files in front of him.

"That's right."

"Okay. Keep working on it. Somebody may have a different story." He knew finding out Nelson's employment status at the CIA, if the Agency wanted to conceal it, would be nearly impossible and certainly hard to demonstrate in court later. But he wasn't going to let Nelson get away with the claim.

He told the task force about Lara's initial outing that morning in front of the grand jury. "The guy's giving us the store, and the jurors love him," Brock reported, the smiles around the table adding to his own satisfaction. He didn't tell them about helping Lara get over dry heaves in the men's room afterward.

Brock put his pen down. "SFPD gave me the word a little while ago. Witnesses, physical evidence, what I provided them about Lara . . . put it all together and he's in the clear on the Kelso shooting. And Jimmy Yee's been commended on the good shoot during the Torrance raid."

The men and women at the table looked relieved. They had understood Brock's point about Lara's grand jury appearance. Denny Lara, soon-to-be father, had gone the distance and made the commitment to go all the way.

Jimmy's news should be plain good news, Brock thought. Except if the shooting review had gone against him, he'd be here now, hauled off the damn Nelson operation.

"Brock"—a hand went up from the Customs rep—"can we go after search warrants now? I've about exhausted all the public record material on Nelson's companies."

The IRS agent nodded and so did the ATF rep.

Brock made a quick decision, based on the morning's success. It was time to very visibly turn the full force of federal law enforcement on Nelson. "All right. I'll put together warrants for all of Nelson's companies, his personal papers, tax records, everything. Let's make him sweat under a spotlight."

"How about Atlantic Industries?" asked the IRS agent.

Brock had alerted him about finding the name on the Perrey auction list last night.

"Yeah. We get under their hood, too." Brock tapped his pen again. "The way Lara is going and what we add from these warrants, I'll indict Nelson and his pals in a week."

He flushed when, for only the second time in recent memory, the men and women around the table broke into stormy applause.

CHAPTER TWENTY-EIGHT

Jimmy Yee stood aside while Lyle Flecknoy and his lone companion Vernon peered at the AK-47s in their crate. Flecknoy bent low over the guns, sniffing at them, like he intended to eat one. He wore a fur-lined buckskin fringed coat, and his hair was uncombed. He muttered something too low for Jimmy to hear, and the other one, Vernon, blew a raspberry.

Ed guarded the storage locker's door just outside. The place reminded Jimmy of the mausoleum where his parents were interred. It had steel-doored rooms here, concrete corridors with ceiling fans open to the gray clouded sky, and on Wednesday morning, June 8, it was sepulchrally quiet.

"I got family in Taiwan," Jimmy said, hands in his red parka pockets. "I can get almost anything from over there."

"Well, I'm really interested in the portable items your people," he smirked, "can send over. Some fragmentation mines would be nice. Grenade launchers."

"We do this sale, I'm going to provide what you want."

Ed glanced back, face impassive, flask dangling from

one hand. Flecknoy's scarred mouth twitched. Jimmy was relieved the Cobra leader had apparently taken the cover story so readily. He'd asked snide questions back at the motel room before they rode here, but Ed's sharp retort that Jimmy was the best supplier he'd run across in dog's years had turned the tide. When they got to the locker, Ed had angrily popped the crate of dud guns himself, demanding of Flecknoy, "Does that look like toy trucks?"

"So," Jimmy said, nonchalantly slipping the crate top over the dud guns again, "I got these puppies all set; you bring me what we talked about, five hundred apiece tomorrow, that's . . ." He grinned as if adding.

"Two hundred thousand American dollars," Ed said, strolling back to them. "Okay, Lyle? You and Sergeant Chang going to do this tomorrow so I can leave your goddamn freezing state?"

Jimmy was astonished and heartsick when Flecknoy shook his head. "I'm not taking the guns, with ammo"— he pointed at Jimmy—"until we get ourselves straight about my mines."

"They're separate items," Jimmy said, showing his genuine anger. He bobbed like a fighter in the concrete corridor, the coming rain's breeze whistling through the fan blades. "I got to move these forty-sevens before we start talking new business."

"Oh, Christ," Ed swore, "I'm freezing my pecker off out here. We'll go to some greasy spoon and figure this out." He pulled his winter coat collar around his throat. "You guys follow us."

He started away, leaving Jimmy to lock up the steel door. Flecknoy and Vernon got into a rattling station wagon parked among the long, wide buildings of the storage facility.

Jimmy was enraged when he got into the car. "What the fuck are those psychos doing?"

"I told you they're funny," Ed said from the passenger seat. "Lyle hears voices." He crossed his eyes and let his tongue hang out.

Jimmy watched the rear sprung station wagon sluggishly

pull out of the storage facility and onto the shoulder of Boise's main highway, waiting for him to pass. He swore and banged the steering wheel. "I'm not screwing around with new deals before this one goes down. I want their asses on this one. We're all set on this one."

"Watch the traffic. I'll fix it." Nelson shivered. "God, I hate this outdoor crap. Slow down, okay? The president failed his last driving test."

They all sat on hard plastic benches near the back of a very busy fast-food restaurant. Jimmy was angry, tense, and he couldn't bear looking at this guy Vernon snuffling his face into a hamburger like a starved hog. It was disgusting to have been patted down by him back at the motel.

Across the table, Ed and Flecknoy were arguing.

Jimmy suddenly thought of One-Eye Piscador. One-Eye had a glass left eye. He was busted for being a crank dealer and firebug. In his incredible garbage pile shack in Amador County, Jimmy and Lila had been astounded to find an incredibly neat basement filled with hundreds of Aunt Jehmima figurines on shelves, all lovingly cataloged. One-Eye had screamed he didn't set any fires, and he might have gotten away with it, but Jimmy had found his glass eye in the ashes of the last blaze.

There appeared to be a lot of One-Eye in Flecknoy, except Jimmy thought this guy had two glass eyes.

"I want to work with you," Jimmy said to Flecknoy. "But I've got responsibilities and I got to pay people now."

Flecknoy sucked his teeth. "I want my mines."

"Later. For sure."

Ed sighed and stared at Jimmy, then said soothingly to Flecknoy beside him, "How about a compromise, Mr. President? The merchandise we inspected stays where it is for a few days; we get together and arrange to sell you additional items. You pay for and take possession of the original merchandise."

Jimmy was about to protest. He knew it would disrupt the schedule, require Alison to adjust backup with local law enforcement. Besides, it was axiomatic that suspects must never control the thrust of an operation. He opened his mouth, but then stopped. It looked like Nelson had it wired.

Flecknoy blinked, scowled, scratched his scar lightly. Vernon poked pensively at the scraps on his paper plate.

"I can abide by that," Flecknoy said. "But I want a deal for my mines the same time I take the guns."

"Voice lower." Ed grinned. "Okay. That works for us, doesn't it?" Ed gave Jimmy a pointed gaze.

"Yeah, fine. Great. Meet at the locker place Friday when they open. That's the tenth. But that's my outside," he said to Flecknoy. "I'll have to go to someone else after that."

"I always thought you people were supposed to be patient. You're the most impatient," Flecknoy hesitated, "Oriental I've ever met."

Jimmy spread his hands to keep from involuntarily making a fist. "I'm one hundred percent home-grown American beef."

Vernon snorted and gagged because he'd blown something into his lungs. Ed swore disgustedly and got up. "We're done. Let's go our separate ways."

Jimmy tried to stay with Ed and Flecknoy, who walked ahead in the parking lot, but it was not until later in his motel room that he realized how diligently Vernon, by chattering and actually tugging on his arm, kept him from getting close enough to hear what was being said. It was annoying, but didn't seem centrally important at the time since Ed had negotiated so well and kept the sting alive.

What Ed said to Flecknoy was this: "Your guns got to Chevy Chase, that storage joint this morning. Little ahead of schedule, but so what? All accounted for, all ready to go."

"What the hell do I need with a couple hundred electric motors? You tell me the goddamn ATF"—Flecknoy lowered his head—"excuse my profanity, is going to violate my land and I will not have a single honest gun to defend it?"

"Not one. The ATF will be all over your place, and they will find no illegal weapons of any kind." Ed held up an admonitory finger, his voice almost a whisper. "That is rule one or we better just forget the whole fucking thing now. And do not excuse my profanity."

"I wish I could have just one of the holy weapons I saw today."

"They're for his benefit." Ed jerked his head slightly to indicate Jimmy Yee behind them. "I thought he was solid, but I'm getting disturbing new information about him."

"Nothing's going to stop the righteous cleansing?"

"Voice lower. No. It's all going to happen on the seventeenth." Ed Nelson's face bore a new grimness. "Just keep moving your people off the compound one at a time in the regular truck trips into town. I want the FBI to keep seeing the same number of trucks going out and coming back. They just don't know how many of your guys are in the trucks. So it's all nothing out of the ordinary."

"Seven have gone out already. Vernon and I tested it last week when we left to inspect the battle site. I'm going out in the final truck, and then I'll join my warriors." He fixed a beady eye on Ed. "If this chink is a betrayer, his punishment will be terrible."

"I'll find out. We'll string him along until I know for certain, Mr. President."

Alison met Val Cantil outside a tall building in San Francisco's financial district, and they took a cab down to Fisherman's Wharf. A cool, wet breeze came off the Pacific, and only a few tourists were around mid-week. They went into a restaurant with a view of the Bay, ordered; then Alison picked up their conversation from every day since Sunday.

"Any good news from your campaign treasurer?"

Val Cantil shook her head slowly. She wore a blue silk scarf around her throat and absentmindedly plucked at it. "Not really. I must've gone to five fund-raisers a day before the campaign and ten every day during the race. I signed anything. If it didn't have a sign saying, 'I'm buying your vote' on it, I took the money."

Alison nodded. "I still don't see a prosecution, Val. That's my professional opinion."

"Alison, this isn't a courtroom. It's a public pillorying. At least in a courtroom I'd have a few safeguards."

The newspaper and television accounts since the story broke had been nearly unanimous in their condemnations. Upstanding Senator Cantil, a symbol of rectitude, had purchased her appearance of integrity with tainted money.

She wished she hadn't told Val Ed's tip about the contributions to her campaign. Lancing a boil sometimes caused an infection that was much worse, Alison mourned.

Their sandwiches and white wine came. A faint salty spray hit the restaurant's seaside windows. Alison nodded when Val thanked her for coming down, being with her now.

"I had a personal reason," Alison confessed. "I want to make the Senate run, Val. No hesitation."

"That makes me feel very good. We'll demolish anybody in the primary, which should only be token anyway. Then you'll romp through the general, Alison." She was quite pleased. "What does Brock say?"

"I didn't tell him."

"You've got to. First impressions matter a great deal. I want to make yours the two of you at the party."

Alison looked out at the sea, then at Val. "Brock and I are finished. So, I guess the first impression is going to be me alone."

She tried to be cavalier, but it sounded hollow and incredible even to her. Val touched her hand.

The next day, in the forenoon, Ed Nelson parked his rented car on a downtown Boise street and started walking. He'd seen the granite and stained glass of an old-fashioned church.

He went inside. Immediately, ancient smells of childhood hit him: musty flowers, candles, wax upon years of wax. He found a pew near the back, in a deep shadow beside a stone pillar, sat down, took out his flask, and drank deeply.

He didn't know what kind of church it was. He didn't care. He hadn't come here to pray. He couldn't see the altar and there were only two people in the pews, a very old man and woman, and the man seemed to be asleep.

Ed liked drinking in churches. They were cool, dark, and quiet. He leaned back on the hard pew. At that moment, everything was in motion as it ought to be. The FBI believed it had the Cobras completely covered. They had watched as trucks holding illegal guns were met by the Cobra's grand high loon.

And me. And an agent of the ATF.

Everybody believed the crates in Boise would head for the Cobra's compound. Yee had seen the bait guns. He thought the crates all contained inoperable guns. But the real guns were waiting just outside Washington, for their ultimate destiny in Chevy Chase at a fancy, spectacular celebrity party. There, lovely Alison would meet her destiny, too. She let a bunch of nuts get AK-47s, the talking heads on TV and secondhand geniuses would scream. She let nuts slip out of their compound right under the eyes of the FBI.

Ed intended for the compound to be searched because all anyone would find, unless Flecknoy goofed, were crates of poorly built Chinese electric motors. A simple magician's trick of misdirection.

Meanwhile. Mean. While. He took a pull from the flask as the old man in the nearby pew began snoring. Whoever's left standing at the U.S. Attorneys Office after the madness on June 17 will be running around trying to find cover, blame Alison. Or Brock. Ed hoped Brock got it in the neck. He assumed that sometime soon, tearing Applied Microavionics and Century Technologies apart, rummaging around at Atlantic Industries, Brock would find Alison's prints on everything, deals she knew about and deals she did not. He'd love that.

Alison or Brock or anyone associated with them would

be so discredited they could shout about some mysterious scrap shipment forever and it would sound like the ranting of undermedicated nuts. All they had to do was flail around for twelve to twenty hours. After that, his ship would be safely in international waters. Revenge complete.

Ed screwed the flask closed, put it in his coat pocket. He was not at peace. He was startled to discover that fact.

What was wrong? He lowered his head. It was Alison. He hadn't counted on her being at old Lurel's party. He could imagine what the crazies would do when they got their hands on her.

He got up, walking up the aisle. When he'd spotted that lovely, lively face in the magazine, he'd had intimations of the hunger for acceptance, the ambition he'd later uncovered. She was self-created, just like him.

He passed a stained glass window, blazing with light.

Something had to be done to save her. It was like saving himself. He indulged in a brief fantasy of wounding her in some fashion so she would stay with him, so he wouldn't be lonely.

But right now, the time had come to spread confusion among the enemy.

CHAPTER TWENTY-NINE

By Saturday, June 11, the search warrants Brock had executed simultaneously at Nelson's two companies and Atlantic Industries had produced a deluge of computerized data and papers. The only incident had occurred at Applied Microavionics when a senior vice-president had locked himself in a bathroom and tried to swallow several incriminating documents. Brock divided up the work so the task force, bringing in more help, could sort through the information and report in once a day at least. He told Lila, "Right now we've got six separate investigations going on Nelson."

"We'd only need one if your wife would open up."

Which, Brock admitted, was so. But Alison wouldn't help crush Nelson; she'd invested too much in him now. There was, he admitted, blame all around. Me, too, he thought. She started out trying to help me.

He worked with little break at the office, slept on the sofa occasionally rather than go back to the stale emptiness of his hotel.

Saturday morning he got a call from the IRS.

"This is an audit made in heaven, Brock," the agent

chortled. "You should see some of these disbursements to members of Congress. We'll be digging for years."

"What about Atlantic tying up to one of Nelson's companies?"

"It's like untangling a spiderweb. Things double back, money goes out, through banks, comes in again, turns around, names change." The agent's breathy delight at the puzzle irritated Brock.

"Have you found any connections?" he broke in.

"Not directly. But I've talked to the Customs people already about these transfers to China Resources. Nelson does business with China Resources. So he's always doing business at arm's length with everybody else. If he buys scrap or anything suspect, it's from this initial purchaser. He retains—"

"Deniability. Did *I* buy guns?" Brock cut in sarcastically. "There's got to be some purchase, some financial tie-in, maybe even a little one."

"We'll find it. This is as good as a steak dinner."

He hung up. He had to see Denny Lara later, to prepare for more testimony. The one bright corner was Mandy and her unalloyed happiness after her first appointment with Dr. Frisch. She had seen her unborn daughter move on a sonogram.

Everyone, Lila especially, was working at their limit, he knew. They had one fixed deadline: the auction on the fifteenth. But there were other deadlines, covert and relentless.

On Monday morning, June 13, Ed hunched over the phone in his motel room. He made a long distance call to St. Petersburg, Florida, and after some initial confusion spoke to Reverend Hayes. In clipped phrases, Ed identified himself as the office manager at Seymour and Clay, the law firm where Mandy worked. She'd moved, as her father knew, and the firm's health plan needed to know which physician was now caring for her. Oh? She called to tell him the good news about her prenatal checkup? How wonderful.

Ed wrote the doctor's name on a small motel pad and thanked Reverend Hayes. He hung up, dialing Dr. Oscar Frisch in Sacramento, California. His voice was slow, bored on this call. Ed identified himself to Dr. Frisch's receptionist as a patient rep for Blue Cross. Her insurance carrier was one of the ostensibly useless bits of information Denny had mentioned sometime about Mandy and Ed filed away automatically.

Did Dr. Frisch have a current appointment for Mandy Hayes? Blue Cross needed verification of a primary care physician to continue coverage.

"Tomorrow at two? Thanks so much, this saves me a lot of running around," Ed drawled, hanging up. He made another call. "Mr. President?" he said brightly. "We need to talk now."

Two hours later, Ed wheezed and sat on a rock after climbing a steep wooded slope. Lyle Flecknoy angrily kicked dirt.

"There's no way to get at Lara," Ed said, swallowing and holding a cramp in his side. "So it's got to be her."

"Fine, fine. It's this government spy I'm mad about. You vouched for that chink!"

"I'm as shocked as you," Ed said, drinking from his flask, shutting his eyes. "Let's keep things in order. Can you take care of her? Because as long as he's testifying, the feds can do us serious damage. Can you hear me?"

"I said it was done. I want the guns for it."

"You'll get them." He stood and handed Flecknoy a small piece of paper. "There's the time and place."

"Right, right, right. Now what about this spy? What about this betrayer?" The scar pulsed whitely against his flushed skin. He kicked dirt wildly.

Ed tried a soothing smile, and from that height looked down at the forest road below. He wondered if it had been wise to climb so high with a man who was obviously insane.

* * *

From a hastily improvised shelter of branches and leaves, two FBI agents stared through powerful binoculars across the wooded floor below at the next hill.

"What the fuck are those bastards talking about?" the younger agent said. He cursed, a dry branch sticking in his leg where he lay. "Get some pics anyway."

The older man, a snoutlike telephoto lens on his camera pointed at Ed Nelson and Lyle Flecknoy, began rapidly snapping photographs. "Crazy Horse is doing a dance. I swear he is. Old Ed must've pissed him off spectacularly."

"*Goddamn*, what the hell are they talking about?"

"Get these feelthy peectures back to Sacramento"—the older agent grinned—"maybe we can arrest their asses soon and you can ask them."

That evening, Jimmy Yee poked and prodded his refried beans and fish taco, hoping he'd feel hungry.

He pushed the plate away, swearing under his breath. The restaurant in downtown Boise was half-filled, pulsing with piped music. He finished his beer and ordered another. This was it. He was ending the undercover operation. He was going to call Alison, then check out of the Sands Motor Lodge and drive all night if necessary to get home and be with his own family, in his own bed.

"Another one?" the pert waitress asked provocatively as she set a full beer down.

"Probably, darlin'," Jimmy said.

"It doesn't have to be such a bad night."

He grinned. "I'll remember that."

But after she left, he realized it was a bad night, the successor to bad nights ever since he got to Boise. The Cobras had broken the meet on Friday, set another for Sunday afternoon, canceled that, each time sending local cops and the ATF Jimmy had alerted frustratedly cursing as they abandoned their positions. Even Ed was furious. "Those fucking crazy bastards," he had bellowed yesterday

and people began hymn singing inside. He couldn't see anybody out in the compound.

"What's that stink?" Jimmy demanded, the door to the windowless building opening. It was dim, grunting squeals and heavy porcine bodies sliding around in the shadows.

Ed stepped quickly to one side.

Flecknoy appeared in the dark doorway, scarred face white. "We butcher our hogs here," he said.

Before he could say anything, Jimmy was roughly shoved forward by the guards, the door slammed loudly, cutting off his yell, and the singing rose over high-pitched squeals.

CHAPTER THIRTY

Alison got up, talked with Porter Ridgeway and Merical again, picked up her third cup of coffee and looked at her watch. It was seven-thirty in the morning. She'd slept less than an hour.

A few minutes later, Brock came into Ridgeway's office. He was haggard and he looked at her accusingly.

"The task force's all here now," he said. "Let's get started." They had gathered just before six. Alison with as much detachment as possible recounted everything from her initial alarm when Jimmy didn't report in, to Ed's frantic call last night at midnight, to her own calls to Brock, then Ridgeway, then the local law enforcement agencies in Boise.

She'd felt numb, caved-in after talking to Brock, but she rallied now.

As they marched into the conference room, she said, "I've got Nelson in his motel room with three Boise city cops on top of him."

"It's a little late," Brock said. "This is all catch-up. He's way ahead of us."

"He called me," she said. "He's scared out of his mind."

"No, Ally. Not now," Brock said, hand up, and she didn't know whether he was chastising or warning her. Ahead of them, Ridgeway and Merical spoke quietly, nodding, and she knew who they plotted over.

Don't panic yet, she thought, coming into the conference room. I haven't lost Jimmy. As if will alone could make a fervent prayer fact.

She stood in front of them all. The windows were undraped, and the new morning's sunlight gleamed on the city's high buildings and across them all the way to the Sierras. The dozen or so cold, anguished men and women at the table only saw her.

She told them, cleanly and concisely, about Nelson and the elaborate undercover operation he was involved in for her and the Department of Justice.

"When he called me last night," she concluded, "Nelson said he and Jimmy Yee were supposed to meet again no later than eleven. Jimmy insisted on working out the final buy with the Cobras alone."

"That's a lie!" Lila Martin spat out down the table. "He wasn't crazy enough to stay with those assholes alone!"

Alison remained calm outwardly. "Special Agent Merical has the surveillance reports. Nelson and Agent Yee entered the Cobra compound. Nelson left by himself about an hour later."

Brock waved down the growing angry murmurs, hands slapped in rage on the table. "The first thing we're doing," he said loudly to capture their attention, "is getting search warrants for the Cobra compound and the storage locker where they've stashed their new guns."

"What the hell about Jimmy?" Lila Martin demanded, jumping to her feet. "He's a lot more important than goddamn storage lockers!"

"Tomorrow morning," Porter Ridgeway pushed to the lectern suddenly, "we'll raid the Cobras, with locals providing support." He appeared to wait for anticipated applause and frowned when there was none. "I think we should try

...ing these jackasses and finding out if they're hold-
...g Agent Yee first," he said sternly to Brock.

"These people don't negotiate. All we can do is surprise
them. We're going to coordinate the raid from here and
Boise," Brock said, moving in front of Ridgeway. "Once
the compound is sealed off, we'll go in massively. That's
why we can't risk going in any sooner or alerting them in
any way." He smiled coldly at Ridgeway, who hovered near
Merical for support. "I'm leaving for Boise right after this
meeting."

Alison felt sidelined as the various liaison and coordina-
tion details were quickly sketched out. But I've got one
indispensable talent. Ed talks to me, she thought. She had
never seen Brock's people work as a team, but he focused
them, directing their fears and anger toward the job. Fairly
inspiring, she thought with a pang because she was outside
it.

When the meeting was about to end, she stepped forward. The room fell silent. "We're going to get Agent Yee
back. I promise you that." She took a breath.

"You screwed him, lady," someone muttered.

She pulled Brock away from urgent commands to Merical and several other people. "I put him in jeopardy," she
said to Brock. "You were right about that."

"Jimmy went in voluntarily. He wouldn't be the first one
around here who got conned."

"I'm coming to Boise," she said. "I can help."

Ridgeway appeared beside them suddenly. "Alison, just
got off the phone with Chris Metzger. Great change of
attitude from the other day. He's very upset about this
sudden turn of events. He agrees you should stay near your
office until the situation's resolved." He gloated, glancing
at Merical, who stared balefully at her.

"Nelson will talk to me," she said to Brock. "He won't
be very forthcoming with anyone else. I'm his ticket out."

Brock nodded. "Any edge is welcome. You've worked
with him close up. Okay, Porter? Any problems?"

"I want you here. Metzger wants you here. To make sure
nothing else gets fucked up."

Alison said bitterly, "Metzger wants me isolated so he can wipe any dirt on me. I'm not sitting around waiting to be his scapegoat. I can still work Nelson. We've got a rapport." She noticed Brock's contained fury even if no one else did. Popeye was on thin ice, even with Merical beside him.

"My wife and I agree on one thing, Popeye," Brock added coldly. "Don't get in our way or you'll get flattened."

She sat with Brock on a 737 hastily rounded up from the Marshal's Service fleet. It was noon, and they were nearly over Idaho, the clouds below silken white, broken through by mountain peaks.

There was endless air telephone traffic. She talked again with Nelson. "Just get up here and get these bums off my ass," he said, a panicky undertone in his voice. He had nothing more to add about the meeting last night. Jimmy's car was found still parked in the restaurant lot, untouched.

Brock paced the packed jet's aisles, talking to the task force members he'd brought, then to the police in Boise. The FBI had mounted overflights on the Cobra compound. There was no unusual activity detected.

Brock finally sat down a few minutes before landing. "I've got an FBI hostage negotiating team standing by," he said.

"Ed's always told me the Cobras are fanatics. They won't negotiate and they won't give Jimmy back easily."

Brock stared out his window. "I like to pretend I have an option besides shooting the place up."

"Sometimes we don't have choices."

"Boxes," he muttered.

"What?"

"Lara said Nelson puts everything in boxes. Just like we do. If we didn't have our lives in these goddamn compartments, we wouldn't be here." He rolled the ring she'd given him. "It'd all be different."

"Maybe it would," she said. "The here and now is the problem."

There was a loud shout behind them, and Brock jumped up. "I've got to talk to her," he said.

Alison wondered what they would do in the next twenty-four hours. *After we're on the cold, solid ground again.*

Brock sat down next to Lila.

"He's mouthing off, saying it's a waste to have hostage rescue along." She shivered, swearing at an FBI agent three seats back.

"Are you going to keep it together?" he asked evenly.

"Oh, yeah." She crossed her arms, glowering at him.

"I mean it. Jimmy's got enough trouble without us acting unprofessional."

Lila leaned back. "You didn't see Trish or the kids this morning."

"I talked to her." The fear and anger from Jimmy's wife had been overwhelming. She blamed Brock for taking advantage of Jimmy's careless exuberance, enlisting him on the task force in the first place. Somehow even tempting him through Alison. "I told her I'm going to do everything to bring him back."

"I *saw* her," Lila said. "It's different, Brock, believe me. I didn't tell her I can't stop thinking about what happened to Camarena when he got kidnapped, the shit they did to him before they killed him." Brock remembered the torture-murder of DEA Agent Camarena by Mexican drug dealers several years earlier.

"Nothing like that's happened to Jimmy," he said with conviction.

"Unless that fucker Nelson burned him to the Cobras. So I'm telling you, and I'm telling Alison, don't try to hold me back when we go in tomorrow."

He loosened his tie. It was almost an affectation to have worn a coat and tie today, with all the crisis sirens wailing. Like Ally, he thought, we both need to keep appearances no matter what. "You shouldn't go into the compound," he said, "unless you get an attitude adjustment. Right now."

She looked at him. "You going to keep me out, chief?"

Brock paused, as if the jet had stopped in midair. "No," he said quietly. The pilot came on and announced they would be landing in fifteen minutes.

The emergency command post was set up in the basement of the Boise Police Department. It rapidly filled with county, city, and federal law enforcement officers, hastily laid new telephone lines, some connected to the mobile command van that would be used during the following day's raid, and computer terminals. Alison followed directions upstairs to a third-floor holding cell.

Ed Nelson, holding his head, sighed with relief when she came in. He wore a sweat-stained blue dress shirt, tieless, and brown slacks with a cheap black belt.

"Christ, Alison," he said, standing up and futilely trying to take her hand. "Everybody's gone crazy around here. They're treating me like the fucking son of Hitler."

Alison pulled up the single wooden chair and sat down. "I gave Brock all of our data, Ed. He's out taking a look at the storage locker where you put the AK-47s."

Nelson swore, sat down. He only had gray socks on, she noticed. Even now, tieless, shoeless, and drenched in fear sweat, she was unsure who or what he was.

"They're going to screw everything," he raged. "They'll blow the whole deal."

"It's blown, Ed. Jimmy Yee is a prisoner. Or worse. So we've got pieces to pick up. Like why Atlantic Industries, your partly owned subsidiary, is buying scrap from DRMOs."

"How the fucking hell should I know," he stopped, hand going across his forehead. "I'm sorry, Alison my love. The excitement. Look, you and I have our transactions; I watch those like a hawk. But my companies, other ones I do business with, they're on fucking autopilot, right? They've got their own business."

Brock had shown her the files collated and cross-referenced thus far about Applied Microavionics, Century Technologies, and Atlantic Industries. What she lacked, of course, was a specific trail of military equipment going through a DRMO. It would take weeks, if not longer, to sort through the millions of entries on computer printouts from the Defense Logistics Agency to determine if equipment was being deliberately miscoded or lost as it went into the military surplus sales system.

"All right, Ed," she said, pretending assent. "We'll come back to that. But I can't get around the simple fact you left Agent Yee with the Cobras, can I?" She stood up and snapped, "You left him. You didn't tell me you were going there."

"Well, you'd forbidden me," he said plaintively, then returned her truculence. "Alison, Jimmy demanded to make this operation work. He demanded we go to that nut farm. I'm not exactly a free agent. You say jump, I start jumping. He says jump." Ed Nelson closed his eyes. "How long am I stuck here?"

"I don't know. Everything depends on the next eighteen hours."

"We've still got the Chinese deal, right? I can still set that up."

She observed him. The anxiety appeared real, hands through his hair, worn features. But if this was a charade, then it all could be, and she had no clear stopping point. "Realistically, Ed," she said, "we're probably finished. DOJ is already making noises of shock and dismay. Nobody's going to buy you anymore."

He did something quite surprising. She expected frustrated rage, curses. Instead, he stretched out on the wobbly steel bunk. "I did what you wanted, my love. I'm entitled to my good conduct letter."

She laughed, harshly and deeply. "Dream on. And forget about blackmail, too."

He smiled at her. "I'm your friend. You never know when you need a friend." There was warmth as he looked at her, and she was unpleasantly reminded of the raw propositions he'd made.

"I don't need your friendship," she said sharply.

He shrugged, then started to say something, and the cell door banged open. Brock barged in, trailing two stocky, belligerent city cops in ballistic vests.

"Where are the guns?" Brock demanded from Nelson. He grabbed him off the bunk, and Alison thought the cops were angry enough to pummel him.

"What's wrong?" she said loudly.

"What the fuck's going on? Get your hands off me," Nelson shouted, shoving Brock aside.

Brock turned to her. "The locker's full of electric motors. One crate of useless rifles and a couple hundred electric motors."

"Jimmy told me he saw the guns. He unloaded them," she said heatedly.

"Well, they're gone now. So where the hell are they, Nelson?"

Ed stared, closed his eyes, mouth working. "It's a goddamn double-cross. That's why the goddamn Cobras wanted Yee alone. Christ, I just missed getting . . ." and he trailed off.

Brock shouted at him, the fists rising and falling before he was restrained by the Boise cops, and Alison. Ed cowered on the bunk. The cell stank of sweat, rage, and terror.

Mandy asked Denny what he'd do while she was at the doctor. He stretched, yawned at the kitchen table. "Maybe a little yard work, pull a weed maybe."

"You don't mind me going by myself?" she asked.

"Some guys say their wives start talking to themselves, eating weird. You want to spend time with the doc alone, that's not so bad." Her grinned at her.

On the ride downtown, Mandy wondered why she preferred these visits to Dr. Frisch without Denny. It was, she decided, like the solitary museum trips, the rare moments she and the baby would have because she and Denny would be together all the time. Their enforced togetherness now while he testified only underscored for her how inextricably bound their lives were going to be afterward.

"Pull around the front like before, Mrs. Lara?" asked the marshal driving her.

"Thanks. Saves me walking like a blimp," she joked, grimacing at her unbalanced, awkward movements.

The car slowed in front of the low, white painted row of medical offices. Several nurses chatted as they headed back into the buildings. The marshal put the car in park, hopped out to get her door. She grunted getting out. Denny needed a little rest time, too, she thought. Brock had called abruptly that morning saying the grand jury wasn't going to be in session until day after tomorrow. Mandy had felt a pang when she'd seen Denny take the news with enormous relief. Like a kid who hears school's canceled because of too much snow, she thought.

The marshal had her arm as he guided her to the sidewalk. "I'll pull around back," he began.

Mandy saw the spray of blood as his face disintegrated and the car's windshield blossomed from a solid, sleek surface into a cracked explosion of shards flying, shining in the afternoon sun.

She heard the nurses screaming. She heard the sputtering, spattering sound, which as the coddled daughter of a prosperous minister, former legal secretary in a prominent downtown Los Angeles firm, she had no way of identifying from actual experience as automatic fire from an assault rifle.

CHAPTER THIRTY-ONE

Brock said, "Settle down, please," raising his hand for quiet. He went on, "Latest witness reports say two men ran off after the shooting stopped. The descriptions are coming in now. You'll have them. The bad news is, no real ID witnesses."

The men and women in the crowded basement command center groaned. Alison sat beside Brock at a cluttered makeshift desk. It was five in the morning, she thought, the darkness holding outside, the real hard to distinguish from the unreal.

"But we do have the stolen VW van they were driving, abandoned outside Sacramento. I bet the print work will give us something. And the target, Mandy Hayes, survived. She's got some cuts and she's upset, but we're all right."

He looked at their assembled tense, uneasy faces. "Now we're going to get Jimmy Yee. Focus on that."

The impatient buzz of voices rose almost immediately, the agents and cops fired to the task by Brock's contagious optimism.

Alison said softly, "One marshal's dead."

"I didn't think that'd cheer them up. They don't need to be reminded."

He was grabbing papers off the desk, cursorily glancing at them. The raid was coming very fast, and she could see he was as nervous as everyone else. Only they didn't see it, she thought.

"I can handle the command center." She stood near him. "You're going to lose your witness if you don't go back to Sacramento."

He shook his head. "I've probably lost him. Lara's a basket case, wants instant relocation, won't testify anymore. Told me I'm a goddamn liar."

"All the more reason to get back and salvage what you can."

He slowly picked up a last paper. He wore jeans and jogging shoes, a hooded sweatshirt. "I can't be in two places, Ally. I've got to be here."

"I guess you do," she agreed, understanding at last that he was a disciple of situations, too. Brock's necessity was finding his lost soldier. "I'm going back to work on Nelson. We didn't knock off until one. He's still saying he's been tricked by the Cobras. He loses if they're off the reservation."

Brock took a last look around the room, already ripe with the ingrained smell of too many bodies, too much fear and worry, burned coffee. "Cobras took the shot at Mandy. We both know it. Who wants Lara shut up? Your man Ed."

"I am going to find out the truth."

"Okay, Ally. Do that. Find out what he and Flecknoy were talking about on the mountain just before Jimmy disappeared and my witness got shot at."

She sat down, fatigue and fear seeping from the room into her. "I hope to God you find Jimmy."

"For both our sakes, I hope so, too." Then he was gone, trailing agents in clipped, urgent dialogue.

Alison steadied herself, then went upstairs to shake Ed awake, and find the secret path through this maze he had hidden in his head.

* * *

From a pine ridge a half mile south of the Cobra compound, Brock saw the raid commence. The sun was now high and bright, and around him bustled FBI and ATF agents who directed the vans and cars that swept like a storm-driven tide through the flimsy barrier around the compound.

Brock watched, through high-power binoculars, as small figures scattered like leaves among the partly tree obscured nest of flat buildings, and black-clad men with rifles smashed open doors, windows, and crept onto rooftops.

From up here, he thought, it all looks so orderly and symmetrical. Like we intended everything.

Fifteen minutes later, the FBI SAC, Merical's Idaho counterpart, said to Brock, "Okay, it's all nice and secure down there."

"Any sign of Agent Yee?"

"Not so far."

"Get me down there," Brock said, already darting to the helicopter kicking up dust around the command center van from its whirling rotors.

Brock strode from one small group of sullen, white-faced women and children to another. An FBI or ATF agent with a submachine gun guarded them. Beside him, Lila, also in a black uniform, her rifle gripped with crushing intensity, shouted to each group, "Where's the man who came here Monday night?" Or she'd suddenly shout, "Jimmy!" and the name would echo among the old pines and birches, then fade into insignificance.

"We'll find him," Brock said. He kept her nearby because she was furious and he could steady her. But his own frustration grew as each batch of silent, glowering women and young children seemed to delight in his inability to locate Jimmy Yee. There was something very wrong.

For an hour he helped Lila and two dozen law enforcement officers tear the compound to pieces, wrenching furniture and floorboards apart. The urgency he felt pulsed through them, their shouts and the rough, brutal search.

Brock said to Lila, "I figured there'd be some shooting. We got them completely by surprise, thank God."

"Fuck surprise." She whirled on him. "They don't have any guns. Not one. The baddest thing they've got here is a hatchet."

Brock immediately yelled for the FBI SAC, who trotted to him. "Have you found any weapons? What about the forty-sevens?"

"Nothing. It's unbelievable."

"They've stashed the guns someplace, and I bet we'll find Jimmy Yee right there, too," Brock said. The raid had been so swift and overwhelming because it was predicated on the grim belief the Cobras had the hundreds of missing automatic rifles and more stockpiled in the compound.

Now he paused in the midst of the organized pandemonium and chaos as the buildings and people were searched. He hadn't been able to pinpoint the unsettling thing until this instant.

"Where are the rest of the men?" he demanded of a haughty young woman, holding a small boy by the hand as they sat in the dirt outside the dining hall. "It's over here," he said more gently to her. "You're all under arrest. Do you want to stay with your son? Tell me where the men are. In the woods? Hiding?"

She wiped the boy's mouth slowly.

"It's not over," she said.

Brock conferred with the FBI and ATF agents in charge in the shadow of a vast pine that nearly blotted out the sky.

"The last intelligence reports said there were between ten and twenty adult males here," he whispered. "They're gone. Flecknoy's gone. The rifles are gone. What happened?"

"All they took were the usual trips into town for supplies,

two men in each truck, two men come back," said the
thin-faced, agitated ATF agent. "We're going to have to
go through these goddamn hills tree by tree. They're out
there."

Brock had been reminded by the woman's sinister gloat-
ing of what one of the suspects arrested outside the Peninsula Hotel in Beverly Hills had said. Maybe this was it.
Guerrilla warfare in the forests of Idaho, waged by a small
band of millenarian militiamen armed with assault rifles.
Cleansing spears indeed.

"I'm going through Flecknoy's office," Brock said, turning toward the closest flat building, a crude flag of Free
America limp beside it. "I want everything boxed up in
there. Even the no-pest strips," he said harshly.

Lila came in while he worked. Her face was damp with
sweat, knuckles looking skinless as she tightly held her
rifle. Brock stopped scanning the raving rough drafts of
articles and manifestoes Flecknoy had been writing. He
took her shoulder and it felt like she was solid metal. "It's
going to take a lot longer," he said softly. "Jimmy's here.
He may even be nearby, but these assholes are hiding so
we're going to have to do it the hard way."

"I want to hear something from one of them," she said
throatily.

"Look, I'm almost done." He gestured at the scattered
papers and upended chairs and table. "This is going to
be a long haul. Why don't we go back to Boise, come back
here later and start fresh?"

"I don't want to go back."

Brock looked at her, touched her face, then said, "We're
going to Boise, Lila. The rest of these guys will keep
looking."

She nodded, almost dazed, and left the office. Brock
gathered papers into boxes. Sorting through this mass of
delusion and defiance might provide answers to what the
Cobras were doing. He found a burlap sack in a corner,
the word BURN raggedly written on it. He gingerly opened
it. The ATF agents had assured everyone there were no
booby traps, but he wasn't entirely convinced.

He pulled torn fragments of paper from the bag, obviously intended for the fire and either overlooked or the raid had prevented it. Brock didn't have time to piece the fragments back together. He held up three bits of a photograph. A brick facade, many windows, trim hedges. Where the house was, why the photo was ripped up and slated for burning, he had no idea. He shoved it all back in the sack. Get it to the FBI, let them put this puzzle together as fast as they could.

Maybe it was connected to Jimmy.

Brock closed the boxes. He knew why Lila was so stunned. She'd undoubtedly spotted the search and rescue dogs being brought in along with the infrared and thermal scopes. All would be valuable if the Cobra militiamen were lurking in the woods.

But you needed the dogs and scopes to find buried bodies, too, he thought.

The first shot cracked, reverberated, then piled onto two more, and shouts, obscene, desperate, angry, spilled over them outside.

The screams followed. Brock ran out and found the women and children being held back by yelling FBI agents. Lila, surrounded by ATF agents, handed her rifle to one.

"What the hell happened?" Brock demanded loudly, trying to be heard over the women praying and shouting at him, shoving to get past the armed men restraining them.

"She started running and she had a gun, Brock," Lila said, head up, eyes wide. "The bitch was going for someone."

"Oh, Christ," he breathed, walking fifty feet away to the crumpled form in the dirt being frantically massaged, infused with breath. The woman's gray and blue blouse was torn open, a naked breast bloody. Brock shouted for more paramedics to get over to her. He leaned down. It was the woman he had spoken to, and her small boy, screeching and tearing to get to her, was lifted by two FBI agents and carried toward a van.

"Killers! Killers!" the other women screamed, then

wailed with an incoherent fervor that made the skin on
Brock's neck prickle.

He said sharply to one of the FBI agents, "She had a
gun. Where's the gun?"

Lila passed him, walking to another van with several
agents both protecting and hustling her forward.

Brock wordlessly took a palm-sized wooden black cross
from the stony-faced FBI agent.

CHAPTER THIRTY-TWO

Brock and Alison, even with Boise police officers flanking them, pushing ahead of them, had to stumble, then roughly force their way into the Police Department building through a surging, yelling mass of reporters and cameras. A microphone boom swept down toward Alison like a great carnivorous insect, and Brock swatted it away.

By mid-afternoon on Wednesday, June 15, the raid's debacle was drawing media from up and down the West Coast, more on the way.

In the lobby, Brock stopped, hands on his hips. Alison looked back in disbelief at the size of the crowd outside.

She said to the FBI agents and Boise chief of police, "You can send some brave soul out there and tell them we'll have a briefing in an hour."

"Until then," Brock said, "no comment. All right?"

The other men nodded. He and Alison took the elevator upstairs. They glanced at each other. She patted dirt and sweat off her face and neck with a silk handkerchief. "You kind of feel like all the lifeboats have gone."

"And the band's stopped playing," Brock said, the elevator doors opening. It was uncertain to Alison whether he only meant the raid or something more personal to them both.

"You're not under arrest," Brock said to Ed Nelson in his cell. "But you're going to be." He was as taut as Lila.

Nelson, knotting his tie, sitting down to put on his shoes, peered at him, then smiled at Alison, who sat on the wooden chair. "Of course I'm not under arrest. Brock," he mangled the name merrily. "You try that sucker punch shit on me again, you just add one more count to my lawsuit. Which you'll be served with as soon as I get home and talk to my lawyer." He stood up.

Alison said cuttingly, "I'm not impressed with the performance anymore, Ed. A good ATF agent is missing, another one suspended, and a woman shot dead. Now, where are the guns? Where are the Cobras?"

He fumbled in his pockets, found a piece of gum and threw it into his mouth. "Yeah, I could hear the boys and girls getting together outside, so I assumed something didn't go right with your raid. Which was to be expected." He grinned at Brock.

This was agony, Brock thought, controlling the uncontrollable desire to punch Nelson bloody, force him to shriek out Jimmy Yee's location, why Mandy had been almost killed. Instead, he grinned back. Something tiny, black, and squirming looked out at him from Nelson's eyes.

"I've still got your letter, Ed," Alison said.

"I still want it. I've earned it."

"Not with Jimmy Yee missing and the guns unaccounted for."

Ed Nelson cocked his head. He listened, apparently, to the inchoate voices from the massed reporters just below his window. "You two have stepped right into the shit, haven't you? We've all gotten fucked by these funny farm Davy Crocketts. They got your guns, but the joke's on them." He nodded to Alison. "Like we planned, all I delivered were duds."

"How the hell do we know that?" Brock demanded. "We didn't find any guns."

"Your credibility's deflating by the second," Alison said, standing up. Her face was flushed. Her plain olive green shirt, partly unbuttoned, rounded over her breasts. "Time's up, Ed. Without that letter, you're hanging out bareass. Nobody at DOJ will back you. I'm all you've got. Persuade me right now."

Brock held himself tighter. Nelson stared at her, obviously attracted. The reckoning would come the instant after Nelson answered Alison's questions.

"Well," Nelson rasped, loosening his just-tightened tie, "you'll have to play hide-and-seek in the hills with the nutlogs. But, on the other business"—he pointed at Brock—"you stay clear, Brock."

"What business?"

"The DRMO down at Perrey. You pawed through my records, all my companies, scared my people shitless. You do not want to connect these dots. Trust me."

Brock said tightly, "You're a smuggler, Nelson. Right now, right here, you can help yourself. Give up your people, lay it all out, maybe Alison's Queen for a Day letter might still work."

Nelson frowned, then laughed. "I'm trying to help *you*." He gestured at Alison. "Here's a little lesson in geopolitics, Brock. What's coming out of the DRMO at Perrey today are some container trucks filled with scrap, and in that scrap there's a shitload of useful hardware the Chinese are practically begging for."

"Repeat that under oath," Brock began. Alison had gone white.

"Fuck under oath." Nelson waved a hand dismissively, started for the cell door. "This is your government talking. Part of it anyway. Look, bud, you're in the White House, you get these frantic calls from China. Got to have this jet, that missile, that black box. But, you go to the Hill, you make it all public, and suddenly every douche bag in the country goes apeshit. Can't give our good military crap to the Chinese, no matter how much we want them to love us, and vice versa. So, what's a frustrated administration to do?"

Alison sat down again, looked up at Nelson. "The lessons of Iran-Contra, right, Ed?"

"Always the first in line, Alison my love. That's an A-plus. You do not want to repeat the mistakes of the past. So you send all of this wonderful military equipment out through a system nobody watches, with unbelievably lax inventory control. The Chinese get what they want; you don't have to sweat a lot of publicity-seeking oversight from Congress. The national interest is served."

Brock thought of Denny Lara's suspicion. Ed never left the CIA.

"It's a lie," he said, coming toward Nelson. "What was all this militia bullshit for?"

"I'm an arms dealer. I have to be seen dealing. Every fucking surveillance picture you've got, that's what I'm doing."

Alison said low and hard, "Get out, Ed. The locals will take you through the back. Put your coat over your head." She smiled, more a twist of pain, though.

Brock said grimly, "Go back to Virginia, Nelson. Or I'll arrest you right now and I don't care if it sticks or not."

"That's exactly what I'm going to do. I'm going to put my feet up by the fire at the old homestead and watch you self-destruct." He paused at the cell door. "I hope you find Yee. We got along. Good guy."

He was through the door, barking at a Boise detective, before Brock could lash out again. In fury, Brock slammed his fist into the cell door over and over, and Alison didn't stop him at once.

They went down to the command center, Alison ordering serial interrogations of the Cobra women, two teams of FBI agents questioning each suspect. The children were dispersed to three local child care centers. There was an electric vibrancy in the command center, people moving and talking faster as if the shock of the raid's failure made them jumpy. Brock was on the phone when she came back to him.

Where's Jimmy, she thought. The big question that makes it hard to think straight.

Brock scribbled on the backside of a pizza menu. He spoke out loud for her. "Okay, the Atlantic Industries jerk showed up, bid on lots twenty-six, twenty-seven, and twenty-eight. All listed as mixed metal scrap and electronic parts."

Alison sat beside him on a chair with rollers. She felt unsteady, like the first time she and Brock went ice-skating.

He said, "Six trucks loaded up, nothing unusual. Total tonnage is ninety-seven. The trucks are seagoing containers." He grinned over at her. "I understand. I'll call you back when I've decided."

Alison saw two FBI agents approaching. She said to him, "It happened?"

"Two and a half hours ago. The trucks were hauling for Atlantic Industries, the bidder on the junk. But right afterward, the drivers notified Cavanaugh at the DRMO, the stuff had been transferred to Applied Microavionics for shipment."

"Where is it now?"

"On I-5 going south. Destination is supposed to be the terminal at Long Beach for China Resources. Delivery tomorrow, Thursday, loading on a ship sailing for Hong Kong early Saturday."

"I don't care if Ed's telling the truth," she said, the FBI agents almost there. "We can just intercept the trucks. None of that military equipment has to leave the country."

Brock nodded, standing up. "It's not going to. I've got surveillance on those trucks every inch of the way to Long Beach. I've got eyes on Nelson, too. He steps one foot off his Ponderosa, he's busted. He's either holing up there or he's lying again and he'll turn up at Long Beach when the scrap arrives." He examined the FBI agents, both just rushed over from the local office.

Alison got up. "The joke's on us, Brock. Popeye, the desk jockey extraordinaire, lucks out. All those pictures of Nelson after he was told to lay off. That'll be the proof against Ed." She shook her head, then said to the agents, "I can give you my information about the raid now," leaving with them. She had her own interrogation to endure, as they all did.

Brock wheeled toward the stairs.

The FBI agent at the interview room on the second floor refused to let him in. "I'm doing mine in about an hour," Brock said to the agent. "I want to see how she's holding up."

"You know the drill. Separate everybody before they're interviewed." The agent was young, his neck so rigid Brock saw veins standing out.

"Come on in with me," Brock replied tartly. "Maybe someone will do this for you in the very remote chance you screw up someday."

A moment later, he and the young agent went inside. Lila stood in a corner, eyes closed. An overturned soft drink can lay on the blue-green metal table. There were four metal chairs around it. The walls were plaster thickly painted white.

The ultimate horror, for most law enforcement officers, was to be where Lila stood, under suspicion, in an interview room with hostile interrogators on the way.

It was that sympathetic recognition that persuaded the novice agent to let Brock in. But, only Brock knew Lila had one additional, perhaps greater horror eating at her.

"How you doing?" he asked, hands in his pockets.

"Good. Anything?"

"We've got the area around the compound broken into grids; we're taking it a piece at a time. On foot, the dogs, couple helicopters."

"Any of the assholes say anything?" Lila opened her eyes. There was an onion skin transparency around her face from tension. "I mean, one word?"

Brock saw the FBI agent's worried expression. An exchange of information was very bad procedure. Screw him. "They won't talk about anything except the thing this morning." He frowned. "But we're redoing every one of them. Alison set it up. It's not quite kosher, but we're asking gentle questions of the kids, too."

"Shake it out of the little bastards," Lila said, sitting down. "Somebody heard him or saw him Monday night."

He sat next to her, saddened at her trapped look. "I'm not going anywhere until we find Jimmy. I'll be here for you; you just call for me."

"I'm going to need a real lawyer." She smiled a little. "We all might."

She breathed hard and fast suddenly, glaring up at the FBI agent; then she said to Brock, "I'm sorry about the way it went this morning. I sincerely am. I am so fucking sorry I didn't hose the whole bunch of those bastards when I had the chance."

Brock, although it was close to being utterly useless, reached out and put his hand on hers. How could you comfort or console a woman who had probably lost part of what passed for her family, and the part she lost was a man she could never admit she loved?

"What do you know about the house in the picture?" Brock asked Merical over the phone. It was nearly six; Alison had gone back to her hotel exhausted.

"We're working on it. I've talked to the agents up there, and even with the original photo, they don't have anything yet. They're checking photo developers, the manufacturer to see if we can place the sale of the film."

"Flecknoy and the Cobras weren't keeping a family album."

"Look, we're trying analysis of the foliage. It might give us the locality, some geography. We're checking the light pattern to get a time of day, running the house against a database of registered homes, like maybe it's a national monument or something."

"I keep thinking Jimmy might be nearby that house."

"Nobody's sleeping until we get some identification."

"What about Nelson?"

"Boarded a United flight for Dulles at three-forty."

Brock sat back. "Stay with him when he gets off, when he goes home, and make sure he's there if I want him."

"The good hands people are handling this deal from now on," Merical said. "People with experience. Not like the amateur night Alison was running."

Brock ignored the jab at Alison. She had started to seem a distant presence suddenly. He drank a cold cup of coffee. Where were the guns? Where were the Cobras? Where the hell was that elegant old home?

And where, dear God, was Jimmy Yee?

An hour later, Brock finished his seventh and, he vowed, last cup of coffee. He had seen the FBI twice more, neither adding nor subtracting from his early account of the raid. He was due, in fifteen minutes, to join the day's last helicopter sweep over the forest north of the Cobra compound.

He sat back. Except for specific questions, everyone else in the basement command center left him alone, like an invisible bubble or lethal contagion surrounded him. He tried Lara again, got the marshal on duty. It was touch and go whether Lara would simply pick Mandy up and walk out the door in the next five seconds, the marshal said.

"Tell them whatever you have to. They're safer at the base," Brock said, knowing it was merely a patch on a great hemorrhage.

The media flood outside the Boise Police Department grew hourly, too. The biggest law enforcement catastrophe since Waco or Ruby Ridge, Brock heard over and over on the large screen TV at one end of the basement, no matter which network an aggravated FBI or ATF agent tried. Finally, with a flurry of obscenities, someone turned the TV off.

He stood, aching from exhaustion. The trucks still moved. Nelson's trucks.

Like an almost inconsequential flaw in an otherwise perfect diamond, Brock suddenly saw the way to answer the

doubts both he and Alison had about Nelson's claim the
scrap trucks were part of a government plan.

He grabbed the nearest telephone and called his task
force rep, who remained doing cleanup on the auction
at Perrey Air Force Base. Then he talked to Cavanaugh,
peremptorily and coldly. "A hundred tons of your best
garbage, right now," he said. Cavanaugh stammered,
resisted, then agreed to Brock's demands.

Finally, he called Merical again in Sacramento. "I need
six agents ready to go. Truck drivers," Brock said, a hard
edge in his voice. "Can the good hands people handle
that?"

"What's the idea?" Merical asked suspiciously.

Brock told him. Then repeated it. "I'm going to play
the way Nelson does."

Merical said grudgingly, "If it works, you're back in
business."

"We all are," he corrected, hung up, and hurried out
to the helipad on the roof.

The June night fell slowly, shadows shooting along the
treetops as the sun dropped and Brock's helicopter along
with the teams on foot below were going to make a last
circuit of the land, and come back the following morning.
Nerves were at the breaking point after the shooting and
the raid's failure.

Brock stared down through an infrared scope. An FBI
agent beside him studied the same landscape through a
thermal scanner, looking for unusual hot spots. Ten minutes later, the agent shouted, and the teams below moved
in.

The digging took just fifteen minutes, even with time to
preserve the area for evidence. Brock landed, trotted the
short distance to the site, a swatch of wild grass and flowers
surrounded by sentinel pines. Flashlights and high intensity lights almost recreated day in the small circle where
men dug. When the last layer of dark, moist forest soil
was removed, and ashen-faced agents stood silently, Brock

turned away. He recognized the still-intact haircut and the red parka with its distinctive Boreal and Squaw Valley ski patches. The hope he'd felt a little while ago, a weakness in Nelson's grand design, was frail against this stark spectacle in the clearing.

He returned to Boise and drove to Lila's motel.

He held her tightly until the wrenching sobs quieted, then came back, as if something were tearing up through her. "What am I going to do? What do I do now?" she managed to say.

"We'll all go home together," he said softly, rocking her on the side of the bed.

On Thursday morning, June 16, Brock got up after a dark, repellent half sleep, showered, shaved, and mechanically ate breakfast at a silvery diner down the street from Alison's hotel. He waited on the sidewalk for some time, watching the cars, sorting through his mind. Then he went up to her room.

She had nearly finished packing.

"I'll say it again. I'm so sorry. I don't know what else I can say," Alison stopped.

"That's all I can say."

"Does it stop hurting this much?"

"I don't know."

She nodded. She wore a green dress, a red bandana and light perfume. She went into the bathroom and came out with her toiletry case.

Brock was nauseated by the silence, so he said, "Talked with Merical late. The house in the picture's definitely East Coast, old. Early nineteenth century. So the operative concept now is that the Cobras have a terrorist attack planned."

"But why that house?"

"The big thinkers, like Popeye and whoever else, think it's something along the lines of a national shrine. Someplace like Monticello or Mount Vernon. The Cobras are after a high visibility target."

"Aren't they hiding in the hills here?"

"Who knows, Ally? Who knows where the hell they are." He watched her close the suitcase, adjust her skirt. She had a worn, scarred look. It reminded him of the wounded expression after her miscarriage, the real pain buried deep, only sending its least damaging signs outward. "Old Ed is sound asleep in his own little bed. That's certain anyway."

"Brock, I've got to go. Val's arranged appointments on the Hill. I'll twist a few flabby arms and turn this around."

"You do what you have to, Ally."

He stepped aside as she put on a gray coat, eyes avoiding him.

"I'm going to give Chris Metzger a spine. He's going to back us up." She reached for her briefcase.

"After that, you go to the big party and let Val make you a senator."

"There's no reason for me to stay here." Her voice caught for an instant.

He nodded. "Not one. The sick part, Ally, is I don't care. I didn't think that would ever happen. But, now I don't care. I hope you become a senator. I hope you get what you want."

He pulled the ring off his finger slowly, handing it to her. Like a kid who can't play anymore, she thought, observing as if from a great depth.

"Oh," she said, holding the ring, fingers closing around it. "I only did what Metzger wanted because," she hesitated and continued when she could, "it was the only way to look out for you. For both of us."

"Yeah. Very ironic," he said.

"So goddamn ironic it makes you want to cry," she said.

But she didn't until much later, on a plane heading east, thousands of feet above the green spaces and silent emptiness of the Dakotas, traveling across the rivers marking the Badlands.

CHAPTER THIRTY-THREE

At ten-twenty on Thursday morning, the salesman at Best Buy Used Trucks in Falls Church, Virginia, who had waited on Lyle Flecknoy, was half-surprised to see him appear in the office, hand over the final payment on the six trucks, sign the papers, take the keys, and walk out.

The salesman saw five men waiting on the lot, one he recognized from the earlier visit, and four others. They all had iron skillet hard eyes, he told one of his mechanics later. When the six men and the trucks had driven away, the salesman shook his head. "Make you a bet," he said to another salesman, "those guys are going back to the Mother Ship."

The six slightly battered trucks traveled through Falls Church, down the main highway for several miles, and turned in single file onto a short, poorly maintained road. A quarter mile down the road, the trucks went into a large aluminum-sided building, the creaking metal doors sliding shut behind them.

Flecknoy and his men got out, put on paper masks, and for the next few hours, spray painted the trucks powder blue. The former general aviation hangar reeked of acetone and sweat. Four more men arrived from the scattered motels they had been staying at. They brought newly made signs with peppermint-striped letters.

Joking, working methodically, the men attached signs to the sides of all the trucks. Flecknoy wiped his paint-spattered hands, his sweaty neck.

Vernon grinned. They admired their work.

ROYAL RENTS PARTY TENTS the trucks now proclaimed, with little balloons and champagne flutes hovering around the letters.

"Just about thirty hours from now," Flecknoy said to the reverently quiet men around him in a semicircle, "we will change history in this nation."

"How about a prayer?" Vernon murmured.

Brock flew back to Sacramento, drove out to McClellan. He went up to the bedroom and saw Mandy. Her face was mottled with tiny stitches and white bandages, and she sat in a chair, looking on the restful backyard below.

"Never says anything," Denny Lara whispered hoarsely to Brock. "I brought her back, and she just sits."

Brock knelt on one knee beside her. He saw the bandaged right hand, laid lightly on her swollen stomach. He patted her arm. "How are you?" he asked softly.

She didn't move; then her face turned to him slowly. "I'm alive," she said.

"Damn right."

"My baby's alive."

"Everything's going to be all right. I promise."

"It doesn't matter what we do or where we go."

"I'm going to make sure you're protected."

Mandy smiled. Then she didn't say any more. Finally, Brock stood up. "Come on," he said briskly to Denny Lara.

He took Lara out of the stilled, stunned house. He dragged Denny Lara around the base, watched whipcord sleek jets take off, felt the rumble in their chests of great engines. It was uncommonly hot.

Brock was waiting and watching for the moment to stem

Lara's increasing panic. If it hardened, there would never be indictments or any way to punish Nelson.

They walked beside a vast hangar, four jets being serviced inside. Brock stopped. "You've got to go on testifying Monday."

"Fuck that. I'll get Mandy killed if I do." Sweat shone on his face. "I've got immunity. We're leaving."

"Where'll you go? You walk out of here, you are dead and so is your family."

Denny Lara flinched. "You're getting us killed," he shouted. "You almost got her shot, at the doctor for Christ sake."

"Walk away and Nelson will find you and he will kill you."

"I'm not testifying anymore; I'm not bothering him. He'll just leave us alone if I do that."

"Denny, Ed Nelson knows you got up in front of the grand jury once. Do you think he'll risk you doing it again?" Brock needed Lara, not only to punish Nelson, but to atone for losing Jimmy Yee. Lara had to testify Monday morning because Brock would be at the funeral Monday afternoon. "Up here"—he tapped Lara's forehead lightly—"you've got information about him. You know where his money is."

"I don't. Swear to God."

"I've got a lot of material on Nelson now. You've got the last pieces about his bank accounts, and that's going to bring him down. I find his money and I can prosecute him."

Lara breathed huskily; then he burst out, "Why the fuck should you? Why can't you just leave me and Mandy alone?"

Brock turned away, swung back and said slowly, "Denny, I prosecute the bad ones all the time. It never stops. I know that. But every so often, like once in a century, I have the chance to really make a dent, to really stop some very bad things and bad people."

"So you want to use me?" Denny Lara said bitterly, walking away. "Fuck you. It's not worth my family."

Brock grabbed his arm, jerking him back. "Every so often I get a chance to stop some bad people," he said intently. "But I never have the chance you do, Denny. You stand up and stop Ed Nelson and what he's doing, you change things more than I ever will in my entire career."

"I don't care about changing anything," Denny Lara snarled. "It's always going to be me and my family on the firing line."

Brock looked at him steadily, sweat beading, stinging his eyes. He didn't blink. "I'll be right beside you and Mandy. Until we lock Nelson up."

"What good is that? Were you right beside your agent up there in Idaho?"

"It's not the same," he said, but the image seared in his mind was Jimmy, whom he had not saved.

"I don't see a damn big difference," Denny Lara said. "I know what Mandy's going through, and I can hide us from Ed a fucking lot better than you can."

Brock tried every argument and appeal as they walked back to the house. But he knew it was useless. When a snitch bolts, it is irrevocable. Even if you manage to wrangle him back, he's gun shy and timorous and juries never trust him. Juries that don't trust don't convict, he thought.

He helped Lara pack, helped the stoical but quietly disapproving marshals gently put Mandy in a car.

"You're making a mistake," Brock said to Lara.

"I'm fixing one. Tell Ed I give up. He wins. Just leave me and my family alone." Lara looked at Mandy. He said to Brock, "What would you do?"

"Not this."

Lara grinned mirthlessly. "First time you've lied to me."

Brock stood on the grass of the once more deserted house on Balboa as his snitch was driven to the airport.

Case closed, he thought.

Brock later went home. Celeste, fixed point in the changing universe, insisted on making him something to eat.

He sat with her in the kitchen, pretending to taste the avocado and cheese sandwich she set in front of him.

"You like my opinion?" she asked, hands on her hips.

"Go ahead."

"Some people I work for, I don't care, they can drop dead. But you and Mrs. Andrews are special."

"I used to think so."

"If you don't fool around, and she don't fool around, married people can always figure it out," Celeste pronounced. "That's my opinion."

In her frame of reference, only adultery dissolved a relationship. Adultery would be preferable, he thought.

"Thanks for the sandwich and advice." He kissed her cheek.

He went into the study. Coming here was a sign he was still tethered to Alison and their lives together. But it was an illusion he had to banish.

He looked at the pictures and awards on the walls, mocked by memory and unfulfilled promises. Then he went upstairs and packed. He called and got a reservation on a flight to Washington, D.C., that night.

Jimmy Yee was dead. Lila was still being interrogated by the FBI in Boise. Lara and Mandy were gone. Alison was gone, too.

Brock reached to the top shelf of the bedroom closet, found his Sig Sauer and added another ammunition clip. He wrapped the gun and clip in a shirt, putting it in the lone suitcase he would check through to Washington.

He carried the suitcase downstairs and had scotch in the study, in the late afternoon. He got a little drunk. He called a cab for the airport.

Before he left, he went into the kitchen again.

"I'm going to miss you," he said to Celeste.

"I'll still be here when you get home." She didn't understand.

In the cab on the way out to the Sacramento airport, Brock logically ordered why he was traveling one-way to Washington.

He was going to tell Chris Metzger in person he was

quitting as an assistant United States Attorney. And maybe punch him in the face, he thought.

I might wait for Ally in the lobby of her hotel. Not to talk to her, just to see her walk by once more. To see her like I did that first fresh day, limitless possibilities for us both stretching to the horizon. I would like to see her like that, for a few moments, he thought.

He stared out the window. The Sierras loomed distantly and whitely. But what I really think I might do, Brock thought, is take a drive out to Virginia.

And pay a visit to Ed on his farm.

I'll tell Ed all the horror he's caused has been for nothing. The trucks that unloaded at Long Beach harbor today weren't carrying what he thought anymore.

There might just be time enough to tell Nelson that and watch his face.

CHAPTER THIRTY-FOUR

At mid-morning on Friday, June 17, Alison slipped through one of the Pennsylvania Avenue entrances at the Department of Justice. Police barricades along Constitution Avenue successfully kept the camera crews and reporters on that side of the building. It was a warm, slightly humid day, and the interior of the vast building was chilly, like her last visit. In the last twenty-four hours she had become nimble at dodging reporters. She was unable to avoid the stark headlines about the disastrous raid in every newspaper she saw.

The associate attorney general wore his charcoal pinstripe and red-dotted bow tie. Dressed for bear, she thought, as he showed her in, seated her, then went back behind his own formidable desk, a gilt-framed portrait of John Randolph to his left.

"You're not returning my calls," she began evenly.

"You're here now. Place's been a madhouse since yesterday. We're in full war mode. I can't even go to the bathroom without a camera crew beside me."

"It's amazing you haven't found the opportunity to put out a positive statement, Chris. Even something like 'This unfortunate incident was part of a DOJ investigation of dangerous domestic terrorists.'" Alison sat back. "This was your investigation."

He cracked two knuckles nervously. "Three committees on the Hill want a piece of you. And Brock."

"I know that," she said, determined not to give him the satisfaction of hearing how fruitlessly she had spent the day before. Slogging down the long corridors of the Russell Building, into offices at the Hart Building, every senator politely listening and showing her the door without any word of support. "I want you to make a public statement today, Chris."

"Saying what?"

"Give the pep talk you hit me with." She was cold.

"We're still collecting information." He got up, jumpy and defiant. "It's too early. There've been a lot of mistakes, Alison."

"I know that, too." She looked into the portrait's unlined, iconic face of the first attorney general. "All right. I've got two things to tell you."

He braced his hands on his desk. "Go ahead."

"First, I'm resigning, Chris. I'll wrap up this catastrophe and that's the end."

She suppressed disgust at his instant and patent relief. "You're a terrific prosecutor. It's a great loss," he said.

Already laying out my public pillorying, as Val called it, she thought. "The second thing, Chris, is that I'm going to run for Val Cantil's Senate seat. It's not a sure thing, of course." She came near him, close enough to see the tiny blot of egg yolk on his shirtfront. "But if I do make it to the Senate, the first thing I'm going to do is launch a very loud and very public inquiry into your activities at DOJ. A real housecleaning."

"You don't have to threaten me," he said unsteadily. "I don't have anything to hide."

"Yes, I do," she said, revolted by him, "and you certainly do."

She left, and Metzger sat still for a few moments. Then he wiped his hands on his handkerchief, locked his door, and opened the safe behind John Randolph's portrait. He removed a stack of files, all of Alison's reports on her meetings with Ed Nelson, the financial records of his companies, the memos, and took them to the largest shredder in his office. He slowly fed each page into the machine, which cross-cut it into confetti.

Metzger saw his hands tremble. There were other files, of course, more records.

But this was a good start.

Alison left the building anonymously in a crush of other people, falling in with a group of tourists going by the National Archives and up Indiana Avenue. No cameras, no questions when you're faceless, she thought.

She walked, thinking about the future. Better that than even the immediate past. She tried imagining what Val would say tonight at the party. They were having a drink beforehand, then riding out to Chevy Chase together.

The last twenty-four hours had been the hardest of Alison's life. She had few doubts about how easy the next twenty-four would be.

Abruptly, she found herself at the National Law Enforcement Officers Memorial. On the three-foot-high wall were names of every cop killed in two hundred years. Alison stared, reading the thousands of names. Three couples, chatting about where to eat lunch, strolled by, glanced idly at the wall, and sauntered away.

Where would Jimmy Yee's name go? she wondered. It would be just his name, not what he suffered, dreamed about, or the shattered family he left behind.

She decided she'd advise every reporter, every member of Congress who would brandish her misjudgments for their political gain on television, to come here.

She didn't call a cab, just walked farther up 6th Street into Chinatown, mingling with more tourists. She found a restaurant, bracketed by boarded-up buildings and graffiti-covered walls, a roast duck hanging by its neck in the window.

She sat down in the dark, ordering a sherry. She and Val were supposed to have lunch, assuming Val could get away from the clinging embrace of accountants, advisers, and media spinners. Val had her own Nelson-kindled fires to put out.

Then there was the party at Lurel's and the start of a new life. Alison sipped the sherry and glanced at the dead duck hanging in the window. It seemed a fitting object for contemplation under the circumstances.

"Where the hell is he?" Brock shouted furiously into the phone.

"Who the fuck knows?" Merical answered from Sacramento. "Nelson drives off the ranch forty minutes ago, our guys have him in sight. They follow him into that little town, Burke or whatever, he gets out of the car, does some grocery shopping, not a care in the world. He goes into an antique store, never comes out."

"He's on foot. He's got to be right there nearby."

"We are looking everywhere, Brock. We will find him."

"He's trying to get out of the country."

Merical laughed hollowly. "This'll cheer you up. If he does skip, he won't be rich. All that financial material you got from Lara, the stuff about his companies? We tracked and accessed his new Cayman accounts. Soon as the trucks unloaded at Long Beach, he got sixteen million deposited."

"Freeze it right now."

"We do think of things like that," Merical said. "There's a lot of talk you should be here, not back there now."

Brock paced his hotel room. "I'm coming back tomorrow," he lied. "Got to see the DOJ honchos later." He hoped he sounded sober enough. "But Jesus Christ, find fucking Nelson before he gets out of the country."

"Do our best, Brock. And we still haven't gotten a decent location for that house in the picture."

"Fantastic," Brock said, hanging up. He wore an Omni Shoreham robe, the uneaten remains of lunch stale on a tray, the TV blaring, and a nearly empty bottle of scotch on the table.

He quickly changed the channel again when news about the raid came on. It was just past five. He took another drink angrily.

He paced. Waited too long, he thought. Sat around here, working up my courage and I waited too goddamn long. Nelson's running. I should've gone straight from the airport, right to his farm.

Brock picked up his gun, lying reproachfully on top of the clothes in his open suitcase. He's getting away, Brock raged.

He tightened his grip on the gun. Working up my courage, Merical scrupulously calling with updates. There's the joke of the world like Ally said. Popeye and Merical stayed in for the long haul. Everybody else bailed out.

He flicked the safety off the gun, feeling it become alive and lethal in his grip. I didn't even have the courage to go to Ally's hotel down the street, watch her walk by. Maybe after the party, when she's high, happy, I can see her for the last time then.

He put the gun down carefully. He tore off the robe, got into the shower, the water as cold as he could stand. His teeth painfully chattered, his skin reddened. He recalled mountain winter cold in the Rockies when he went deer hunting with his father.

I let Nelson out of my sights twice, he thought, face burning under the icy water. But he will be caught again. I must believe that.

He opened his mouth, eyes tightly shut. I won't let him out of my sights again.

But where the hell is he right now?

Nearly seven, Brock lay fully dressed on top of the bed. The TV was black, Washington glittering outside his window.

The phone buzzed and he snatched it instantly.

"Go ahead," he said.

It was, as he hoped, Merical. "We got him, Brock. Sono-fabitch, we got the bastard."

"Where?" The gun lay companionably beside him.

"Jesus, listen. Maryland trooper's doing security at this society party out in—" Merical burbled.

Brock interrupted. "Chevy Chase. Paulette Lurel's annual party." He sat up in bed. "Is Nelson there?"

"Yeah, right. Lurel's party. This trooper is at the gate and he waves a black Lexus in and the driver is Edward Nelson. In a tuxedo, you believe that? Fuck must've stashed the car and change, planned the whole deal."

"Is he in the house now?"

"Sure as hell, and he is not, I guarantee you, going anywhere. The trooper told his commander and he got on to me." Merical finally stopped his burst of excited chatter. "But why'd he turn up at that party? Every damn celeb and pol is there, couple hundred people. He must've known he'd be recognized."

Brock said, "Thanks, Merical. I'm going out there myself." He got off the bed, holding the gun.

"Check in with the troopers. I'll get a couple agents over, too. You know what Nelson wants at the party?"

Brock hung up without answering, took the elevator down to the underground garage, and sped out into the capital's jeweled dusk. The gun, without a holster, notice-ably bagged his right coat pocket.

He knew exactly why Ed Nelson was at the famous celeb-rity gathering in Chevy Chase. He had seen Nelson's frank interest in Alison in his Boise jail cell. He had heard Ali-son's rancid, sad taunt at him that Ed Nelson wanted her.

Brock swerved in traffic, leaving a wake of blasting horns as he sped out of downtown Washington.

For what he was going to do, he knew there was no justification or excuse. And that made no difference any-more.

* * *

Cubby Merical agitatedly left his desk at Sacramento's FBI office. He motioned to several other agents, and snapped his fingers, asking for the printout of the Maryland state police commander's report on Nelson's sighting.

He didn't like Brock's odd, flat responses.

"I want to know where this party is," he said to an agent. "State cops say it's some old place, Slade House. Get me something on it."

When the FBI computers produced a wordy description, with color picture of historic Slade House in Chevy Chase, Merical stared at it. He had seen this building before, the brick facade of the central portion flanked by smaller elegant wings. The venerable trees. The sweeping driveway.

He had been vainly trying to identify the beautiful old home in the torn photo brought back from the Cobra compound until that moment.

The other agents stirred nervously at his obvious astonishment.

Merical looked up, all energy suddenly. "We've got a full alert. Right now. Every tactical and SWAT unit in the damn Maryland and D.C. area."

It was almost seven-thirty, sunset little more than a rosy blush against darkness, when the black woman at the U-STORE-U office saw six cheerily decorated trucks roll up, open the gate, and drive down toward the large locker in D-Building.

Although it was about time for her to leave, she curiously followed the trucks. Lord knew strange people rented lockers from her, but there was something just a little stranger about the duo who had rented the big one.

She stayed sheltered by C-Building, holding the edges of her sweater with one hand. The trucks were in a line, the locker's metal door open. She counted ten men, in plain blue coveralls, taking several large crates out of the locker and putting them in three of the trucks. The two odd ones she'd seen were there, motioning, closing the locker door.

It was all so quiet, she thought. Not a word spoken. Like they had rehearsed it all so much it was automatic.

She hurried back to the office. When the first truck came to the gate to be let out, she went over to the driver's side.

"Excuse me," she said firmly, studying the orange-haired driver, his white hands on the wheel marked with tattoos. "There's a problem. I want to tell you now so there's no complaint later that you didn't know or something."

He stared at her. "What problem?"

"I can see from these trucks you're in business. You can't run a business from your locker. It's not in the lease."

The driver's mouth twisted, he turned and slapped the back of the truck's cab. She went on, explaining why even unobtrusive businesses like party tent rentals were not permitted, when the scarred man was suddenly beside her.

"We didn't know. We're sorry." He was polite, coveralls buttoned to his chin.

The driver whimpered. "Time, time, time," he said.

"There's time," the scarred man said in his skin-crawling gurgle. "We'll move the items out of your locker tomorrow. Does that solve the problem?"

"Well, there won't be any refund," she said.

"I understand. It's our fault."

He turned. She knew there were ten or so men in the trucks, but the silence was peculiar, as if they were poised in there, waiting and listening.

"Well," she softened, "I'm sorry about this. You look like you're doing a good business. Lot of summer parties tonight, I imagine."

The scarred man didn't answer. He got back into the truck, the driver muttered something she didn't understand, and in a convoy the trucks moved into the busy early evening traffic.

It was only a few minutes later, as she was locking up the office for the night, that she conjured up what struck her as most unusual about the men she'd seen loading the trucks.

They're all white, she thought. Every one.

Not black or anything else. Not even one.

For a service business in Maryland, so close by Washington, this was a rare thing and worth mentioning over the family dinner table.

CHAPTER THIRTY-FIVE

"Well, that's one dead soldier," Val Cantil said. She held up the empty champagne bottle to Alison.

"Luckily we're here," Alison said. "I could handle a few more genteel tipples. We need a little walk first." She asked the limousine driver to stop and let them out. They were a city block away from the busy stone gate to Paulette Lurel's estate. The street was lined to the gate with limousines discharging guests.

Val feebly protested, but they got out. The evening air was fragrant, a faint pleasant babble drifting from the brightly lighted house partly glimpsed through the trees.

As they walked Val said, "I intend to sweep all criticism aside tonight." She took Alison's arm. "Did I tell you you look fabulous?"

"No"—Alison smiled—"*you* look fabulous."

Alison allowed, though, that she was pleased by the compliment. She wore a black silk sheath dress, three strands of small pearls, and antique topaz silver earrings Brock had given to her. Her blond hair was teased, full, the product of her hotel salon's best art, and she framed it with an exquisite jasmine scent. It was armor against the nightmares all around.

"Let's forget everything else for a while," Val said, hugging her as they got to the gate. They joined a line.

"Trade you one of my investigating committees for two of yours."

"That's what I mean. There are no obstacles. This is your night, Alison."

A small press of men and women in high fashion and tuxedos was slowly being admitted by solemn servants.

She nodded. "I thought there would be more security," Alison commented as they showed their identification and invitations and strolled up the gravel driveway toward the house.

"The State Police have always been enough. You just need someone in uniform to keep reporters from getting in and ravaging the food."

For the first time, Alison chuckled. The music was light, the babble louder. She glanced at the mass of famous faces just inside the white-columned entrance portico.

"I know this is lousy, it's awful, it's wrong," she lowered her voice, "but I think I feel horny right now."

Val patted her arm as they went in. "Power does that. Enjoy it."

Alison was shuttled from one knot of people to another. She held on to the same warming glass of champagne. As Val Cantil predicted, there were endless offers of vague support, much public affection, and then quiet whispering.

"This is as bad as being a trained bear," Alison grumbled.

"Paulette's beside herself. We can avoid her for a while. Instead of two modestly well-known guests, she's bagged a whole national scandal." Val slipped easily into chatter with anyone who begged an audience.

Val continually pointed out the sights. "The secretary of state and wife. Seven of my stalwart colleagues."

Alison peered around. "Couple network anchors, couple actors, and all the folks who used to advise presidents who are out now.''

''Paulette's parties are the kind where people are insulted if they have to introduce themselves,'' Val said, and they both laughed.

''Let's make the announcement pretty soon. I can't maintain this smile.''

''All right. How about a half hour?'' Val looked at Alison. ''How much is my endorsement worth now? I wonder. Do you want to run for the Senate that much, Alison?''

''I have to start over anyway,'' she tried to sound callous and witty, ''so I might as well start at the top.''

But she couldn't maintain the pose. Only wizened Paulette Lurel appearing beside her, clutching her arm for the grand tour, prevented her from blurting out how desolate she really felt.

Alison and Paulette Lurel went up a curving, mahogany balustraded staircase. They looked into many charming rooms.

''Last but not least, this was Guy's,'' Paulette Lurel quavered proudly to Alison, holding her arm tightly at the final stop. ''He hit a tree in Aspen.''

The tour of the grand old eighteenth century home was almost over, so Alison allowed herself to be convoyed into the second-floor boy's room. Guy Lurel had died in a skiing accident thirty years before, but looking around the adolescent decorations, pennants, posters, baseball bats, it was like Paulette Lurel assumed her son would come back any minute.

Alison made the right noises, happy to be out of the crush downstairs that spilled over the living room, across a gaily lighted terrace, filling the lawn. Waiters still added large fruit baskets and great bouquets outside. She could see it all from the window, the ivy trellises just below and the cunningly shaped hedges and bushes.

''It's very pretty, Paulette,'' she said. ''I know Val Cantil's talked to you already. How about near that big carnation display for my announcement? Do you mind?''

They walked out to the landing. "Oh, no. Launching a Senate career is going to be unique for me."

"How do you mean?" Alison caught the acid slyness below Lurel's quaver.

"Incidents at my parties have ended several Senate careers in the past. But I don't think . . . No, I'm positive, I've never launched one before."

"I hope I start a new trend," Alison said. I hope I start something, she thought.

"Assistant United States Attorney Brock Andrews," Brock said to the sallow man at the gate, taking back his identification. "My wife's a guest inside. I've got to see her."

He waited impatiently in his car, perfumed and well-dressed people passing by. Finally, a state trooper, uniform leather belts creaking, bent to him. "What's the problem, sir?"

"This is Department of Justice business."

The trooper was young, flat-faced. "Do you need any assistance?"

"I need to get in there now."

"I just mean, sir"—he rubbed his chin nervously—"if it's about the other guy who went in, if there's going to be some difficulty, we've got orders to keep everything really calm. So nobody gets upset."

"There won't be any trouble," Brock said, gunning his engine. "I'm just going in and coming out."

The trooper nodded. "Okay, sir. Go on through." He waved at the four other Maryland state troopers who stood across the street holding reporters behind barricades.

Brock honked his horn and drove up the gravelly driveway, forcing the stylish and famous partygoers to cleave aside.

The six ROYAL RENTS trucks followed a series of small country roads threaded around Chevy Chase. They came up behind the Lurel estate, at the edge of deep woods, on a dark and quiet road. Three of the trucks parked just off the side of the road. From them, six men emerged carrying AK-47 rifles at port arms, more ammunition slung in packs on their backs. Their coveralls melted into the cobalt darkness of the woods.

The men began trotting forward, then ran and were lost in the dense stands of trees.

The three remaining trucks drove a quarter mile toward the front of the estate.

"Slow down," Lyle Flecknoy barked to Vernon in the lead truck.

"They'll get there ahead of us," he said, moist hands slipping on the wheel.

"I do not want to get stopped for speeding. You're only driving because I don't have a license. A nation's destiny isn't going to be diverted by a traffic citation." A fierce exultation built in his voice. "I don't believe anybody's going to call me a psychopath tomorrow."

He gently laid his own AK-47 at his feet.

Alison found refuge in a dark, book-lined room, a single Tiffany lamp colorfully bright on the desk. It was quiet here and she closed the paneled doors. Val had advised a few moments solitude before they made the announcement.

She studied the leather-bound books lining the walls, burgundy easy chairs. She tried to summon composure from years of public performances. Maybe, she thought, I can pull it off. Maybe I'll care afterward.

She turned when the doors opened. Ed Nelson slid in, closing the doors. He had a wide, wild smile.

"What the goddamn hell are you doing here?" she spluttered in sudden shock.

"The old babe told me where you were hiding." He walked to her quickly. He stank of liquor, his face redder than usual. "Listen, there isn't any time."

Alison swore again, pushing by him. But Ed reached out, yanking her toward him with astonishing strength.

She jammed a palm swiftly under his chin, then snapped a fist into his throat, and he staggered back, gurgling, gagging, bouncing off a chair.

Alison stared at him, fists clenched, as he shook his head, coughing raggedly. "You goddamn bastard." She tried to hit him again, but he ducked behind a chair, hands up. Outrage turned into farce. He kept changing position, keeping a chair or the desk between them.

"Listen, Alison. Listen. Calm down. I want to help you. Any minute, some of the Cobra nutlogs are going to come whooping in here. We've got to get out right now."

There was, for once, a genuine pleading look on his face.

For the first time since her mother gave lie to what she had stumbled on, Alison knew she could kill another human being. She had considered childish plans to kill her uncle for weeks before giving them up.

"The Cobras?" she repeated, knowing it was true. It matched the grotesque facts. "Why are they coming here?"

He stood, hands protectively in front of him. "Old Ed's magic act. Keep everybody looking in the wrong places. You, Yee, Brock, FBI. Nobody's looking where they're supposed to. This's a little visual diversion, that's all."

"The scrap equipment in Long Beach," she said, moving to the door. "You've put everybody's life on the line for a damn con."

"There's time right now, right this instant, for you and me to get out of here, all right?"

"You're out of your mind."

"I came to get you!"

She opened the door. The crowd was in high gear, boisterous, voices mingling with the large band's show tunes.

Nelson had his hand on her shoulder, begging again, arguing.

Alison half turned. Near the foot of the stairs across the foyer, vehemently gesturing at Val Cantil, was Brock.

He saw her. He saw Nelson. He shoved people aside and thrust toward her. His hand went to his coat pocket.

* * *

"Got one of those emergency calls," Lyle Flecknoy explained to the state trooper and dubious servant at the gate. "Not enough tents, tables, you name it."

"I helped supervise the preparations," the servant huffed. "There was no problem."

"Well, we're here. We got the stuff." Flecknoy shrugged. His left foot nudged the AK-47. Vernon's eyes were wide on the trooper.

"Yeah, yeah, go on in, take care of it." He waved the three trucks past the gate.

The servant said sourly, "There was nothing missing as of this afternoon."

"You want to argue about it? You know how bad celebrity types can screw you up if they're unhappy about something?"

Behind her, Alison heard the library door slam and lock.

Brock began pounding on it, and people moved away from him.

Alison blinked. He knew about the Cobras. He had come to warn everyone. She grabbed his arm. "How much time do we have?"

"What?" he barked, looking at her finally.

"When are they getting here? Did you bring backup?"

"What the hell are you talking about, Ally?"

She understood. "Oh, Jesus. The Cobras are coming here. Nelson set it up."

He seemed dazed; then his mind refocused. "Yeah," he said. "We've got to get to a phone."

As he turned, Val said, "You should do any arguing in private." She had a strained expression for Brock.

They all started when screams and loud shooting exploded outside and several windows shattered inward. The guests froze and, a moment later, moved in a great, terrified wave toward the front of the house.

Alison was pushed back against the nearest wall. The

front door burst open, and four men in camouflage uniforms ran in, shouting. She recognized Lyle Flecknoy. He
walked in, mad, distant gaze raking the mass of terrified
people, his rifle pointed at the ceiling.

She yanked Brock's hand, pulling him forward. The
Cobras were busy herding and shouting, forcing men and
women back toward the living room. Like wolves in a sheep
pen, she thought.

She started up the stairs. "There's a way out up here,"
she gasped to Brock. Val was beside him.

"Go, go, go!" he said, pushing Val forward. He had a
gun, she saw. His eyes snapped down the stairs, more shots
ringing and the yells more frenzied.

He's guarding the stairs, she thought, pulling Val by the
arm. He'll follow us. Of course.

She and Brock had handled kidnapping cases. In hostage seizures the critical time was always the first moments,
before the hostage takers consolidated their control over
the people and secured the area.

"Upstairs, down the hall to the right. There's a bedroom,
we can get down to the lawn, get to the trees," she yelled
to Val.

"I'm right behind you," Val said in a strangely calm
tone.

Rifle fire erupted below, more glass splintered, and the
sharp smell of cordite grew strong.

It was only when she got halfway down the carpeted
second-floor hall that Alison realized Val was not with her.

Brock was partly up the curved staircase, his Sig pointed
down at Lyle Flecknoy, who did not notice him.

An instant later, a half dozen maddened guests, faces
contorted, ran from the living room, and made for the
stairs. The first woman slammed into Brock, clawing to
climb over him, to get away.

He pushed, arms beating back the bodies shoving and
shouting. He was shouting, too, trying to get down the
stairs.

Brock saw a Cobra militiaman, mouth open and shriek-
ing, rush from the living room, take a firing stance, and
begin shooting.

Something jerked Brock's left leg from under him, and
he pitched onto the other people on the stairs. They all
fell in a tangle of arms and legs, pearls from a necklace
spattering like rain on the parquet floor.

Hold the gun, hold the gun, Brock thought frantically.

A blow knocked the wind out of him, and he felt a sharp,
bone-cracking pain in his side; his right arm went numb.

The gun fell away like a leaf blown by the wind, and he
tumbled with the other bodies down the stairs.

CHAPTER THIRTY-SIX

Alison heard the sputter of shots at the same moment she reached the bedroom door. Neither Val nor Brock was in sight.

An upsurge of terror and wrenching nausea filled her. She thought of going back. But she immediately recognized that the sooner she got out and away, the sooner she'd bring help. There were troopers just outside. She would tell them how many invaders were in the house, how they were armed.

She kicked off her slight, fashionable dress shoes. She hurried into the bedroom, screams resounding downstairs and more angry shouts following. The window was only feet ahead of her now.

Behind her, Alison heard, "Where you going, lady?"

She turned. Vernon, assault rifle pointed at her, stood in the bedroom doorway, then came toward her, motioning her away from the window. He grinned, his head an odd, stove-in shape.

Alison meekly nodded. She fluidly grabbed one of the late Guy Lurel's baseball bats beside the bureau nearest her, and swung with home run fierceness.

The bat hit Vernon on the side of his misshapen head, and she felt the impact all the way to her shoulders. The rifle flew to his left, and he pitched backward with amazing speed.

Alison didn't pause to see if he was stunned or not. She dropped the bat, then nimbly climbed through the window. She clung closely to the ivy trellises on the rear of the brick building, her nearly bare feet fumbling to find purchase.

Below her, several of the Cobra militia were taking positions near the overturned buffet table. Large fruit baskets and bouquets had been torn apart by bullets. A struggling woman, and a man groaning and holding his side, were dragged into the house. Alison held her breath, watching it happen through the ivy frame just below her.

The black dress helped, she realized. As long as she moved carefully, in the night, with the confusion, she blended in. She hung onto the trellises, then continued climbing down, freezing whenever one of the Cobras passed. All one had to do was look up and he'd spot her instantly.

After years, she slid down the last few feet, behind a clipped boxwood hedge. She crouched there. Through the screen of trees at the edge of the lawn, she saw armed men scurrying around the police cars in the street. From the house, AK-47 fire kept the cops from moving nearer.

I've only got to make it to the yard, then to the trees and I'm safe, she thought. I can cut around to the street and Brock and Val are all right and that's all I have to do and it's nothing and I can do it right now. Her heart thudded. A Cobra, screaming "Free America!" knelt just in front of her concealing hedge and began shooting, on full auto, at the lights behind the police barriers.

Brock was on his side, a dead woman's glassy eyes staring at him, a large red chunk gone from her neck and shoulder. An emerald earring still dangled coquettishly from one ear.

He could move his left hand a little. The butt of his Sig protruded from the armpit of a man, sprawled facedown, three feet away. He reached slowly for the gun. Then he passed out.

When he opened his eyes again, he heard a whistling sound. It came from him, from a hole in his chest, and he felt a skyscraper pressing down on him. He reached for the gun again.

It was, he realized, much quieter. People cried, men shouted, but it was more orderly. Time had passed.

What he saw next was fragmented, as if the fine tuning in his eyes was gone.

Two Cobras dragged Ed Nelson from the library. He was protesting, twisting, fighting in their grip.

Brock nearly had his fingers to the gun.

"Christ Almighty," Ed shouted, stepping on people trying to press themselves into the living room carpet, "what the fucking hell have you done?"

He counted five bodies; blood sprayed copiously. Through the window, he saw three more bodies on the lawn.

Flecknoy, giving orders, came to Ed. Other Cobras bustled setting up paint buckets, wiring them around the living room, up the stairs, in the library Ed had just left.

"The time has come," Flecknoy said dramatically.

Ed spotted the placement of explosives, probably some home brew the loons had made up, taken from boxes lugged from the trucks. They planned to bring the whole fucking house down, with everyone inside. He cast a hasty look to find Alison. On your own, my love, he thought with regret and anger.

"You just killed hostages," Ed said evenly. "You've screwed your bargaining position, Mr. President."

He was startled when Flecknoy replied, "I'm glad you're joining us, Ed. I worried about you. But you're our Samson after all, bringing down the temple."

"Listen to me," Ed said calmly, aware of the eyes on him

as people silently begged from the floor. "Your demands aren't going to fly now. The cops are going to come in here like bats out of hell, so it's time to pack up."

"Our manifesto to free this nation was sent to all the news organizations. They will understand fully when this place is put to fire and sword."

Ed's gaze snapped to the buckets and bundles being fixed to furniture, walls, and doorways. Not just explosives, probably incendiaries, too. Flecknoy was going to ascend to heaven on a fiery chariot.

He began edging away. "Then I better go," Ed said, clearing his throat.

"We're all one now. We all remain to the end." Flecknoy's rifle raised. Ed had figured the Cobras wanted so many AK-47s because they intended to sell most of them. But he counted more than enough inside the house to keep anything short of a massive rescue assault at bay.

He straightened his shoulders, shuddering a little. "Mr. President," he said formally, "your manifesto won't have the importance of a live witness. You must have someone testify to the world how you stood in your shining hour of glory."

Flecknoy blinked. Rifle lowered slightly.

"I'm willing to make the sacrifice of remaining behind now," Ed said with as much conviction as he had ever put into a pitch.

He'll buy it, he's biting right now, Ed thought.

"No," Flecknoy said between clenched teeth. "I believe you've earned the honor of staying with us."

Ed swore, and Flecknoy's rifle butt instantly flicked toward him. It smashed the left side of his mouth, and his eyes widened in shock and pain.

Ed didn't struggle when he was shoved down into a shivering group of guests. He huddled, spitting broken teeth and blood to the carpet, his face swelling rapidly, wondering how the hell he was going to get out of this.

* * *

Brock could barely breathe. The whistling was softer, but a wetness covered his neck and shirt.

He moved his head slightly. He wondered where Alison was, whether she had gotten away.

He passed out again. Saw another fragment. Val Cantil, sleeve of her dress torn, walked calmly to Lyle Flecknoy. They talked in the foyer, the living room packed with panicky, terrified celebrities just behind them.

Val pointed at the stairs, at him, he thought. He couldn't hear. She might be asking to see how he was. Asking for help. Offering to mediate for the Cobras, convey their demands to the authorities. After all, she was California's senior United States senator.

Brock's hand crept to his gun. He had to roll slightly to reach it, the pain making him dizzy, then paralyzing him.

Lyle Flecknoy punched Val in the face. She staggered. He made an adjustment on his rifle. He pointed it at her and squeezed off three very slow shots.

The first snapped her large body to the right, the second yanked her right arm as if on a string, and the third blew the back of her head off.

Alison finally moved, crouching, bursting with speed, making for the trees. She expected to hear gunfire, but there was none. She ran, feet pounding first on the grass, then bitten by the rocks and roots when she hit the trees.

She ran farther, cutting to the right, making for the growing line of vans and trucks that were arriving on the street. Suddenly there seemed to be a hundred men surrounding the house.

She shoved branches away and nearly collided with a black-clad man, mask covering his face, who grabbed her.

"Oh, Jesus," she gasped. He motioned her to be quiet, pointing at the dozen and more other nearly invisible men with sniper rifles, creeping through the trees toward the house. "Oh, God. Listen. Let me tell you who's in there, where they are."

She spoke quickly and as softly as if telling a bedtime

story, and the black-clad man murmured it all into a whisper mike at his throat.

Brock could see Val's body every time he opened his eyes.

His fingers finally stretched to the Sig, closed around the butt, pulled it slowly to him. He wasn't breathing anymore, making no sound, and yet he saw and heard everything as if it was blazing with halogen light.

He saw Lyle Flecknoy, rifle pointed to the floor, run from the living room. Something was happening both at the front and the rear of the house. The Cobras in the living room started firing, and a hundred screams rose.

Brock lifted himself partway up. "Hey!" he shouted at Lyle Flecknoy at the foot of the stairs.

Flecknoy paused and looked toward him reflexively. Brock brought up the Sig and started shooting and didn't stop until the clip was empty.

Jimmy had told him that trick, a stunt from his earlier incarnation as a street cop. The pukes always hesitated for a split second and turned to the sound of a voice.

Brock stopped thinking suddenly because the foyer and the whole world ignited in a white, all embracing flash, and a roar of thunder swallowed the shooting, screaming, and awareness.

CHAPTER THIRTY-SEVEN

A day and a half later, drained and somber, Alison stepped to the lectern in the cavernous auditorium of the Department of Justice. The attorney general, FBI director, ATF supervisor, and Porter Ridgeway stood behind her. He winked at her.

The auditorium was bursting with TV cameras and reporters, tangles of cables laid everywhere. The crowd grew silent.

Alison spoke firmly. "I don't have anything to add to what the president said last night. This was a cowardly attack, and our prayers are with the families of those killed and wounded."

Thirty-two Killed, Eighty Injured: Secretary of State "Critical," read one of a hundred headlines that morning. The roll call of famous dead and dying filled the television.

"I did want to commend a very brave man," Alison said, looking at the rows of faces. "He worked undercover to provide information about this militia group. I wish he could have discovered more sooner, but he was only one man. He was also instrumental in stopping the theft of our country's most sensitive military equipment. I think it's only fitting to honor him today. He is among the missing, but I hope, I pray, we will find him soon."

Alison straightened. "We owe a great debt to Edward Nelson."

She took questions, shouted from the crowd. It went on, frantic and unbridled, until the attorney general waved his hand and showed Alison through a side door.

"Come to my office," the attorney general said to her.

"I don't have time."

He was nearly seventy, white hair parted sharply, dark suited. "As a favor, Alison. I think you'll want to see this."

She allowed him to escort her to his private elevator. As they rose slowly in the ancient, paneled car, he said, "What actual consequence do you expect from that little performance just now?"

"I turned Ed Nelson into the biggest snitch on the face of the earth," she said. "As my husband used to say, I burned him to the ground."

"You think he's still in the country?"

"I don't know where he is. We've tracked him being brought to George Washington University Hospital with dozens of other wounded guests. We've got his treating physician's notes, the work he did to stabilize Nelson's jaw. Then—" she went silent as the door opened.

"He walked out into the balmy Washington evening," finished the old man, shaking his head. "What a bastard."

"Ed's very good at patter. I'd love to listen in when he tries to explain why we love him," she said coldly.

They went into the attorney general's large office. It was blue carpeted, hung with oil portraits and brass sconces, antique breakfronts and a great desk.

"Is he likely to talk his way out?" asked the attorney general, handing her a letter.

"Ed's business associates probably aren't happy with him after Brock's stunt with his trucks." She began reading. "I like to think I just put a gun to his head."

She looked at the old man, then obviously at her watch.

"So Chris Metzger's resigning." She dropped the letter on the desk.

"More than that. He's going to have significant trouble wherever he goes. Nobody likes an obvious liar. Your computer records were detailed and voluminous enough to vindicate you."

"Lucky me."

"I don't want your resignation."

"Yes, you do," she said. "If you think about it. I've got to go."

He nodded sadly. "I know where to reach you, if you change your mind?"

Alison stopped at the door. "I'll be at the hospital. Nothing changes there," she said.

It was better now, she saw, the signs of bloody mortality swept, washed, disinfected away. But they invisibly hovered everywhere, echoes of a great crime.

Alison walked through the vast downtown hospital's corridors. She still saw the red-stained dresses, torn starched shirts, shoes, and underwear scattered wildly over the floors thirty-six hours earlier. And an endless procession of ambulances, cars, cops bringing mangled, keening victims. Pails of discarded syringes, gloves, blood-spattered hospital gowns. On one gurney, she remembered a man stripped naked, gaping abdominal wound tended by frenzied doctors and nurses, his shockingly white legs ending in black sheer stockings and shiny black pumps.

She went to the fourth-floor Intensive Care Unit. There were still a dozen Metro cops guarding the people, keeping reporters away. She nodded to FBI agents compiling, questioning everyone.

Brock was in a room with three others. He was prone, connected to machines and bottles of fluids. His left leg was swathed from hip to foot. His face against the blue sheet was opalescent, like he glowed inside. Tubes ran from his nose, and the one taped in his mouth seemed oddly like an infant's pacifier.

Alison felt a hush inside herself, even with other relatives or the FBI prowling into the room.

She sat down, draping her coat on the chair.

Outside this room, this hospital, the city and nation were in agonized turmoil. She took Brock's hand. It was heavy, cold and inert. The thick and wide white bandages across his chest made him look like a knight Templar, brought home from the Crusades.

"Hello, sweetheart," she said. "I'm back. It's been another crazy day. You'll like this. Do you know what I did?"

She went on, as if he could hear her, and his silence was merely ardent concentration on her words.

A sturdy, jowly American in a white shirt, sleeves rolled up against the merciless late August heat, emerged cautiously from his modest hotel off Rome's Via Veneto.

He walked slowly, watching people. He took this walk nearly every day, sipping from a little flask, studying those around him deeply. He ate at a nearby inexpensive restaurant, and the only thing he bought regularly were English language newspapers and magazines from a small stand.

He paid for three papers that day, eagerly reading as he walked back to his hotel. He wiped his face with a handkerchief, grimacing when he gingerly touched the distended jawline on the left side of his face. As he stood at the corner, heedless and frenzied traffic swirling by, four broad men surrounded him.

The American lowered his newspaper.

Six hours later, from thirty-four thousand feet, Ed Nelson stared emptily at the slate gray ocean below. He held his flask but didn't drink. He still wore the same shirt and pants for the Roman summer, but in the jet's dry coolness, his sweat dried faster even as it beaded on his face. He sighed, fingers running over the twisted bones of his jaw.

"Why so glum?" Deng Li said, sitting down beside Ed.

"Cut the crap," he answered. "I'm not in the mood."

"We'll have a great deal of time to brighten your spirits."

"Oh, yeah," Ed said, drinking, pulling down the shade on his window. Except for eight armed plainclothes military guards, he and Deng were alone in the cabin. "Listen, one more time. I did not fuck you on the sale. I did not steal your money. Christ, look at me. I've been living in a fleabag hotel for five weeks, and I've got one suit. I had to get some fucking *Italian veterinarian* to fix my mouth."

"Nonetheless," Deng said blandly, "we didn't receive the equipment and we paid you for it."

"Look, I'll run it for you again. The fucking U.S. Attorney did a switch. He took your trucks of scrap with the equipment in it and switched it with everyday plain scrap. He just switched trucks!"

"How, Ed? Why?"

"Somewhere between Perrey and Long Beach. Probably. Look, he figured out the scrap's in sealed containers. Nobody can look at it until it's opened at the destination. The buyer's relying on—" He got no further.

"Trust. Yes. We trusted you to deliver what we paid you for."

"I am being hung out," Ed said slowly, sarcastically. "We're both being screwed."

Deng Li's slash of a mouth tightened. "You and I will have many long days and nights to explore every detail of what happened, Ed. And then, we will explore each detail again. And again if necessary."

"I can work for you," Ed said, sweat dripping down his face, a drop hanging ludicrously on his nose. "You know what I can do." He grinned lopsidedly, wiping the sweat. "Nervous flyer." He shakily raised the flask for a drink.

"You will work very hard," Deng said quietly. "For how long is impossible to say. Perhaps we should begin." He lifted Ed's flask from him. "You won't need this now."

Ed started to speak, but Deng Li stopped him by putting a tender, almost maternal finger on the poorly reset jaw.

"Yes. This will need correction. We have doctors, Ed, who are very good at reconstructive surgical techniques."

He shook his head. "And, unhappily, we also have many who are quite unskilled."

Brock brought the small catamaran angled toward the dock, clumsily tacking with the late September breeze. Although Alison reached down quickly to prevent them from hitting the dock, the catamaran scraped along the planking's edge with a dull groan.

"Good sailing, Captain Queeg," she said, hopping into the water.

He furled the sail and tied down the catamaran, joining her in the hip-deep warm blue water. Delicate waves foamed and curled on the nearby white beach. He ran his hand along the ugly black scrape.

"That's going to add a little to the rental," he said. "Couple more weeks and I might get it right."

"One more week, Captain. That's all we've got."

"I don't want to go back."

"One more week," she said. "So we'll obviously have to spend most of it on the water." She started for the beach. He put his arm on her shoulders. They chatted as they walked toward the rented bungalow beneath palms, framed by high bamboo and ladyfinger banana trees.

"Let me sit down," he said.

"It hurts?" She sounded worried.

"Damn right, Ally. I mean it. I do not want to go back."

He disengaged his arm, and she let him slide gently to the fine sand. One leg was noticeably shorter than the other, a dead white scar extending its length, stark against his tan. He wore frayed cutoffs. The scar on his chest began on his back and came around until it girdled him.

"I'll get the crutches," she said. "Old man."

"I'll be right here, missy," he said in a mock quavering voice. He stared at the ocean and the spongy clouds promising the day's rain later. He watched her go to the bungalow. She wore a blue halter top, cutoffs, and rubber sandals. She had freckled and tanned in equal measure. Her hips gracefully shifted as she walked.

Brock got up very awkwardly and followed her as fast as he could manage.

She wasn't inside when he got there. He heard a Jeep's grumble, and Alison came in, a bundle of envelopes in her hand.

"Mail call," she said. "Joy got ours again by mistake." The island's postal service was somewhat erratic, and their closest neighbors, about a half mile away, often got letters meant for them.

"Want a beer?" He hopped to the kitchen.

"If you're there," she said, looking at the letters.

He braced himself on one aluminum crutch kept near the sink, opened two beers he got from the tiny refrigerator, and brought them to her. She sat in a rattan chair, her legs under her. From the bungalow's three open sides a veranda looked out on the Pacific's expanse.

"Don't read them, Ally. I'm warning you. None of it's good news." He drank long from his beer.

"Not so. Here's another one from Popeye. Another job offer, more money than last time." She held it out to him as proof.

He looked out to the sea. "I guess he doesn't believe you're really going to start at Stanford next week. Teaching the next generation of Popeyes."

"He wants you, too. He doesn't believe you're starting your own practice."

"Contractors should almost be finished remodeling my office. But, I don't believe any of it," he said, finishing the beer. "Another one?"

"I'm still working here," she said. She knew the signs, the restlessness, and no longer actively resisted them. It will play itself out, they had told her at the hospital. But she never talked to him about the funerals, and they rarely mentioned Jimmy or Val. "One for you," she said. "Lila again."

He came back, hunched forward on his crutch. He took the letter unopened and laid it carefully with the first ones

he'd read, all cheerful and bright with news about her new
job with ATF in Boston. "I'll look at it later," he said.
"Christ, throw the rest of that shit out."

He drank again, clumping to the veranda. At least he'd
read some of Lila's letters. Denny Lara's first letter, without
return address, postmarked in Ohio, and forwarded from
Sacramento, he'd glanced at. Baby fine. Mandy fine. Working as a farm equipment salesman.

When Brock spotted the apologies, and lachrymose
handwringing in the letter, he'd torn it up. The later ones
he simply threw out.

Alison got up, the rattan creaking.

"Trouble in River City?" she asked, touching his waist.

"Thunder woke me up again last night," he said, his
voice quavering for real.

"I thought so."

"I thought I didn't make any noise this time."

"Not so much," she said softly.

"It's the flash bang grenades again. Right after I shot
Flecknoy. And Popeye keeps sticking his nose in here so
I keep thinking about it again." Brock wiped an eye angrily
with his wrist, taking another drink. "I keep thinking what
if. What if Merical hadn't made the house in the picture,
what if he hadn't called out the cavalry? What if I'd gone
in there and shot Nelson?"

"You didn't."

"I do not want to go back, Ally. No jokes. No faking. I
don't want to go back to a practice. I don't want to go
back and have them start slicing again to fix the leg either.
Why not just stay here?"

"We can't. You know that. This is a dream."

"The other stuff's the dream."

She kissed him. His hair had sun bleached lighter than
hers. "We'd be beach bums, Brock. Doing what? Running
a bait shop or bar? It wouldn't work."

"I've got a start on a money-making buccaneer routine,"
he said, flourishing the crutch and squinting with one eye.

She didn't smile. "It wouldn't work."

He dropped the crutch with a clatter, and stumbled

down the beach. He stood, canted to one side, holding his beer.

They drove over the winding mountain road to Bainbridge, the island's closest town, for dinner that night.

It started to rain, and they had to hurry inside the loud, busy tin-roofed building. The downpour sounded like bullets.

They had to move tables twice when the roof leaked. They ate spicy roast chicken, drank rum and beer, and fed scraps to the brown dogs the owner let roam freely.

Brock touched the ring on his hand. "Sometimes I actually think I know when you put this on my finger."

"Doubtful. The docs said you'd be gone by morning. So I had your morphine drip maxed and I—" She stopped. She grinned finally. "Well, you tricked everyone again."

He leaned across the table and kissed her, holding it for a long time.

When they got back to the bungalow, the sky had cleared, and a half-moon, eerily glowing above the water, shot fantastic shadows of the palms and trees everywhere.

They made love quickly, then more slowly, concentrating on each other. He pulled a sheet over them both afterward.

The phone rang before dawn. Gulls swooped over the sea littered with floating trash from passing cruise ships and the island's eccentric refuse disposal.

Brock got up. They hadn't brought cell phones. There was only an antique rotary dial near the front door. He glanced at the water, where pelicans and terns joined the gulls squabbling over the bounty.

The phone went on ringing. Brock didn't pick it up. Alison padded to him, naked.

"Want me to answer it?" she asked.

"Yeah, why not?" He stepped back, leaning against a wall.

She picked up the phone. "Hello? Hello? Hello?" she said, then stopped.

Brock shook his head. The calls had started a month

ago, followed them from Sacramento to Hawaii, finally even here. Whenever he answered these insistent predawn calls, whoever it was hung up wordlessly.

But when Alison answered, the silence remained, as if someone listened only for her voice.

After a moment, she hung up. She shrugged. "You could probably get connected to Eisenhower with these phones."

They got back into bed. A breeze rattled the rattan matting at the windows.

"I still think it's Nelson," Brock said, pulling her closer.

"If it is, why doesn't he say something?"

"Maybe he can't." Brock hardened. "Maybe he doesn't have anything left to say."

She traced the bony knob of his hip. "We've got one more week, all right? Let's get ourselves as fucked up and fucked out as we can. Because then it's back to the real world."

"Meeting those standards is going to be rough." He smiled.

"Seriously. I don't want to make the same mistakes again."

He shivered, kissing her neck. "No. I promise if we make any they'll be new ones."